Colin P Brown

Effect and Cause

For Eve

Prologue

Cocooned within a small tent, two men sat, relaxed, aware of the steady pitter-patter of light rain against canvas, comforted by the cool but dry atmosphere inside, one heavily laden with the aroma of tinned Irish stew.

Although Ian Bradshaw considered Roland and Roland's wife, Faye, to be very close friends, he classified David Utteridge, his current companion, as his best friend, the distinction made possible merely by the length of time the two men had known each other.

Adding to the noises of the rain and the occasional light flutter of fabric, another sound became apparent.

'What the fuck is that?' Dave asked, startled, moving his head this way and that, his ears working in unison to pin down the source of the noise; an intermittent but persistent sound, capable of creating anxiety and then feeding it.

Even though he said nothing by way of reply, it was clear his companion harboured at least some of the same feelings, evidenced by Ian reaching for a torch, before unzipping the entrance flap and crawling out into the darkness on all fours. His bottom half remained inside, presenting his friend with a view of mud-stained buttocks; the result of a mishap earlier in the day.

Seconds passed during which the beam of Ian's torch could be seen scanning the area immediately outside the tent.

'Jesus!' You scared the shit out of me. Go on, off with you.'

The tent shook slightly under several blows from the torch against its side.

'Go on.'

After a short pause, Ian reversed back inside, fastening the zip before returning to his low, folding stool.

'It was a bloody fox trying to get in,' Ian explained in disbelief. 'Must have smelled the stew.'

'Cheeky little bugger,' Dave responded, relieved.

Nothing more was said on the subject, both men quickly returning to their pre-event state; relaxed; carefree. In fact, so relaxed were they that conversation did not restart until after the first few spoonful's of stew had been consumed and savoured.

'So,' Dave announced, quite without warning, 'the butterfly effect has it that an insignificant little butterfly, beating its wings in some wood somewhere, starts a chain reaction of seemingly insignificant events that land up providing some fella in Bangkok with a bowl of steaming hot owls' nest soup – no butterfly; cold soup.'

His four word summation was punctuated with two nods of the head; the first to the left, the other to the right.

Ian was thrown for a moment, before making the connection between his friend's reference to soup, and the soup-like stew they were both now enjoying.

'Owl's nest soup?' Ian responded, overemphasising and rounding the word 'owl', tightened facial features requesting further explanation.

'The point I'm making is that an insignificant event can have a major effect. I could have stuck with convention and said birds' nest soup, but I've always found owls useful for comic effect. I could equally have cited an ant farting in the underground causing a crane to fall over in the German Rhineland; it makes no difference to the proposal.'

Ian smiled.

'For a roofer, you're quite the professor, aren't you?' he said, placing his spoon in his enamelled mug. 'However, with regard to your original proposal, the butterfly effect would only work if the butterfly was killed by a lepidopterist who, having decided to take up killing butterflies as a hobby, found that he couldn't get a girlfriend and therefore ran off to Bangkok, got sexually frustrated because not even the lady boys would entertain him, and landed up murdering the chef.'

'Exactly.'

'There's no exactly about it. The theory's pants,' Ian responded, leaning towards his friend, shaking his head from side to side animatedly.

Having delivered his opinion, Ian returned to the upright position and took another spoonful.

'Oh, yes?' Dave challenged.

'Yes,' Ian replied, waggling his spoon in front of him, having delivered a steaming hot piece of minted potato to his mouth. 'I've given this some thought. In life, there are two kinds of event: those that have an effect while you're alive; those that have an effect beyond your grave. For example, my two kids are the next generation and by definition will affect life beyond mine. In order for me to have had Stephen and Ann, I first had to meet Debbie. To meet her, I had to attend the school reunion, and you had to have brought Debbie with you as a guest. For you to have introduced me to her, I already had to know you as a good friend. For us to have been friends, we first had to meet, and we did that on the first day at junior school some forty odd years ago. Nothing else matters – choosing tea or coffee; holidaying in Sri Lanka or Scarborough – nothing else matters. I had to go to Acorns' Junior School; meet you; attend the Cardle's reunion; hit it off with Debbie and get jiggy, jiggy – twice. End of story. That's why my family means everything to me; it's the only thing that matters – my two kids are my purpose; my wife is just as important to me as she was vital in providing that purpose.'

'That's not very romantic,' Dave responded, somewhat shocked at what he was hearing. 'It makes Debbie sound like a tool; a vessel.'

Ian realised he had not explained himself as well as he might.

'I guess that in my summary of events I didn't mention that I fell in love. I wouldn't have done so had I not met her, and you gotta keep loving the person who produces the ultimate purpose in your life, haven't you.'

'Whoa, now you're getting a bit too soppy for comfort,' Dave said, holding his spoon and mug in front of him to ward off any feminine traits that might otherwise infect his entirely masculine persona.

'It's true and I'm not ashamed to say it. I love Debs and my kids more than anything else in the world, and I'm not exaggerating.'

'What about me?' his friend asked, feigning hurt.

'It goes without saying; I love you too – not in the biblical sense of course – but given the difficult choice of losing you or my family, Debbie and the kids would win every time – unless they'd just raided my bank account that is – which happens quite often, so you would still be in with a chance.'

'Fu-nny,' Dave responded, exaggerating both syllables. 'On a serious note though; I know what you mean. I've always said that if anyone hurt my family, I'd do time for them. I'd kill for them.'

Ian threw his hands wide, screwed up one cheek and nodded to one side, indicating he was not entirely in agreement.

'All dads say that, but if the worst ever did happen, how many of us could actually do something?' In the heat of the moment, maybe - you might lash out and kill the person who had harmed them, but doing it in the cold light of day is an entirely different matter – I don't know if I could.'

The conversation paused just long enough for both men to consume another spoonful.

Dave then began waggling his empty spoon, indicating his intention to speak as soon as his mouth was clear.

'All this proves one thing,' the roofer observed.

'What's that?'

'Blokes don't need a pint of lager in their hand to talk utter bollocks; a mug of stew is just as good.'

1

Sunday, 21 June 2009. 18:09 hours.

The heavy, glazed aluminium door engaged its frame with a single, decisive click. Releasing his grip on the handle, Ian Bradshaw moved further into the hall, parting the press-studs on the front of his weatherproof coat as he did so, subconsciously synchronising each pop with a single footfall.

To the rustle of the coat being stowed on a crowded hook in the hall cupboard, another sound was added - that of the kettle being filled in the kitchen.

'Ian, is that you?'

The voice was that of his wife, Debbie; Debs, when Ian was feeling particularly affectionate.

'Who else would it be?' he replied, putting sufficient force into his voice to carry it through the lounge and on to the far end of the kitchen.

He could hear the distant chink of mugs as he seated himself, perched on the edge of a small armchair that stood beneath the stairs, ready to do battle with his boots. Fed up with the laces working loose - despite them being tied with a double bow - in a fit of pique, Ian had knotted them, over and over, rendering them almost impossible to undo without the aid of a sharp knife and a steady hand.

'What you been up to?' he called, trying to disregard feelings similar to those experienced by a man held in a straitjacket.

'Nothing really.'

He could hear the clunk of mugs impacting gently on the table.

'Thought you might have been seeing that soppy old battle-axe of a mother of yours.'

This was no mumble. It came, squeezed from the pit of his stomach.

Debbie's response was no whisper either. It was loud and shrill.

'Ian! That's a horrible thing to say.'

'Well she is,' Ian whined, placing his Swiss army knife back in his pocket and his boots on the rack beneath his coat. 'Her only redeeming quality is that she stays well away from here when I'm at home.'

Surprised this last remark did not evoke the reaction he had intended, Ian padded across the living room carpet, holding back further conversation until he could see his wife face to face. There was nothing in particular he wished to say, but their meeting was guaranteed to spark off idle chat on some subject or other, and besides, he was keen to plant a kiss on her lips.

Debbie stood in the kitchen waiting for him, her face a mixture of dumbfounded shock and intense embarrassment. Beside her, sitting at the table, was Beryl, Debbie's mother, who looked on in disgust. Neither woman spoke a single a word.

At that moment Ian wished, more than anything else in the world, that a masked assassin would suddenly break cover from a hiding place in one of the kitchen cupboards and put a bullet through the back of his head. Maybe two, just to be sure.

***

Sunday, 21 June 2009. 18:09 hours.

The front door clicked shut. It did so in much the same way as it always did, but this time the sound carried with it significance - a memory. Ian was no stranger to the feeling. On many occasions the merest hint of a fragrance, or a song's core riff, had reminded him strongly of events in the past. Flavours often had the same effect. They were all links between the events of past and present. The closing of a door was not. If it had been, he would have experienced the current sensation every time he stepped from the porch through to the hall.

'Ian, is that you?'

He knew Debbie was going to say those words.

'Who else would it be?' he replied as he walked up the hall.

Having placed his coat in the cupboard, he seated himself and began to remove his boots with the aid of his knife.

'What you been up to?' he called, his words tailing off. He had said those exact same words before. He was almost sure of it.

'Nothing really.'

'Thought you might have been seeing that soppy old battleaxe of a mother of yours.'

No sooner had the words passed his lips, he was regretting having said them. He knew that when he stepped through the lounge to the kitchen, Beryl would be there, waiting for him.

'Ian! That's a horrible thing to say.'

By the shrill, awkward and outraged tone of her voice, Debbie had confirmed his fears without the need to see for himself. There was only one thing to do and that was to face the music. Sure enough, on reaching the kitchen, both Debbie and Beryl were waiting for him.

***

Sunday, 21 June 2009. 18:09 hours.

Ian Bradshaw closed the front door behind him, applying sufficient pressure to ensure the spring bolt engaged the doorframe. The resultant click had an unusual effect. On countless previous occasions it had served merely to confirm the door was secure. However, on this occasion it provoked such a premonition that Ian remained standing on the coir doormat for some moments, his eyes slowly scanning the hall, his mouth partially open.

He had lived this moment before. He knew he was about to remove his coat; nothing unusual there. He knew he would then sit down to remove his boots; nothing unusual there either. He knew he would then insult his mother-in-law who would be sitting in the kitchen waiting to make him wish he were dead.

'Ian, is that you?'

Stunned, Ian did not answer. Instead he walked through the lounge to the kitchen, still wearing his fastened coat and walking boots. As expected, Beryl was there, sitting at the kitchen table, near empty glass of white wine in hand, reading a magazine. Debbie was at the far end of the kitchen making hot drinks.

Ian stood in the doorway.

Beryl managed to break away from an article on celebrity lifestyles long enough to offer a feeble greeting. Debbie's reaction was more welcoming, but she was surprised to see her husband still wore his outdoor clothing, and by the bewildered expression on his face.

'Is everything all right?' she asked, placing a hot mug gently down upon the table in front of her mother. 'I hope those boots of yours are clean.'

Ian failed to acknowledge the mild reprimand.

'I've done this all before,' he replied, still trying to come to terms with what was happening.

'That's just déjà vu. You must have had that before,' Debbie said with authority. 'No pun intended.'

'Yes, of course I have, but this is different. Déjà vu is all about feeling you've done something before. What I am feeling is that I was about to do something I've done before, but managed to stop myself.'

Beryl had never thought much of her son in-law and made no attempt to hide it. Closing her magazine, she stood up and grabbed her handbag.

'I won't stay,' she said, sneering at Ian. 'I'm running a bit late so I shouldn't stay for coffee after all. I wouldn't want to miss my bus.'

With that she left, making a point of saying goodbye to Debbie while at the same time ignoring Ian.

'What on Earth was that all about?' Debbie asked once she had seen her mother out.

'She's never liked me. I'm okay with that.'

'No, not Mum – all this stuff about stopping yourself doing something you were going to do. It sounded very odd. No wonder she made such a quick exit.'

Ian shook his head, lips distorting as he searched for the best way to describe the strange sensation he had just experienced. He began slowly.

'It's weird. I came in and while I was removing my boots I made an insulting comment about your mother, not knowing she was sitting right here in the kitchen. I was mortified and wished I'd never said it. Then my ears started buzzing, I felt disorientated and lo and behold, I am coming in through the front door again, realise she's here and stop myself blurting out that I think she's a soppy old battle-axe.'

Debbie's lips narrowed visibly at this comment, but Ian ignored her and finished what he was saying.

'Somehow, I was given a chance to take things back.'

'Don't be so ridiculous. You came in here with your boots on, saw Mum, felt like insulting her, but thought better of it. End of story.'

Ian felt foolish. His wife's quick analysis was the only explanation.

'I suppose you're right.'

'Suppose? Of course I'm right,' Debbie retorted, confidence permeating her every word. 'Now stop acting all strange. You've already made Mum feel so uncomfortable she had to leave.'

'Rubbish. You know how much she dislikes me. I didn't have to say anything.'

Debbie could not deny her husband and her mum had next to nothing in common and had never quite bonded with each other.

'Okay, let's say nothing more about it,' she suggested, picking up the mug intended for her mother, and offering it to her husband by way of closure.

Ian took a sip and changed the subject to that of the hiking expedition from which he had just returned.

Two days of bracing walks, interspersed with one chill night in a two man tent, was not to everyone's taste, but to Ian and his companion it offered far more than being cosseted in a warm house ever could. They had been denied television, but they had experienced the satisfaction of achieving a goal, and Ian, albeit temporarily, had been released from a society that forced him to work in an environment that daily caused his chest to constrict to the point he believed it to be his last.

Debbie was understanding and feared for her husband's health, but she also understood they had bills to pay and two children to support as they went through years of expensive university education. Once Stephen and Ann had finally emerged from their respective seats of learning and established lives for themselves, Ian and Debbie's options would open up. Until that time, they would have to make sacrifices. That meant Ian continuing to turn up for work, however much he detested it, his wife's wages making a useful contribution to the household income, but being insufficient to permit her husband to remain at home, idle.

For Ian, the evening passed all too quickly, a sense of dread building within him, brought on by the thought of returning to the office in the morning. The closer it came to bedtime, the less he could be bothered to speak. It was not fair on his wife, but there seemed nothing he could do to snap himself out of his ever darkening mood. At ten o'clock, unable to concentrate on his favourite programmes, and certainly in no condition to give the extraordinary events of the day a second thought, he retired to bed.

The alarm clock sounded eight hours later. Ian's reaction was to award himself an extra five minutes in bed; then another; then another. He was not in the least bit tired; rather, he could not bring himself to face the prospect of yet another working week.

His reluctance to start the day solved nothing; it merely made things worse. When eventually he threw back the covers, time had become so short he was forced to bolt down his breakfast - tea and toast - without having had the chance to sit down and enjoy it.

Hastening out of the door, his sense of urgency was short-lived, failing completely as he slumped into the driving seat of his car.

The hand holding the ignition key lay lifeless upon his lap as he stared at the controls before him, trying to summon up sufficient motivation to commence the journey. None was forthcoming.

With blank disinterest, Ian's eyes followed the movement of his left arm as it reached round for the seatbelt hanging above his right shoulder and clicked it into place down by his left hip. His right arm, bored with lying idle, reached forward and inserted the key into the ignition and turned it, bringing the car to life. It seemed his body was conspiring against his mind, forcing him to comply with what was expected of him.

The journey to the office was short. Two minutes took him through the small village that lay half a mile from his home. A further eight minutes was enough to cover the remaining four miles, it consisting entirely of unbending, uninspiring, dual carriageway that brought him to within a hundred metres of the office block in which he toiled daily. A short journey, but nonetheless one of sufficient duration for Ian to start questioning himself as to whether or not he could be bothered to complete it.

On many occasions he had considered pulling into a lay-by, abandoning the car, and walking away across the fields to where, he knew not; rather that than subject himself to the inevitable tightening in his chest he experienced every morning on turning in through the gates of the car park.

With the engine switched off, it was all Ian could do to force himself to let go of the steering wheel, leave his vehicle and enter the building.

Arriving at his desk, he removed his suit jacket, hung it up, sat down on his swivel chair and reached forward to switch on the computer terminal. Apart from exchanging the usual politeness of bidding each other good morning, Ian could not be bothered to engage in any further conversation with the two clerks who made up the rest of the section. He might be in charge but thankfully they were sufficiently self-motivated to get on with their work without needing his input.

From his top drawer, Ian took a packet of indigestion pills and crunched two of them between his teeth in a vain attempt to quell the nausea that rose from the pit of his stomach.

The in-tray, an unpleasant shade of shiny brown plastic, sat silent and still, filled with the source of all misery - a great pile of paper that never got any higher or any lower and every piece essentially the same. An order, whether great or small, was always processed in the same way. Details of customer and quantity were entered onto the computer. A phone call to ascertain the date and place of shipment and then there would follow the printing of a thousand documents for distribution to as many places: accounts; transport; packing; customer; file, et cetera, et cetera, et cetera. The list went on. It was always the same. No matter what day of the week or month of the year, the job was always the same. The orders sapped hope and brought a living death to all whose eyes fell upon them.

'Kill me,' Ian said quietly. He had intended for the words to stay within his head, but somehow they had escaped.

'Pardon?'

At least the other staff on the section knew he was there. He wondered if they had heard what he said or if they had only heard him speak, but had not caught the words. Either way, he doubted very much if they cared why he had said what he had.

'Nothing,' he replied.

It was difficult to relate to them, separated as they were by a generation of cultural differences. The two clerks' ages combined did not total his own forty-eight years, and it showed.

The door opened at the end of the office. Mr Greeve had decided to leave the inner sanctum and venture out on patrol; something he did at least once a week. Even from this distance, Ian could see the man was openly displaying his usual sense of superiority. Today he was even worse, having a brace of junior management in tow to impress. Both attendants were managing to do fine impersonations of Uriah Heap, never straightening their backs fully, never stepping more than a micron from their master's side. Section by section, the three men wafted through, Mr Greeve taking great delight in belittling the staff in front of his understudies. He revelled at the remarks of the few unctuous sycophants who had sold their souls to the devil to secure early promotion. Now was not a good moment for Ian to speak to the company director, but there was no avoiding it.

'Ahh, Mr Bradshaw. And how are we doing in your area of the world? Hmm?'

Mr Greeve was very animated when he spoke. His eyes, his mouth, indeed his whole head were needed just to put this simple question. The animation ended with him looking down his nose, the muscles surrounding his mouth bunched up, his head tilted slightly back.

Ian stared at this squat, inadequate, self-important little man with the greatest of contempt in his eyes, gently biting the inside of his lip as he formulated the exact words he wished to say.

'It would appear by the way you speak to your staff, you were either born to a race of arseholes, you are suffering from a serious mental health problem, or you have an exceedingly small penis. By the cut of your trousers, I'm minded to think it's the tiny dick.'

Mr Greeve's mouth fought to strike back, but only managed a splutter, showering Ian with a fine spray of spittle.

Ian had not finished.

'I, for one, have had enough of your company, its lousy pay, the monotonous, soul destroying, repetitive work and in particular, you sir! It would give me the utmost pleasure if you would take this and see just how far you can shove it up your anal passage.'

As he ranted, Ian held a shatterproof plastic ruler up in front of him.

'I'm betting you can take it all.'

'HAVE YOU QUITE FINISHED MR BRADSHAW?' the director exploded, emphasising each and every word.

Calmly, Ian replied, wrapped in a sense of being fully in control of the situation.

'Yes, thank you, I do believe I have.'

2

Ian burst into the kitchen, eager to see his wife.

'It's happened again,' he announced excitedly.

Debbie looked confused and said nothing.

Ian stared at her as though she should know what he meant.

'It has happened again,' he repeated, his mouth stretching sideways more than was necessary.

'It?'

Exasperated, Ian expanded his explanation.

'First I told the boss to go fuck himself. Then I heard that buzzing sound again and then I didn't.'

'Didn't what?' Debbie asked, still confused.

'Didn't tell my boss to go fuck himself, of course.'

'Ian, slow down,' Debbie began at a steady pace, placing one hand on his upper arm and looking directly into his excited eyes. 'Let's think about this logically. You saw your boss and were rude to him. Then you saw him and were not rude to him. We can conclude that either you did actually tell him where to go and somehow managed to rewind time so you could retract your statement, or you were only fantasising about what you would like to have said to him. Which do you think sounds the more plausible explanation?'

Having quickly considered the two options, Ian's shoulders slumped, his chin sank to his chest and his eyes fixed on the middle distance, his body crestfallen. His head, ever so slightly, began moving from side to side.

'Of course, you're right. Just like last time,' Ian conceded, his lifeless voice bearing all the qualities of a man about to launch himself from a bridge. 'Debs, what's wrong with me?'

Stepping closer, Debbie's arm slid round behind her husband's back, pulling him towards her. The embrace lasted until she was certain she had established calm at which point she pulled away, her hand drawing across her husband's arm, soothing him further.

'I'll run you a nice hot bath and put some of my aromatherapy oil in it. You're probably over tired; that's all.'

For once, the evening did not seem to pass quickly. Tormented by fears for his sanity, the minutes dragged by until, at last, it was time to sleep and perhaps to be free from worry for a few hours.

The remainder of the week dragged on, all the while with him trying to suppress his desire to burst into tears. It was not a moment too soon that the weekend came around again.

Saturday was uneventful: shopping with his wife in the morning; a drink in the pub in the evening, Roland and Faye making up the foursome.

Sunday saw Ian wandering round the house as though he had something on his mind. Debbie tried several times to find out what was wrong. Each time she was either assured it was nothing, or she had her head bitten off.

'Is it the thought of going back to that place again?' she asked, pleading. 'Please let me help. It's not fair to treat me this way. I've done nothing wrong.'

She was right. Telling her would undoubtedly lead to upset, but keeping it from her any longer would be doubly damaging.

'I know you think I'm going mad, but it's happened again. This time it was different though.'

'I'm listening,' Debbie said, looking at her husband suspiciously, failing to inject any hint of sensitivity.

'Yesterday, Saturday, I confided in a so-called friend, giving him some information regarding a third party. This friend and I were in the bar next Sunday…'

'Next Sunday?' Debbie cut in.

Irritated by the interruption, Ian continued.

'As I was saying, this friend and I were in the bar next Sunday when in walks the subject of our conversation. Peter, my so-called friend, let me down and told this person what I'd said. It was just like the first time when I was rude to your mother. I wanted the ground to open up and swallow me whole. Then I found myself back at yesterday, having the opportunity to tell him the secret all over again. Of course, knowing what that would lead to, I didn't.'

Debbie was shaking her head, looking deep into her husband's eyes.

'Ian, I really think you need to make an appointment to see the doctor. Listen to yourself. You're really beginning to worry me.'

His reply was spoken with passion and at the rate of knots.

'I know it sounds weird, but I can prove what I'm saying. I'll write down everything I can remember that has happened over the coming week. You can keep hold of it until next Sunday and you'll see it has all come true and the only way that can have happened is if I've lived that week before.'

'That wouldn't prove anything,' Debbie said, speaking far more slowly than her husband. 'Take for example you playing golf. You could write you'll play at noon on Thursday and then go there just to make your prediction come true.'

'No, I wouldn't do that. Anyway, I'll write down all those things I have no control over. Like the milkman dropping a bottle of cream soda on our doorstep on Friday morning and leaving the tiles all sticky for you to clear up.'

Reluctantly, Debbie agreed to her husband's suggestion, if only to diffuse the moment and to give herself time to think. Ian immediately began rummaging through a draw full of papers, searching for a pristine notebook in which to commence writing his predictions.

'I'm off to bed now,' Debbie said. 'Don't stay up too late.'

Ian could only manage a mumble by way of acknowledgement, wrapped up as he was in his task.

Debbie woke to find her husband bending over her in the half-light, attempting to plant an affectionate kiss on her forehead. His breath smelled minty-fresh, highlighting the fact hers was not. She felt a book being thrust into her clutches.

'Don't lose this. I've been up half the night trying to remember. I've been racking my brains for all things I could have no influence over. You try remembering details of the week you've just had. It's really difficult.'

Debbie reached to one side, located her bedside lamp and switched it on. Ian looked smart in his best suit; clean-shaven, hair neatly combed back, but his eyes were bloodshot and framed by dark shadows.

'Are you going to be all right?' she asked, genuine concern written all over her face.

She realised immediately her question had sounded ambiguous. It might have referred to his ability to drive having had insufficient sleep. Equally it could refer to his mental condition, a subject best left unexplored.

'I mean, are you fit to drive?' she added quickly.

His reactions were noticeably slower than she was used to. Again, was this due to fatigue, or mental incapacity?

'I'm a little tired, but other than that I feel the best I have done so in a very long time.'

Her eyes alone asked the next question.

Ian smiled benignly back at herm   .

'Don't worry about me. That book is proof I'm not mad and it has given me something other than work to think about. It will get me through the week in small doses as I wait for my next prediction to come true.'

'Give me a proper kiss,' Debbie instructed, a small but pleasant smile creeping across her face.

Ian leant forward, pressing his lips to hers. Then he turned and left the room, calling back from the safety of the landing.

'Brush your teeth; your breath's minging.'

She smiled again; this time more broadly, sat up in bed, supported by all four pillows, and began to read.

'Monday: You're not at work. We will receive a letter from Aunt May in Australia. It will contain a photograph of her new ginger cat.

When I get home, you will tell me you had plans to go to lunch with Sandra but she locked herself out of her house and had to wait next door for the locksmith to come. Sue called round so you had lunch with her instead.

On the news, a tanker has gone aground and threatens to spill oil down the Scottish coast.'

Debbie decided not to read on. The text contained references to what she would be doing over the coming week. If she was aware what she was supposed to be doing, she might make them happen without realising it. Closing the covers, she slipped the notebook into the drawer of her bedside cabinet and went downstairs to have breakfast. Within half an hour the washing machine was on the go; the ironing pile had been taken upstairs; she had hoovered throughout, and was now in the process of boiling the kettle for a well-earned mug of coffee to accompany the toast that was beginning to brown under the grill.

Settling herself at the kitchen table, Debbie bit into a slice of toast. The crunch was synchronous with the sound of the post dropping to the mat in the hall. She froze. Receiving mail was not uncommon, especially with all the unsolicited, unwelcome, junk that was shoved through the door these days, but this was the first test. She felt silly. It was obviously not possible for her husband to turn back time. The book she had so cheerfully accepted from him this morning contained the jottings of someone well on his way to having a nervous breakdown. This thought saddened her, causing her to pause both what she was doing and what she was thinking, sitting blankly for a moment before shaking herself free from her melancholy.

Whatever was to happen to her husband, she would always love him and would take whatever action was necessary to make him better. She wondered how best to present the results of his experiment - to break to him the inevitable conclusion his predictions had simply been a figment of his imagination. It might be wiser to do so directly on his return home from work in the evening, or it might be kinder to play along with him at least until the end of the week. On balance, it seemed the right thing to do to put an end to his delusions as quickly as possible. She would tell him the moment he walked through the door. After all, he would be eager for confirmation he had been right all along. Anything she might say to delay giving him negative results would be a lie and that would not be right.

Debbie stood up, wrapped her dressing gown tightly about her and went to fetch the post. There was quite a lot of it, the majority fallen to the floor as a bundle, with one or two additional pieces scattered elsewhere. Gathering the mail in her hand, she made her way back into the kitchen to finish her coffee.

'Junk, bill, bill, junk, more junk,' she listed aloud as she sifted the envelopes for anything of interest. She would put the junk in the bin and leave the bills for her husband.

'Insurance quote, holiday cottages…' and then she stopped.

Her fingers shook at the sight of a single, brightly coloured stamp bearing the word Australia, adorning the top right-hand corner of an otherwise normal, manila envelope. The handwriting was not entirely familiar but she had the uneasy feeling she had seen it before. One thumb penetrated beneath the flap of the envelope, slid along its length and assisted the other to pull apart the front and back to allow the contents to flop onto the table. A folded letter enclosed several photographs. Parting the missive with the fingers of a bomb disposal expert, the subject of the snapshots was revealed. They showed a ginger cat in three different poses: standing; sitting; sleeping.

Kicking her feet into the quarry-tiled floor, Debbie pushed her chair away from the table with one sharp movement. She looked at the pictures lying there, unmoving, somehow sinister. They seemed to be shouting back at her, 'now who's mad?' Her heart was pounding; her whole body shaking; her breathing erratic. She nodded to herself several times as if to agree to a plan she had suddenly conjured up out of thin air. Gathering the debris of paper and plastic sleeves, she stuffed everything into one of the kitchen drawers, not having read a single word other than the phrase 'all my love, Aunt May'.

The next task on her agenda was to shower and dress before popping down to the local supermarket for some normality. It was close to midday before she returned, laden with the essentials: potatoes; bread; cheese - foods that could be relied upon; nothing out of the ordinary. As the last of the heavy bags was hoisted up onto the worktop ready to be sorted away, the phone rang. Flustered, Debbie trotted the length of the kitchen, picked up the receiver and said, 'Hello'.

'Debs, it's me. I've locked myself out of the house and I'm in next door's waiting for the locksmith.'

For the second time that morning, Debbie found herself thrown into a state of stunned silence. It took a moment for her to rediscover her ability to speak, at which time she apologised to her friend and told her she hoped the locksmith would arrive without too much delay. No sooner than she had hung up, the doorbell rang. It had to be Sue - Ian had spoken and apparently whatever he said always came true.

It was indeed Sue. She had been in the neighbourhood and dropped in when she saw Debbie's car on the drive.

'Sue, do me a favour. While I make us a sandwich, check the news and tell me if there's anything about an oil tanker.'

It took a minute or two to find the remote, to turn on the television and to find the right channel. Meanwhile, Debbie finished putting the shopping away before gathering together the makings of lunch from the refrigerator.

'Yes, here it is. An oil tanker has gone aground off the coast of Scotland. They're saying…'

On hearing the first four words of her friend's sentence, Debbie dropped the butter knife on the chopping board and made her way through to the living room where she snatched the remote from Sue's hand and used it to terminate the picture. Sue looked surprised.

'Sorry,' Debbie said, failing to explain her actions further. 'Come through. Lunch is nearly ready.'

As soon as Sue had left, less than an hour later, Debbie went upstairs, retrieved her husband's book of predictions, took it into the garden and burned it on the barbecue.

Ian returned home some hours later.

'Well, did my predictions come true?'

Debbie could not look him in the face. Then he noticed she smelled of smoke and began to eye her suspiciously. A black smut sat on her cheek, just below her right eye.

'They did come true, didn't they,' he spoke as if to coax a confession from her.

She remained silent. He looked at her knowingly, took her hands in his and tried again.

'It's all right. You can tell me. I know anyway.'

She was not beaten yet.

'You say you have lived this week already. What if it is just a premonition? You obviously knew what is going to happen this week, but it doesn't necessarily mean you have the power to turn back time.'

Ian thought hard before answering.

'A premonition is a foreknowledge of an isolated, dramatic event that happens at some time in the future. What I have predicted are the small, everyday events that lead up to a non-event, and it will be a non-event because I travelled back through time to prevent it. On Sunday there isn't going to be a plane crash. There isn't going to be an explosion. What there will be is someone who isn't told something because someone else wasn't told it in the first place. That's all.'

The force of his argument was confusing, but nevertheless overpowered that of his wife. She was forced to accept what he was saying, even if she did not like it.

'Okay, but it gives me the creeps and I don't want you doing it again,' she said, her trembling voice indicating she was close to tears. 'Promise me Ian. Promise me you will never do it again.'

Astonishingly, she was blaming him for something over which he evidently had no control. His first thought was to vehemently protest his innocence, but using self-control and an educated guess that such action could only provoke further admonishment, he settled upon an alternative stance.

Sat, hunched at the table, Ian displayed an appearance normally associated with a schoolboy receiving a stiff reprimand.

'Sorry,' he mumbled, weakly. 'I promise.'

His body language indicated compliance, but the contradictory crossed fingers he held, hidden behind his back, mirrored his true intentions.

3

The promise lasted eight days, the intervening period being divided equally between two trains of thought. Why had no further rewinding occurred and was it possible somehow to initiate the process, perhaps by the power of thought?

To the first question, there seemed only one answer. Nothing really embarrassing had happened since the moment when a friend had let slip Ian's juicy bit of gossip to none other than the subject of that gossip. No embarrassing situation; no resulting desire for the ground to open up and swallow him. As the process appeared to be triggered by this emotion, it should have come as no surprise that further supernatural events had remained absent.

This simple conclusion raised an additional question. If another awkward circumstance arose, as he felt it was sure to, would he be given the same opportunity to take things back as he had been on the previous three occasions – insulting his mother-in-law; insulting his boss; insulting the recipient of the gossip Ian had spread? Keen for an answer, Ian was sorely tempted to insult someone just to find out, but with the situation staged, he would not truly be horrified by his own actions and therefore regression might not be triggered. That said, having issued an insult which could not be retracted would cause real embarrassment. Might then it cause the phenomenon after all?

As to the second question, the thought of being able to control the process excited him greatly, causing much loss of sleep and an inability to concentrate on any other subject. He had assured his wife he would not do it again, but from the outset it was clear it was going to prove an impossible promise to keep. That is to say, if he were able to rewind time, he most certainly would.

Debbie was spending the evening at the theatre with her very good friend, Carol, leaving Ian with the house to himself for at least four hours. It was the perfect opportunity to take a freak of nature and determine whether or not it could be tamed.

Punctual as ever, Carol arrived at exactly a quarter to seven. Debbie, anxious not to keep her friend waiting for a second longer than necessary, rushed out through the front door. In her haste, she tripped over the threshold, her upper body adopting a horizontal, mid-air pose that looked certain to end in a collision with the concrete driveway. Even as she flew, Ian could see how this was going to end: severe grazing to both hands and feet; a wasted evening in the accident and emergency department of the local hospital, and a lost opportunity to conduct his experiments. Thankfully though, Debbie's feet, working hard, somehow managed to keep up with the rest of her body, long enough for her to slam against the boot of Carol's car, embarrassed but unhurt.

Keen as a cat to make out the incident had never happened, Debbie scooped up her clutch bag and clambered into the passenger seat. Not waiting to fasten her seatbelt, she could be seen signing frantically, urging her friend to drive on without further delay.

Sure they had gone, Ian switched off the ring on the telephone, locked the doors, turned out all the lights, closed the curtains and made himself comfortable on the bed. He lay with his eyes closed, arms by his sides, and thought about what he should do next. Opening his eyes again, just long enough to glance at the glowing green display of the bedside clock, he took note the time was now 7:02. The house was warm, the light subdued, the duvet beneath him soft and welcoming. With the addition of a pillow placed gently over his eyes, Ian slid into a state of relaxation long unknown to him.

It seemed a sensible place to start would be to concentrate on the feeling of time rewinding, but just what that sensation was supposed to be, he had not a clue. As far as he was aware, nobody had.

Allowing the image of his most recent movements to fill his mind and thinking how they might appear in reverse, Ian's unseeing eyes began mimicking the regressive motion of his imagination. All the while, he was aware of the bed, the slight pressure of the pillow on his forehead and the frustrating fact that nothing unusual was happening. Another glance at the clock confirmed he had stubbornly remained in the present. In fact, he had slipped three minutes into the future, the digits of the clock now reading 7:05.

He tried the same approach again, concentrating very, very hard, enough to tense every muscle in his body, causing him to grunt under the strain.

The clock read 7:09. A respite was needed before a further attempt could be made.

Changing tactics slightly, Ian thought hard about situations that would make him cringe with embarrassment and how much he would like to change them if they became reality. Nothing. It was a quarter past seven, he was exhausted both mentally and physically and there had not been the merest hint of success. The sense of intense relaxation that had eluded him for years once again vanished.

It was too soon to give up. The evening was still young and it would be hours before his wife returned. Hence, his hands interlocked and came to rest on his chin, the two index fingers touching the opening of his nostrils, elbows drawn into the sides of his ribcage. All conscious thought was allowed to slip away, restoring composure. Soon, the state of relaxation he had experienced earlier was back, welcomed like a long lost friend. The moment had come to try again and this time it would be different.

As if to reset the experiment to zero, Ian took another look at the bedside clock. 7:20.

Placing the pillow back over his eyes, resting his hands across his stomach, he began to will the surroundings into himself, sucking in his buttocks with the effort. The atmosphere in the room pressed inwards upon his head. He was willing himself backwards, imagining he was grabbing at his clothing without letting himself physically close his hands. The muscles about his eyes became tight, forcing his mouth into an involuntary, twisted smile. The tip of his tongue pressed upwards against the roof of his mouth, drawing backwards while maintaining firm and constant pressure. Deep within his ears he could feel a hum, a sensation so pleasant he would have been happy for it to stay with him for hours, but this was not the right sound; it was not the same sensation that had accompanied his previous rewinds, and he could still feel the bed beneath him. Nothing had changed. Not yet.

Tensing his muscles ever so slightly, trying to contract them to the bone, he imagined his eyeballs were receding into his head. Not upwards, not sideways, but back through the bone of the sockets that held them. He was afraid to breathe out, frightened any movement away from the core of his body would prevent what he desired so badly. He inhaled slowly, smoothly, under total control. He exhaled, trying to do so in a way that his breath would not condense on a mirror if anyone should examine him to determine whether he was, in fact, dead.

The buzzing returned, but this time it was different. Low in frequency, it filled his eardrums, spreading to envelop the sides of his head and penetrating to the very depths of his eyeballs. He no longer had any sensation of being on the bed; of weight. The only sound was the buzzing; low and constant. He could feel his eardrums closing together to meet at the centre of his skull. Every muscle fluttered without moving, like a butterfly trapped beneath the skin. The sensation was both vivid and brief and stopped the moment Ian opened his eyes.

What he saw was not the underside of a pillow, but the bed as he approached it and the clock next to it reading 6:59.

'Shit! I've done it!'

Exhilaration counteracted both exhaustion and the fear that had made him open his eyes so quickly.

Keen to repeat the experiment - to build upon his initial success - he returned immediately to the starting position: hands folded on his stomach; pillow placed gently over his eyes. This time he was starting with an advantage. He knew the sensations he sought, a knowledge that would surely increase the potential for further success.

As he had anticipated, it proved far easier to trigger the process on the second occasion, the low frequency buzzing returning almost on command. There was no fear. There was nothing to be afraid of. He was in control and was thoroughly enjoying an experience that was becoming more and more familiar with every passing second.

Then, quite without warning, the frequency changed, becoming no less pleasant, but a great deal higher. The fluttering of his muscles quickened to a startling rate, enough to make his eyes burst open, frantic to see what had happened. The bed had gone; indeed the bedroom had gone. He was now in the driving seat of his car, travelling in excess of eighty miles per hour in the outside lane of a very busy motorway and he had absolutely no knowledge of where he was going, or where he had just been.

Reactions induced by severe panic brought the speed down to a more modest fifty, while, at the same time, manoeuvring the vehicle into the inside lane, across fast moving traffic, with only scant regard to the mirrors. Several pairs of headlights flashed wildly and at least one horn streaked by, operated by the incredulous driver of a white company van.

Beads of sweat dotted Ian's forehead and upper lip; quick breaths vibrated in and out; trembling hands clung to the steering wheel. Within a few minutes though, the traffic that surrounded Ian's car on three sides had either not witnessed his appalling display of lane control, or had forgiven him, leaving him to continue his unidentified journey in peace.

Inside the car there were no clues to his whereabouts except that he was on his own. Externally, it was late afternoon and there were no junction signs that might be of help. Thinking back, he remembered having been on a motorway journey only three times during the preceding month, assuming of course he still was within the preceding month. That thought alone could easily have sparked off another panic attack had it not been for a sign for the motorway services coming into view. Not only would he be able to soothe his nerves with a hot drink, he now knew on which road he was travelling. This had to be the last of the three trips, on the Saturday only three days before, and he was heading home.

The facility Ian was keenest to visit was the men's toilet. It was a strange fact that less than fifteen minutes earlier, his bladder had been empty, but having travelled backwards, it was suddenly full - uncomfortably so. Having emptied it again, under the same circumstances as before, Ian washed his hands, as he had done before. Presumably in an attempt to save the planet, the dryer produced only a waft of lukewarm air, cutting out every few seconds, causing Ian to finish the job by wiping his hands on his trousers. He was not alone in adopting this solution. In fact, it was possible for those outside the toilet area to determine who harboured sufficient concern for their personal hygiene to run their hands under the short-duration taps. Those who emerged from the men's room, the front of their thighs a shade darker, had; those whose trousers remained dry, had not. With his hands still damp, Ian made for the shop. A newspaper confirmed, if confirmation were needed, that this was indeed the Saturday he had assumed it to be – the fourth of July; Independence Day across the pond.

Noticing the shop had a lottery terminal, he decided to invest a pound, as he normally did, once a week. However, this was not a habit set in stone. He would only play if he found himself conveniently close to an outlet that catered for it. This casual attitude towards buying a ticket made it unwise to choose the same six numbers. That method might lead to him discovering his numbers had come up on an occasion when he could not be bothered to place them; an unfortunate occurrence that had happened to a work colleague who had never been quite the same since, every argument with her husband ending with, 'Well, if you'd only bought the ticket as you were supposed to…' It was unfair, particularly as he had promised never to mention it again, accepting it was simply not meant to be.

An alternative would have been to let the terminal choose the numbers for him, but, Ian reasoned, being more superstitious than he cared to admit, it must heighten the odds stacked against him. It seemed somehow particularly unlikely that one lottery machine would pick the same numbers as another.

Ian's preferred method was to use random numbers, but possessing a mind more suited to sequences, he relied upon his surroundings. On this occasion, six numbers presented themselves without much searching: the date was the fourth; a magazine fell open at pages sixteen and seventeen; a sign read 'buy one, get one free'; a newspaper heading told of twelve having died; and forty-two was his favourite number, his favourite author having suggested it was the answer to the meaning of life.

Having purchased the ticket, Ian realised that regressing had not only brought him a full bladder, it had brought him thirst.

It was not until he had purchased a coffee and returned to the car to drink it that it dawned on him what having rewound three days meant. He would now have to live them all over again. The thought of having another Sunday off was neither here nor there, but there would follow two days at work that had been intensely boring the first time. Filling the same orders twice would doubtless be almost unbearable.

Ian arrived home late in the evening, just as he had done before. He ate the same meal and followed his wife to bed when she made the same excuse about having to be up early the next morning. The meal was fine. It was not an obvious clone as he ate the same recipe often. Debbie retiring to bed early was nothing out of the ordinary either, excuses or no excuses. What was different though was the way he felt. Ian was suddenly alive and not merely in the biological sense. His very attitude to life had been changed - recharged.

With the lights out and having exchanged a goodnight kiss, Ian was eager to see whether he could use his new found ability to go forward, returning to the bedroom of three days hence, avoiding the repetition he was so keen to avoid. The first step was to rewind a few more minutes - to make certain he still knew how and could do so without disturbing his wife. Fearing he might accidently regress another three days – or more – Ian opened his eyes almost as soon as the low-frequency buzzing returned. This time he managed to return to the point only seconds before she rolled over to exchange their kiss. It meant that even if he made all the noise in the world, his wife would be none the wiser because that reality would no longer exist. Furthermore, each successive rewind was proving to be easier than the last. If it was possible to go forward as well as back, he was confident he now had the skills to do so.

Allowing his head to sink deep into the pillow, eyes closed, Ian concentrated hard on the future - to the bedroom scene as it appeared at the time of his first success. However, no matter how hard he applied his arsenal of newly discovered techniques, skipping forward remained stubbornly unproductive. Debbie, annoyed by the grunting and squeezing coming from her husband's side of the bed, kicked him in the shins and asked him to stop playing with himself.

'Leave it alone,' she mumbled from beneath the duvet. 'I'm trying to sleep.'

Rewinding again ensured Debbie slept soundly, but it also meant, for the time being, further attempts to go forward were out of the question.

The next opportunity arose the following morning as Debbie showered, the noise of cascading water and the shrill notes of her singing voice disguising any sound he might make.

Ian alternated each unsuccessful attempt with a brief step back in time to confirm the process still worked and to ensure the shower would continue for as long as necessary. By the time he finally admitted defeat he had relived his wife's butchered rendition of a pop classic at least a dozen times and could take no more of it. For now he would remain stuck in the past, forced to move forward at the natural rate of mortal man.

As anticipated, Monday and Tuesday crept forward with such languor that inane conversation, acknowledged briefly the first time round, warranted none the second. For two days, Ian remained almost totally silent, uninterested in his work, his surroundings, or those with whom he shared the office. Despite having practised their completion once already, it took longer to process the orders again, Ian spending much of his time staring blankly at the computer screen, drinking coffee and, as a result, paying frequent visits to the men's room. Every moment that passed was unwelcome, even though it brought him that little bit closer to uncharted history.

Finally, Debbie was saying goodbye as she left for the theatre with her friend, Carol, leaving Ian alone in the house again to put behind him the nightmare of the last three days. This time he left the curtains open, the doors unlocked, the lights blazing and the phone free to ring at will. All he desired was to watch television he had never seen before.

At ten o'clock, Ian made his way upstairs to prepare for bed. Having bathed, he lay in his robe on top of the duvet, allowing his skin to air dry. He felt relaxed - as relaxed as the moment when he first tried to control his ability.

Now the subject was back in his mind, it was very difficult to ignore. A gift such as this could not be ignored. It had to be conquered whatever the danger - however strong the fear. He had to experiment again - having achieved so much in only one short session, how much more was there still to learn?

Ian reasoned there had to be a way of going back in time without there being the danger of seriously overshooting the point to which he wished to return. Perhaps if, when triggering the process he were to concentrate on something specific in the past, he would return straight there. It was worth a try.

Not wishing to go back too far just for the sake of testing a theory, the specific event had to be in the near past, preferably within the confines of that very evening. However, having spent the last three hours glued to the television, it was difficult to pinpoint one particular occurrence that might suffice. Then, he hit upon the image of his wife sailing through the air, her arms flailing, her legs striding to prevent her from impacting with the hard ground. It seemed perfect. It had only happened once – although he had witnessed it twice - it had happened very recently, and the image was still fresh in his mind.

Ian lay back, his eyes closed, a confident smile upon his face as he first pictured his wife's moment of embarrassment, then triggered the process he hoped would allow him to witness it again. This time the low frequency buzzing in the centre of his head, associated with a short trip, was absent. Instead, the higher frequency that had previously whipped him back three days kicked in instantly, ceasing again even before he could open his eyes.

The lifting of his eyelids was but the end of a blink to those who might have seen it, and went entirely unnoticed.

A sense of elation gripped him as he saw again Debbie heading at speed towards the back of her friend's car, her miraculous recovery, and her rushed exit from the scene. The fact he now had to re-live the evening, having already exhausted two alternative ways of passing it, did not cause great frustration - a video or two would see him through to bedtime. Besides, it had been a major achievement and was therefore worth it.

4

Over the coming days the clerks that worked on Ian's section noticed a distinct change for the better in their leader's mood. For him, the subtle differences between one order and another had been temporarily magnified to the point of being almost interesting. Never before had the adage a change is as good as a rest rung so true.

Time proceeded at a steady pace, heading smoothly towards the final hour of the day. Then the telephone rang. Force of habit forbade Ian from answering without first pausing. Firstly, it allowed him to determine, by the ring, whether the call was internal or external, and secondly, it demonstrated he had not yet become subordinate to a plastic box. The palm of his flattened hand rested on the cool, silky-smooth back of the receiver for a moment before fingers and thumb curled round, gripped and raised the device to his ear.

The fact this was an external call made no difference to the way he answered. The response to an internal call would have sounded equally disinterested.

'Ian Bradshaw speaking.'

His introduction was barely punctuated with a full stop before the caller began spewing forth a torrent of unintelligible words, delivered at deafening volume, distorted as a result of the phone being held too close to the lips. As if the experience was not distressing enough, the words being spat into his ear were interspersed with the unmistakable sounds of sobbing.

'Debs?' Ian shook as he spoke. He would recognise her voice however it was disguised. 'What's wrong?'

'It's our house. It's gone,' she shouted, her voice jerking lower with every word.

The colour instantly drained from Ian's face. He felt sick.

'What do you mean, it's gone?'

'There's been a fire,' Debbie spoke slowly in a quavering whisper. 'It's destroyed everything.'

The grief in her voice built a picture of a woman with a tear soaked face; mascara running; nose bubbling; excess saliva strung between distorted lips.

'Stay put. I'll be right there.'

Having slammed the receiver down and grabbed his jacket, Ian sped out of the room, much to the surprise of his fellow workers.

Even before the door closer had finished its job, he had reached the lift at the far end of the corridor where he could be seen impatiently jabbing the call button, cursing. After ten seconds and a dozen presses, the wait had become intolerable. The fire door burst open with the force of Ian's shoulder being driven hard against it, the sound of the handle impacting the wall echoing down the sparse concrete stairwell. At the bottom, a second fire door received similar mistreatment as Ian, by this time sweating profusely, swung himself around the open door by its handle, into the foyer.

The startled receptionist had no time to speak before he was gone, the automatic doors to the car park only just managing to open in time as he sped through.

The drive home appeared to take longer than usual. Every minor delay - a child crossing the road in the village; having to navigate past a parked car - saw a disproportionate rise in the level of Ian's frustration. He gripped the steering wheel tightly, his nails digging into the padded vinyl. Taking more chances than usual, he pulled across in front of oncoming traffic, earning the disrespect of people ignorant of his plight. Miraculously, the journey ended without injury, points being added to his driving licence, or sustaining damage to the car, with the exception of a scuffed tyre.

Two large red fire engines were parked in the road outside his house. A small crowd had gathered across the mouth of the drive, their cars abandoned along the grass verge as though visiting a garden fete that offered insufficient parking. The bystanders looked on with dispassionate interest, their shoes partially submerged in a stream of soot-contaminated water that flowed away from the smouldering remains of what had been the Bradshaw's home.

Debbie was there, head bowed, looking tired and tearful. Someone had thought to wrap a blanket about her shoulders and an old lady had come out of the woodwork to offer tea from a thermos flask.

Ian threw off his seatbelt, clambered out of the car and with the momentum of slamming the door shut behind him, launched himself towards his wife. The instant she saw him, the expression on her face altered to that of relief. The burden could now be shared. Burying her head in his shoulder, they embraced, his left arm holding her tightly, his right hand free to gently stroke her hair. Her sobbing returned, dampening the lapel of his suit jacket.

'We've lost everything,' she said, her words muffled by a breast pocket that pressed against both her nose and mouth.

'I know,' Ian replied simply.

Even at a safe distance it was clear this was no chip pan fire with soot damage to the rest of the house. Windows were broken, whether deliberately by the firemen, or by the savage heat of the fire, Ian did not know. Either way, the thick smoke that had billowed forth had blackened the walls above the lintels and darkened the remaining glass to a dull, impenetrable filthiness. The front door had been forced, the roof had partially collapsed and the remainder was still steaming. Every surface within the property was coated with colours chosen from a pallet of shades of black. Light could not escape from such a place.

'Don't worry,' he said in a smooth, reassuring voice. 'I'm going to make it so that none of this ever happened.'

At this, Debbie's crying ceased instantly with one final sniff, before her head slowly lifted, her reddened eyes fixing upon his.

'What do you mean?' she asked suspiciously.

By the tone of her voice, she had not taken this to be the empty promise of a father placating a son who had just pulled the arm off his favourite toy. It sounded as though she knew what he had in mind, but dared not believe it.

'Are you trying to tell me you can turn back time and prevent this from happening?'

Ian nodded slowly.

'I know you told me not to mess with it, but I couldn't help myself. I've only deliberately gone back a couple of times and it taught me a lesson. I never intended to do it again.'

Debbie did not speak. The mind behind her eyes was working hard but she gave no hint as to what her thoughts were.

The silence made her husband feel uncomfortable.

'The thing is, whatever you say, I will not let this happen,' he said, determination encompassing his every word. 'I will go back and you will never know about the fire and you will never know I broke my promise.' He paused before finishing in a more moderate tone. 'Debbie, I can do this with or without you, but it would mean a lot to me if I had your blessing.'

To such an impassioned plea, she could have but one answer.

'Ian Bradshaw, it's at times like this that I love you so much it hurts. Of course you have my blessing and I can live with the deceit as long as we can get back to the way things were.'

A smile spread across his face as he leant forward, found a relatively dry patch on his wife's forehead and kissed it.

'Great. First of all, I need to know what caused the fire.'

'They think it started in the dining room but as yet have no idea what the source was. That's going to be the job of the investigator to work out.'

It seemed the best way to prevent the fire was to be there when it started, but before that could be accomplished the answers to a few more questions were needed. To provide a degree of privacy, Ian took Debbie's arm in his and guided her to the car, the doors closing out some of the distractions.

'Right, what time did you leave the house this morning?'

Debbie looked confused but needed no further coaxing.

'Let me think. About ten o'clock I suppose. My shift started at midday but I had to do some things in town first.'

'Okay, so I'll skip work after ten so you won't know I'm home. It might change things if you did.'

It was unnerving that her husband was telling her how he intended to deceive her.

'Now I need you to help me think of something specific that happened this morning - something I can concentrate on when I'm regressing.'

'You put the bins out,' Debbie suggested after a moment's hesitation.

'Not specific enough. Knowing my luck I'd accidentally rewind to the first time I ever put the bins out. I have to be careful. I seem to have mastered the rewind but I haven't discovered how to fast forward again.'

'Look Ian, if this is going to be dangerous, maybe we should just claim on the insurance and be done with it.'

Ian wanted to put things right as much for himself as for his wife and was not about to be put off by his wife's insecurities.

'Insurance companies can't replace keepsakes. Besides, it's not dangerous, it's just that I've been given a gift without an instruction book. From what I know so far, the first twenty minutes or so rewind slowly, but then the process picks up speed and if you're not careful, you go too far. However, I've also discovered that time appears to be indexed, so you can go straight to the right spot. All I need is the right marker. If I can't think of something suitable, it's no drama. I will just have to resort to tried and tested methods that might not be so convenient; rewinding a little, working out how far I've gone and then rewinding some more. Simple.'

Debbie relaxed a little, reassured by her husband's casual manner.

'I know,' she said excitedly. 'You put that awful picture out for the dustmen that aunt May gave us.'

'Perfect! Well done, I'll have no problems fixing my thoughts on that monstrosity.'

The couple exchanged a smile.

'No time like the present then.'

If his wife experienced second thoughts, Ian did not witness any change of expression, for no sooner had he announced his intention did he recline in his seat, close his eyes and fill his mind with memories of his fist punching through the hideous landscape his aunt had burdened them with. Now she had emigrated to Australia, there was little chance she might ever discover its fate.

Even before his eyes had opened, he could feel his arm was again protruding through his aunt's gift, right up to his elbow.

Shortly afterwards, Ian went to work as before, but by ten in the morning was showing all the signs of having succumbed to a non-specific illness and was forced, at the suggestion of the office manager, to return home. Thankfully, Debbie's recollection had been accurate and she had already left the house.

The sole purpose of being at home was to detect the cause of the fire that was due to start within the next few hours. Ian reasoned that merely by being there he had the potential to alter the future in such a way he might only postpone the start of the fire without knowing it. For example, by using the electric kettle he might jolt a loose wire, putting off the inevitable spark to a later date. If that were to happen, the effort he had expended just to be there, and the further effort of manning a stakeout for hour after lonely hour, would all be for nothing.

To be on the safe side, Ian sat at the kitchen table and began to read a book by the natural sunlight that poured through the window, unwilling to activate anything that used either gas or electricity. He did, however, allow himself the luxury of a glass of water as logic dictated it was no more likely to be the cause of the fire than had been the opening of the front door.

Ninety pages were digested before the merest hint of smoke could be detected. Under normal circumstances it might well have remained unnoticed at this stage, but to a nose primed and waiting in anticipation, this was the moment it had been waiting for.

The general vicinity of the source was easily detected.

The dining room was situated off the kitchen, accessed by a wide door-less opening, effectively making the two rooms one. Although its primary purpose was as a place to entertain dinner guests, it doubled as a library and as a place for Ian and his wife to carry out their respective hobbies. Debbie enjoyed making her own clothes and to this end, had left a half-finished black dress pinned to a tailor's dummy close to the window in the south-facing wall. A wisp of smoke rose around it and before Ian could raise himself to his feet, the sleeve closest to the window suddenly burst into flame.

Despite having foreknowledge a fire would start, and his reason for being there was to witness it, the sight and suddenness of flame, where flame should not be, still came as a shock. However, it was not enough to prevent him from acting. Grabbing his glass, Ian leapt towards the fire and dowsed the infant blaze with water before it was able to gain hold. A second glass, more carefully administered, was needed before he was confident the destruction of the house and its contents had been averted.

The obvious next step was to discover what had caused an inoffensive dress to spontaneously combust. The answer was plain to see.

Sitting on the windowsill behind the mannequin was a large, decorative glass paperweight. The rays of the sun had been focused through it and had burned an arc in the varnished wood as the sun moved across the sky. When the arc had intercepted the sleeve material that lay in its path, it had only been a matter of a few seconds before sunlight became fire. For the accident to have happened, it needed a combination of a sunny day and for the dress material to be lying in just the wrong place.

Marvelling at the power of coincidence, Ian considered what he should do next. The natural time line dictated he should be at work, not at home preventing a fire. It seemed logical to rewind to the previous day and prevent the accident before it happened. In that way his unblemished sick record would remain intact and his wife's new frock would be saved.

With minimal effort, Ian found himself watching his wife flying through the open front door on her way to the theatre for the fourth time. Far from being a nightmare scenario, experiencing this moment again was beginning to feel like visiting an old friend. If all four occasions had been exactly the same, Ian would be tearing at his thinning hair, repetition being his most hated enemy. However, all four had been different.

The first time he had discovered how to control an incredible gift. On the second occasion, he had enjoyed a quiet night in, slouching in front of live television. On the third, he had caught up on some unwatched videos, and now he was about to prevent his house burning down.

It occurred to him, had he not disobeyed his wife's wishes, the house would still have been destroyed by fire the following afternoon. He would have been powerless to do anything more than to ring the insurance company and live the rest of his life with nothing more than memories.

As Carol's car disappeared out of view behind the thick boundary hedge, Ian closed the door, turned and made straight for the paperweight. He discovered that, although the mannequin was not yet in place, the carbonised track of the sun, burned into the wood, clearly was. One half of the formulae had been present all along, waiting only for the second ingredient for potential disaster to become reality.

So, coincidence had not played such a great part after all, with the glass ball sited on the window sill, any number of things might have brought about the same fate.

Ian's first thought was to continue back in time to undo the damage to the wood; to obliterate any evidence of what might have been. However, that would mean having to relive yet more days at work. Not knowing when the damage had first occurred, it might mean having to rewind weeks, or perhaps months of his life and all for very little gain. Besides, by keeping the scorch marks, he had something to show his wife when he instructed her never to place such an object in full sun again.

Debbie returned home several hours later, her natural, positive, emotional state boosted somewhat by the ingestion of a moderate amount of alcohol.

By contrast, she discovered her husband on the settee, both surrounded by and buried beneath the family's entire collection of photograph albums. When he looked up to welcome her home, the tracks of tears could clearly be seen as glistening stripes, superficially scarring each of his cheeks.

'Whatever's the matter?' she asked, sobering considerably, anticipating tragic news.

'Nothing really,' he replied quietly, calmly, trying his hardest to force a smile. 'While you were out, I thought I'd have a look at some photos and they made me think. That's all.'

Debbie pushed a pile of albums to one side so she could sit down beside him. Something was troubling her husband, more so than usual. She had not seen him cry since the birth of their youngest child. Why he should do so now was a mystery and a concern.

With the warmth of his wife's bare arm pressed against him, Ian felt able, or perhaps compelled, to explain what caused such a rare display of vulnerability.

'Looking back, we've had some good times, especially with the kids. Now they're both at uni and have all but flown the nest, all we have left are our memories and a few keepsakes. Imagine how awful it would be if we lost those too.'

'That will never happen,' Debbie comforted, snuggling up closer.

Ian felt secure, soothed and relaxed. There was no need to comment aloud, or even in his head. Nevertheless, the thought was there - a vague blanket of knowing. Debbie was right. They would never lose a single memento of their lives they did not want to; their children could live their lives to the extreme and never come to any harm; and he and his wife's relationship need never be tainted by a single thoughtless word – not while Ian had the ability to undo his life at will and try the same scenario again and again until it was erased or perfected.

5

The following day was pure repetition, save for the fact it did not end with a dash home to a distraught wife and a smouldering home. Balancing increased monotony for the duration of a single day, against the loss of a lifetime of accumulated memories, Ian felt it was a good trade off. Nevertheless, an evening of new experiences, all be they very similar to those of every other evening, was most welcome.

Sitting blankly next to his wife as she enjoyed yet another cookery programme, Ian's mind focused on what might have happened had he not been gifted his new ability. His train of thought soon moved on to what other uses he might put it to. It would be nice, for example, to tell Debbie's mother, Beryl, exactly what he thought of her before retracting the statement. He might go to an expensive restaurant and overindulge by eating all his favourite foods until fit to burst, before rewinding to a point before the event, and instead choosing a more affordable eatery where he would order only a single portion. In this way he would remember the delightful flavours, but not suffer the weight gain, or the financial loss; something akin to bulimia, but without the medical implications. Other similar, amusing, but otherwise unproductive thoughts sprang to mind every few minutes causing the corners of his mouth to twitch upwards in a series of short-lived smirks.

It was only when the mid-week lottery result flashed up on the bottom of the television screen that the true potential of his gift suddenly came to him.

A smile that had been absent for far too many years spread across his face.

'Eu-bloody-reka,' he said aloud, refusing to elaborate further, despite several requests from his wife.

The hastily hatched plan was not a complex one. He had in mind to return to seven o'clock that same evening at which point he would buy a lottery ticket with the foreknowledge of the numbers that were to be picked an hour later. Unfortunately, the jackpot was not as sizeable as could be hoped for. To make matters worse, this smaller sum had to be shared between five lucky winners; Ian would make a sixth if all went well.

'God, you'd be gutted if your numbers came up and you had to share it with that many people,' he commented. 'They won't even make a million apiece.'

'I know. Don't get me wrong, it's still a lot of money, but they must have thought they'd get at least a couple of million each,' Debbie agreed. 'And if any of those winners are in a syndicate, they might hardly make anything at all. They should have won on Saturday. Nine million pounds and all to one person.'

She had a point. If Ian went back to the Saturday just gone, knowing the winning numbers, his share would be a guaranteed four-and-a-half million pounds. Yes, it would shorten the other chap's winnings by the same amount but, in Ian's opinion, he would still be left with more than enough.

Thinking back, he remembered the Saturday in question was the same one he accidentally revisited once before. Then, he had only narrowly avoided being killed when he suddenly found himself in the driver's seat of his car as it sped along the motorway. Not wanting to experience a repeat of that incident, he instead closed his eyes and concentrated on the events during the period following his safe arrival home. A moment later, he was there.

A fragment of guilt glanced his conscience. In his excitement, he had acted without first considering or consulting his wife; had not secured her blessing. Surely it was wrong to force his decisions upon her. On the other hand, Debbie would be left none the wiser and stood only to benefit from life changing winnings. Even if he subsequently confessed what he had done, he was sure she would forgive him as she considered how best to spend their millions. And if her reaction was that bad, he could always tell her she had agreed to the plan, or make it so he never disclosed his actions in the first place.

Another Saturday might have found him camped in the middle of a field, miles from the nearest lottery terminal. However, on this particular Saturday, he was at home, with access to the television. The information was there: the six numbers; the confirmation of a nine million pounds jackpot and the fact there was only one winner.

The next task was to commit the numbers to memory, learning them by rote until he was confident he was able to recite them backwards, forwards and even upside down, if the need arose. There was little point expending too much energy on the exercise, though, the string of numbers needing to remain fresh in his mind for only a very short time. The buzzing at the centre of his head would last but a moment and he had then only to find a pen with which to jot down the numbers, before his memory of them faded, and he always kept one of those in the car's door pocket in case he ever needed to jot down another motorist's number plate.

Once he was confident the numbers were sufficiently deeply ingrained in his memory, the next step was to rewind to a time shortly before the cut-off for buying the tickets. It was then he realised he had been travelling all day and the only time he had come close to a lottery terminal was at the motorway service station. Returning there might mean having to suffer the last two-hours of his journey again, but having to do so in the knowledge he was now four-and-a-half million pounds richer, he was confident he would cope.

Relaxing in an armchair, eyes closed, Ian thought back to the feeling of damp palms, having given up with the hot air dryers provided in the gent's toilets. He thought of the service station shop with its shelves of last minute gifts for those who had been forgotten. He thought of the newspaper headline declaring the deaths of a dozen innocent victims of a civil war that was tearing a country to pieces. He recalled the taste of the overpriced, excessively hot coffee that had dripped on his shoe. Then, when he was sure his mind was fixed upon just the right moment, he triggered the high frequency buzzing sensation that returned him directly there. There was no question, making accurate jumps was becoming easier.

Three visits to the same service area, days apart, yet all at the same time. Three different experiences of the same occurrence. On the first occasion he had merely pulled in for a rest; to empty his bladder; to return feeling to his buttocks; to waken his mind with a dose of caffeine. The second rest stop was required to calm shaking hands, the result of excess adrenalin surging through his veins. This third visit excited desire to get on with the business in hand. To this end, Ian fumbled in his pocket for a pen as he weaved through crowds of tired, irritable travellers, towards the newsagent. There he grabbed a blank lottery slip, laid it flat on the surface provided, and allowed the tip of his biro to hover millimetres above the printed boxes. It was only then he realised he had not the faintest idea what the six vital numbers were. He remembered having known them; he recalled how he had committed them to memory, but just as a dream seeming vivid in sleep becomes a haze on waking, so his carefully selected connections now seemed distant and weak.

There was definitely something right about the number eighteen; he was sure of that. Then there was also something to do with a month, pregnancy, and a connection with the…something…and a… No, it was no good. Everything had gone. None of it made any sense. A man full of supreme confidence rapidly became a student turning over an exam paper to find he had revised the wrong subject. Standing motionless, Ian tried to ignore the sense of panic that was surging outwards from deep within his core.

He was not permitted to stand and panic for long. A queue of hopeful would-be millionaires had formed behind him and each of them was looking increasingly impatient.

'What's wrong mate? Forgotten your numbers?' the man standing next in line chirped.

Snatching the blank slip and walking from the shop, Ian felt like informing everyone they were wasting their time, but why should he bother? He had more pressing things to consider; like what to do next.

In Ian's experience, ideas often presented themselves as he performed the most mundane of tasks - having a shower; brushing his teeth; standing at the toilet, urinating. In this instance, as had been the case on both previous occasions, his bladder needed emptying. The act not only served a purpose – relieving internal pain; producing a degree of pleasure along the way – it highlighted a simple fact. Previously, a fat, ugly man had stood at the adjacent urinal. Ian was sure he had glanced down and to one side, perhaps in an effort to compare like for like; perhaps he had forgotten what one looked like because he could no longer see his own. Ian had no idea how he had fared, keeping his eyes fixed on his own stream until the job was done and everything was shaken, squeezed and tucked away. On this occasion, not only was the fat voyeur not present, Ian was forced to use a different urinal. There was no reason to believe the fat man had not stopped there, but their actions had become asynchronous. A small point but one that monopolised a moment that should instead have been dedicated to finding a solution.

Ian left the men's room, his hands damp, his trousers a slightly darker shade about his thighs.

Despite his previous experience, Ian opted to purchase another cupful of overpriced coffee from the concession stand, situated outside the main entrance. This time he was more careful, avoiding any spillage.

From there he returned to the car where it felt right to thump the padded portion of his clenched fist against his forehead. Frustratingly, this failed to dislodge memories that presumably clung to the inner recesses of his brain, merely causing pain that threatened to linger and grow into a headache. Still Ian could not recall the numbers. There was only one thing for it; he had to see them again.

There were two options: Ian could complete the journey as he had done twice before, commit the numbers to memory as he had done once before, and then wish himself back to this same moment for a third time – a fourth visit - or he could stay put, ring his wife to tell her he had been delayed, listen to the results on the radio, memorise the numbers again, and have another go. He naturally favoured the second course of action, partly to avoid having to drive even a single metre again unnecessarily, and partly because it offered the shortest rewind possible, so reducing the likelihood of memory loss.

Ian went back into the building to ring his wife and explained he was feeling tired and would have forty winks in the car before he continued his journey. She thought it a good idea.

Having taken the opportunity to tell her he loved her, he then returned to the car where he sank into in the passenger seat, moving it back to provide more leg room. Having turned the radio on there was nothing more to do than wait, poised with pen and paper in hand.

'Tonight's lottery numbers are: eighteen...'

'I bloody knew it,' Ian cursed himself.

'…forty-one, twenty-one, nine, thirty-seven, and eight. The bonus ball is number five.'

The numbers were re-ordered and repeated. Ian noted them down again.

'First indications show only one person has won tonight's jackpot, estimated to be nine million pounds.'

'Of course; I remember now: eight, nine, eighteen, twenty-one, thirty-seven and forty-one. I know them off by heart.'

Why the numbers seemed so familiar now when, ten minutes ago, they had been so elusive, he could not say. All he could do was accept it as fact and try harder. This he did using a three-pronged approach: chanting the numbers over and over again; visualising the connections he had already established; and repeatedly writing the figures down as though he were completing lines as punishment.

It would have been nice if he were able simply to slip a piece of paper into his pocket and for it to still be there once he had returned to a point a couple of hours in the past. A time traveller would be able do such a thing, if one existed. The clothes a time traveller wore and any other item within his machine would accompany him. Where Ian's abilities were concerned, where only his mind could move back through time, this was not the case.

It was now nearly nine o'clock.

To reduce the chance of a lengthy rewind degrading his memory, Ian chose not to fix on the moment when he originally stepped up to the lottery desk. That method would mean a single leap of some two-and-a-half hours. Instead, he decided to fall back on the first technique he had encountered.

Sitting comfortably, he effortlessly induced a low frequency buzz at the centre of his head that accompanied a slow but controlled regression of approximately twenty minutes duration. As soon as he felt the higher frequency sensation about to kick in, Ian opened his eyes and checked the clock. Then, before repeating the process, he took the opportunity to test his knowledge of the winning numbers, quickly running through them in his head; re-filling a previously used page of his notebook. All was well.

The second rewind took him to within twenty-two minutes of the draw. Once again, Ian passed the test with such ease he was confident of being able to recite the numbers blindfolded, while heavily under the influence of alcohol, if the situation arose.

The third rewind edged the clock back to the moment less than a minute after the radio presenter had announced the results. He still knew the numbers. The connections were indelibly established, filling Ian with a sense of anticipation, excitement and supreme confidence.

He settled back in his seat, preparing himself for the most important single action of his life. The buzzing began, low in sound and central to the inside of his head. Detecting the cusp between this and the higher frequency, he stopped and opened his eyes only to discover to his horror the memory of the numbers had once again vanished.

For the next few minutes Ian could be seen pounding his fists on the seat, his knees, the dashboard and the steering wheel, much to the surprise of other travellers using the car park. Thankfully, the close-fitting doors of his vehicle muffled the endless stream of profanities that burst from his lips.

No longer able to curse without repeating himself, or ignore the pain that throbbed within his hands, there was nothing left to do but cry. Tears ran down his cheeks; his mouth and nose wet and sticky, filled with a mixture of thick saliva and mucus.

With his hands held out as wide as the cramped conditions allowed, like those of a priest, his head tilted back to face the heavens through the windscreen, Ian questioned the motives of one in whom he had never held faith.

'Dear God, are you taking the piss?'

There was no answer.

As the initial disappointment and frustration ebbed away, Ian began to consider what had gone wrong. Why had he been able to recall the numbers clearly during the regression, only to experience total memory loss when it really mattered? On reflection, there seemed to be only one logical explanation.

From the moment the numbers had been announced, Ian had begun to learn them, repeating them over and over for the best part of an hour. Creeping back through time in stages, when he tested himself he had not been relying on a memory forged over the entire evening, only on what he had recited at that same moment the first time round. As soon as he regressed to a point prior to the announcement, his powers of recollection had become dreamlike, relying only on a vestige of memory that should not exist. What he was trying to do was to remember something before it had actually happened.

All was not lost though. If this theory was true, a rule written in stone, then he would have no knowledge of his future and, of course, he did. Perhaps he just needed to live with the numbers for much longer than an hour in order for the vestige to become a memory clear enough to retain, however far back he went.

Driving home from the service station for the third time was only as dull as any normal long motorway journey. After all, this was an hour later than on the previous two occasions, so in many respects was an entirely new experience. The manoeuvres of other drivers and the radio programmes that kept him company were all different. In fact, the journey could be seen as a positive thing. With the radio switched off, it provided valuable time to ponder alone, without distraction, other than the occasional sudden brake light requiring attention. Even then, the necessary reactions could be left safely to his subconscious and muscle memory.

The first thing to consider was how long he should study the winning numbers before returning for another attempt at the jackpot. Reciting them to himself for one hour, on two separate occasions, had been boring enough; living with them for any greater period was bound to feel like a lifetime; a form of torture. Nevertheless, there was a job to be done. In the end, Ian settled on the arbitrary period of three days. His studies would officially end when Debbie left for the theatre on Tuesday. It seemed somehow appropriate to choose that particular evening as it had attached to it the significance of being the first time he successfully controlled his ability.

Then there was the matter of whether to tell his wife.

Not being able to face reliving either Monday or Tuesday at work again, Ian quickly concluded the only option was to report sick; a course of action that would immediately raise Debbie's suspicion due to the simple fact he never went sick. Even when he had sustained a painful tendon injury to his ankle, he had turned up for work and sat at his desk with his leg resting on an upturned wastepaper bin. It was not that he liked work; nothing could be further from the truth; more, it was a matter of personal pride.

There were other considerations too. Trying to memorise the numbers in an obsessively intensive way, attempting to do so in secret, and revising his studies without the aid of his wife, would be almost impossible. On balance, she had to be told, but that task could be left until the morning.

6

When the moment arrived, Ian settled his wife at the breakfast table with a mug of freshly percolated coffee in hand, a rack full of toast, and a pot of her favourite strawberry jam. Satisfied he had put her in the best possible mood, he then sat down opposite her.

As pleased as Debbie was to be pampered in such a way, she was no fool and could tell instantly from her husband's body language he had an ulterior motive.

'What have you done?' she asked, in much the same way a mother would ask a school boy who wore guilt upon his face, standing with his hands hidden behind his back.

Ian could see there was little to be gained by protesting his innocence, and chose instead to come straight to the point.

'Last Monday, I proved to you I could rewind time to undo mistakes, and that evening I made a promise to you I would never do it again.'

This was not the first time Debbie had looked into her husband's eyes with suspicion.

'Well, I'm afraid I've broken that promise,' he said, his voice trailing off as if shamed by his confession.

'What have you done?' Debbie repeated, adding slightly more force to her delivery.

Ian explained the phenomenon no longer happened involuntarily and that he could now go back in time at will. He assured her there was nothing to be scared about, citing the fire as an example of its potential for good. At first, his wife found difficulty accepting what he was saying until Ian showed her the burn mark that partially encircled the paperweight.

Strangely, the revelation had a more profound effect on Ian than it did his wife. She recognised such a simple thing as leaving a paperweight in direct sunlight had the potential to destroy absolutely everything they had accumulated over the course of their lives; both replaceable possessions and irreplaceable mementos. For her, the thought was unnerving, but not as unnerving as the conclusion Ian suddenly reached. He realised the prevention of the fire could not be taken as read. If he did not remove the ornament from its place of danger for a second time, then the fire would inevitably happen again. It meant there existed a default timeline, one he had been continually trying to alter. His immediate reaction was to question himself as to whether it was wise to meddle with fate, but then it hit home - the thought of him having to see through another nineteen years until retirement. If his life were to be left to continue unaltered, he was sure he would be dead of a heart attack long before then; that, or safely incarcerated within the confines of a padded cell. There was nothing to lose, even if it meant upsetting the Lord God Almighty himself.

Sensing his wife was in two minds - to be angry at his admission of deceit, or to be grateful he had prevented a great loss – Ian decided to tip the balance in his favour by explaining he had been attempting to win the National Lottery, that he had failed, and to succeed he now needed Debbie's help. The prospect of suddenly becoming exceedingly rich brought the balance crashing down on the side of forgiving all trespasses, catapulting his transgressions into the ether, never to be spoken of again.

'What went wrong?'

Glad to see his wife had apparently accepted four-and-a half million pounds as fair and reasonable recompense for any upset he may have caused her, Ian related the problem.

'On two occasions now, I have memorised the winning numbers, but when I go back to buy a ticket, my mind goes blank.'

His wife's reaction was unexpected; she sounded annoyed with him.

'I don't understand,' she said, 'you've already told me you lived a week and returned to the beginning just to prevent an embarrassing situation. You even managed to write a diary of what was going to happen. I've seen that for myself and it all came true. Your memory was intact then, so why not now?'

One minute Debbie had expressly forbidden her husband from using his newly discovered ability, believing it to be the work of the devil; the next she was blaming him for not having mastered the technique, pushing Ian onto the back foot from where he was forced to defend his position.

'What I recalled of that week were the events. I never gave the minute details a second thought.'

Before continuing, Ian leant forward, took his wife's hands in his and looked directly into her eyes. 'Have you ever tried reading a book in your dream? You can see the book, turn the pages and see they have words written on them, but attempt to read those words and it all gets very confusing.'

'Is that it then?' Debbie asked, leaning back in her chair, breaking hand to hand contact. 'Why build my hopes up if there's no chance of winning?'

She sounded hurt.

'But there is a chance of winning. I just need your help.'

Her hope restored, Debbie listened intently to her husband's suggestion, agreeing in principal but making modifications of her own design.

Having mutually agreed a plan of action, Debbie and her husband quickly fell into a routine. Mornings were spent reciting the numbers and writing the sequence down over and over within the pages of a notebook until it was full, front to back. The only respite to be had was by way of a pause for a cup of tea once every hour.

The afternoons were spent focused on individual numbers. Ian and his wife would sit together trying to think up as many links to each as they could, writing the words or phrases within the pages of six other notebooks, one dedicated to each number.

Evenings were set aside for revision. Among other methods, Debbie would test her husband, asking him to repeat ten links for each number.

By Tuesday evening, Ian was sure he knew the six numbers more intimately than anyone else on Earth ever had, or ever would, and that the knowledge of them would remain with him until the day he died. As confident as he was, only by returning to the previous Saturday would he find out whether or not all the hard work had been worth the effort.

Debbie tested her husband until the last possible moment before her friend was due to arrive. She had chosen not to dress for her evening out. Convinced her husband was indeed able to snatch back time, it seemed certain she would never make the performance.

'Well, this is the moment of truth,' Ian said, his hands placed affectionately on his wife's shoulders. 'If I'm successful then we have been millionaires for the past three days. If I'm not, at least you'll be unaware of the hell all this has been.'

Debbie smiled.

'Good luck,' she said, planting a kiss on his cheek. 'You've put so much into this, you deserve every penny. We deserve every penny.'

Ian managed a half smile and then, without moving from his position in the middle of the living room floor, closed his eyes.

'Wait!' Debbie said, startled. 'Your hands are still on my shoulders. Won't I be dragged back with you?'

Ian opened his eyes again, smiled and gently shook his head. His response was spoken softly.

'No, it doesn't work like that.'

Pulling his wife closer, he wrapped his arms around her, his chin resting lightly on her shoulder. She did not see his eyes close a second time; she did not share the buzzing sensation that filled the centre of his head; she did not feel the flutter of myriad muscular movements activating in reverse.

As soon as Ian's eyes reopened, he could see he was standing in front of the lottery desk, pen poised over a piece of paper, one that bore numerous blank tick boxes.

A moment of inaction passed.

'What's wrong mate? Forgotten your numbers?'

With one smooth choreographed movement, Ian turned round and drove his right fist hard against the nose of the man who had spoken. The victim of Ian's outburst remained standing solely due to the fact the people next in the queue had caught him as he staggered backwards. The man looked bewildered as his hands inspected a nose that was no longer perpendicular to his face.

Then, as if it had been his first experience of correcting a wrongdoing, Ian found the man putting the same question again, his nose restored. This time, Ian ignored the comment and made directly for the concession stand to consume the same cup of coffee as he had already drunk three times before – perhaps not the exact same one, but it tasted just the same.

In all that had come to pass so far, Ian had learned there was little to be gained by pounding his fists, crying, pleading to God, or feeling sorry for himself. He was faced with a problem. Now what he needed was a solution.

Settled back in the passenger seat of his car, Ian crossed his hands on his lap, kicked his legs out as straight as he could manage - crossed at the ankles - let his head fall back and closed his eyes. Regardless of what anyone else who saw him might have thought, the seemingly dozing passenger was not asleep. Inside his head, Ian's mind was allowed to wander; to go wherever it pleased; to think of nothing at all if that is what took its fancy.

Left to its own devices, free from badgering input and suggestion, the unhampered mind processed the problem, providing a promising solution in very little time at all, evidenced by the appearance of an expression normally reserved for an atheist who had suddenly discovered the existence of God.

The passenger sat up, his hand reaching for the wheel that brought the back of the seat to the upright position.

'Of course.'

He spoke aloud, his eyes moving from side to side as though reading the proposal from an imaginary sheet of paper.

He would engage the help of a hypnotist, one who specialised in regression. He would pay the man, or woman, to use the same technique, but to attempt to recall his future, not the past – simple; elegant.

Being sat in a motorway service station on a Saturday evening did not present the best opportunity for making a start. That would have to wait until Monday morning. In the meantime he was once again faced with the same two-hour drive home and once again the exhilaration of success was not there to help him on his way. At least there was time to think how best to achieve the next step.

Ian's alarm did not sound on Monday morning, having been switched off deliberately the night before. Debbie, worried her husband might be late for work, was surprised when she learned he was taking the day off sick. She put questions, but received only diversionary answers. Readying herself for work, her only clue as to what might be wrong came when she found Ian at the kitchen table, flicking through the telephone directory of businesses, his finger running down columns of advertisements listed under the heading, 'HYNOTHERAPISTS'. Debbie was in two minds as to whether she should comment. The decision to remain silent was influenced by her need to leave the house.

Having kissed his wife goodbye, Ian was almost grateful she had gone, allowing him to continue his research in peace. He was pleased to see there were many practitioners to choose from, but without recommendations from friends, he had no idea which one to approach first. Some advertisements specifically mentioned regression. Of those, some were based nearby, others, further afield, cutting the choices down to a more manageable number. Then it was just a case of ringing up the first on the list and seeing whether or not they could help.

It was disappointing to find that every practice had a waiting list and he would be lucky if they could fit him in for an initial assessment inside a week. That meant he would have to return to the previous Monday if he had any chance of booking in a session before Saturday's draw. If that were not enough time, he might even have to go back further.

Without wishing to worry his wife any more than he had done so already, Ian closed his eyes, thought of the moment he had presented her with the diary that would prove the validity of his claimed ability, and returned there in an instant. The fatigue he had experienced the first time round was still there. The Ian Bradshaw of that moment had been up most of the night preparing the contents of the notebook he now held in his hand. He had to go through the motions of presenting her with it again -there was no other choice. He would go to work and by the time he returned home in the evening she would once again think he was in league with the devil.

The morning was spent phoning one hypnotherapist after another, working through the pages he had ripped from the phone book at home. He spoke normally to the receptionists and with scant regard to what the other members of the section might overhear. Progress was slow. In all instances, the waiting time before he could be seen was more than he cared to suffer. That is, until he reached an advertisement half way down the second page. Doctor Uddin could manage Friday afternoon.

With the booking made, Ian would dearly have liked to return home without further delay, suffering with some hastily manufactured, non-specific illness. Whatever he concocted would no doubt be believed by everyone in the office, including the manager, as, so far as their surviving experiences were concerned, he never went sick. However, his wife would be there and she would be only part way through day one of his diary. He could not go home, and he was mentally incapable of filling the same orders for a third time.

Overhearing their section leader's telephone conversations was enough to keep the clerks' heads down, they exchanging sideways stares, silently wondering what was going on with their boss. Further speculation grew as a result of his subsequent behaviour, Ian deciding to split the rest of the day equally between meticulously tidying his desk drawers - so that, for example, all paperclips were oriented the same way, with the large end facing inwards - and swivelling on his chair, finding different ways to develop initial impetus.

Not only had he decided he could not bring himself to spend the rest of the day re-processing the same orders as he had done twice before, he had absolutely no intention of repeating those he had previously completed over the remainder of the week.

Sure enough, on returning home that evening, Ian found his wife upset by what she had read, and that his predictions had all come true in every detail.

'Changing the subject,' Ian said, trying to slip a snippet of information into the conversation without it being noticed, 'I shan't be going in to work tomorrow, or for the rest of the week for that matter. Would you like a cup of tea? I'll make some toast to tide us over until dinner.'

Had the tables been turned, Debbie could have let slip the world was about to end, and that she intended spending her last moments on Earth sleeping with each and every player in the local rugby club, both A and B teams, and still Ian would not have detected the news if there had been the smallest of distractions present: a squirrel running across the road; a TV advertisement for women's shower gel; a leaf fluttering past the window in the middle of summer. However, it was Ian who was trying to take advantage of his wife's emotional state to bury some news, and he failed miserably. Debbie was instantly made doubly suspicious.

'Why's that then?' she asked, raising her head from a damp three-ply tissue.

'I'm taking a little time off sick,' Ian explained, trying to sound casual and thus avoid further questioning.

By his tone, Debbie knew something was definitely wrong and would not rest until she had extracted a full explanation, or a full confession.

'I suppose that snippet of information was in the diary I burned? If I'd read to the end of it, I'd probably know what is going on wouldn't I?'

'No, I worked the week the first two times round. I just can't face doing it again. I'm booked into see a hypnotherapist on Friday and I shall remain home until then.'

'Hypnotherapist? Are you going to let me in on your little secret?' Debbie asked, indignantly.

'Look, I'm hoping the fella will be able to retrieve next Saturday's lottery numbers I spent the best part of next week learning.'

'You're what?'

'Look, it's no use. I've briefed you on events many times now and you even spent three whole days helping me further my plans, but that was all in the future. I'm tired of having to remember what you know. It's not your fault, but I'm asking you not to push me on the subject any further. Let's just enjoy my time off together and say no more about it.'

In contrast to the upset of Monday, the following three-and-a-half days proved idyllic. Debbie was not one for taking time off either but rang in to inform her colleagues she had caught whatever Ian had. It had been many years since she and her husband had spent so much quality time together: walking along the riverbanks; picnicking in meadows; reading together in the garden under the shade of the apple trees. Each day their skin was bathed in warm summer sun, mending both their tired bodies and their even more tired minds, and not once was any mention made of Ian's gift.

However, Friday afternoon was soon upon them and with it came the return of Ian's quest to become rich beyond the dreams of avarice. With the millions he stood to gain, he could alter their lives permanently, making these last few precious days the first of many.

The hypnotherapist seemed to be a nice man with a soothing voice; not sickly, just reassuring. Without giving away specifics, Ian explained he was sure he had already lived a future and was keen to know if he could retrieve any recollection of it. Any mention of the lottery numbers could wait until later.

Doctor Uddin was intrigued. He had carried out many regressions in the past, but this was the first request he had received asking him to help someone remember something that had not yet happened.

To ensure the doctor did not keep the lottery numbers to himself if they were retrieved, Ian insisted Debbie be permitted to stay in the room throughout the session. There was one other point on which Ian could not be more emphatic.

'Doctor,' he said, locking his eyes with those of the hypnotherapist, 'whatever you do, do not try to regress me. I do not want to think about my past under any circumstances. Concentrate only on the future. Is that clear?'

It had occurred to Ian the doctor's actions might accidentally return him to some distant time in his past; a scenario that would undoubtedly be unimaginably disasterous.

Doctor Uddin was not used to being spoken to in such a manner, but he agreed to his patient's terms nonetheless. Clearly his patient had issues.

With his fears allayed, Ian allowed himself to relax further and further until, eventually, he was in a state of deep hypnosis.

'Ian, I want you to think yourself forward into the future as far as you can go. What day is it?'

'It's Wednesday,' Ian replied drowsily.

'And the time?'

'Evening.'

'You have gone forward five days? Is that right Ian?'

'Yes.'

'And what are you doing?'

'I've just decided to go back and win the lottery.'

'That's interesting,' Doctor Uddin commented, looking confused. 'How do you propose to do that?'

'I'm going to go back to Saturday evening and learn the numbers before I go back again and buy a ticket.'

The hypnotherapist's posture changed noticeably. He sat forward in his seat, his left hand grasping the fingers of his right hand, rolling them firmly against each other. His expression had changed too, from one of professional interest to one of personal curiosity. He paused before asking the next question and when he did, it was as if he were broaching a delicate subject.

'Okay Ian, you're moving back closer to my time. It is now Saturday evening. Can you tell me how you intend to find out what the lottery numbers are?'

'I'm listening to them being announced.'

'Can you tell me what the numbers are?'

'I'm confused. I can see and hear them on the tele at home but I can also hear them on the radio in my car.'

'Is it possible you are getting similar occasions mixed up?'

'Yes, I have been here so many times now, I've lost count.'

Doctor Uddin's eyebrows raised a little.

'How many times have you listened to the announcement on the car radio, please?'

'Once.'

'Right Ian, I want you to concentrate on that one time only. Can you hear the announcer's voice clearly now.'

'Yes.'

'Can you tell me what the six numbers are, Ian?'

Ian spoke slowly; drowsily.

'Eight, nine, eighteen, twenty-one, thirty-seven, forty-one.'

The session ended swiftly.

***

Ian remained at home for the whole of Saturday, refusing to go anywhere near the motorway or its service station. He drank and enjoyed several really good mugs of coffee at home and went to the toilet whenever he felt the need, never in fear a pervert was trying to size him up. He washed his hands, running the tap for as long as necessary, before drying them on a towel. Consequently, he emerged from the bathroom on each occasion, his trousers remaining bone dry. After lunch, Ian and Debbie took a casual stroll in the sunshine, round to the local newsagent, Ian adding six ticks to a blank lottery ticket, his wife checking the chosen numbers against those she had written on a piece of paper at the hypnotherapist's surgery. She checked them again, against the printed ticket, handed to them over the counter by Mr Patel, the proprietor for many years.

After enjoying a late tea, Ian and his wife sat together in front of the television, an unopened bottle of champagne and two crystal glasses placed on the low table before them. It was only a matter of minutes now before the cork would leave the bottle with a yelp.

The counter-rotating arms within the machine were spinning. The balls were released at the push of a button, and within seconds the first of seven emerged from a hole in the casing and rolled to a halt at the end of the collecting trough. Eighteen.

Ian, who had been holding his breath for longer than was natural, relaxed visibly. His eyes remained fixed to the screen.

Forty-one.

Debbie's fingers curled under and pressed into her sweating palms.

Twenty-one.

Ian's eyes darted between the screen and the ticket that he held tightly within the index fingers and thumbs of both his hands.

'That's a tenner we've won anyway,' he commented.

Nine.

'That's probably at least eighty quid.'

Thirty-seven.

'We're into the thousands.'

Eight.

Debbie turned to her husband as the bonus ball dropped neatly beside its brothers.

'Have we got all six?'

'We certainly have.'

'Phone them then.'

'In a minute, I'm shaking too much at the moment.'

The balls were re-ordered into the correct numerical sequence, following which the announcer made the usual statement.

'First indications show three people have won tonight's jackpot, estimated to be nine million pounds.'

'Not a bad bonus for a hypnotherapist,' Ian commented, sardonically. 'Still, I can live with three million.'

Having had a moment to collect his thoughts, Ian picked up the telephone receiver, ready to claim the Bradshaw share. Hearing the dialling tone, his index finger poised over the keypad, but suddenly he was no longer there; he was back at the same newsagent as before, buying his ticket from Mr Patel, as before. There was no explanation as to what had happened and only one course of action to be followed. Bewildered, Ian purchased the ticket for a second time.

The numbers came out as before, much to the surprise of Ian who had expected there to be a sinister outcome to the unexpected rewind.

Once again he waited for the numbers to rearrange, and for the announcer to make the statutory statement.

'First indications show four people have won tonight's jackpot, estimated to be nine million pounds.'

Ian immediately looked to his wife for confirmation he had heard correctly. It was true, there were now four winners.

7

By the following morning, most of the national press and many of the local papers had chosen for their leading story the man who had won the National Lottery for a second time. Every article included the man's name, his age and the village in which he lived. Both the lucky winner and his postman could be pitied as they were both about to be inundated with many thousands of begging letters, interspersed with a significant amount of hate mail.

The original winner was unaware he had once been the sole claimant of the nine million pounds jackpot. Not being a greedy man, he had the sense to remain anonymous while he waited for his bank balance to jump by a cool two-and-a-quarter million, more than happy to share the total with the three other, equally lucky, prize-winners. Likewise, the hypnotherapist, who had been rewarded so very well for half an hour's work, also chose to remain clear of the limelight. Of the four men, though, Ian was the least likely to be hounded by reporters as he had not yet informed the lottery's claims department. He had money in the bank to tide him over and had allowed himself the pleasure of withdrawing his services from the company at which he had worked for many years. However, as Ian could not be bothered to ring them either, it would take perhaps a few days, or even weeks, and many unanswered phone calls before his boss finally concluded his seemingly loyal employee no longer worked for him. For Ian, the knowledge he had achieved financial independence was enough for now. Obtaining the money could wait until the dust had settled.

The two-time winner's desire for notoriety went further than would appear unwise even to the most ardent attention seeker: Mike Summerbee made a guest appearance on every daytime television programme that needed a five-minute filler; he agreed to a photo shoot for a Sunday magazine; he even agreed to open a supermarket, advertising the fact to the world whenever the opportunity arose. Here was a man who had declared to the nation he had more money than he knew what to do with, and if anyone wanted to take a pop at him for being so self-satisfied, he had told them where and when to find him.

Ian had no intention of having a pop at Mr Summerbee, but he was curious to meet the person who had so mysteriously stolen a part-share of his money. Having had time to reflect, there could be only one interpretation of the events that had taken place. Ian had a rival; there was someone else who had the ability to rewind time.

The opening of the new superstore drew crowds larger than might normally be anticipated. Having cut the tape, Mike Summerbee insisted on mixing with the crowd, handing out twenty-pound notes at random from his own wallet. It was a small gesture, five hundred pounds being a miniscule portion of his multi-million pounds personal wealth, but it was enough to make the gathering and the media warm to him instantly. Evidence of their growing affection manifested itself as a continuous barrage of flashes firing from a bank of cameras, both amateur and professional. Such activity suggested he would receive favourable coverage in the morning.

With the ceremony having come to a close, the crowd began filtering into the store, passing their benefactor on their way. Despite the danger that among their numbers there might be those whose resentment drove them to wish the affable Mr Summerbee harm, he remained stalwart and smiling at the entrance, protected only by members of the senior management team and a single store detective.

Ian approached his co-winner.

'So, you can rewind too,' he said casually, looking into the man's eyes for any sign of reaction.

There was a noticeable pause during which Mike's expression remained unchanged. Then his eyes dropped to follow his own hands as they worked in unison to pull an envelope from his suit pocket, pressing it firmly into Ian's unsuspecting palm.

There followed another pause as though the act of handing over the envelope had been frozen in time, caught by a distant surveillance camera fitted with a telephoto lens.

Turning to the store manager, Mike spoke.

'Right, must be off now. I've got a busy afternoon ahead of me.'

The group hardly had time to express their gratitude for making the opening such a success, before their star guest was sliding down into the seat of his waiting Aston Martin, and was gone.

Within the folds of the envelope was contained an introduction and a set of instructions telling Ian when and where they were to meet. The wording made it quite clear this was no request. It was a command and one that offered no option of negotiation. The document closed with the name Mike Summerbee, the only informal concession to an otherwise business-like contract, giving a hint the author might not be as unfriendly as he had first appeared, so far as Ian was concerned. Michael Summerbee or Mr M. Summerbee would have been more in keeping with the body of the text. This subtle difference served to calm Ian's indignation, allowing him to accept the invitation without feeling he was the obedient subordinate. In truth, even had the instructions been many times more discourteous, he would still have attended, his curiosity having been roused so strongly.

The chosen venue for the meeting was the Summerbee country retreat. The lanes leading to the property were narrow and winding and on a number of occasions the brakes had to be applied firmly so as not to overshoot concealed turnings. However, the map that had been provided proved to be of an extremely high standard and led Ian's car straight to what he assumed to be the correct address. A plaque bearing the words The Grange, embossed in gilt on a background of enamelled British racing green, offered welcome confirmation.

A neat row of orange traffic cones, butted up against each other, lined the feathered border between spreading gravel drive and the unshifting tar macadam surface of the single-track lane that ran past the property. Their purpose was clear – to prevent vehicles straying onto the property the cones sought to protect. However, why anyone should wish to take such precautions when gates already barred access beyond the first few metres, Ian could only guess.

Driving slowly on, he looked anxiously for a place to park. After twenty metres, in the shade of a mature oak, he came upon a muddy lay-by, worn into the grassy verge. Deep tyre tracks scarred the area, retaining water in long, narrow puddles. It was by no means ideal, but it would have to do.

Ian was able to step from the doorsill of his car, across to the farthest reaches of the lay-by, avoiding the worst of the mire. What mud he did encounter formed a thin layer of paste, spread evenly over consolidated, drier, soil beneath. Fallen twigs prevented the worst of the slurry from lapping over the soles of his shoes, but it was still necessary for him to shuffle through the grass before continuing. The delays were small, but mounting. A quick glance at his watch showed it was fast approaching seven o'clock, the time of his appointment.

The end of the long driveway was protected by a pair of imposing wrought iron gates set at the narrowest point between two neatly finished, curved brick walls. Ian noticed an intercom built into the right-hand wall, pressed the button and introduced himself as the man from the supermarket opening.

'Good, glad you could make it,' a voice responded in a confident manner. 'Walk down the drive, follow the tape and that will bring you straight to me. Oh, and as you come in, would you be good enough to stack the cones inside the gate for me? Thanks.'

With a hum, the gates swung open, allowing Ian to stagger through under the weight of a stack of cones. He had not appreciated how heavy they might be. Three trips back and forth were needed to clear the entrance, leaving the invited guest wondering why he had so readily agreed to the task. As soon as he was clear for the last time, the hum returned and the gates once more filled the breach in the estate's defences. Although he could not see a camera, it seemed likely there was one as the timing of the gates closing could not have been so well achieved had it been left to chance.

The view that opened up before him was impressive. Never before had he set foot on such a piece of land without having first paid an entrance fee. Perfectly manicured lawns of emerald green stretched away on either side. Peacocks roamed beneath an old cedar tree whose branches fanned out high above the drive. Away in the distance, Ian could make out tennis courts, paddocks and a swimming pool. There was no doubting the man who lived here had a lot of money.

One hundred metres down the drive, a length of red and white plastic tape indicated progress beyond it was not welcome. It continued round and appeared to completely encircle the main residence. Mike Summerbee's detailed instructions had forewarned Ian of the cordon that had apparently been laid out to keep reporters at a comfortable distance during their recent siege.

The instructions stated Mike could be found in an outhouse at the far right-hand end of the tape, tinkering with one of his vintage cars. With so many buildings fitting the description, Ian was glad he had something to guide him to the right one.

The route took him off the hard surface of the drive and onto the lawn. In contrast to Ian's grass which crunched under foot due to summer sun and drought, this lawn looked and smelled fresh. It had reaped the benefit of the garden sprinkler, and recently. Water droplets still glistened in the diminishing evening sunlight, moistening the leather uppers of his shoes.

The lawn stopped at a freshly dug flowerbed. It too had received its fair share of water. Not wishing to walk across wet mud, and with the bed being slightly wider than a natural stride, Ian sprung off his back foot in an attempt to land on the gravel path that lay on the far side. However, without a run up, he fell short, his shoe impacting the mud close to the terracotta rope-edging that defined the border. His immediate thought was to rewind and try again, but it seemed impolite to do such a thing while a guest of someone who shared his ability. Instead, Ian scraped the sole of his shoe clean against the edging as best he could and continued on his way.

The path and the tape led down to a group of buildings, one of which was showing light from an open door. Inside, Mike was to be found, as promised, bent over the front wing of an E-Type Jaguar, tinkering with its engine.

'Mr Summerbee?'

'Please, call me Mike.'

Ian smiled awkwardly, standing just inside the door, wondering what etiquette demanded he do next.

'Pass me that knife on the side, would you?' his host asked, casually, without raising his head.

Ian looked round. A long-bladed kitchen knife lay on the workbench. It seemed a strange tool for a motor mechanic to be using, but he picked it up nonetheless and offered it forward, turning it handle-first as he did so. Mike lifted his head from the engine bay, took one look at the knife, then directly at Ian's face.

'No, I meant my utility knife. Over there on the bench,' he said, pointing to a cluttered work surface some distance away from both of them.

'Sorry,' Ian replied, feeling foolish.

He replaced the kitchen knife where he had found it and began rummaging round until he uncovered a small blue-handled knife, the retractable triangular blade exposed in its housing.

Mike used the knife to trim the end from a length of insulating tape he had finished wrapping round the wiring loom.

'That should do it,' he said, gently closing the bonnet, before returning his tools to their proper places. 'I see you have my instructions.'

There was something in the way Mike spoke that suggested the maps and corresponding notes had only been meant as a loan. Ian waggled them awkwardly in front of him for a moment before laying them on the bench next to the kitchen knife. His suspicion was immediately proven to have substance as Mike unceremoniously gathered up the bundles of papers, put a lighted match to one corner, and dropped them, flaming, into a galvanised bucket that sat on the garage floor, a short distance from his feet.

The two men stared at the flames until they died down and extinguished with a final puff of wispy smoke. Then, without comment, Mike picked up the bucket and emptied the contents into a flip-top bin, crushing the ash into fine flakes as he swept them in with his fingers. Still not a word passed his lips as he carried the bucket into an adjoining room from where the sound of metal could be heard clanging against a hard surface, and of running water rinsing the container clean.

Seconds later, Summerbee re-entered the workshop, drying his hands on a small towel which he then cast aside on one of the many worktops. Seeing the expression of surprise on Ian's face, he then appeared to feel it necessary to offer an explanation.

'Don't worry,' he said. 'It's just that I'm quite a secretive person and I don't like the thought of there being anything out there that might bring unwanted snoopers scurrying to my door.'

This statement was clearly at odds with Mike's actions ever since he had won the lottery. For a secretive person, he had behaved in a very public way, a contradiction Ian was quick to point out.

'Ah yes,' Mike began, his arms folded across his chest, the fingers of his right hand rapping the bicep of his left arm. 'I would normally, as I say, keep myself very much to myself, but when you came along, I had to meet you.'

His face was alive with expression; his body leaning slightly towards his guest; his voice smooth.

Mike let his arms unfold, then raised his right index finger, lowering his head slightly so that he appeared to be using his fingertip to sight his target, his elbow pressed against his rib cage, offering steadying support.

'You could not help but notice the extra winner and I suspected you would then realise the significance,' Mike said, his finger rising and falling with the beat of his sentence. He let his arm drop casually to his side before continuing. 'I imagine you had thought yourself to be the only person on the planet to possess such a gift. When you discovered it was not the case, you had to meet the person who shared it. I was right, wasn't I?'

To indicate he had finished making his point, Mike brought the crooked index finger of his right hand up to rest on his lips, his right elbow supported by his left hand. He stood up straight, his eyes challenging his guest to tell him he was wrong.

Ian could not and simply nodded.

Summerbee, seemingly satisfied, relaxed visibly. However, Ian was not about to let the stranger have it all his own way.

'But if I hadn't come...'

Ian's suggestion brought about a sudden and noticeable change in Mike's expression, but he could not pinpoint exactly what emotion it portrayed.

'Then I would have found some other way of flushing you out,' Mike replied, coldly. 'People are quite predictable when many lives are at stake.'

Mike looked serious, but the sinister stare quickly melted to a warm grin.

'Just kidding. I knew you'd come. There is not a man on this planet who could have resisted after the stunt I pulled.'

Ian's reaction was to laugh, but there was no force behind it.

Without warning, Mike suddenly turned away and casually wandered across to the far side of the garage where he leant forward towards a small mirror on the wall, pulling the lower lid of his right eye down as he did so. Moving his head up and down slightly, he appeared to be checking the surface of his eye for foreign bodies. As he made no attempt to remove anything, Ian could only assume that whatever had been causing the problem had gone.

Returning to his guest, Mike continued his explanation for having brought Ian to his house in such a manner.

'I needed to talk to you as you are the only other person alive who knows what it is to have our ability. I can discuss things with you. I have theories and questions I could share with no-one else. Do you understand?'

Ian felt more at ease. He could sympathise with the man, having to live daily with such a power, but unable to talk openly about it for fear of ridicule and misunderstanding.

'I must admit,' Ian said. 'It is nice to be able to mention the subject at all. My wife thinks I've sold myself to the devil and it would be hard to make anyone else believe me.'

'Come with me,' Mike said, reinforcing his request with a nod of his head to one side. 'We can talk it all over while we walk.'

Mike led the way outside, across the front of the house, to the far end of the tape.

'Now the reporters are gone, I won't need this anymore,' he said, easing the first steel rod from the ground, before winding in the plastic tape tied to it.

'These reporters; they didn't make much of a mess of your lawn did they?' Ian observed.

By the tone of his response, Mike was clearly annoyed by the question; defensive even.

'It's a well-tended lawn. It's been mowed, rolled, watered and pricked since then. A good lawn always makes a speedy recovery. Enough of that. Let's concentrate on the matter in hand.'

Having been put squarely in his place, Ian felt uneasy again, certain his host was hiding something; convinced he had an ulterior motive.

Neither spoke again until the rest of the poles and tape had been gathered, and the two men had returned inside, at which point Summerbee stowed his bundle in a box, and pushed it beneath one of the worktops.

'I have always been curious as to how I got my powers,' Summerbee said. 'It may be we can discover something we have in common that might explain it.'

At that moment, a telephone rang, cutting the conversation dead. Mike produced a handset from inside his overalls and answered.

'No, no, I'm fine. I've just returned from a stroll in the garden. I've been getting some fresh air. Look, I've got company so I'll have to go. See you soon. Yes. Give it fifteen maximum. That's right. Bye.'

Mike did not feel the need to tell his guest who had rung, or the topic of their conversation. Instead, he returned the handset to a pocket hidden within his clothing and carried on as though the conversation had never taken place.

The two men moved through to the area in which Summerbee had cleaned his bucket. It turned out to be nothing more sinister than a small but well equipped kitchen. Mike put the kettle on and while the water heated, he made his way back to the small mirror to check the same eye that had previously been troubling him. Seeing Ian wondering at his actions, Mike felt compelled to comment.

'I keep thinking there's something in it but I can't find anything,' he said, casually. 'Must be a scratch.'

Ian nodded nonchalantly as though it had never been an issue.

Settled at a workbench on a couple of bar stools, mugs of tea in hand, Mike and Ian began to exchange life stories.

The first thing that tallied was they were born within six months of each other and in the same county. One connection led to another, it quickly transpiring both men had attended Cardle Street Secondary School, and were in fact in the same year together, although neither remembered the other from that time. As far as they could determine, this and the school reunion they both attended eight years after they had left Cardle's, were the only times they had shared the same environment.

Establishing this connection hinted at an answer to their question, but did not provide enough evidence to draw any solid conclusions; especially when, in most other respects, the differences far outweighed the similarities. Whereas Ian had technically first encountered his ability less than a month ago, Mike had been using his for twenty-four years; since approximately one month after the reunion, to be more precise.

'So, what can you do?' Mike asked, before draining his mug.

'Well,' Ian replied innocently, 'I can go back to any point in my life, as far back as I like, and as quickly as I like.'

'But you can't magic yourself forward again?'

'No.'

Mike nodded, appreciating the significance of his guest's reply, he himself having never conquered that problem either.

'Have you discovered different ways to go back?' Mike asked.

'Yes, I can simply conjure up the process, go back a bit, and then open my eyes to stop it. Gotta be careful though; if I don't open my eyes, it suddenly goes into superfast mode and I can find myself going back a lot further than I had intended; or, I can concentrate on a memory, so long as it's clear enough, then activate the process and go straight there. I don't even have to open my eyes to halt the process. That's far safer as I can't overshoot. The problem is, I can't always think of an event clearly enough.'

'When you go back, do you have difficulty remembering details?'

'Yes.'

'I imagine remembering the lottery numbers was difficult.'

'It was.'

'Ingenious – using a hypnotherapist. I just had to wait until I had sufficiently mastered my ability to such a degree that memory of the future was no longer a problem.'

'You know about the hypnotherapist; how?' Ian asked, his face a mixture of confusion and concern.

'My dear boy, I have experienced that particular lottery win as many times as you. Every time you go back, so do I. First we had one winner, and then we had three. It took a while to trace down the hypnotherapist, but my men found him. You proved a little harder to find because you didn't declare yourself.'

Something in the way Mike spoke made Ian feel guilty. Apparently, he was the noisy neighbour that had not realised his loud music had been bothering the man who shared the party wall. However, judging by his host's actions, whatever he had done was seemingly forgiven; either that or his behaviour had not been classed sufficiently annoying to warrant holding a grudge. Rather than glare at him with an evil eye, Mike Summerbee flicked his gaze towards a wall clock, and then casually got up from his stool to examine his eye in the mirror for a third time. Ian wondered if it was more a compulsive disorder than a genuine scratch as Mike repeated the actions of the last two times in every detail.

Having confirmed once more there was nothing in his eye, Mike returned to his stool.

'I have a theory,' he said, settling himself down for the long haul. 'Until you discovered your ability, for more than two decades I was the only person alive who knew I could rewind time. On every occasion I did so, the whole world remained oblivious to the fact it was experiencing the same period over again. Sure enough, some people would have a feeling of déjà vu, but nothing more than that.

Now, here's my point. Déjà vu has been around since long before either of us discovered our gift; probably since God created the power of thought. So, my theory is there must have been people like us around for at least as long. We are just the latest in a long line.'

Mike paused for confirmation Ian was following his argument.

'Sounds like a reasonable conclusion to make,' Ian said, nodding with the authority of a world expert.

'Here's where I get to my second point,' Mike continued slowly, adding definition between sentences. 'There can only ever have existed one of us at a time. When two exist, each time one rewinds, it affects the other against their will. Unlike the situation with normal people, those having the ability would know their lives were being toyed with and would find it intensely annoying. I should know, you've been doing it to me for weeks.'

Ian's guilt returned; he felt embarrassed, despite his transgressions having been entirely accidental.

'Don't you see,' Mike continued, emphasising every point. 'Every time you turn back time just to avoid stubbing your toe, or saying something you wish you hadn't, you are doing so for the entire universe. Think about it; the entire universe.'

By now, Ian's face was red with shame; shocked at the concept of what his ability truly was.

'That's quite a conclusion to jump to. How do you know it affects the entire universe?'

'Simple. Because you don't find different parts of the world living out of synch do you?'

The point was valid, but hard to comprehend.

'I can't believe my mind is powerful enough to affect the whole planet. That's just mad.'

Mike looked upon Ian with belittling contempt.

'You don't get it, do you? You don't find planets suddenly becoming out of sync either,' he said forcefully, highlighting the seemingly obvious. 'Their movements still tally with the tables printed in almanacs, don't they?'

Ian conceded and fell silent.

When he next spoke, he did so sheepishly.

'So, I can rewind the entire universe just by the power of my thought. What does that make me?'

'It demonstrates to be true,' Mike replied, 'what mankind have always suspected; that we are the single most important creatures in the universe. The Bible always maintained we were. Now we know for sure.'

Ian was quick to pick up on the point.

'And if the universe was made primarily to suit mankind's purpose and we have powers no other man has, then we must be the crème de la crème.'

'You do us an injustice,' Mike said, shaking his head and raising one hand to guard against Ian's short-sighted conclusion. 'We are nothing less than Gods.'

Ian sat motionless, trying to comprehend the enormity of the suggestion.

Mike slid from his stool and slowly paced round behind Ian as a lecturer might do for dramatic effect. Ian did not know whether or not he was supposed to follow Mike's progress and chose to remain facing the empty seat, his head turned only slightly to indicate he was still listening.

Mike's hand rested for a moment on the grip of a long, thin screwdriver.

'Twenty-four years ago I won the football pools. Two years ago I topped up my bank balance with a win on the National Lottery. On both occasions I managed to remain anonymous and continued to live my life in peace. Then you came along and I had to expose myself to flush you out. I'm sorry Ian, but we simply cannot co-exist.'

Ian's back arched violently in response to a sensation of having been punched hard in the kidneys. Then he felt the tugging of the screwdriver being withdrawn from deep within his body. He tried to stand, but instead slumped to the floor, landing heavily, face upwards. Mike stood over him, coolly wiping blood from the shaft of the screwdriver with an oily rag, looking satisfied at a job well done.

Too weak to twitch even the smallest muscle, Ian's eyes closed as all expression on his face began to melt away. Inside his head, his mind felt relaxed as his thoughts started to drift. Then, from the depths of his consciousness came a pulse of defiance, and with it, the ability to make the low frequency buzzing return once again.

Ian opened his eyes abruptly, slid from the stool, turned and jumped back just in time to avoid being stabbed for a second time.

'Hmm, I hadn't foreseen this happening,' Mike said calmly, with no more than a hint of disappointment in his voice; disappointment in himself for making such a schoolboy error.

Relying purely on impulse, Ian grabbed for the closest heavy object to hand. The weight and momentum of the club hammer shattered Mike's skull with a sickening thud, spattering blood across every surface within a three-metre radius. The body staggered sideways, slid along the edge of the workbench, fell across the stool it had recently been sitting on, and rolled onto the floor, landing face down.

The bleeding was profuse. Fresh and free flowing, it cascaded down from a clearly defined depression among an area of matted hair, to join a steadily growing pool centred beneath the motionless head. The ear directly below the breech deflected the flow, presenting the pale whiteness of the folds it protected as an unspoiled oasis in a sea of scarlet. Then, from the route to the inner ear, there began to trickle a straw-coloured fluid, a symptom to cause anxious concern in any paramedic.

The shock of seeing what he had done initially blinded Ian to the priorities of diagnosis. It was almost a minute before he could tear his gaze away from the indentation he had caused and from the flow of blood. Only then did other senses begin to come back on line. Only then did he realise, despite the obvious trauma, and against all the odds, Mike's body was still breathing. Lungs filled noisily and slowly, but nonetheless steadily, giving no indication the process was about to stop.

There was no telling whether or not the damage to Mike's brain was sufficient to prevent him reversing the course of events, placing Ian in mortal danger for a second time. He could take no chances.

Kneeling over the body, his eyes focused on the back of Mike's head. Ian raised the hammer high, intent on bringing it down with as much force as he could muster, but to do so was against his nature. Inflicting the first blow had been a reaction to a deadly situation and had been executed without the need for conscious decision. The second blow would be quite different; premeditated; aimed; extremely unpleasant.

A black plastic refuse sack had dropped to the floor as the stricken man swept his arm along the workbench during his short but untidy journey to the ground. Ian picked it up and draped it over the injured man's head, smoothing it down to reveal the outline off the target beneath. Now he was aiming at a bag, not at the skull of a living human being. It could just have easily been a coconut awaiting destruction for the flesh it contained.

Ian concentrated on the bag, ignoring the body protruding out from beneath it. He held the hammer sideways on, hoping to generalise the damage in preference to causing one single, deep penetration. The heavy weight swung down and met with a thud and the rustle of plastic. The definition of the target disappeared.

One final blow would ensure the job was done. He smoothed out the plastic for a second time, his palms sensing a sponge-like quality where they had encountered firmness before. The hammer, a full kilogram of hardened steel, rose and fell, transmitting vibrations from the impact through the handle and on into Ian's arm. From there, nerve responses relayed the information to the areas of his brain that controlled feelings of nausea and activated them to spectacular effect. As the hammer dropped to the ground, Ian's stomach retched, and then there was silence.

Taking a paper handkerchief from his pocket, Ian mopped at the strings of saliva that hung from his glistening lips, spitting several times to rid his mouth of the acidic taste that irritated his tongue. With trembling hands, he then wiped away the tears that trickled down his cheeks. He was not a man who took to crying easily and even now could not bring himself to produce the sounds that normally accompanied a man in torment. His fingers gently caressed his lower face as he knelt, rocking back and forth on his heels, his eyes staring into the middle distance.

Then, with a single gulp, a brief clenching of his fist, and a slow exhale, Ian's composure was restored as quickly as it had been lost.

'Okay,' he began reasoning quietly to himself. 'This was self-defence. I have nothing to worry about.'

The fact he had not automatically rewound meant his subconscious was in agreement. This was a justifiable killing about which he had little or no regret. After all, only minutes ago the man now lying dead on the floor had tried his best to make Ian the victim.

He looked at his blood-stained hands and then at the weapon. Doubts began to surface.

'But what if they don't believe me? I'll go to jail for life.'

There were two options: to go forward and risk imprisonment; or to go back so the murder never happened. The latter was impossible. Going back would resurrect the true murderer, putting his own life in mortal danger. At least going forward did not necessarily mean certain capture. As far as he knew, no one was aware he had visited Mike Summerbee that evening. He could simply deny everything.

There was little to be done at the crime scene other than to dispose of anything that showed he had been there. That meant washing his cup and wiping the fingerprints from the handle of the hammer. The instructions leading him to 'The Grange' had already been destroyed.

Ian was not a stupid man. He knew however careful he might be at covering his tracks, he would still be leaving plenty of forensic evidence for the police to digest, including the erstwhile contents of his stomach. What mattered was that if he were not a suspect, all the scientific evidence in the world would not lead to him. He had led a law-abiding life up to now, giving the police no reason to keep his prints on file. He had no motive. He had no connection with the man except they were both lottery winners and, so far, only he and his wife knew he was.

The worst scenario would be for Ian to be discovered bent over the victim. As if to heighten the possibility of this happening, the telephone rang from within the corpse's clothing. It was time to leave.

The gates offered the only resistance to a quick getaway, but despite being nearly fifty years old, Ian was a fit man and scaled them with less difficulty than some half his age.

Trying not to draw attention to himself, he pulled away smoothly from the lay-by and kept within the speed limit all the way home. The journey was uneventful by normal standards, but paranoia brought threat from every direction. A police car cruising past on the opposite carriageway induced a brief panic attack that saw Ian repeating oaths to himself under his breath.

'Oh, My God. Oh, My God. What have I done? Please forgive me. Oh, My God.'

8

Debbie, unable to find anything of interest to watch on the television, got up from her seat as soon as her husband stepped through the front door. She could not help but notice instantly the blood spattered over him.

'What's happened?' she said quickly, her eyes scanning his body for injuries.

Detecting his wife had jumped to the wrong conclusion, Ian brought the palm of his right hand to rest gently against her cheek.

'It's all right. I'm not hurt.'

Her expression immediately changed to one of confusion.

For Ian, there was no avoiding the truth. If things were to work out, he needed his wife's unconditional support.

'Let me get cleaned up and changed out of these clothes and then we need to talk,' he said, solemnly. 'Can you bring me up a dustbin sack?'

Several times, Ian closed his eyes against the warm water that cascaded down from the shower rose overhead, his hands cupping either side of his nose, moving up and down his face in an act of self-reassurance. On each occasion, the closing of his eyes was accompanied by the most grotesque flashbacks, detailing in slow motion the results of bringing a heavy object into violent contact with a human skull. The shower continued only long enough to rid his flesh of the other man's blood, before he could bear no more. Stepping from the shower tray, Ian looked drawn – ill. Were it not for the heat of the water bringing colour to the surface of his skin, he might well have blended in totally with the white towelling bathrobe he wrapped himself in to dry.

Back downstairs, Ian sat beside his wife on the settee, ready to confess all, intent on speaking without knowingly withholding any piece of information, large or small. He began with how he had concluded the fourth winner must also have been able to rewind time. Debbie picked up that her husband consistently spoke in the past tense. However, any attempt to interrupt him was met with a hand gesture, asking her to wait until he had finished. As frustrating as this was, it was not long before she had her answers, Ian continuing to recount details of his evening to the point when he had climbed the gates and had driven off at a steady twenty-eight miles per hour.

The explanation took a full fifteen minutes, but it took Debbie just one short sentence to sum up the salient points.

'Ian, you've killed a man,' she said incredulously, looking down at the hearthrug.

'I had to. It was either him or me,' he replied, firmly.

Debbie was angry with her husband for being so stupid.

'I told you not to do that thing again. Now look what mess it has landed you in.'

So far, her reactions had neither blamed nor exonerated him. What Ian needed to know was whether her intentions were to support him or cast him to the wolves.

'Well, do you think I should go to jail?'

'Don't be so stupid. I don't want to lose you. I just want to know where we stand.

'I understand you can't bring him back, and from what you say, it would be unwise to cash in the lottery ticket. So, where does that leave us? With no money and no income; that's where. I heard the way you spoke to your boss on the phone. Even claiming a nervous breakdown wouldn't explain that little outburst.'

'Don't worry; I have enough put by to tide us over for six months, if we're careful. Something will turn up by then. In any case, in a few months we can always pull the same trick with the lottery again. Summerbee told me himself it gets easier.'

Debbie was not listening; she had other troubles on her mind.

'What also worries me, Ian, is there might be more people out there who can mess with time just like you. Will they come looking for you too? Will you land up having to murder or be murdered for the rest of your life? And what if you're caught? You'll go to prison and I'll be left out here, alone and penniless.'

Ian shuffled along the sofa, put his arms round his wife's shoulders and buried her head in his chest.

'Let me put your mind at rest,' he said gently. 'Firstly, there are no others out there because neither Summerbee nor I detected them. Secondly, if I am arrested I shall think of something else. I assure you, I will not be spending years in jail and you will not be spending years coping on your own.'

Silence fell. In that silence, Ian had an unwelcome opportunity to think. He had lived the events first hand, he had relived them unwillingly in the shower, he had recounted them to his wife and now he did not want to dwell on the subject anymore.

'Have we got anything to drink in the house?' he asked, desperate to obliterate his thoughts.

Debbie, disapproving, but at the same time understanding her husband's reasoning, retrieved a bottle of cheap cooking sherry from a cupboard in the kitchen and offered it to her husband.

'I'm sorry, this is all we have.'

Ian poured a tumbler full of the harsh red-brown liquid, drank it and immediately poured another.

'This is disgusting,' he complained, wincing.

The quality of the drink was no barrier to him draining the second glass, or to him pouring a third.

Debbie looked on, worried.

Within ten minutes the sherry bottle sat empty on the kitchen worktop, but Ian remained horribly and reluctantly sober.

'My jaw aches from talking too much; my head feels numb from thinking too much; I need to rest,' he pleaded, feebly, begging for deliverance from his torment.

It was Debbie's turn to offer solace. She did so by placing her arm firmly round her husband's back in order to guide him up the stairs to bed.

Half an hour passed during which time Ian lay staring into the darkness, trying unsuccessfully to change the subject that filled his head. There followed the sound of his feet shuffling across the landing to the bathroom, the sound of the cabinet doors sliding open and shut again, and the sound of the foil backing from a blister pack of medication being popped open.

Ian returned to the bedroom where he could just make out, by the dim glow of the bedside clock, his wife, who was now sitting up in bed, clearly experiencing similar difficulties in getting to sleep.

'What was that you've just taken?' she asked, curious.

'Flu pills. One always knocks me out so two should do the trick under the circumstances, don't you think?'

'Ian,' Debbie responded, shocked and annoyed at her husband's recklessness. 'They contain paracetamol. You should never exceed the dose stated on the packet. It might lead the brain damage, or liver failure, or something. Besides, I'm sure you're not supposed to take them with alcohol.'

'Nag all you like. Within half an hour, if I'm lucky, I shall be away in the land of nod. So, if you have anything you wish to say, do it now.'

Ian could hear his wife talking of things that did not matter even after his eyelids had fallen shut. Then he thought of nothing.

When he awoke the following morning from a dreamless sleep, the events of the previous evening seemed a million miles distant; as though they had happened to somebody else. His tongue felt arid and swollen, but otherwise he felt marvellously rested.

Debbie, herself unwilling to induce sleep through drug abuse, had not fared nearly so well. She had remained awake for most of the night and her skin was now pale, with the exception of the redness surrounding her eyes.

Ian could only think to help by providing a cup of tea in bed. Strangely, however, on his return to the bedroom, he found the coming of daylight had finally allowed her to succumb to her need for sleep. As she lay peacefully, he set about making amends for the anxiety to which he had exposed his wife, tending to those household chores he could carry out without making any noise: the ironing; the polishing; washing the dishes.

Debbie remained in bed until late afternoon at which time Ian carried out the noisier duties he had been prevented from doing so for fear of waking her. He ran the vacuum cleaner over the carpets, filled the washing machine, and tidied the bedroom. All the time, Debbie lay sprawled upon the sofa, watching the television with little interest, occasionally sobbing to herself.

As much as Ian regretted what had happened – what he had done; what he had been forced to do – his wife's inability to cope was making matters worse.

'Debs, we can't carry on like this. We need to talk,' he said, sympathetically, perched on the edge of the settee, his wife's ankles stretched out behind him.

After a short delay, she slowly folded her legs, swung them round, and sat up. Ian embraced her with a reassuring hug, one arm across her shoulders, the other across her front, his hand gripping her upper arm tightly, pulling her towards him.

He had nothing to offer but words of comfort and understanding. When he spoke, he did so without script; the words forming not in his head, but coming straight from his heart.

'I can only imagine how you feel,' he began slowly; earnestly. 'Rest assured, whatever you're feeling, the guilt I'm suffering is probably a hundred times worse. It hits me in waves; constantly; whatever I'm doing; however much I try to think about something else. It's not just guilt though. I'm also being eaten away by the injustice of it all. It wasn't my fault; it was self-defence, but I am going to have to live with this for the rest of my life – our lives. It's not fair I should suffer this torment; it's not fair society should punish me. For God's sake; I'm not a murderer.'

Fighting back genuine tears, Ian continued.

'I know you will never be able to forget what has happened, but try to accept it; find a place for it and store it away somewhere. I need you now more than ever. I need you to be strong for me, and I need you to help me think about where we go from here.'

Ian spoke with his head bent forward, trying to achieve eye contact, but instead had to be satisfied with a view of the top of his wife's head, her face nestled into his chest.

The couple remained locked together in silence, long enough for Ian to begin to feel physically uncomfortable. Despite shifting his position more than once, his back grew ever more painful. Eventually, after several aborted attempts to unravel his arms, Debbie let him go, having extracted a promise he would come straight back.

At least there were no more tears, and she managed to remain sitting up, although her reddened face remained grotesquely distorted, and her hands performed a contorted dance on her lap, knotting and unknotting a handkerchief Ian had fetched from her bedside drawer.

Ian went to the kitchen, returning ten minutes later with a teapot, their best bone china cups, and a plate of his wife's favourite biscuits, all neatly presented on a tray.

'This is a treat,' Debbie said weakly, but smiling. 'I don't recall when you last pampered me like this.'

The evening meal, prepared by Ian's novice hand, came and went. To his relief, Debbie's appetite at least had returned to near normal. By nine o'clock she was almost her old self again. It was as though she had tried to sustain an argument over something she had slowly concluded was not worth letting ruin her life.

In fact, by half past nine, Debbie felt sufficiently restored to answer the door in response to a rapping on the glass panel.

It was the police.

9

For a short while, Debbie knew more than her husband. Warrant cards had been presented to her; formal introductions had been made. Whereas, from his position perched on the very edge of the settee, curious to know who might be calling at such an hour, Ian could tell merely that at least two people had interrupted their evening, the feminine voice of his wife contrasting the much deeper voices of more than one man. Ian heard nothing of the words that passed between them, but his wife sounded flustered, sufficient to increase her husband's pulse rate so that he became aware of his heart beating within his chest.

The doorway that appeared more than adequate for his wife to pass through, seemed less so for the two towering men who followed her, both suited, both unmistakably plain-clothed police officers. Their chosen combination of trendy suit, shirt, tie and slick haircut might have been worn by any ambitious young businessman, but salesmen did not travel in pairs; salesmen did not intimidate Debbie to the degree she failed to insist they remove their shoes – a house rule, advertised through the medium of a friendly, decorative placard hanging on the wall opposite the front door.

Ian rose politely to greet his visitors, a look of genuine surprise and confusion described by every nuance of his expression.

'I am Detective Constable Bramworth,' the elder of the two men announced, holding forth a warrant card that looked horribly official; not at all like the nametags worn by counter staff in building societies.

'And this is Detective Constable Andrews.'

The second man offered forward his identification. Ian ignored it but nodded towards him to acknowledge his presence.

The group sat down, Ian and his wife huddled close together on the settee, the two officers each taking an armchair opposite them.

D.C. Bramworth was quick to get to the point.

'We are investigating a serious crime and were wondering whether either of you might be able to further our enquiries,' he stated, clutching an open notebook.

'And how might I be able to do that?' Ian asked, trying to control his voice which, to his own ears, was shaking noticeably.

The detective made a mental note of two observations that interested him. Firstly, Mr Bradshaw had failed to enquire as to the nature of the crime; surely a natural question to raise under the circumstances. Perhaps he did not ask because he already knew. Secondly, he had referred only to himself in his reply. Was this man assuming the investigation would only involve him? If so, was the man's assumption based on the fact he had knowledge of, or even a connection with the crime?

For the time being, the detective remained undecided, weighing up Bradshaw's verbal response with the look of utter surprise Bramworth had noted on the face of the potential suspect when he and his colleague first entered the room.

'Well sir,' Bramworth continued, 'we believe either you or your wife may have seen something.'

Ian sat silent and motionless for a moment, sizing up his situation and the abilities of the two detectives who sought to discover him. Despite being faced with the prospect of having to answer the most difficult questions of his life, he felt suddenly and strangely at ease. However good the police might be at their jobs, he could not help but feel he held the upper hand. In fact, it was the best hand it was possible to have. If all else failed, he could rewind time so the crime never took place. Then where would their case be? Sure enough, taking such a course of action would resurrect a man determined to kill him, but he could cross that bridge when he came to it. At the very least he could rewind to a point half an hour before the police arrived, giving him time to flee.

Having no special powers, his wife lacked the same confidence. She sat beside him, head bent forward, knees together, her fingers twiddling on her lap.

Ian was interested to know the extent of the policemen's knowledge. If it was sufficient to arrest him, they would take fingerprints and that would lead to an inevitable guilty verdict at court and a mandatory sentence of life imprisonment.

Settling back into the cushions, Ian delivered a defiant response, bordering on flippancy.

'Tell me when and where it took place and I'll try to be of help, but I don't remember seeing any crimes of late, serious or otherwise.'

The quavering was no longer present in his voice. His pulse had returned to normal.

The detective considered Mr Bradshaw's sudden change from whimpering simpleton to an arrogant man brimming with confidence. Then he considered the man's wife, Debbie. Everything about her oozed guilt and had done so from the moment she opened the front door. Everything she did, the way she did it, everything she said, or did not say, pointed to a suspicion she was hiding something. Experience suggested to Bramworth she might be covering up for her husband.

'The crime took place at a remote house near the village of Arkleston, at around seven o'clock yesterday evening.'

Bramworth released information only as it was necessary, hoping Mr Bradshaw would refer to information he could only know if he had been at the scene of the crime.

'I don't recall being there,' Ian responded, innocently.

'What about you ma'am?' Andrews asked, keen to demonstrate he was not present merely to take notes.

'My wife was in all evening,' Ian interjected, denying Debbie a chance to speak for herself.

She nodded when the detective's expression begged confirmation.

With Ian refusing to crumble as he had hoped, Bramworth felt it time to reveal the first of his trump cards.

'I must inform you that your vehicle - the one that currently stands outside on your drive - was seen near the property in question at about the time the offence was committed.'

Still Ian did not enquire as to what had happened.

An awkward silence fell during which Ian was supposed to react, but did not.

Andrews was next to speak, hoping a barrage of questions from two sources would be more effective than one.

'Are you not interested what crime has been committed?'

Ian hesitated before answering, but there was no indication he had been placed on the back foot.

'Of course I am. I just didn't think you were allowed to tell me. Up to now you seemed to have been at pains to keep if from me.'

Bramworth paused for a moment before putting his next question, pregnant pauses usually working in his favour.

'We are talking about murder; a particularly violent and seemingly premeditated murder. Does that jog your memory?'

Ian squirmed a little; revealing an involuntary chink in his armour.

'I may have been there. I enjoy the outdoors, you see. Camping and walking keep me sane. Yesterday evening I was driving back from one such trip, taking the scenic route, and I got lost. I stopped in a lay-by somewhere to look at the map. I don't know exactly where I landed up, but thinking about it, it may have been where you said.'

'Hmm, that's interesting,' Bramworth considered. 'Can you explain why then, at the time your vehicle was seen, nobody appeared to be in it?'

Ian shook his head lightly, his lips pursed, giving himself time to concoct an answer.

'No,' he replied, looking defiantly into the detective's eyes. 'It may be I was bent forward studying the map closely. The light was not particularly good inside the car.'

'No sir,' Bramworth responded, his eyes equally fixed, upping the ante by leaning forward one degree. 'Our witness states she approached the vehicle and found it to be empty.'

Ian tilted his head and upper body back, opened his mouth, and then brought his lips together again as he rocked forward, returning to the upright position. One hand remained unflinching on his lap; the other rose briefly in a sweeping motion before dropping back to bounce on his thigh.

'Oh, I remember now,' he said brightly. 'I needed to use the toilet. I was probably still in the bushes at the time. I dare say my footprints are still in the mud. Awful stuff.'

Silence returned as the lead detective considered what he had heard. Evidently he was not satisfied.

'Ian Bradshaw, I am arresting you in connection with the murder of Michael Summerbee. You have the right to remain silent...'

Ian did not hear the caution. The worst had happened. His fate was sealed. Arrest meant fingerprints. Fingerprints would connect him with the scene of the murder; a scene that would give up other forensic evidence - body fluids; fibres; all sorts. Then he would go to jail and he would remain there for a very long time. At this point, rewinding the universe offered a solution, but not a simple one. He needed to consider choices: how to avoid being murdered himself; what was best for his wife and children.

The cell was small; only three paces by four. Its walls were of bare brick that had, over the years, lost their sharp edges to many, many coats of paint. The bed was of normal height but cast in concrete, topped by a thick board of varnished wood, and cushioned by a thin vinyl-coated easy-wipe mattress. A pillow of similar fashion to the mattress and a blanket completed the cell inventory.

Incarceration was entirely alien to Ian. Lacking freedom; lacking choice; lacking the simplest of creature comforts and, most of all, lacking companionship. It did, however, offer hours of uninterrupted solitude, providing time for reflection and the opportunity to plan. On waking though, the only conclusion the night had drawn was he should wait and discover exactly what the police knew and determine whether it was possible to return to the scene after the incident and cover his tracks.

The interview was delayed until mid-morning and took place in a very large, bleak, room. The levels of light were good, but not so the acoustics. The high ceiling encouraged an echo; not the sort associated with shouting 'hello' at a distant rock face; more that of a lounge stripped for redecoration. The analogy was strengthened by the lack of furnishings; a table, a few wooden chairs and a recording device, loaded with two tapes, being the only objects of note in the room. The walls, painted gloss, were divided top from bottom by way of a rubber dado rail, running horizontally, a metre from the floor. A warning from D.C. Andrews not to lean on it revealed it was the means of activating the alarm.

The room was cold; a fact at odds with the intensity and quality of the light that streamed through the window in the rear wall, but explained by the presence of a portable air conditioning unit situated on the floor beneath the window. Its silvery flexible hose, draped through a fanlight opening, was working too efficiently and had reduced the temperature such that it caused goose pimples to stand proud on Ian's forearms.

Apparently the choice was to be cold, but bearable, or hot to the point of passing out. D.C. Bramworth, being in charge of the interview, chose the former. Ian, his top half dressed only in a short sleeved shirt - made of the thinnest material - and a summer jacket, gave himself a firm embrace, placing his hands under his armpits in an attempt to maintain the blood supply to his fingers.

While waiting for a much needed cup of warming tea to arrive, D.C. Bramworth began with the preliminaries.

'Can you confirm for the record you do not wish a solicitor to be present?'

'Yes.'

What was the point? It would only delay procedures further and Ian was keen to know how much evidence was stacked against him.

'If you change your mind, let me know and I shall halt the interview until one can be obtained. After all, you must understand these charges are of a most serious nature.'

Ian nodded.

'When I saw you at your home last night, you didn't seem sure whether or not you had been in Arkleston at around seven o'clock the previous evening. Now you have had time to think, are you any clearer on the subject?'

Ian paused to consider his response.

'Okay, I was there, but it was at Mr Summerbee's request.'

D.C. Bramworth leant forward to rest his elbows on the table, and began manipulating a metal-bodied pen between his fingers, seemingly more interested by the pen than the answer his suspect had just given. Having chewed his bottom lip for a few moments, he clipped his pen to the opening of his inside jacket pocket, before leaning back in his chair, his chin resting on his chest, his eyes fixed on Ian.

'At his request?' he prompted, trying outwardly to remain calm, but inwardly screaming with excitement, having driven another nail into his suspect's coffin.

'Yes, I met him at the opening of a new out of town superstore and he gave me instructions on how to get to his country house.'

'And why would he do that?'

'Because we had both won the National Lottery.'

D.C. Andrews looked surprised. D.C. Bramworth remained unflinching. The interview was going well. So far the interrogation had provided means and a possible motive – money.

'So, you're a rich man?' Bramworth continued.

'No, I hadn't claimed the money and after last night I destroyed the ticket.'

'Why would you do that?'

'There was no connection between Mike Summerbee and myself and I wanted it to remain that way.'

'That's a high price to pay for anonymity isn't it?'

Ian shrugged his shoulders.

'Do you still have these instructions?'

'No, Mr Summerbee destroyed them shortly after I got there.'

'Destroyed them?'

'Yes, he set fire to them and disposed of the ashes.'

'That's convenient for your story.'

'Hardly. If I still had them, I could prove what I am saying is true. I could tell you where to find the ashes. Perhaps your forensic people might be able to retrieve something.'

Both interviewers appeared unconvinced.

'If, as you say, you were a guest, why didn't you park up near the house? Why choose a passing-point.'

Ian looked as though he did not understand the question, forcing Bramworth to explain.

'A lay-by provided so motorists can pass each other on a single track road.'

'I didn't realise that's what it was for. Anyway, I would have pulled through the gates but they were coned off.'

'The drive was coned off?'

The elder detective's habit of using a statement as a question was beginning to annoy Ian who tensed his arms and gritted his teeth until the feeling passed.

'Mr Summerbee asked me to stack them just inside the gates. They're probably still there now.'

There was a pause, long enough for Ian to become aware of the fan within the air conditioning unit -by its low, ceaseless noise and by the draft it exerted upon the exposed portions of his skin. He was reminded at once of the cold that had somehow been forgotten since the questioning began and tucked his hands back into his armpits. By doing so, his arms crossed his chest as though he were receiving a hug. Somehow, this simple physical contact gave him comfort, as though his own limbs were in fact those of his wife.

The whereabouts of the cones was dismissed as if of no consequence. Instead, Bramworth chose to come in on another tack.

'It would seem from what Mrs Summerbee has told us, her husband was indeed expecting a visitor, but an unwelcome one.'

'He must have been referring to someone else then,' Ian said defensively, treating the detective's statement as a question.

'No, he made plans to check in with his wife every fifteen minutes, for the duration of your visit, and he activated those plans on your arrival. That suggests to me you were the anticipated unwelcome visitor; the person he feared sufficiently to make preparations to protect his safety. Unfortunately, it seems they were not good enough.'

Ian looked genuinely confused. Bramworth, sensing his line of enquiries had finally put his opponent on the back foot, followed quickly with another provocative statement.

'Mr Summerbee told his wife he was being pestered by someone regarding his lottery win and that someone was coming over to see him. He must have been concerned as he made arrangements to check in every fifteen minutes, either by phone or via a video link between the workshop and the main residence.'

'Video link?' It was Ian's turn to ask a question by way of statement.

'Yes, it seems they had it installed so Mrs Summerbee could tell her husband when dinner was ready. As it turned out, it meant she was on scene within ten minutes of her husband being murdered. The blood was still flowing from his crushed head when she found him. Can you imagine how she felt?'

It was apparent the detective was trying to paint a graphic scene, hopeful it would awaken subdued feelings of guilt that might lead to a quick confession. Ian shuddered inwardly as an image of the brutal killing burst into his conscious thought, but there was to be no let up. The detective continued, revealing an overwhelming weight of evidence that was sure to seal a conviction, whether or not the suspect came clean.

'Mrs Summerbee saw a man climbing over the gate at the end of the drive. The description she gave could easily be a match to you.'

There was nothing for Ian to do but bluff his way through.

'I don't know why Mr Summerbee should have been so concerned when he was the one who invited me.'

'So you keep saying. Why then did you feel the need to creep through the flower beds instead of using the paths?'

Again, Ian looked confused.

'A footprint was found in a flowerbed near the workshop in question. It appears to match another print found in the lay-by where your car was parked. I'm guessing we'll be able to link those footprints to you.'

'I had to go across the lawn. There was a tape cordoning off the house from reporters. Mrs Summerbee will be able to confirm that.'

D.C. Bramworth produced a look that asked if that was the best Ian had to offer.

'Where is this tape now?' he asked, enjoying the moment; a Spanish bull fighter thrusting yet another barbed stick into the creature's wounded shoulders.

'Mr Summerbee and I walked together in the grounds. He gathered in the tape as he went.'

'What did you do as you walked?'

'We talked.'

'About what?'

'Things we have in common.'

'Had, don't you mean?' Andrews corrected.

Ian had been concentrating so intently on Bradshaw's voice, the comment, thrown from the side, had him staring at the second detective with an expression of utter confusion upon his face.

'Had,' Andrews reiterated. 'He's dead.'

Ian stared all the more, but now with disbelief the constable would try to score points so cheaply.

Bramworth quickly regained his attention with yet another set of questions.

'What did you have in common?'

'Not much. We did discover we had been at school together and in the same year, but that was about it.'

'You knew Mr Summerbee at school?'

'No, that's just it. We were there together, but did not remember each other.'

'So why did a man you did not remember from school invite you to his house?'

If this were a rehearsal for his day in court, Ian was sure he would be convicted of the premeditated murder of Michael Summerbee, even without a whole host of forensics reports that would surely be available to damn him further. D.C. Bramworth was good and Ian was sure the prosecution barrister would be even better.

'I believe he wanted to kill me.'

Bramworth's eyes interrogated Ian with as much ferocity as had his ceaseless questioning.

'Look,' Ian began, exasperated; 'you can corroborate some of what I've been saying. The cones: there are three stacks of them to the left of the driveway, just inside the main gates. You'll find the tape bundled round a bunch of metal stakes at the back of the workshop. How else would I know they were there? And if his wife is telling the truth, she'll be able to confirm the tape was in front of the house when I arrived. You'll find the remains of the ashes in a flip-top bin and the galvanised bucket next to it. The lottery people won't be able to confirm I won a share of the jackpot, but they will be able to confirm the unclaimed ticket was bought at Mr Patel's newsagent, just round the corner from my house.'

The interviewers let Ian finish but were clearly not impressed, indicating this by way of their body language: D.C. Bramworth idly staring at the table throughout; D.C. Andrews shaking his head ever so slightly, a half-hearted smile developing on his lips. Ian looked at the two men, each in turn, with pleading eyes, but it was obvious neither man was about to give quarter.

Bramworth then explained why he had difficulty believing the story he was hearing.

'Mr Bradshaw,' he began, 'even if we accept all of that, none of it explains how Mr Summerbee came to meet his death.'

Ian took a deep breath.

'I killed him,' he spoke quietly. 'But you have to believe me; it was done in self-defence.'

'Mr Bradshaw, the man's head was pulverised with a club hammer. If you'd hit him once, we might have believed you, but you struck him multiple time, didn't you? How can that possibly be self-defence?'

'He stabbed…went to stab me with a screwdriver. I went for the nearest thing at hand and hit him.'

'So, why did you then cover his head with a bin liner and proceed to reduce his brains to pulp?'

'He wasn't dead. I was scared that if I didn't finish the job, he would try to stab me again. I was squeamish. I had to cover his head or I wouldn't have been able to go through with it.'

'Game over', thought the detective, almost bursting with a sense of self-satisfied smugness. The case was complete and in almost record time. He had forensic evidence that no jury would be able to ignore. He had a motive - Bradshaw had been angry his money had been reduced by the greed of Mr Summerbee in winning the lottery for a second time, unnecessarily. And if that were not enough, he now had a taped confession. Despite this evidence though, the murderer, Ian Bradshaw, still seemed hell bent on trying to convince his captors of his innocence.

'Don't you see? Right from the moment he bought the lottery ticket, Mike Summerbee was engineering the situation with the intention of killing me. The bastard went to great lengths to set me up. I was supposed to turn up, leave a trail that made me look like an intruder and all so he could murder me and make it look like self-defence. If I was there to kill him, what was I supposed to have done it with, anyway? I wasn't to know he'd have a club hammer, left lying about.'

Bramworth, weary at Bradshaw's refusal to accept it was all over, could not be bothered to answer. That duty fell to Andrews.

'A large kitchen knife was found at the scene,' the detective began, making reference to his pocket book. 'Mrs Summerbee claims she has never seen it before. It certainly doesn't match the knives she has in her kitchen. A set of fingerprints were recovered from the handle.'

At this point, Andrews looked straight into Ian's eyes. 'What's the betting they belong to you?'

'Yes, of course they do. That just goes to show how clever he was. He made me handle that knife. I'd never seen it before that night.'

'Mr Bradshaw,' Bramworth snapped, slamming his hand against the table. 'Why might Mr Summerbee go to all that trouble to murder you?'

Ian flinched at the impact, but then tried to answer the question as calmly as he could.

'Because, as Mr Summerbee explained himself, we could not co-exist.'

He spoke as if this would make sense to any normal man.

Both detectives had heard enough. The interview had reached its natural conclusion. Sure enough there would be other bouts of interrogation, but effectively the need for talk was over.

Ian was left to consider what had happened. From the detectives' point of view, it was clear. They had forced a confession and had established a watertight case on which no jury would hesitate to convict. From Ian's point of view, he had a similarly clear understanding of the outcome. He had explored an avenue and had reached a dead end. It could be likened to navigating a garden maze, and as with all mazes there comes a time when the only option is to retrace ones steps and explore another path. In this case, it meant returning to the previous evening where he would be able to discuss his options with his wife. She might be useful only as a sounding board, but he hoped her input would be far greater. He valued her opinion and she deserved to have a say in any decision that was bound to have an enormous effect on both their lives.

The Inspector spoke briefly to the tape recorder, formally ending the interview.

With the click of the off button, Ian could not help but make one final comment, which he delivered in a most matter-of-fact way.

'So much for me being the most powerful man in the universe. Why couldn't I have been given something more useful; like being able to make you forget all about this little unpleasantness?'

With that, he produced a grin that annoyed the policemen intensely.

'This is no laughing matter,' Andrews said seriously. 'A man has died in horrible circumstances and I believe you are solely to blame.'

Still exhibiting a contemptuous smile, Ian, now full of confidence, sat back in his chair, his arms folded. Any further conversation would be pointless for in a few moments the words would be sucked back into the windpipes of those who spoke them. Nevertheless, he could not help himself. He wanted someone to know he was more powerful than all other men. He wanted to believe, however briefly, he was in control. He had the opportunity to show off and he intended to take it.

'I have the gift all men desire. How many times have you wished you could have your time again; to undo the countless little mistakes we all make?'

He delighted for a moment in the detectives' confusion before finishing his point.

'Well, I can.'

With that, Ian closed his eyes and brought back memories of the clunking of china as he served his wife with tea and biscuits the previous evening. There followed a momentary buzzing in his head.

10

'Debbie,' Ian said, taking his wife's hand in his. 'We need to discuss our options.'

She looked at him strangely, her eyebrows taut, her lips slightly parted.

'Ian,' she replied, a mixture of distrust and confusion shaping her every word. 'We have just spent the past half an hour discussing our options. The way you're talking; that never happened.'

'That was then, this is now.'

Ian's words were delivered slowly as if to emphasise their gravity – their meaning – but still his wife looked confused.

'Everything we spoke about was based on the police never linking me with the death of that bastard, Summerbee. Our options now must be based on the fact they do.'

The penny finally dropped.

'You've done it again haven't you?' Debbie said, horrified.

Ian looked awkward.

'There's no easy way to say this, so I'm going to give it to you straight.'

Ian paused as he drew together pockets of courage that were dispersed throughout his body, concentrating them so he might recount events that were destined to happen, unless he made alterations to the past.

'Later this evening, the police will pay us a visit and they will arrest me. A witness saw my car. They have enough evidence to take my fingerprints and they will match them with those found all over the murder scene. So you see, I will be convicted and I will go to jail – if we do nothing that is.'

The news came as a shock; one of many jolts to her system Debbie had received of late. She fell silent for a few moments, preferring to do that than commit to yet another bout of crying.

'So,' she said, eventually, 'what are our options?'

They were numerous and could all be put before her for consideration; all with the exception of one; that being suicide.

Taking his own life would provide the definitive solution. After all, the police could not arrest a dead man. Ian was prepared to make the sacrifice if needed; that being defined as the most effective action to take to prevent his family suffering as a result of his failings. Suicide, though, had its shortcomings. However low his self-esteem, his family would no doubt miss him greatly. Debbie would have no one to support her. Stephen and Ann would no longer have a dad. Then there would be the stigma; not only that brought about by the suicide itself, but also by the general acceptance he had been a murderer and one too cowardly to stand before a jury.

In effect, this option was not an option at all.

There was another way. Ian could return to the point when he first mastered his gift and vow to himself never to use it. As the days rolled back, Mike Summerbee would be resurrected, but, without the lottery win, he would be denied the tools needed to flush out his adversary and kill him. This choice seemed an instant clear favourite, but it too had its limitations. Some event might happen in the future - like the house burning down - that would make the continued suppression of his ability almost impossible. It might also happen by mistake; as a result of an unintentional deeply embarrassing situation, for example.

However it happened, Summerbee would experience any rewind Ian triggered; he would realise its significance; he would find it intensely annoying, and he would make it his business to track down the perpetrator and despatch him post haste.

It was then Ian remembered the conversation he and Summerbee had exchanged when they met at 'the Grange'. If Ian had not responded to 'the stunt', reacting to the sudden appearance of a fourth lottery winner, Mike Summerbee, as he himself had stated, would have used alternative means, hinting it might result in the loss of many lives.

Debbie asked her husband what he thought the deceased had meant by that statement. Ian considered what he himself might do; at least what tactics might work to make him come out in the open if they were used against him.

'I imagine he could cause some sort of accident that would result in many deaths; tens; hundreds; maybe thousands. He could then make a broadcast and challenge anyone out there to rewind time and prevent the event from happening. He would then lie in wait and see who turned up to save the day - simple.'

'Then you would just have to resist the temptation to go back,' Debbie said, desperation forcing her to settle for the simplest solution, without giving her opinion sufficient thought.

'And let a whole load of innocent people die? Even if I could live with the guilt of letting him kill all those people, what would stop him doing it again; and again; and again; and each time he might up the stakes, slaying more and more people until I complied with his wishes? The man has ice running through his veins. I didn't know him long, but I'm pretty sure he's capable of anything.'

'All right then,' Debbie responded, as though her husband had overlooked the obvious, and it was her duty to bring it to his attention. 'He stays dead and you go back to the scene of the murder and clean up all the forensic evidence before you leave.'

Ian appreciated his wife was only trying to be helpful. He did not want to shoot her suggestions down in flames, but her latest was a non-starter. Had he remained in the garage for a minute or two longer, he would have been caught red handed by Mrs Summerbee, and the only way to prevent her testimony would be to kill her too. Then there was the car. Even if he got rid of all the other evidence, his car would still have been seen. If he went back far enough to move it elsewhere, dear old Mike would come back to life to kill him.

'How about you return us to the moment you got home that night. We could cash the lottery ticket and get the hell out of here.'

Again, Debbie had not thought it through.

'Firstly, it takes time to get hold of the cash,' Ian said, tapping his right index finger against the fingers of his left hand in turn, marking off his points as he made them. 'The police were on to me within less than twenty-four hours. That's not long enough. Even if we managed to get away, we'd either have to split the family, or sentence us all to a life on the run.'

Debbie could see her husband was right on all counts and sank back into the sofa, crestfallen.

'Then what do we do?' she implored, her eyes shedding fresh tears.

Ian wiped his wife's cheeks with a fresh tissue and then took her hands in his. His face became the definition of earnest.

'Of course, I could simply put my hands up to the murder, tell them I'm sorry, and hope to be free again in fifteen years. I'd understand it if you didn't wait. I'd restore the lottery ticket first, so you wouldn't have any money worries.'

'Don't be so bloody stupid!' Debbie shouted, as though chastising a child who had offered his pocket money to pay for the boat he had just sunk. 'Firstly, you didn't murder anybody; it was self-defence, and you shouldn't be punished for it. Secondly, I couldn't cope without you being here; you're part of me. Thirdly, I don't give a damn about the money. In fact, it was our greed for it that brought us to this in the first place. If they left a pile of bank notes in front of me right this second, I'd burn the lot.'

Although Ian was fully prepared to relinquish his freedom to save his family, he was relieved he was not expected to do so. The sheer monotony of his job had almost driven him to suicide; the routine of prison life would doubtless finish him off.

One final option had been in his mind from the first. It had begun as a seed, growing steadily until fully matured. Ultimately it offered the best solution, but at the same time, it was the hardest to accept. Discussing other options had been a way of preparing Debbie for that which had to be endured. It was also a means of convincing himself, the enormity of the solution being so very great.

The plan would be to return to a point before the murder, but not hours or minutes; he would have to rewind twenty plus years of his life; of his family's life; of the lives of every living thing in the universe. Mike would be brought back from the dead, sure enough, but at a time before he inherited his ability; at the time of the school reunion, shortly before Summerbee discovered his powers. So long as Ian went straight there without stopping at any point en route, there would be no murder charge to face and no fear of him being murdered.

For a time, the two men would be able to co-exist as Mike would be unaware of Ian as a threat. Regrettably, to prevent future events repeating themselves, Ian would be forced to kill him again, but with a little planning he had a far better chance of making it look like an accident. Clearly, this part of the plan could not be related to Debbie - she would never give her consent to a premeditated murder – but everything else could be put forward for discussion.

In practice, Ian did not need his wife's authority to carry out his plans, but to satisfy his own peculiar sense of morality he sought it even if it meant disguising his full intentions.

Having explained his plan in as much detail as he dared, Ian fell silent. Husband and wife then remained seated on the edge of the sofa, each sideways on so they faced each other, their knees touching.

Having given Debbie time to absorb his words, Ian gently took his wife's fingertips in his. He spoke, focused on her bowed head, sounding like a politician who was trying to be sincere.

'I don't wish to hurry you, but in a few short hours the police will arrive and we need to make a decision before they get here. I can turn back the clocks as many times as I need and that would give me infinite opportunity to mull it over, but you would not remember your thoughts and would have to start all over again. Time will never be any longer than it is right now.'

Debbie raised her head and looked sorrowfully at her husband's face, tears building in the corners of her eyes; tears that were readying themselves for a swift journey down her cheeks.

'How can you be certain we will be together again; that we will have our children again?' she asked, voicing only those concerns most dear to her.

'You only have my word we will and next time round, it will be so much better. I promise. None of you will suffer; you won't even be aware what I've done; you know that. I've just endured a police interview from hell and you know none of it other than what I have told you. You have no memory of the mental torment you suffered following my arrest either. Aren't you glad none of that has happened; that you have no memory of how you felt?'

'Yes,' Debbie conceded, 'but that was deleting bad events. You're proposing to get rid of decades of the good times we've had together; of me and you and the children.'

Ian's thoughts immediately turned to his career, the misery he had experienced during a succession of dead-end jobs overriding his memories of the good times; and that was the problem – those dark thoughts masked the good times of which he was sure there had been many, but of which he found difficulty in recalling any.

Debbie read the expression on her husband's face.

'You don't agree do you?' she said, accusingly, shocked and hurt the thought of losing those years did not mean as much to him as it did to her.

'I was thinking of work. You'll never understand what it does to me; how it makes me feel each and every day.'

'So, this is all about you. You're happy to wipe our lives clean so you can pick a better one. Does that even include us?'

'Don't say that. Of course it includes you and the kids. It's all about us as a family. That's why I want to return to the night of the school reunion so we'll meet again, just as before. I want everything to be the same; all except work. Wouldn't you like your memories of me to be happier?'

Debbie avoided answering the question.

'This is so easy for you isn't it?' she said, shaking her head from side to side.

'Easy?' Ian replied, suddenly more animated. 'It fucking terrifies me, and what terrifies me the most is when I meet you again for the first time, you won't see that spark that set us on our path together. Maybe I won't say that one word, or do that one action that originally made you fall for me. Maybe you'll go off with my best friend, Dave. That's why he took you there as a guest. That was his intention then and that's what his intention will always be, however many times I return to that damned reunion.'

For the first time since the long debate began, Ian looked scared; vulnerable; close to tears. His appearance instantly mellowed his wife's attack.

'You silly old fool,' she said, managing a smile. 'It wouldn't matter how many times we met for the first time, or how many other people you were up against, I'd always pick you. You're my soul mate. Surely all these years of marriage have shown you that. You will meet me again. I won't be able to believe my luck and we shall be together again forever.'

'Then you agree?' Ian asked, placing a hand on each of his wife's shoulders. 'I should go back to the reunion?'

Having spoken, he looked deep into her eyes, awaiting confirmation.

'Debbie, I promise we will be together again just as we are now, only it will be better. I promise.'

He spoke slowly; deliberately.

Debbie looked down at her knees.

'It sounds as though you've already made up your mind,' she whispered. 'I don't know why you even bothered asking me.'

'Debs,' Ian pleaded, 'I know you're scared but you mustn't be like this. I asked you because I was hoping you might come up with an alternative solution I hadn't considered. I don't want to do this anymore than you do.'

Debbie offered no response other than to sniff and dab her nose with a tissue.

'If I do have to go through with this, I want to do it with your blessing. I don't want the most recent memory of you being one of hysteria; crying; tears; knowing you hate me. I want to feel it is the right thing to do; a positive thing – for all of us.'

'I don't hate you. That's the whole point. I love you and I don't want to lose you.'

She paused before saying anything further, reluctant to issue the words aloud she now spoke in her mind on a continuous loop; practising them; testing them. In the end, as much as it pained her to say them, Deborah knew they were the right and only words.

'You must do whatever has to be done,' she said quietly. 'We will be together again and hopefully under better circumstances. I know we will.'

The couple fell silent once more.

Her faith in her husband, her willingness to hand her life over to him, and those of her children, touched Ian greatly. Her acceptance was welcome, but in some ways premature. Had she taken a more defensive view, one that challenged his plan, he would have been forced to argue the good points and the bad. He would have been made to research his own views and feelings regarding what he was proposing to do. As it was, he had the consent of his wife, but not his own.

What would regressing twenty-four years mean? What would he be leaving behind: the prospect of prison; the misery of work; living from day to day, hoping that life would someday be better? As much as he would surely miss his wife and children, at least he would experience the joy of them all over again, and this time he would do it better.

The plan had other merits too. He had been experiencing a mid-life crisis of late, overwhelmed by the fact his life was speeding through the second half without him having achieved even a small percentage of the things he wanted to do. Reliving a quarter of a century would give him the opportunity to make amends. He could change his career, live the contented life he always longed for, and bring his wife and children up in a better, more prosperous environment.

He thought of all the stages of his life, all the decisions, all the hardships he had endured to get to where he was: the nappies; the days when money had been scarce; the recession; the funerals he had attended. Could he face them again?

Arguments and counter arguments could have continued to battle, one against the other, for a night and a day, but the conclusion would always have been the same. Of all the options, this seemed to be the only viable one.

'I'm going to do it,' he said suddenly, his voice determined, his body animated.

The statement made Debbie start. They had been sitting in silence for several minutes now, she with her head bowed; he staring across the room as if in a trance.

Then, almost as quickly as it had burst into the open, Ian's enthusiasm died.

'The kids. How do I explain it to the kids?' he asked, looking to his wife for an answer.

'You don't,' she said. 'Remember, they know nothing of any of this.'

'But I have to tell them something.'

Debbie, trying to be the tower of strength she knew her husband needed, squeezed his hands gently and began to speak; softly; tenderly.

'Talk to them,' she said. 'Tell them you love them, but don't say anything else. Soon your conversation will never have taken place and you alone will carry the memory of what was said. Let them be happy memories.'

'You're right,' he said, solemnly.

Picking up the receiver, Ian chose first to speak to his daughter. At nineteen years of age, she was the younger of his two children and, because of her age, seemed in his eyes to be the most vulnerable.

'Dad?'

Ann was pleased, but surprised to receive the call.

Ian tried to sound casual, natural, limiting the topic of conversation to the everyday. They joked; they exchanged news; they discussed how her studies were coming along. Then it came to the moment when he had to say goodbye.

He was going to say, 'remember, I will always love you,' but realised it was exactly this - her ability to remember - he was about to rob from her.

'I'm going now,' he chose to say instead. 'I want to ring your brother.'

Then he paused, choking back the urge to cry.

'Is there something wrong?' Ann asked, detecting just a hint of the emotional state her dad desired to remain hidden.

His overriding wish not to worry his children was the boost he needed to restore his voice to normal.

'No, no. Nothing's wrong. I hope to speak to you soon. Love you.'

'Love you too, Dad.'

Then, as though an afterthought, 'Ann?'

'Yes.'

'I really do love you, you know. I like to think everything I've done and everything I will ever do will be for you, your brother and Mum. I just wanted you to know that.'

'Dad, you're the best. We all appreciate everything you've done for us.'

'Thanks, you've cheered me up,' he said, bravely. 'Bye then. Love you.'

'Love you too, Dad.'

Having replaced the receiver, Ian's entire body began to shake. To avoid total collapse, he sat down on the armchair chair beneath the stairs, took a few calming breaths, picked up the receiver again, and dialled.

'Hello son,' he said, brightly.

Stephen too was surprised to receive the call, it not being the usual night of the week for such an occurrence.

'Dad, listen, I don't want to seem rude, but I was just on my way out of the door. Would it be all right if you rang back tomorrow?'

'Sure, no problem.'

'Okay Dad, I'll speak to you then.'

Ian just managed to catch his son before he hung up.

'Stephen?'

'Yes, Dad.'

'Just in case I don't manage to talk to you tomorrow, I wanted to tell you that I love you.'

Stephen sounded suddenly uneasy. This was not something he was used to hearing; not in such a formal way.

'You too,' he said, sounding suspicious. 'Is everything okay?'

'Fine,' Ian replied, his voice placed at a higher pitch than normal. 'Anyway, I must go. If I don't speak with you tomorrow evening, I'll speak to you as soon as I can.'

'Okay, Dad,' Stephen said, not entirely convinced something was not wrong, but distracted from enquiring further by his need to get going. 'Bye then.'

'Goodbye son. Love you.'

It now remained for Ian's mind to fix upon the school reunion, his memories of which had been diluted by the passing of twenty-four years. The only recollection he had of the evening that came close to being sufficiently vivid was of him meeting Debbie for the first time, but even that was hazy. Any mistake might lead to him stopping off at another point on the way and that would surely spell disaster. Even the briefest hiccup in his journey would resurrect Summerbee with his superior ability fully fledged. At best, the opportunity for Ian to eradicate his enemy before he became a threat would be lost. At worst, Summerbee would track Ian down and kill him as he had always intended, and if Ian was killed young enough, Stephen and Ann would be denied their existence.

Ian racked his brain, trying hard to dislodge a suitable memory, his fingers gently tugging at his lower lip as if it might help, his eyes flickering this way and that.

'Eu-bloody-reka!' he shouted eventually, breaking the silence with a single word, shot from an animated face.

Debbie had not attended the same school as her husband. She had gone to the reunion as a guest of his best and most enduring friend, David Utteridge, who himself had desires upon her. The fact she had no better reason than that to be there, and the fact Ian and Debbie had so readily identified themselves, each as the other's soul mate, had left them always believing their meeting was fate.

However, it might have been so very different had the forces of anti-fate managed to skew matters their way, and it was one such attempt to do so that now promised Ian a memory of sufficient clarity to meet his purpose.

It began with an enormous clap of thunder from a cloudless sky. Ian had been sitting watching the television in the living room at the back of his mum's house. Glancing through the window behind him he had seen only clear blue skies filling the horizon. Further investigation revealed the noise had, in fact, been generated by the impact of a box-sided lorry with the edge of the driveway at the front of the property.

Running parallel to the road for a quarter of a mile, a sleepy stream cut deep across the front of a dozen gardens. Shallow water babbled peacefully over a bed of pebbles at the bottom of the two steep banks that confined it. At intervals, driveways spanned the gap via simple humped back concrete bridges. However, the drive leading to and from the Bradshaw's property had been laid on solid ground, owing to the direction of the stream changing course sharply half way across their lawn, and disappearing into a brick tunnel built beneath the road.

Originally, pedestrians had been protected from the dangers of falling into the brook by means of a chain link fence. Over the years it had become entangled with columbine, nettles and brambles. The wire had become rusted. Children passing by on their way to school had trodden down great sections. Then, as the road became busier, accidents began to happen. On three separate occasions, a car had taken the bend too fast and had landed in the stream, each adopting an unnaturally vertical pose. Miraculously, none of the occupants of the vehicles had been seriously hurt.

To the local residents, these night time events were a nuisance, but at the same time, a highlight in their otherwise average lives. The council took a more dim view, deciding to fortify the stream against such attack by erecting an ugly, galvanised, crash-resistant fence. It was this fence that made possible the memory to which Ian referred.

Evidently, the lorry had mounted the pavement at speed, crashed through the steel safety fence, used the distorted metal as a ramp to jump the stream and adjacent flower bed, pivoted on the edge of the driveway, and had come to rest, standing vertically on its nose, centimetres from Ian's car.

The driver had crawled, dazed but otherwise unhurt, from the cab to be led away to a neighbour's house who had a first aid box and a kind heart.

Closer inspection showed the windscreen had remained intact. Popped from its seating, it had lain neatly on top of the rubber seal that had held it in position.

This extraordinary event had occurred on the evening of the reunion, nearly preventing Ian's attendance. If the lorry had landed only a few centimetres over it would have written off Ian's car, or if the recovery team not been so efficient, Ian might have been so delayed he decided not to bother going. Either way, the accident came very close to preventing him meeting his future wife.

'I remember you telling me about that,' Debbie said, seemingly cheerier for the memory. 'I'm sure there are some photos of it in one of your old albums.'

'Yes, I remember seeing them the other night when I landed up getting all emotional,' Ian agreed, slightly embarrassed at the recollection. 'Although, we have so many albums, it will probably take the rest of the evening to find them.'

Certain she would not only be able to locate them, but also in a far shorter time than her husband predicted, Debbie immediately scurried off into the dining room to conduct a search. By the time Ian followed her through, she had reached the shelf on which the albums were stored, had studied their spines, narrowing the possibilities to two fat volumes that she reached down and lay open on the table. She flicked through the first quickly, but without success. The second took a little longer, its pages sticking together just enough to prevent a casual 'flipping' action. Excitedly, Debbie peeled the pages apart one by one until, towards the end of the book, she discovered what she had been looking for.

'There, you see?' she said, smugly.

Ian did see. The three portrait images represented a hard copy of his memory. The particular shades of orange and turquoise used for the company's livery were as he remembered them and were as true now as they had been over two decades ago.

Debbie took the pictures from their safekeeping and handed them to her husband. Studying the first one closely for a moment, he then flipped it over to see if anything had been written on the back.

'Fourth of May, eighty-five,' he commented, idly.

Then, turning the photograph over again, he began staring at the other two pictures, each in turn, remembering with increasing detail not only the event itself, but also what it felt like to be there. He had been amazed how the vehicle managed to perform the jump without sustaining more than superficial injury to the lorry, the driver, or the flowerbed. Despite being absent from the pictures, he could still see clearly the expressions on the faces of the onlookers and of the man tasked with the job of recovery. He could see the state to which the pristine vehicle had been reduced having had a chain attached, first to its back axle in order to topple it sideways, and then re-positioned in order to right it. He could see and still mourn the destruction of the shrubs and bedding plants as the battered lorry had been dragged through them, reducing the flowerbed to a ploughed wasteland.

Already there in mind, it now only remained for him to be there in body.

Closing his eyes, Ian prepared for his journey. A serene expression spread over his face as thoughts of the past flooded his mind. He was ready for the final step.

At that moment, Debbie panicked.

'No! Stop! I'm not ready,' she spoke loudly, quickly, desperate to be heard before it was too late.

His concentration broken, Ian opened his eyes and looked to his wife.

'Perhaps we shouldn't be so hasty,' she said, panting. 'Perhaps we should talk it over some more.'

It was a fact there was still plenty of time to negotiate before the police arrived, but such discussion would always lead to the same conclusion. In Ian's judgement, more talk would only serve to prolong his wife's torment.

'I'm sorry,' he said. 'It's for the best.'

Debbie witnessed his eyes close for a second time and was in no doubt as to his intentions.

'Stop! What are you doing? You can't do this. Please Ian, you've got to stop for a minute.'

She was crying almost hysterically, begging her husband to have a change of heart, helpless in that she could do nothing to prevent him stealing her life. Ian heard every penetrating word and fought to ignore them, trying desperately to concentrate on what had to be done.

'I'm sorry,' he said, sadly, his eyes remaining shut tight. 'I'm doing this because I love you.'

Then, without another word, he returned to the business of blocking his mind to all but the image of the lorry and the day it landed in his life. Debbie, though, was not about to give up without a fight. Leaping on her husband's back, her hands cupped his forehead, her fingers spreading, working to pull open his eyelids.

Ian's mastery of his ability had improved daily ever since he first discovered he could activate it at will. However, no amount of practice would allow him to continue such precise work while his wife was gouging his eyes.

'Stop it! Get off me and listen for a minute.'

It was Ian's turn to shout.

Such was the ferocity of his delivery that Debbie came immediately to her senses, dropped her weight to the floor and backed away, happy she had at least won a reprieve.

Ian turned, stepped forward and put his arms round his wife - one behind the small of her back, the other diagonally leading from his right hand to her right shoulder, embracing her, pulling her towards him. Their heads locked side by side, her hair soft against his cheek.

'You must understand me,' Ian said, speaking over her shoulder. 'I don't want to do this anymore than you, but it is simply the only way of getting all of us out of this mess. I could wait until I'm alone in that cold police cell; I could wait until you go to the toilet, but I don't want to do this behind your back. I don't want to remember having tricked you.'

'But Ian,' Debbie spoke pitifully. 'I'm scared.'

'I'm scared too. Can't you feel I'm shaking? Let me do this and your fear will last no more than a few seconds; then it will all be over and I can begin to build better lives for us.'

Debbie's response was swift.

'Do it then, but don't expect me just to stand here while you wipe me from your life.'

'Listen, I won't do it while you're like this. I won't do it at all if that's what you want. If you want I'll go to jail, or go on the run – whatever you choose. You must believe me, I don't care about me. I only want what's best for us.'

Ian relaxed the embrace so he could look into his wife's eyes and show his sincerity. Her wet eyes looked back at him.

'I know that going back is the most logical solution,' she said, more calmly, 'but think of all those happy memories that will be lost: the kids growing up; our time together. You can't tell me we'll have those exact same memories again.'

'No I can't, but for the most part they'll be pretty similar. If all goes well, they'll be better and they'll be more of them.'

Debbie pulled her husband close.

'Okay,' she said, her voice muffled against Ian's chest, 'you have my blessing. I love you. Whatever happens, I will always love you.'

'Not as much as I love you.'

Still firmly embraced, Ian closed his eyes, squeezing tears onto his cheeks. Silently he took a deep breath and began to concentrate.

Rapidly, the generalised memory of the lorry accident became sharper. As soon as Ian was sure he had fixed upon the right moment he triggered a brief, high pitched buzzing sensation inside his head. In an instant, Debbie's fears had ceased to exist; Ian's had only just begun.

11

Ian found himself reintroduced to his past through the viewfinder of a Kodak Pocket Instamatic camera, the index finger of his right hand activating the shutter release button at the split second the rewinding process ceased, capturing the image that had facilitated his return.

Less than a second later, the repercussions of his determination to go through with his plan hit home, with a force that stunned his body into a state of almost total immobility. This was not the brief parting of a few days away on a business trip. He had opted for a separation of no less than twenty-four years, and there was no way of reversing his decision. It was true he would see his wife again - in fact the same evening - but she would not be the woman he had loved for so many years. Would it, could it, ever be the same? Debbie would share one set of memories with her husband while he would always carry the burden of at least two. How could he reminisce with her about things that had never happened, at least as far as she was concerned? As for his two children, they no longer existed.

Ian managed to lower the camera, but only slowly. In a daze, he scanned the scene one element at a time, concentrating on the details his memory had long forgotten.

A line of onlookers had formed, one deep, on the far side of the lorry, obediently respecting the boundaries of the Bradshaw's property. The steel fence, erected to segregate the dangers of fast moving traffic from the dangers of a deep-cut stream, lay flattened and useless, protruding out over the babbling, shallow, brook below. Ian's mum was there, looking much younger; taller too, her posture unaffected by the rigours of old age. Bengie, the family's Scottie dog, lay cradled in her arms, being shown the spectacle as if it were a child. The sight of her talking to her dog, as if it were human, induced a wry smile, bringing life to an expressionless face, gently easing away Ian's temporary paralysis.

Only an analogy hoped to describe his feelings. Ian's head had been centimetres from a church bell when it was struck. The noise it produced had been overwhelming, pinning him, helpless, to the spot. As the vibration subsided, so he was able to think more clearly, but he suspected it would be days before the ringing in his ears would stop. Worryingly, he feared there might be permanent damage.

For the first time since he arrived back in his past, Ian noticed he felt different. As a forty-eight year old man, he had considered himself fit. He ate a well-balanced diet, exercised more than most his age, and drank only in moderation. By comparison though, his body now felt renewed. A stiffness that had gradually grown within him had suddenly disappeared. The skin on the backs of his hands was smooth and snapped back into place when pinched. He felt lighter, invigorated, and as he swept a hand across his head, he found his hair line began several centimetres further forward of his crown than he was used to. He flexed his biceps discretely and felt powerful, mighty, and then sad and angry to think how the fitness of his youth had been robbed from him bit by bit over the years, despite his best efforts. That was something he had to look forward to again, regardless of what other changes in his life he was able to engineer for the better.

Abandoning his self-assessment, Ian continued to scan his surroundings.

His car sat close by – an ageing Ford Escort, its roof covered in droppings from birds that perched hidden among the branches of an overhanging tree. The silver paintwork was dulled with age and showed evidence of botched attempts to fight the onset of the rust that ate away at the wheel arches and doorsills.

'Look at the state of that,' Ian whispered.

Then, turning his attention to the gap between lorry and car, he spoke aloud again, this time wincing.

'Jesus.'

The lorry had, as had been his memory, landed very close to his car; so close in fact it would be difficult, if not unwise, to pass between the two vehicles.

Up to this point, the act of acclimatising to his surroundings had pushed to the back of his mind the reason why he had made the journey in the first place. However, seeing his car triggered a train of thought that first reminded him he had a school reunion to attend, and then led him swiftly to the sickening realisation he could not remember where the reunion was being held, or at what time it was due to start.

Ian's body reacted with a twitch as if it were subjected to a false start off the blocks. His eyes began moving erratically, trying desperately to access and fix upon memories that were clearly absent, or incomplete.

Looking down the length of his body – casual shirt to shoes – Ian realised he was already dressed for an evening out, confirmed by the forgotten aroma of a designer aftershave he remembered his mother had bought him as a gift. Ian patted his hands against the outside of his pockets and then drove them in, both hands grabbing simultaneously at the contents – a tissue and a few coins in one; his wallet in the other. The latter held some plastic, a quantity of bank notes and some receipts. It did not hold any information pertaining to the reunion.

Thankfully, not everything had been forgotten. At least Ian could remember which town had played host to the venue. The organiser, John McGahan, had chosen it as the hub most equidistant between the ex-pupils' current addresses. It also happened to be the hometown of the organiser himself. Ian had always considered this as being the deciding factor when choosing the location for the event, but in the man's defence, John had arranged the whole thing, and none but a handful of the Cardle Street alumni still lived close to the school in Chelderham; Ian being one of the few who remained in that locale. Nevertheless, in Ian's opinion, any one of the available venues in Chelderham would still have been the obvious choice, the town being the one place they all shared in common; the place where they had all spent so many years together. As it was, he now faced a drive of at least an hour to get to Flayton.

Driving there was the easy part. Ian knew the lorry would be extracted successfully from the drive, without any damage being caused to his car. He could then set off in the knowledge there was time enough for him to reach the venue without being late, having completed that exact journey before. However, Flayton was a big place; home to many function suites. Twenty plus years ago, the chosen venue had been known to him prior to the event. The recollection of how he came to discover the name of the place, and the directions to it, now evaded him. It might have been by telephone conversation; it might have been by way of written invitation. Either way, he felt there must now be something in writing, somewhere among his possessions, that would provide the when, the where and the how.

Staring towards the upturned lorry, but not focussed upon it, Ian tried desperately to recall more information. His mind thought of nothing else until he sensed the arrival of his mum at his side.

'Isn't it lucky the lorry missed your car,' she said, brightly.

Her comment was meant for her son's ears, but her eyes were not fixed upon him, instead flicking between the upturned vehicle and Bengie who still lay comfortably in her arms. The dog's eyes were alert; his expression one of utter joy and excitement.

'Very lucky,' Ian agreed distantly, idly stroking the animal's head, massaging a handful of white fur, a single ear protruding up through thumb and forefinger.

'You look really worried,' his mum said, sounding concerned. 'I'm sure they'll be able to move the lorry without damaging your car. They must have loads of experience with this kind of thing.'

'I'd be very surprised if they do have experience,' Ian replied, doubtfully. 'It's not often you see a lorry standing on its nose in someone's driveway. Anyway, I'm not worried about that. I have every confidence the car will escape unscathed. In fact, I can guarantee it.'

'What then?'

Ian seemed to be trying to find the best way to broach a sensitive subject.

'Mum, have you seen the letter regarding the reunion?' he asked, fishing for clues.

'I think it was in your bedroom, dear.'

So, there was a letter and it would no doubt contain directions. He had to find it.

'Thanks.'

Leaving his mum to chat with the neighbours, Ian went indoors, heading for his bedroom with the intention of conducting an immediate and systematic search. However, on entering the house, he could not help but take a few minutes to explore what felt like a living museum of his premarital years.

Much of the furniture was the same, but in better condition. As his mum had grown older, she had seen less and less reason to replace expensive items merely because they were becoming dated. Over the years, settees and beds had either become superfluous, or had broken and been replaced, or disposed of, but bookcases, the sideboard, tables and chairs, had all survived. The worn carpets he, as a middle-aged man, had trodden upon during his visits to see his mum, were now in their youth; springy and clean. The wallpaper and paintwork had remained largely untouched too. Generally, the place was tidier; not due to Ian being there to help with the chores - he recalled painfully, he never did any - rather, his mum was not yet as frail as she was destined to become.

Ian would happily have spent time sucking in memories from each room in turn, until they had nothing more to offer, but there were more pressing matters to attend to. He had to find the invitation to the reunion and he had until the lorry was removed from the driveway – not long if his faded memory could be relied upon at all.

Ascending the stairs, Ian felt suddenly uncomfortable, as though he no longer had the right to be there, inviting himself into parts of the house that visitors would not normally see unaccompanied. To contain his discomfort, he avoided his mum's bedroom altogether and headed straight for his own. It was still his, not yet having been re-designated a guestroom as it would in later years. As he stepped across the threshold, Ian felt the warm glow of familiarity.

'My own little sanctuary,' he said, quietly; ruefully.

He paused for a moment before commencing the search; partly to give him a chance to relish the emotional hug he was experiencing; partly because, even though it was his own property, it felt wrong to be rummaging through unfamiliar drawers. In the end, though, an overwhelming sense of urgency drove him to begin.

The bedside cabinet, being closest to the door, made the obvious place to start. On it Ian found a book, a marker gripped between the pages, keeping a place he had reached more than two decades ago. Previously serving a purpose, the passage of time – both forwards and backwards - had rendered its position superfluous. Not only had Ian forgotten the story so far, but science fiction no longer interested him.

In the drawer of the cabinet he found a personal diary, containing entries for the first week only. His hopes for the year ahead were recorded on the first day, as was his determined intention to keep the journal going for the whole of the coming twelve months. The six subsequent entries became gradually less detailed, finishing with a mere two lines on the seventh day.

'Still finishing up the chocolates left over from Christmas. Had to clear snow off the car this morning before going to work.'

Hardly comments future historians would appreciate in the same way they did those of the great diarists such as Samuel Pepys.

The drawer also contained a magazine - 'Airgun World'. Not only had his taste in literature changed, his pastimes had too. This particular hobby had ended abruptly when he met his wife. She hated guns of any description and made him sell his prized air rifle, complete with hand-finished stock and personalised strap, even before they had moved in together.

Beneath the airgun magazine was another periodical, although of an entirely different nature. Seeing it, and the box of tissues that accompanied it, made him wince at the thought of what he used to do under the same roof as his mum. That too had stopped when he began dating Debbie.

Moving round the room in a clockwise direction, there was nothing on the bed, and the space beneath it was devoid of all but a quantity of carpet fluff, pushed there by the vacuum cleaner. Tucked out of sight at its foot, partially hidden by the edge of the bedding, Ian discovered a green leatherette case that contained a number of suspension files. In them, he found documents pertaining to his car, payslips, and a variety of other important pieces of paper: letters and receipts. However, there was absolutely nothing relating to the reunion.

The wardrobe contained only clothes; shabby ones at that. The long-sleeved work shirts looked tired, the area about the armpits discoloured yellow. Ian remembered the grey suit he had been forced to wear beyond its natural lifespan, unable to afford a replacement.

A thought popped into his head, prompting him to dip his left hand into the jacket's inside pocket, instantly causing him excitement, his fingers closing upon a folded piece of paper. It was a letter, enclosed within an envelope, one that bore his name and address. Surmising he must have taken it to work to show his friends, or to use the company telephone to confirm his intention to attend the reunion, Ian felt both relieved and confident he had at last found what he was looking for. However, the letterhead quickly revealed he was sadly mistaken.

Signed by the secretary on behalf of the office manager, it thanked him for showing interest in the vacancy for Section Head, and invited him to attend for interview at ten o'clock on the sixth; two days hence.

This was a double blow. Not only had he not found the instructions he needed if the night were to end in success, he now had an interview to attend on Monday. History, as it had been, recorded he had passed the interview. However, that would not necessarily be the outcome this time round. Of course he remembered where the offices were and was confident he would remember the names of those he worked with, especially when triggered by seeing them face to face. He also knew the job entailed completing customer orders. What he was less certain about were the details of his employment: the routine of his working day; who should be sent what, and when. He was not even sure what time the day started.

Originally, Ian had passed the interview by displaying a thorough knowledge of his job and had inspired confidence in his manager he was capable of passing that knowledge onto others. How could he repeat such a performance if he were not even sure which desk he sat at? Unfortunately, that was no exaggeration, the office having been moved round on several occasions during his time with the company.

So far, Ian's plans to put his life in order were not proceeding as expected. At this rate he might never meet his wife, and if that were the case, his children might never come to exist either. Not only that, his promotion and his job were now in jeopardy simply because he could not remember what it was he was supposed to do.

If he had nothing else in his favour, Ian retained his ability to prioritise. At that moment, the interview was not as important as the reunion. Worrying about it could wait.

The search continued.

Adjacent to the wardrobe, a chest of drawers held jumpers, socks and underpants, all except the topmost drawer where Ian found such things as his belt, electric shaver, wrist exercisers, binoculars and ammunition for his air rifle. No paperwork at all. Next in line, the bookcase was packed beyond capacity, titles slotted in sideways on top of others that were more conventionally displayed; some rows being two deep. The few areas that remained free from books had been covered with ornaments and other bits and pieces. Still Ian found no instructions.

There remained only the area behind the door. There he discovered a wicker waste paper basket, frayed around the top edge and containing nothing but an apple core; brown and disgusting. There was also an odd sock, hidden in the corner, and a calendar upon which a single word had been written, next to the number four - 'Reunion'.

'For fucks sake,' Ian cursed aloud. 'Can't you give me more of a clue than that?'

In truth he was criticising only himself, unfairly blaming version one for not foreseeing a time in his future when he would need to return; failing to appreciate how useful it would be to leave pockets of information to be rediscovered.

Frustrated, Ian drifted from his room onto the landing where he stood for a moment, his fingers massaging his mouth, wondering where to look next. Out of the corner of his eye he became aware of an orange light intermittently illuminating the net curtains at his mum's bedroom window. The recovery vehicle had arrived. Time was running out. Of course, Ian could manufacture as much time as he needed to conduct a successful search, but he had drawn a line in the sand, deciding he had gone back as far into his past as he was ever going to. His return to 1985 was the last time he would ever use his ability. Determined not to go back on his promise to himself, Ian's mind continued to look for inspiration as though this was his only opportunity.

The letter did exist - his mum had confirmed that much - but it was clearly not in his room as she had thought. There were only a limited number of places left where it could be. It would not be in his mum's bedroom; of that he was quite certain. There was no reason for it to be in the bathroom either. Nevertheless, he could not resist giving each of the two rooms a quick scan from the doorways. Nothing.

Downstairs offered equally few hiding places, it consisting of a kitchen, the hall, and a room divided between the lounge at one end and a dining area at the other.

Ian quickly established the kitchen was devoid of anything resembling a letter, a map, directions, or even a simple envelope. In fact, the only pieces of paper of any description to be found in the kitchen were a few recipes, torn from magazines, attached to the door of the refrigerator by means of magnets disguised as large, red, ladybirds, and realistic-looking but fake sweets.

In the lounge, a TV paper lay open on a nest of tables that stood between two armchairs. Reading through its pages would undoubtedly be an interesting trip down memory lane, but again there was no time.

A large display unit stood against the outside wall, most of its shelves filled to capacity with books, old and new, all of them acting to attract dust, causing Ian to sneeze violently. The base of the unit consisted of three drawers with a double-fronted cupboard to one side. The cupboard contained ornaments that had fallen from favour and the combined record collection of both Ian and his mum.

The drawers contained artist's materials, reminding Ian of another of his hobbies that had fallen by the wayside. The only paper to be found there was held between the covers of a number of quality sketch pads. Seeing the drawings for the first time in more than twenty years, impartial eyes judged them favourably. It begged the question, given he possessed such natural talent, what had gone so very wrong in his life that he had found himself tied to a succession of dreary office desks for his entire working life? The answer provided the first positive thought Ian had experienced since his return, his creative side perhaps offering an alternative career path. However, none of that mattered if he were unable to ensure he would share his new life with Debbie, Stephen and Ann, and that meant first finding the elusive invitation.

In his search, there remained only the hall.

The under stairs cupboard provided a home to the ironing board, the vacuum cleaner, and bundles of free weekly advertising newspapers, stored ready for recycling.

That left the coat rack – half a dozen hooks with a small shelf at waist height. The shelf supported a dish and in that dish Ian found his car and house keys, held on a ring, attached to a fob bearing the Ferrari logo. It seemed the best place to have left the invitation, but clearly his old and new minds did not think alike

Above, each hook was laden with one or more of his mum's coats. She had always had a special fondness for this particular item of clothing and rarely took them off, sunshine or rain, indoors or out. Among the many were her favourite, including her dog-walking coat and her dog-sitting coat. Perhaps it was subconscious rebellion that made Ian her exact opposite in this respect; perhaps it was a lack of money. Either way, he never owned more than one coat at a time until he married, at which point he suddenly grew to share her passion. By the time he had reached his forty-eighth birthday he could boast: a calf-length raincoat for travelling to and from work; a waterproof hiking jacket; a coat fit for formal evenings out; a coat for the pub; a gardening jacket, and a thin summer jacket, not to mention a clear plastic poncho, there to protect him in the event of unanticipated downpours.

What was most noticeable about the coat rack was not how many more items belonged to his mother, but the fact not one of them belonged to Ian, begging the question, where was his coat?

At that moment there was a loud crash as the recovery vehicle pulled the stricken lorry to the ground.

'The car!' Ian said aloud, considering kicking himself as punishment for his stupidity.

Having grabbed his keys, he was through the front door just in time to witness the lorry being dragged clear of the drive and on, twenty metres up the road. It looked helpless, lying on its side, its back axle chained to its master, over whose actions it had absolutely no control. The breakdown truck was large and brutish and accompanied its every exertion with a great belch of black smoke from an exhaust, mounted vertically behind the cab, and a harsh roar from its massive diesel engine. The grating noise – the liveried sheet metal of the lorry's bodywork against tarmac - made it possible to believe that even inanimate objects could feel pain.

As much as the spectacle continued to grab the attention of the gathered crowd, Ian's was focused instead on his own car, the gymnastic lorry no longer acting to block his line of sight, or prevent access to the door. To his great relief he could see the elusive jacket discarded casually on the front passenger seat. A turn of the key and a tug on the handle revealed that beneath it lay a dog-eared road atlas, a hand-written invitation, and a photocopied sheet of instructions leading to the door of the Jubilee Suite at Flayton – a complex that had been demolished to make way for flats eight to ten years ago – or would be, fifteen years in the future. No wonder he had forgotten the venue.

Ian's sense of relief was palpable, although there was still cause to delay counting his chickens until they were hatched. History, as it had originally been written, recorded his car made it to the venue without breaking down half way up the motorway. However, as he would not depart for the Jubilee Suite at exactly the same moment as before, he would not encounter other road users exactly as before and so there was still the possibility he might be involved in an accident with a vehicle or vehicles he had not previously come across. Further, history recorded the car did not run out of petrol, but Ian had no recollection whether this was because there was already plenty of fuel in the tank, or he had stopped to fill up en route. This was a matter easily resolved, but an indication nothing could be taken for granted. Nevertheless, at least for the time being, Ian was a happy, confident man.

The driver of the smoke-breathing beast jumped down from his cab and set about rearranging the shackles so he might pull the dying lorry back onto its wheels. The man, dressed in oil-stained blue overalls, appeared to be in a hurry, conducting every part of the operation at the double. So versed was he in his particular field, the recovery went seemingly without him once consulting anybody: the police; the crowd; the driver of the stricken vehicle. No sooner was the lorry upright than it was secured for a journey of unknown destination, and gone.

There remained nothing more for the police officers to do than pass a broom over the worst of the debris that littered the road, and then remove their cones, restoring the flow of traffic. The crowd dispersed almost immediately. The unfortunate driver was taken off in an ambulance at a carefree pace. The police, having closed their notebooks, climbed into their respective vehicles and returned to their patrol.

It was half past seven; the invitation was for eight. With an hour's drive to the venue, Ian could see he would be late, but only fashionably so.

Driving his car again after such a long absence was not a pleasurable experience: the engine was noisy; clearly the valve clearances were incorrectly set, or simply much worn; the gear stick offered as much play when engaged as it did when in neutral; and the brakes were woefully inadequate. Then there was the stereo - a crackling FM signal, or a worn audio cassette, both offering music he had tired of more than a decade ago.

Under normal circumstances Ian would have cherished the opportunity to drive a car from his past, allowing him to reminisce about a fading chapter in his life. Under normal circumstances there would have come a time when he would say, 'thanks for the drive, but can I have my own car back now, please?' Under normal circumstances, his request would have been granted. However, since the discovery of his ability, normality had been in short supply. The car was a heap and he was stuck with it, at least until the engine blew up, sometime in the future, a hole suddenly appearing in the side of the crank case – a journey destined not to be repeated. Yet despite the backward step with regard the quality of material things in his life, the situation was far from hopeless. Even if he lived his life just as he had done before, Ian knew he would eventually have a house to call his own, new clothes and a decent vehicle. None of them would impress the neighbours, but he and his family would be comfortable.

On the other hand, although following his original path would restore to him all those things he missed, it would come at a price; a heavy one. Life would be even more predictable than was the daily trip to the office he had endured for so many years, and there he had found only misery and thoughts of suicide. Even then, Ian could see ways in which his life could turn out worse than before, two of which acted to counter his enthusiasm. The first was the prospect of having to attend an interview he was incapable of passing. That failure would no doubt have an adverse effect on his career, such that it was, making it harder to regain what he had lost in the future, never mind improve it. The second related to his imminent meeting with Debbie, the woman he hoped would again become his wife. Would they have anything in common? Would she see the middle-aged man in his eyes and be put off by the maturity that had dulled his zest for life in later years? Would she be put off by the anxiety that wracked his body?

Only time would tell.

12

To those unfamiliar with the 'Jubilee Suite', the name conjured up images of sophistication, or at the very least, premises fit for a conference. The building behind the name did not live up to expectation. It was merely an annex of a public house - The Jubilee - and would suffice for lower end wedding receptions, parties and discos. The lobby was not home to well dressed, smiling, women, there to take guests' coats. Instead, it was an area between the outer and inner fire doors; the location of the ladies' and gents' toilets, a few coat hooks, and a large notice board, A4 posters stapled one on top of another.

Through the inner set of doors, at least a hundred men and women of similar age stood in groups, drink in hand, or sitting on chairs placed around the edge of the room, chattering wildly. The air, filled with noise and smoke, bewildered Ian's senses. He stared at faces, concentrating on their features, hoping to recognise someone; anyone. He desperately wanted to see a familiar face; someone he wanted to talk to; someone who would want to talk to him; anyone that meant he did not have to remain at the door looking like a man without a friend in the world. His search was so intense that for a while he did not see the man who was sitting at a small table next to him. Having established eye contact, the man smiled pleasantly and spoke, his voice raised in order to be heard over the din.

'Evening. Glad you could make it,' he said. 'Write your name on one of these badges and enjoy the evening. The first drink is free in exchange for your invitation.'

The man, leading by example, was himself wearing a badge and had a half empty pint glass of lager next to him.

'John McGahan?' Ian said, reading the name from the cardboard label pinned to the man's chest. 'Sorry mate, I didn't recognise you. Blimey, you've changed.'

John already knew Ian's identity, having glanced at the invitation he held clutched in his hand.

'If you think I've changed then you're in for a few surprises tonight, I can tell you,' he replied cheerily. 'As for you, you still look much the same as I remember.'

'Listen John, have you seen David Utteridge?' Ian asked, moving his mouth closer to John's ear.

'Sure, I think he's over there in the far corner with a lady friend of his,' replied John, his arm indicating in which direction David was to be found. 'Gorgeous bit of stuff she is, the lucky so and so.'

Dave had only brought one guest; Ian remembered that much. It stood to reason, then, that the gorgeous bit of stuff to which John referred was Ian's Debs.

'Cheers mate. I'll probably catch up with you later in the evening. I've got to see this girl you're on about.'

With that, Ian began weaving through the crowd, no longer interested to see whether he recognised any of them.

There was Dave, standing in profile, smiling like a lovesick school child into the face of a dark-haired woman who stood beside him, her back to Ian. It was less noisy away from the bar and he could see and hear she was engaged in conversation. Indeed, she had the full attention of the small group in which she stood: Dave - his best friend since his earliest days at school - and two other men he did not immediately recognise. The woman wore a pure white, close fitting tee-shirt that clung to her body, accentuating the inverted triangle of her upper torso. The short sleeves left exposed skin that was toned and blemish-free. Below her waist, she wore tight blue denim jeans that exhibited her buttocks and slender thighs in the best possible light. In short, she was perfect.

Ian was close enough to reach out and grab her, but managed to check himself. However, that was as far as self-control was able to help him.

'God, Debbie, you look even better than I remember.'

The subject of his lustful words looked round in surprise.

'Sorry, do I know you?' Debbie responded, genuinely intrigued, not a hint of sarcasm in her voice.

Thrown for a moment, Ian's mouth idled, his mind frantically searching for an adequate explanation.

'Er, no,' he began awkwardly but gaining confidence. 'Sorry, it was just a really bad line from a really bad film. I'm always doing that.'

Debbie stared at him, her face a picture of confusion.

'If we have never met before,' she replied, slowly, 'how did you know my name?'

It was a good question. Again Ian paused, his lips moving silently.

'I didn't,' he responded finally, his attempt at nonchalance failing miserably. 'The woman in the film was called Debbie. What sort of coincidence is that?'

Any credibility his explanation might have carried was lost almost immediately, blown to pieces by the unintentional addition of a nervous laugh at the end of his sentence. Even Ian could hear how ridiculous he sounded. The group were staring at him, each of them clearly uncomfortable in his company. If left unchecked, there was very little chance Ian's future wife would agree to date him. Indeed, there was every possibility she would go further, insisting one or other of them leave the reunion.

Forced to draw a fresh red line – another final use of his ability - Ian closed his eyes as if in meditation. A moment later, the man at the door was pointing to the far corner of the room, just as he had done before.

'Cheers,' Ian said, distantly, as he moved away through the crowd to find Debbie for a second time.

Now Ian was worried. Firstly, it was no longer clear he would be able to secure a first date with Debbie, without which there would be no marriage, and the parts of his future life he wished to retain would be lost. Secondly, having rewound time, he had announced to Summerbee's predecessor that he too had special powers and was therefore a threat to their mutual existence. In his favour, Ian was sure he had not yet done enough to lead any potential adversary to his door, but if such a person did exist they would certainly be aware of him. On the other hand, there might not even be an adversary. Summerbee had never made it clear what had happened when he discovered his abilities. Had he killed his predecessor, or had he merely been the natural heir when the predecessor had come to the end of his life? There may even have been a period between the end of the previous incumbency and the beginning of Summerbee's reign, when there existed no one who possessed such powers.

This train of thought ended abruptly with Ian's eyes meeting Debbie's perfect physique for the second time in as many minutes. For all the problems his ability had caused, this was an occasion to appreciate its benefits. Who else could have made such a mess of asking this woman out and then be given a second chance, or a third if need be, or a fourth? Indeed, who else could boast they were able to replay each stage of the dating game over and over until they got it just right?

'Dave,' Ian said brightly, as if pleasantly surprised to see his old friend.

'Hello mate,' Dave responded, his voice starting on a high note, swooping down low and finishing back where it began, sounding genuinely pleased by Ian's sudden arrival.

'Sorry,' Ian said, turning to Debbie, 'I didn't mean to interrupt you.'

'That's okay,' she responded, before turning to the man who had brought her to the reunion. 'Introductions, David, if you please.'

'Er, sorry,' apologised David, before pointing, with a flattened hand, at each member of the group in turn. 'Ian, this is Debbie, a friend of mine. She didn't go to our school so you won't know her.'

Ian looked at her, hoping the smile on his face was a friendly one, trying hard not to let his eyes wander from hers.

'I expect you remember Gary and Robert,' David continued. 'Debbie, this is Ian. We were inseparable at school, but we seem to have drifted apart of late.'

'Don't worry mate,' Ian said, jovially, 'that was just a blip. Twenty years from now people will think we're conjoined twins.'

Debbie smiled. She looked so natural; her teeth so white.

'Nice to meet you,' she said, pleasantly, her eyes twinkling.

David noticed Ian did not have a drink. 'I'll get another round in shall I?' he asked, reaching out to collect the empty glasses from the rest of the group.

'Cheers Dave. I'll have a pint of whatever real ale they have on tap,' Ian said, handing over his invitation by way of payment. 'I'll get the next one.'

'Blimey, how old are you?' Dave joked, snatching the slip of paper from his friend's fingers.

With Dave at the bar, it felt natural for Ian to start idle conversation with the remaining members of the group.

'I wonder what triggered John to arrange the evening now? I mean, eight years after we finished our 'O' levels is an odd length of time. Why not ten?'

Although Ian had no recollection of having done so, it occurred to him he might have asked that exact same question before, but there was little time for the concept to take control of his thoughts, the conversation waiting for no man.

'I don't think he could wait any longer to rub it in our faces how successful he's been,' Robert suggested. 'He got in to Cambridge; came away with a first and a masters; got some amazing job; made oodles of money; and now he's jetting around the world. I'm just surprised he's found the time to mix with plebs like us.'

'Speak for yourself,' Gary responded, feigning indignation. 'I may not have a degree but I started with British Gas and now I've got my own business. Doing quite well actually.'

Ian acknowledged Gary's achievement with a nod.

'It's a shame I can't toast you, but Dave seems to be taking his time.'

'Boo to Dave,' Robert said, his eyes flicking in the direction of the bar. 'Probably still trying to get his wallet open.'

Ian turned his attention to the only female in the group; the only person who really mattered.

'What about you, Debs? You don't mind me calling you Debs do you?'

Debbie smiled.

'Actually, I like you calling me Debs. It's friendly.'

She paused, allowing a sweet expression to linger, melting Ian from the inside out.

'If you must know, I'm a sales assistant in a clothes shop – McNab's. I doubt if you've been in there. We only do women's clothing…unless, of course, that's your thing.'

Her sweet expression was replaced with a mischievous smile, melting Ian still further.

'No, female clothes don't suit me. Not with these legs. Mind you, I might pop in now I know you work there.'

'Maybe I could help you choose something for your girlfriend.'

'Sadly no one has filled that position yet. God knows I've tried – advertisements in the national papers; a sandwich board in the High Street; a card in the newsagent's window – very demeaning, that one.'

Debbie responded with no more than a prolonged smile, the opportunity for a delayed verbal reply being denied by the return of Dave, who ferried two batches of drinks from the bar to the group with only the shortest of absences in between.

'Okay, what have I missed?'

'These two were just about to get a room,' Robert replied, nodding his head in the direction of Ian and Debbie, each in turn.

All five raised a smile, Dave's being the least pronounced. Something that did not go unnoticed by Ian who remembered his best friend had brought his guest to the reunion with desires to win her affection. Although it raised a pang of guilt, Ian knew his friend would get over it, and in time, come to find the right woman for him; someone with whom he would live happily ever after.

Dave handed a glass to his friend, his face looking decidedly less happy than when Ian was first invited to join the group.

'I got you lager. The barman said you need a working man's club if you want anything else.'

Ian accepted the substitution with a smile.

Conversation returned, future husband and wife quickly forming an unspoken alliance; each adding to what the other was saying; each making the other more interesting and fun to be with. Soon, without realising it, they began mimicking each other's actions, and it was noticeable to anyone who cared to look that they stood closer together than did anyone else in the group, their shoulders frequently bumping together as they laughed.

From time to time conversation lulled, only to be reignited by one or other of the party. Robert changed tack with some news.

'Has everyone heard about Jim Bedford?'

Gary had, but said nothing, the mere mention of the name causing his eyes to shift their direction towards the floor; his arm to withdraw his drink from his mouth. David had not heard anything and Debbie knew nothing of the other pupils who had attended Cardle Street, other than those she found herself in the company of.

Robert explained solemnly that Jim had been in contact with John McGahan. He had expressed an interest in coming to the reunion and had looked forward to receiving his invitation. However, instead of Jim subsequently confirming he would be coming, he wrote a letter explaining he had been suffering from severe headaches and tests had diagnosed a brain tumour. Jim Bedford had died two weeks ago.

David looked shocked. Gary appeared pained at hearing the news for the second time. Debbie, even though she did not know the man, was visibly upset. Ian looked sad too - a true reflection of his feelings at that moment. Unfortunately, by speaking, he ruined everything.

'That's terrible. I'd forgotten.'

His comment drew upon him the curious gaze of four pairs of eyes.

'What did you forget?' Gary asked, confused.

'I'd forgotten Jim died two weeks before the reunion.'

Rather than provide clarity, Ian's reply served only to share Gary's confusion among the rest of the group. For a while, nobody spoke. It was not odd that Ian had already heard of Jim's untimely demise, but it was strange his memory had not been jogged with the first mention of the deceased's name; stranger that he was able to forget so tragic an event in such a short space of time; puzzling that his choice of words suggested both the death and the reunion were events of the past.

As conversation stumbled back into full flow, Ian regrouped his thoughts, reminding himself why he had gone to so much effort, and caused himself so much distress, to return to the Jubilee Suite of 1985. Firstly, he was there to meet and woo Debbie. Secondly, he was there to find and kill Summerbee. With regard to the former, progress could not have gone better, although he would still need to remedy his latest faux pas over poor Jim. With regard to the latter, Ian had made no inroads at all. Up to this point he had not even seen the man, let alone made contact with him. Putting aside the delicate matter of hooking up with Debs, it was time to think about how he could achieve his second aim.

Having finished his drink, Ian placed the empty glass down on a nearby table. He then reached into his jacket pocket, pulled out a cheap ballpoint pen and began twiddling with it between his fingers. As Robert, Gary and Dave began reminiscing about the life of their lost friend, ringing his praises to Debbie, Ian held the hexagonal clear plastic barrel in both hands, flexing it repeatedly, bending it a little more each time. At the next lull in conversation, he applied an extra burst of pressure, causing the pen to snap. All eyes fell on the two jagged broken halves and on the man who held them.

Ian produced a sheepish smile as he tucked the pieces away, one in each of the jacket's two outer pockets.

'I'm a bit of a fiddler,' he confessed.

Then, as if trying to change the subject, he asked if anyone knew Mike Summerbee?'

'Yes,' Gary replied, craning his head, scanning the crowd. 'That's him walking towards the bar.'

Ian's eyes looked in the direction of Gary's stiffened finger. It would have been difficult for him to identify this near-total stranger in the crowd by himself, but having had the younger Summerbee pointed out to him, he could now see he definitely had the right person in his sights. The man's features had not yet felt the effects of middle age spread, or suffered as a result of too many hours in the sun, but they were otherwise recognisably the same.

Ian froze for a moment, his attention drawn to the curvature of Summerbee's undamaged skull, triggering the retrieval of recently stored mental images and sensory memories – so much blood; a black plastic bin liner hiding the worst of the injuries from sight, but doing nothing to disguise the sudden change in texture from hard to unnaturally soft; the weight of the hammer meeting resistance but passing through with a dull thud. His stomach clenched, pushing breath through his nose. A tremble passed through his body, stifled by a silent gulp. The memory took hold for just a moment, but was then dismissed.

'Time I got the next round in then,' Ian said quickly, gathering the empties before setting off to replenish them.

Summerbee was at the bar, leaning on his elbows, a five pound note held between his fingers to indicate to the barman he was ready to order. Unfortunately for him, there were many other customers whose growing impatience had led them to adopt stances that required more immediate attention. The delay presented an opportunity for Ian to introduce himself.

A narrow gap remained between Summerbee and the man who stood beside him, just wide enough to allow Ian to stake his claim by resting a single elbow on the counter. This forced him to stand sideways on to the bar, facing his adversary.

'I don't know about you but I don't remember half the people here,' Ian said, directing his seemingly idle conversation at Summerbee.

It worked. Bored with waiting, Summerbee welcomed the distraction.

'Me neither, and I have to confess,' Summerbee said, looking at Ian's name badge, 'I don't remember you either.'

'What house were you in?'

'Newton.'

'Ah, that explains it,' Ian concluded quickly. 'I was in Churchill. I don't think our lot shared many lessons with yours.'

'No, we were paired up with Darwin mainly,' Summerbee added in agreement, his head bobbing this way and that, unsuccessfully trying to gain the barman's attention.

Ian quickly followed up with the first of many questions he was eager to ask.

'So, how has life treated you since leaving school?'

The two men, although seemingly utter strangers, shared a common heritage, and besides, by attending the reunion they had effectively consented to openly discuss their private lives with anyone who cared to ask.

'Not bad. I have a wife and a daughter, with another on the way. I work in a bank and I like to scuba dive in my spare time.'

Summerbee's reply was given in such a way it was clear this was not the first time during the course of the evening he had provided a summary of his achievements.

His features might have been the same, but this was not the man who had driven a screwdriver into Ian's back: he had a family; he had a wife who was expecting; he had no aspirations of achieving world domination; he was a normal, everyday, family guy. Despite the mortal threat he posed to Ian's future – not only Ian, but his entire family - it was going to be difficult to kill him.

Ian reciprocated, offering a brief outline of his life since leaving school, as far as he could remember it, establishing a two-way flow of information that paved the way to Summerbee answering further questions.

'Do you live locally?' Ian asked, casually.

'No, Fringely.'

'Really? Me too,' Ian lied, acting surprised. 'What part?'

'Outward Fleet Road.'

'No! I live at number four.'

'Really? I live down the other end at four-eight-two.'

'Amazing.'

The two men's conversation was cut short by the barman who pointed at Summerbee, indicating it was his turn to be served. Had there been more time to chat, Ian would have chosen not to, his motive for engaging his enemy having been entirely satisfied. Besides, speaking further would surely have revealed Ian's deception.

Closing his eyes, Ian concentrated on the memory of his hand gripping the ballpoint pen, and on the act of snapping it in two. As soon as the image was clear in his mind, he casually regressed the entire universe to a point before he had asked the group for the whereabouts of Mike Summerbee, eliminating any connection between himself and the man he intended to murder.

This was to be the first of two short journeys: an indexed jump to the pen snapping; a controlled rewind to the moments before his inappropriate reaction to the news of Jim Bedford's death. For a millisecond, Ian felt smug at the successful use of his clever idea to create a book mark to which he could return again and again, but then devastated to discover his mind had failed to retain his enemy's exact address. He still knew Summerbee lived at Fringely, but this was hardly sufficient to lead him to the man's door. It was tempting to follow the loop again, repeatedly extracting Summerbee's address until it lodged in Ian's brain, but his experience of retrieving the lottery numbers had taught him a valuable lesson. Perhaps in years to come, when he had mastered his ability, it would be worth the repetition, but for now, given he did not have a hypnotist to hand, he had to believe there would be another way. At least knowing the name of the town in which Summerbee lived was a start.

In the meantime, there was that other little matter to attend to.

Robert retold the tragic story of how Jim had died, the other members of the group reacting exactly as they had done before. Despite this being the third time he had received the bad news, Ian found no difficulty joining them in expressing his sadness. Jim had been the only one of their friends, who from an early age, had known exactly what he wanted to do with his life; who had not floundered when it came to making his subject options in the third year. He had been the only one who had followed his ambitions, leaving school to embark on a life dedicated to conservation and wildlife. It was such a waste of a talented, dedicated, deserving life, not to mention how devastating his death had been for the man's wife and their baby daughter.

The mood of the group had plummeted; the opportunity for asking Debbie out on a date temporarily suspended. Something had to be done to raise their spirits.

'Time I got the next round in then,' Ian said, gathering the empty glasses together before setting off towards the bar.

Summerbee was there just as before; Ian filled the gap, just as before.

This time though, it was Summerbee who spoke first.

'Don't you hate it when you get that feeling you've done something before?' he said, directing his question to anyone that cared to listen.

'Déjà vu?' offered Ian, indicating Summerbee's words had not simply been lost to the ether.

'That's the one. I've felt it twice this evening.'

'It's really unnerving when that happens isn't it.'

The two men did not speak again. Of course, it was extremely tempting for Ian to con Summerbee again; to obtain his address by deception, but he could see how this could only lead to an unproductive repetition of hope and failure.

The second encounter had not all been in vain. Ian was far more interested by Summerbee's comment than he let on. When they had spoken together in the future they theorised déjà vu was in fact the slightest detection of an otherwise undetectable rewinding of time. His adversary had felt it twice in the same evening, detecting both occasions Ian had used his ability. In all probability, this was a precursor to Summerbee discovering his own.

At that moment, Mike Summerbee - father of one-and-a-half children, loving husband and recreational diver - was clearly no threat to man or beast. However, with the coming of Summerbee's new ability almost upon him, Ian could once again see him as a very real and dangerous threat. Unwittingly, by speaking openly of something seemingly as insignificant as déjà vu, Summerbee had allayed Ian's doubts and had sealed his own fate.

Ian gathered the drinks from the bar, holding them awkwardly between his hands, fingers pointing in all directions in order to maintain a stable grip. As he headed back towards the group, his eyes alternated between the surface of the drinks and the crowd through which he navigated, trying not to spill a drop. On the third occasion he looked up, he found himself staring directly at a familiar and very pleasant face. Rather than dwell on it, his immediate reaction was to break contact and cast his eyes to the floor.

Nicola Appleby had caused Ian's pulse to quicken many times back in their schooldays together; especially in the practical physics lessons when the class had gathered round the bench to see an experiment being conducted by the teacher. On many such occasions, Ian had experienced the pleasure of her ample chest pressed against his back as she fought to see the demonstration, it being obscured by her classmates; at least, that is what Ian had always believed. At no time had he guessed her actions had been for his benefit, looking upon them merely as a welcome bonus. It was not until his last few days at school, when his friends and classmates had written farewell messages in his autograph book, did he begin to see the incidents in a new light. Nicola's entry had read, 'Goodbye and thanks for the physics lessons', at which point Ian could have kicked himself.

Even had he realised sooner that her erotic displays were deliberate, he would have done nothing about it, being painfully shy and unsure of his attractiveness towards women.

When he had first attended the reunion - as a twenty-something in a twenty-something's body - he had bumped into Nicola in much the same way as he had now. Originally, the intervening period between leaving school at sixteen, and meeting up again eight years later, had done little to dispel Ian's shyness; certainly where women were concerned. He had seen this picture of loveliness, been too scared to say hello, captured an image of her in his mind, and walked on by, believing he would never set eyes upon her again.

There was much to admire too. From the floor, his eyes were instantly drawn to her jeans, the faded creases of which drew inwards towards her crotch. If anything, she had an even better figure than Debbie.

Moving his gaze slowly up her body, Ian's eyes finally met hers. She smiled.

'Ian, how nice to see you again,' Nicola said, breaking away from her group with the merest gesture to them that she would be back shortly.

'Nice to see you too; and I mean that literally. You're very nice to look at.'

Far from being taken aback by such effrontery, Nicola looked as though she had expected a complement and was satisfied with Ian's attempt.

Twenty years plus had dulled Ian's shyness, making him every bit as capable of flirting as the next young man. As a forty-eight year old, though, flirting was nothing more than an attractive girl willing to humour him; to bring a smile to the face of a man who had grown so old as to render him 'safe'. His wanton mind, stuck inside a middle-aged body, was safe. However, with that same mind now inside a young body, flirting had become very dangerous; especially when the woman he wanted to take as his wife was standing only a few paces away. Now was not the time to test his pulling power; to see what might have been if he had read the signs in the physics lessons.

Looking at his drinks and then into Nicola's eyes with an exaggerated motion, he made his excuses.

'I'd really like to stop and chat, but I'm going to drop this lot if I don't get rid of them pretty damn quick.'

His face was a picture of remorse.

'Maybe I'll see you later in the evening then,' she replied, with more than a hint of seductiveness in her voice. 'Just in case I don't, here's my telephone number.'

She pulled a small business card from her pocket, and an attractively decorated lady's pen. Hiding the card within her palm, she wrote on the back of the card and slipped it into Ian's jacket.

'Call me,' she said, smiling softly.

Then, touching his cheek with a light caress, she moved away, returning to her friends without saying another word.

Ian felt strangely ill at ease as he distributed the drinks among his group. It was understandable that such a meeting should have aroused him - after all, he had just been on the receiving end of the biggest come-on of his life - but it was important these residual feelings of lust were put to the back of his mind if the evening with Debbie was to conclude as he intended.

Such was his innate desire to be with Debbie - his one true love - within a very short space of time, Nicola had been forgotten and Ian was bumping shoulders with Debs once more, each laughing and enjoying the other's company.

The rest of the evening passed without event, save for the occasional interruption from ex-pupils who were circulating, briefly meeting up with old faces to see how they had fared, before moving on to catch up with someone else in the crowd.

Ian, David and Debbie stayed to the end, by which time Dave was keen to get going.

'I'll be in the car,' he informed his guest, sensing she wanted a moment alone with Ian.

He was right.

'So,' she said awkwardly, turning to face Ian, 'time to be going. It's been a nice evening.'

'It certainly has. Thank you.'

'Why thank me?'

'Because having you for company made the evening nice.'

Debbie smiled, directed her eyes at Ian's chest, and began twiddling her fingers together.

'I'd like to see you again,' Ian continued, feeling almost as nervous as he had done the first time he had asked her out.

She paused, but not for long.

'I'd like that too,' she said softly. 'Have you got a pen? I'll give you my phone number.'

Ian reached into his jacket pocket and pulled out the pen that had been broken and then not.

'Here, write it down on a beer mat,' he suggested, finding a suitably dry coaster on the table that stood next to them.

Pocketing the piece of card, Ian and Debbie left the hall, stopping outside beneath a wall light that illuminated the entrance.

'Bye then,' he said gently, not making a move to leave.

Debbie smiled sheepishly. Then, as though she had needed a moment to pluck up the courage, she leant forward to plant a gentle kiss on Ian's lips, her hands placed on his upper arms to steady herself. It was all the recipient could do to stop himself plunging his tongue into her mouth. After all, he was not supposed to know her that well. Instead, he satisfied himself, placing his hands against her back, feeling the softness and warmth of her body. The clinch was brief, but it meant everything.

'Ring me,' she said.

'I will.'

Ian watched as Debbie got into David's car, remaining motionless until the headlights swept out of the car park and were gone.

A sense of inner warmth blanketed Ian's body as he returned to his own car to begin the long drive back to his mum's house. Thoughts crossed his mind; thoughts of what an extraordinary day it had been; thoughts of Debbie and of what the future held for them.

As the journey wore on, comfortable feelings began to fade, replaced by those associated with the problem he faced of how to find and kill Mike Summerbee. At least he now knew what the victim looked like as a young man and in which town he could be found. Ian would need to formulate a new plan, but that required thought, something his brain was not capable of at this hour. Believing it to be more productive if he were to sleep on the matter, he tried his best to put the subject out of his mind.

It was midnight before he pulled onto the drive, extremely thankful to be home. The intensity of the day had drained every last drop of his energy reserves. Another ten minutes on the road would probably have seen him falling asleep at the wheel, crashing the car and landing up in hospital, or the mortuary.

Walking slowly towards the front door, he found it impossible to stifle yawns that came, one after another.

Upstairs, Ian felt, at the same time, both familiar with, and a stranger to, his bedroom. It felt almost as though he was staying over in a friend's spare room.

Pyjamas poked out from beneath his pillow, something he had not worn in many years, but the thought of sleeping naked under the same roof as his mum made him don them without complaint or hesitation.

Sinking beneath the bedding, Ian vowed to himself to spend the next day planning. In the meantime he desired only to sleep.

13

Gradually the depths of Ian's sleep lessened, dreamed-thought giving way to an increasing awareness of the real world. The temperature beneath the bedclothes could not have been more perfect, dispelling any desire to wake fully. Although natural sleep had nearly run its course, Ian was determined to hang on to the feeling of wellbeing for as long as possible. However, a conspiracy was already building. Senses, becoming more alert, detected that all was not as it should be. The sunlight that forced its way through the fabric of the curtains was too strong and coming from the wrong direction. The sheet, the duvet upon his shoulder, the very pillow on which his head lay, all felt wrong. Then there was the absence of his wife, her body pressed against his, her breathing an indication she remained asleep when he could not.

It had become the norm for Ian to rise before Debbie and to bring her a cup of tea to help ease her back to consciousness, but this morning the tables seemed to have turned. As he lay on the brink of opening his eyes, he heard the distinct sound of a cup being placed gently down upon his bedside cabinet, close to his exposed ear.

'I've brought you a nice cup of tea, dear,' a voice said, pleasant, but not that of his wife.

With his eyes open, he could see it was in fact his mum who had spoken, but for a moment could not comprehend why she might be in his bedroom, bringing him tea, or even why she might be in the house. Then, quite suddenly, it all made sense and he remembered everything.

'Thanks,' he said, too late to be heard, his mum having drifted from the room.

Lying on his back, fingers interlocked upon his chest, Ian stared at the ceiling, taking stock of where and when he was and all that had happened to get him there.

The feelings of shock were not nearly as severe as they had been at the moment he set eyes upon the upturned lorry the previous day. In fact, given the success of the previous evening, he could now begin to look on his situation in a positive light.

As uninspiring as it had been the first time round, if all he did now was to rid the world of Summerbee, without getting caught, and if he never used his ability again, he could at least expect to live his life as before, but without going to jail, or being murdered, at the age of forty-eight. And surely with his knowledge of the future, he could make at least some improvements along the way.

Spoken quickly, it sounded easy. For the price of one murder – one displaced act of self-defence - he could remarry the woman he loved and they would have two children together - Stephen and Ann - who would go to university and make their parents proud.

Ian smiled as he recalled the faces of his family as they would appear twenty-four years hence, but the smile soon evaporated at the thought he would not experience those images afresh for a very long time.

Realising no good could come of dwelling on that which he was powerless to change, Ian made the conscious decision to think upon a different subject, the obvious one being the removal of Summerbee. Continuing to drop the man's given name kept things impersonal; avoiding use of the words kill and murder made the task less daunting. World War Two pilots did not kill or murder other pilots; they brought down planes.

Ian was confident he would recognise his adversary when they met again and knew in which town Summerbee lived. Unfortunately, that was the sum total of his knowledge. As for a plan to find and dispose of him, his unconscious mind had let him down. So much for sleeping on it. And if that was not enough, Ian had yet to secure a date with Debbie, and then there was that bloody interview in the morning. With regard to the latter, Ian considered whether he should attend, determining he should not, almost before he had finished asking the question. Boycotting an interview he could not hope to pass avoided the humiliation of failure and provided an opportunity to seek out Summerbee instead. However, the act of removing his adversary from the scene, without being discovered, was bound to take time – perhaps weeks, but not a month, as by then Summerbee would have discovered his powers. In the meantime, a decision would have to be made whether he should return to work at all, at least until Summerbee was no longer an issue. In that respect, it was impossible to know how badly his career would be affected by not securing promotion at this stage, but as his working life had already been relatively unsuccessful, he doubted it could be made much worse if he were not put in charge of two of his colleagues. If he was forced to go sick for several weeks, not only would he be denied promotion, he might lose his job. On the other hand, if he called in sick for the day of the interview only, his bosses might simply reschedule, and if they were not inclined to do so, he would be expected to carry on as he had been at this age, performing everyday tasks he had forgotten entirely. The only solution he could think of was to attend work to observe his colleagues, reminding himself how it was done. He would appear unproductive, but a quick rewind at the end of the same day, multiple times, would help get him back up to speed. This was not ideal as it would prevent him making progress towards his other goal – that of winning the heart of his soulmate.

It was only with regard to Debbie that Ian felt he was on track. He had made first contact with her and found the spark that originally ignited a life of blissful marriage was still there, shining with the same brilliance as before. She wanted to see him again; he had her telephone number; all was looking well.

As a bonus, Nicola Appleby, the woman he had lusted over during their school days together, had also furnished him with her telephone number. Of course, he had no intention of using it, but the fact she too wanted to see him provided an immense boost to his ego. For this reason and this reason alone, her card would remain in his wallet; a sort of, 'in the event of needing a confidence boost, break glass'; a card to look at, but not use.

Ian swung his legs out of bed and took a slurp of tea. It had sugar in it, his liking for which had faded ten years ago; now ten years into his future. Abandoning the cup to go cold, he padded across the landing to the bathroom, intent on doing something that needed no concentration. It was not to be. Immediately upon arriving in front of the sink, another question presented itself - which of the toothbrushes was his; the green one, or the blue? The bristles of the green brush were worn but retained their original white colour. The bristles of the blue brush, however, were equally worn but were stained red. Then he noticed the two tubes of toothpaste, one with white paste crusted about its nozzle, the other with a red gel oozing from beneath the cap. The latter contained a preparation designed to counter sensitive teeth, a complaint his mum had suffered for many years until finally they had been extracted sometime in the future. Therein was his answer.

It was rapidly becoming clear that living in his past, with only the memories of his future to help him, was not going to be easy. He would have to conduct himself as would a sleuth: being observant; making deductions; trying to fit together the pieces of a seemingly incomplete jig-saw puzzle. The luxury of allowing his mind to go blank would be a rare thing.

Downstairs, his mum had already poured him a bowl of corn flakes. Next to it, she had placed the sugar jar and a freshly opened pint bottle of chilled milk; unshaken so he might have the pleasure of pouring the cream of the top of the milk onto his cereal; just as he liked it - sweet and creamy. Ian would have preferred a slice of wholemeal toast, coated with a generous portion of rich, thick-cut, marmalade, but did not even consider saying so.

Holding the foil cap firmly over the neck and using both hands, Ian inverted the bottle several times to disperse the cream before adding the milk to his bowl and taking his first spoonful.

His mum was surprised to see the tea spoon, imbedded in the surface of the sugar, remained undisturbed. She was surprised further to witness her son drinking a freshly brewed cup of tea she had made him, without first sweetening it. Most of all, she was surprised that he thanked her, and offered to do the washing up once he had finished.

'What's all this; you lost your sweet tooth all of a sudden?' she asked, jovially.

Thinking quickly, Ian explained a friend's father had been diagnosed with diabetes and the news of it had shocked him sufficiently to consider adopting a more healthy diet.

'Sounds more like you've got yourself a girlfriend at last,' his mum replied, dropping her chin so her eyes looked over the rim of her glasses.

'Not yet, but I'm working on it,' Ian responded, with a smile.

Standing in front of the sink, his hands immersed in warm soapy water, Ian was able to clear his thoughts, enough to know he needed to clear them even more. In fact, what he needed was complete isolation.

Many years into the future, David Utteridge would introduce Ian to the pleasures of hiking; or so it had been the case the first time round. Ian had quickly taken to this quiet activity as a way of getting temporary relief from the rat race in which he had been forced daily to compete. It provided a means of putting things into perspective; a chance to think unhindered. This time, though, he would discover hiking, not in ten years, that very day.

By mid-morning, he was ready to set off. Bewildered by her son's sudden interest in the outdoors, his mum watched as he left the house.

'She likes walking then,' his mum said as Ian bustled past her in the hall, laden down with coat and rucksack.

Ian smiled.

It was unnecessary to take the car as the entrance to the local network of public footpaths lay less than half a mile from the house. Inadequate footwear limited the length of his walk, but it was still well into the afternoon before he returned, refreshed and with a plan for the disposal of his enemy clear in his mind. Tasks had been prioritised and would be acted upon in turn.

Firstly, he would ring Debbie; establishing a relationship with her being central to all else. Secondly, as already decided upon, he would take the following day off sick to avoid the interview and provide an opportunity to commit the necessary act. Thirdly, he would take steps, by some means not yet decided, to tackle the interview at a later date, or to improve his career in some other way.

From his bedroom, Ian retrieved the beer mat that bore Debbie's telephone number, and strode confidently downstairs to the living room where he settled in an armchair to make the call. His mum was out, affording the privacy he desired. Having placed the beer-stained card on the table beside the telephone, he picked up the receiver in his left hand and held it against his ear. Phase one of his master plan was progressing at pace, but at the point of execution, the momentum failed suddenly. Ian had butterflies.

His eyes scanned the first digit written on the card, while his finger hovered over the corresponding button on the telephone's keypad, but there it stayed. His mouth was dry, and inwardly, he was shaking. The tip of Ian's finger bobbed above the button, enough times for Ian to become angry with himself. As if to chastise his finger, his hand slapped the padded arm of the chair several times, raising a cloud of dust into the air. When sufficient angry words had left his lips, the instruction was given to try again. This time his finger plunged forward and struck the first key. Thankfully, the rest followed without further hesitation. There was a pause and then the sound of a telephone ringing at the other end. Five, six, seven rings and then a click as the call connected.

'Hello,' a young feminine voice answered.

'Is that Debbie?' Ian asked, tentatively.

'Yes.'

'Hello, it's Ian; we met at the reunion last night.'

Much to his relief, Debbie was pleased to hear his voice and before long each was probing the other's social diary for a suitable opportunity for them to meet. Monday was obviously out as Ian had a murder pencilled in, although he kept the real reason to himself. Tuesday was out too as Debbie had already arranged to see her grandmother who was in a home and would be expecting a visit. Wednesday was free. Eight o'clock. He would pick her up at her house. All was arranged. He was a happy man.

As the day drew to a close, Ian readied himself for bed. He was tired and elated by his success with his future wife, but the positive thoughts he had for her were in conflict with those he had for the task in hand. Sleep came, but not easily.

The alarm clock activated, pulsing with a harsh, rhythmic tone, devoid of bass. Ian was lying curled up on his side, his hands clamped between jack-knifed knees. He made no movement, other than to stretch his uppermost arm out from beneath the bedding in order to silence the noise that sought to tear him from his sleep. A restless night had left him feeling no more refreshed than he had been when his head hit the pillow eight hours previously, but at least he woke knowing where and when he was, and what was on the day's agenda.

Taking the day off sick was his only course of action, but it was too early to ring the office, or at least he assumed it so. The unnerving reality was that he did not know at what time he was due to start work, or to whom he should report sick. Recalling the department to which he belonged was easy – 'Export'. He also knew he was one of a team of three, comprising of two clerks and a section head – his line manager. His was one of four sections and dealt with orders from customers whose company name started with the letter G through to...., but that is when the detail ended. He could hardly contact the switchboard and ask for 'G to...' and then mumble.

Alternatively, he could ask for the head of his section by name, but here was another problem. During his time with the company he had worked under two section heads. At first, Barry had led the team: Ian and his colleague, Roland. At some point, Barry had moved on to pastures new, leaving a void that Roland had filled, his experience making him the only logical candidate. So, who was in charge now, Barry or Roland? The clues were there. The interview that Ian was meant to be attending was for the position of Head of the American Section; a separate department altogether. He had applied for the job knowing his only competition, Roland, had already been promoted. Therefore, Roland was in charge.

Having resolved the problem, Ian felt much better and swung his feet out of bed, ready to attack the day.

Having attended to his ablutions, Ian wandered downstairs, still wearing his pyjamas, where he helped himself to a bowl of cereal before taking it through to the lounge to eat alone.

A few minutes later, his mum entered the room, placing a freshly brewed mug of tea down on the nest of tables beside her son, using the TV paper as a coaster.

'You'll be late,' she said, in a matter of fact way. 'You normally leave about now and you're not even dressed.'

This simple comment resolved another question, without there having been the need to ask it. It was now twenty-five minutes to nine. The journey to work would use twenty of them. He knew this through years of experience, continuing to drive the same route even after he had left the company, it forming part of the journey between his mum's house and his own. He was also aware of his lifelong aim of getting to where he should be right on time, never wishing to give his employer a minute more than was necessary. The conclusion: his start time was nine o'clock.

'I'm not going in today,' Ian said, picking up the mug, blowing away the steam with pursed lips. 'I've taken a day's holiday.'

'That's nice for you dear,' his mum replied, before shuffling from the room, her slip-on footwear making it difficult to walk any other way.

Ian had not thanked her for the drink. He would have, had it been his wife. Shamefully, he had always taken his mum for granted, expecting her to look after his every need without reward. Debbie had refused to accept surrogacy as a part of her wedding vows, insisting on being treated as an equal. As a result, Ian had been forced to develop into a man who was prepared to pull his own weight.

Washing up the breakfast dishes the previous morning, to help his mum, had seemed the natural thing to do. However, being back at the point in his life when he had been most pampered, he was quickly slipping back into his old ways. Somehow, the lessons he had learned were being forgotten. In his defence, the situation had arisen unexpectedly, catching him off guard. Vowing to himself not to let one misdemeanour become a habit, Ian let the matter go and turned his thoughts to the more pressing matters at hand.

By nine-fifteen, Ian knew his colleagues would have noticed his absence, and would be speculating wildly as to the reason. Had he overslept? Had his car broken down? Had he been involved in a serious road accident – perhaps fatal? Whatever the excuse, it had to be something big to keep him from work on the day of his interview.

It was time for Ian to use the telephone and disappoint those who harboured a secret lust for a good tragedy.

Making sure his mum was out of earshot, he dialled the number that he found at the top of the letter advising him of his appointment with his departmental manager.

'Hello,' Roland answered the call, clearing his throat before he spoke, as he did so on every occasion he answered the telephone. The small distinct sound was enough to tell Ian he was through to the right person.

Ian spoke feebly of the illness that had stricken him during the course of the night. It sounded less than convincing, but he could hardly tell the truth that he needed the day off to murder someone, or that he could no longer remember how to do his job. In an attempt to sound more believable than his limited acting abilities would permit, he began asking advice on what to do regarding postponing the interview. Roland uttered a string of comforting words and promised to make things right with their mutual boss. The conversation ended with Roland wishing his colleague a speedy recovery, and the deed was done.

Not knowing how the day would pan out, Ian tried to cover as many eventualities as he could, slinging a sports bag into the boot of his car, containing a torch, a warm jumper, a bottle of diluted orange cordial and something to eat.

The first step to finding Summerbee's home was to drive directly to the town in which the target lived. That much he remembered from their brief conversation at the bar.

It was a working day so it was likely Summerbee would be out, affording a good opportunity to carry out a recognisance of the property and of the immediate area in which it was situated.

The thirty-five miles between Chelderham and Fringely took little more than three quarters of an hour to cover; sufficient time to consider how best he could narrow down the search on his arrival.

The plan was simple - to find a telephone box with a directory, and interrogate that directory, looking for the name 'M. Summerbee' and its associated address. In his favour, Ian felt it unlikely the name would appear more than once.

Unfortunately, although Ian was able to find many telephone boxes - one after another - none of them contained the necessary book. The only other place to find one was the library.

The car park in the centre of town was a pleasant one - a square of tarmac set in one corner of some playing fields; a border of birch trees separating the two. The tariff for parking was reasonable when compared with the fee Ian was used to paying for a three-hour stay. However, by the standards of the day, it was still dear, and when compared to the amount of lose change in his pocket, it felt extortionate.

Knowing he would be buying drinks at the reunion, the Ian of the past had obviously been to the bank in preparation, prior to the Ian of the future slipping back into his body. The money he had withdrawn had been all but spent in winning the favour of his old school friends, and more importantly, of Debbie. He would soon need fresh funds.

On inspection, Ian found his wallet to contain: a bank card, for use in its automatic telling machines; a credit card, and a cardboard organ donor card - a fraction of the number of cards he was used to carrying around with him.

The credit card could be used to replenish the petrol tank on the strength of his signature alone. That was one less worry to contend with, although he would need to practice writing his name before using it, his signature having altered considerably over the years. The credit card would also allow him to borrow money via a hole-in-the-wall machine; an expensive, but easily available loan. The cash machine card, the forerunner of the debit card, differed in that it would let him draw money directly from his personal bank account, at least until it was empty. In both cases though, he would need to know the personal identification number appropriate to each, but he remembered neither.

There were alternatives, and for a while Ian had overlooked one of the more obvious.

Being more used to paying by direct debit, having money automatically taken from his account by prior arrangement, and by plastic, he had not written more than half a dozen cheques in a year. If he could find his chequebook now, he would be able to simply walk into his bank and hand over a written order made out to 'cash', receiving that sum as banknotes of his choice. However, with there being so many details about his past missing, Ian had no notion as to its current whereabouts.

In the hunt for the invitation and instructions relating to the school reunion, he had thoroughly searched his mum's house less than forty-eight hours previously. If his cheque book had been there, he would have found it. That left only his car.

Back behind the steering wheel, Ian rummaged about in the door pocket on his side of the car, and then in the pocket of the passenger's door - nothing. The only remaining hope lay with the glove compartment.

With a twist of the catch, the hatch, set low down in the dashboard, burst open under the pressure of the many items of paper, pens and other paraphernalia it had been forced to contain. Boiled sweets spilled down onto the mat below, along with several empty wrappers.

Ian reached across awkwardly, his head resting on the front passenger's seat, the gear stick pressing uncomfortably against his ribs. However, the discovery of the missing chequebook, stuffed between the owner's manual and the top of the glove box, was well worth the discomfort.

The obvious next task was to pay a visit to the local branch of his bank. Thankfully, its logo was easy to spot among the stretch of shops that lined the High Street. Inside though, Ian found himself at the wrong end of a very long queue that snaked back and forth three times; something else he was not used to. Two decades on, there would be no need for him to visit his bank in person at all, the majority of his dealings with them being conducted across the ether.

The crowd moved slowly forward, Ian among their numbers, patiently waiting his turn. But then, with a free teller almost in sight, another thought occurred to him. If he cashed the cheque now, there would be a paper trail leading to him being in the same town as Mike Summerbee on the day of his murder. It was a slim connection, but Ian wanted there to be none at all.

Feeling awkward, he began patting his pockets and upper torso with both hands, and made a suitable facial expression to indicate to nobody in particular that he had forgotten something vital. With that, he stepped out of line and exited the building.

Obtaining funds had been of secondary importance. The primary purpose of stopping in the centre of Fringely had been to visit the library, the location of which Ian had not yet determined. Loathed to ask for assistance in case the conversation was later remembered, he chose instead to walk the length and breadth of the street and of the smaller roads that spurred from it. Eventually, he came upon the welcome sight of a tourist information centre. In its window, some nice person had pasted an A4 photocopy of a map of the town centre. Symbols annotated the positions of the police station, toilets, car parks, and more importantly, the elusive library. Fortunately, not only was it nearby, it was open.

Inside, people of all ages stood quietly among the bookshelves, respecting the silence that libraries used to enjoy. This one, at least, had not yet become a meeting place for pensioners who, in later years, would gather and speak among themselves, making no attempt to lower the volume of their voices.

A woman sat at the enquiry desk, the epitome of a bookworm, wearing a tan cardigan, thick, dark-rimmed glasses, and sporting a self-administered haircut, approximating a bob. Her desk guarded a row of shelves that bore the weight of numerous reference books, including those that interested Ian most: dozens of telephone books, covering a vast area. Ian would very much liked to have accessed these volumes without first seeking permission, believing the less people he spoke to, the better. However, the librarian's presence made that impossible.

He approached the desk, wondering how she might react to being disturbed, especially by someone beneath the age of thirty. She turned out to be delightful, helpful and to have a smile capable of preventing a war.

The research paid off. The surname, 'Summerbee', was listed only once; the full entry recording the telephone number of one M. Summerbee of 482 Outward Fleet Road.

As with the fiasco of the lottery tickets, rather than the sight of the address informing Ian of something he did not know, it merely reactivated the knowledge that Summerbee himself had given him during the school reunion. It was infuriating he had been forced to go to so much trouble only to find that he knew the answer all along. However, had he not hunted down the telephone book, the address would undoubtedly have eluded him forever.

Ian returned the book to the very pleasant librarian, and in doing so, noticed the shelves behind her desk also bore a huge variety of maps.

The complete collection of Ordnance Survey maps, covering the whole of the British Isles, was of no use. The folded sheets showed everything from contours to bridges; rivers to windmills. They also showed roads, but their identification was limited to a colour, a single letter, and a number, and then only if they warranted recognition at all.

What Ian needed, and what he found, was a street map. In fact, between the pale blue covers of a single book, he found not only a plan for the town in which he was interested, but for every town in the county. The extensive index took him swiftly to one in particular that illustrated the location of Outward Fleet Road, Fringely.

The photocopier took the last of Ian's change before it was time for him to return to his car, triumphant.

14

Outward Fleet Road was a road of two halves: the longest section running between properties on either side, with pavements providing pedestrian access; a shorter section acted as a scout, inexorably leading the town into the countryside. Along this stretch, a high, pathless grass verge separated a row of post-war terraced houses from the traffic that flowed by, fast and unceasing, perhaps ten metres from their front doors. On the opposite side of the road, a hawthorn hedge, interspersed with oak and beech, shielded the arable fields beyond. There was nowhere to stop, not even the opportunity to slow down without drawing attention. The best that could be achieved on the first pass was to produce a mental shortlist of properties that might belong to Summerbee. Thankfully it was still early afternoon.

Half a mile past the last house, a narrow lane leading in from the left, splayed its end to join the main road at a T-junction. A triangular grass hillock cleaved the mouth of the road in two, allowing Ian to pull off, swing his car round the back of the island, and land up facing in roughly the direction he had come from. There he waited patiently for a gap in the traffic. When it came, he set off for a second drive-by, sighting the terrace barely a minute later. Easing his foot off the accelerator, Ian slowed the forward momentum of the car as much as he dared, trying not to upset the drivers that closed on his bumper. Still he could not see the house numbers, his ability to search being hampered by the need to keep his eyes on the road.

Forced to continue back towards the centre of town, Ian sighted a small parade of shops with its own, free car park. There he was able to stop. Other cars and vans drew in, their occupants popping in to one or more of the half-dozen businesses that plied their trade, before returning to their respective vehicles and leaving again. No-one stayed long enough to notice how long Ian had been there, making it appear, at least at first, to be the ideal place to abandon his car while he dealt with the small matter at hand. However, he soon realised the car might be parked in the same position well into the evening, long after the shops had pulled down their shutters. At that point, it would stick out like a sore thumb and Ian wanted very much for it to remain invisible.

A side road offered a logical alternative. The space was not overlooked, did not cause nuisance to anyone, and was entirely legal. There would be no reason for anybody to notice his car among so many others – his was not the only banger in the neighbourhood. The spot was perfect, or at least as good as he was going to get, the only apparent drawback being he was now over a mile from Summerbee's house, although this was a fact he thought might work in his favour.

Ian opened the car's boot and grabbed his sports bag. Thinking what else he might need, he took spanners, a knife and a junior hacksaw from the car's resident toolbox and dropped them into the bag. He then set off on foot along Outward Fleet Road, in the direction of number four-eight-two.

At this point, houses lined the road on both sides. Further along though, urban sprawl gave way to open countryside on one side of the road, where it was screened from full view by the hawthorn hedge that Ian had observed on his first pass through the neighbourhood. Between the last of the houses on the far side, and the beginning of the hedge, a sign marked the entrance to a public footpath that ran perpendicular to Outward Fleet Road. Having crossed over, Ian followed the narrow, foot-trodden track for less than a dozen paces before stepping from it to disappear from view.

The hawthorn hedge was at least three metres tall. At first glance, it appeared to be formed of densely packed, bright green foliage, but this was not so. The small leaves were merely a veneer, hiding a core network of viciously spiked twigs. Cars passing by on the other side were clearly visible, almost as though there was no barrier at all. If Ian could see the faces of the drivers as clearly as he did, he reasoned they would be able to see him equally well.

Running parallel to the hedge, a drainage ditch continued the length of the field and beyond. Being both clear of obstruction and dry, it offered an immediate solution to the problem. Without further consideration, Ian dug one heel into the earth bank, took two quick, jerking, steps to the bottom and ducked down so that his head was no longer visible to anyone unless they happened to be flying low in the sky, binoculars peering towards the ground. Tentatively, his head then rose just above the parapet, so that his eyes could survey the area, looking to detect anyone who might have seen him. To his relief, he appeared to be alone.

At the base of the hedge, the foliage was at its sparsest, although tussocks of dry grass conspired to obscure his view. Ian fell quickly into a routine, uprooting parched clumps of grass that in most instances came up easily, before peering between the trunks of the hawthorn to see if he could detect a house number on the opposite side of the road. When he could not, he would move along several paces before trying again. From this distance and angle, most of the house numbers were too small to read, or were hidden by any number of obstructions. However, there were two that Ian's eyes could make out. The first, number 472, was carved into a sliced section of tree trunk, its figures painted white in contrast to the background of varnished natural oak. The plaque was no larger than on many of the other properties, but it was attached to the gatepost at the front of the drive, rather than to the house itself. The other, number 486, was screwed to the wall adjacent to the front door. This plaque might have been further back than the first, but the size of the individual figures more than compensated. They were huge - at least thirty centimetres high - suggesting the occupier had either experienced problems with his mail being mis-delivered, or was simply a wild eccentric.

Knowing the address of these two houses alone allowed Ian to extrapolate the identities of all others in the row, revealing the exact whereabouts of number 482. Having shuffled along the bottom of the ditch to a point opposite Summerbee's property, there was nothing to do but stay hidden and wait.

Having established his position, there was now time to look around and take note of his immediate environment. Not far from where he crouched lay a few medium-sized branches, their leaves crisp and curled as if left to die in the hottest of deserts. These he used to fashion a crude roof that spanned the ditch, and a wall of sorts, so as to protect his flank from the casual glance of passers-by.

He was not accustomed to the work of a private detective and soon discovered just how slowly time was capable of passing. The only relief came from the occasional bite of food, and a swig from his bottle of orange.

From five o'clock onwards, the flow of passing traffic became steadily heavier. Every so often a vehicle would slow, at which point Ian's glazed eyes suddenly, but only temporarily, became more attentive. Then, as the traffic moved on, he would quickly slip back into a state of stupor. The majority of the time, the sheer weight of traffic was the cause of cars braking. Twice though, Ian's level of excitement was raised when the deceleration was accompanied by the winking of orange indicator lights. Both times, his hopes were dashed when the cars swung off the road, but onto the driveways of Summerbee's neighbours.

Finally, just before the little hand reached six, an ageing, gold-coloured Chrysler Alpine clattered to a halt on the driveway in front of the Summerbee residence. The man that alighted from the vehicle turned to lock the driver's door and stood for a moment side-on to Ian's position. There was no mistaking it; this was indeed the man Ian had come to remove.

The purpose of Ian returning to a point, more than two decades into his past, was threefold: to avoid jail for the murder of a fellow lottery winner; to avoid being murdered by that same man; to murder that man again, executing the killing in such a way blame did not fall upon Ian's shoulders. With regard to this last point, murder could be conducted as before - at close quarters and brutal - relying on the police failing to connect the two men, but this had not gone well in the future. Back in 1985, although there were no cameras to record his movements, there were links. Even the briefest of investigations might bring detectives to interview everyone who attended the reunion. If so, they might question why Ian had gone sick on the day of a very important interview – the day of the murder. One thing would lead to another and he could be heading for jail for the second time within a week – two separate murders of the same man, years apart; it was a bizarre concept. The preferred alternative, therefore, was to make Summerbee's demise look like an accident, the most obvious means of achieving such a twisted goal appearing to be the target's own vehicle. After all, it looked like a death trap. The plan, such as it was, was simple. It entailed interfering with the Alpine's braking system, and then waiting for Summerbee to go for a drive. The target would get up to speed, need to slow quickly in order to navigate a hazardous bend, and find himself unable to stop, causing his car to leave the road, preferably in the direction of a brick wall. There were a hundred or more things that might go wrong, but having the ability to rewind time, Ian had the option of trying again and again, making tweaks each time until he was successful.

Clearly, such interference would take time and stood to attract attention if it were carried out during daylight. This meant there lay ahead another very long wait, until Summerbee and the rest of the neighbourhood had retired to bed for the night.

Not wishing to leave evidence at his observation point, Ian had been careful to return all food wrappers to the sports bag. Now, with hunger setting in, he rummaged about for something more to eat, but his fingers found only screwed up paper and pieces of torn plastic. The residue in his mouth, a lasting reminder of the bottle of drink he had long since drained, served to accentuate his thirst. Then there was the aching in his knees; the result of having remained crouched at the bottom of a ditch for several hours. He was hungry, thirsty, increasingly cold, and bored to the point he could not dismiss the idea of causing himself harm, simply to reduce the monotony. At least the jumper he had stuffed into the bottom of his bag brought him warmth.

At seven-forty, Mike Summerbee emerged from his house, dressed in casual attire: jeans; tee-shirt; lightweight jacket; and training shoes. He turned to close the front door and waved goodbye to someone who remained unseen inside the property. Summerbee then stepped towards his car, straightened the chrome aerial that protruded from one wing, and got in. A few moments later the vehicle reversed into the road and drove off.

For the time being, the target had gone, taking with him Ian's intended instrument of execution. Even if Summerbee were to return soon, there would not be the opportunity to tamper with the brakes until the early hours of the morning. Waiting that long, in the conditions Ian now found himself, would be unbearable. Besides which, every moment he remained in the ditch, he ran the risk of being spotted by someone walking their dog.

Checking the coast was clear, Ian threw off the branches that had camouflaged his position and scrambled up the side of the bank, the task made more difficult by the sudden, inevitable onset of pain associated with the restoration of blood circulation. Nerve endings fired indiscriminately, creating a bout of pins-and-needles such that he had never suffered before. Ian tried to ignore them, but every footfall brought new agonies, causing him to hobble and stamp his feet for several minutes. Only when his gait had returned to normal did he set off back towards his car, aware a man with a limp would be more memorable to potential witnesses than one without.

It took twenty minutes for Ian to reach the vehicle, all the while his mind active to the problem of how to spend the next six hours. There was time enough to return home, but the journey would waste petrol he could ill afford. Then again, not returning home would undoubtedly cause his mother worry; worry that might lead her to reporting him missing to the police; disastrous for someone who sought to maintain anonymity. Whatever else he did, he had to contact her to provide assurance all was well. However, there was a problem.

Telephone boxes were everywhere, but without change to feed them, Ian might as well be living in the Stone Age. A reverse-charge call was an option, but as it might raise her suspicion, it was not a viable one. All he needed was a single coin; something he was pretty sure he did not have. The only things available that might yield one were the clothes he wore and the car he sat in. He knew his pockets were bare because he had used the last of his change to feed the photocopier at the library. As to the car, he had now searched it twice, firstly when he had been desperate to find the invitation to the school reunion, and secondly, when he had rummaged through the pockets and glove compartment looking for his cheque book. The glove box had been extremely full and had given up the latter with only minimal disruption. If it were emptied, there was still a chance a coin or two might be hiding at the bottom.

Under compression, the contents of the glove box consumed a finite space. However, once released, the single pile of paperwork expanded upwards on the passenger seat until the force of gravity caused it to collapse and spill into the foot well.

It took seconds to empty the compartment completely, and all for nothing. A single penny languished in a sticky pool of dust, fluff and crumbs at the very back, but it was of no use to anyone wishing to make a call. Slipping it into his pocket, pushed home with his left thumb, Ian sat back, his head resting on the top edge of his seat, his neck not appreciating the absence of head rests; something he would not have again until several cars down the line.

Having nowhere to rest his hands, Ian slipped them into his trouser pockets and relaxed his arms, allowing his elbows to hang freely by his sides. Almost immediately an itch demanded attention beneath the overhang of his nose. Without conscious thought, his left hand freed itself, intent on swiping away the irritation. Dragged with it, the pocketed penny fell between the seats, hitting something metal, out of sight. On many occasions in life, Ian had lost money this way. Coins would spill from shallow pockets onto the floor beneath the seat, or land between the seat runners and the centre consul. Here they would remain, sufficiently difficult to retrieve as to be written off, considered lost forever; unless, that was, he happened to be desperate.

Instinctively, Ian's hands felt for the lever that controlled the front-to-back adjustment of the driver's seat. Having located it, he braced his feet against the bulkhead, his back pressing firmly against the seat, and pushed. It was stiff, but yielded. Then, having gained the extra space he needed, he got out of the car, knelt in the road, and buried his upper body beneath the steering wheel. To search the passenger side, it was necessary to contend also with the gear stick pushing painfully against his rib cage, but the end result was worth it. Three coins - a five pence and two ten pence pieces - gave themselves up involuntarily, their chosen position being responsible for several minor injuries to Ian's knuckles and fingers. However, the inventory of scrapes and scuffs mattered not; he had what he needed.

The closest telephone box to hand was at the nearby parade of shops he had parked at earlier in the day. The interior smelled of stale smoke and urine and was littered with cigarette butts. As with every other phone box he had been to of late, this one had no directory. Thankfully his mum's number had not altered in thirty years; or so he thought. Having dialled just three digits, a continuous tone emitted from the earpiece, indicating the number was unobtainable. Angrily, Ian stamped two fingers down on the cradle that held the receiver, terminating the failed call.

The decision to rewind such a large portion of his life had not been taken lightly. Plainly, there were always going to be difficulties readjusting to a time he had not been familiar with in more than two decades. However, he could be forgiven for having so greatly underestimated the number of problems he would then encounter. He had foreseen the larger problems and had mentally prepared himself to deal with them, but it was the apparently endless stream of minor hiccups that was rapidly reducing him to a state of utter despair.

Taking a single, calming breath, Ian cleared his mind before assigning it to determine what had gone wrong. The sound from the earpiece had occurred even before he had finished dialling the area code, so that was obviously where the problem lay. Then he realised what must have happened. Due to the need for expansion of the network, at some point over the coming years, a 'one' had been inserted between the first two digits. Simple. He dialled again, this time omitting the offending digit. To his great relief he heard first the ringing tone, then the voice of his mum answering, and finally the sound of his coin being accepted as he pushed it home.

'It's me. Listen, I'm going to be late. I might even stay over at a friend's house, so don't wait up.'

'Okay, dear. I was worried about you. Your dinner's ruined.'

The call was short but of sufficient length to leave Ian with two opposing thoughts. He was glad to have put his mum's mind at ease, but guilt-ridden for having put her to the effort of cooking him a meal only for him to let it go to waste – there was no microwave to resurrect it whenever he eventually arrived home.

Putting his guilt aside, the rest of the evening went without a hitch, Ian parking up to listen to the radio for a while before moving to several other locations, hoping to avoid suspicion.

Finally, at half past eleven, Ian allowed himself to settle back in his seat and drift off to sleep. There was never any danger he might remain in such a condition through until morning, the facilities for sleep being so uncomfortable. Midnight passed. At around two o'clock, having glanced at his watch in the moonlight on numerous occasions, Ian decided enough was enough. He sat up, waited for feelings of near death to subside, turned the ignition and set off in the direction of Summerbee's house.

As before, he parked his car in a convenient side road, some distance from his target's home. The absence of human activity, traffic and natural daylight, all served to bolster his confidence.

On foot, the pavement soon ran out, forcing Ian to walk in the road, but thankfully, not a single vehicle drove by. He reached the entrance to the driveway of number 482 and approached the target vehicle from the passenger side, ensuring he remained in deep shadow.

From his bag, he took a torch and an adjustable spanner. He then lay on his back and shuffled beneath the car. Although severely restricted, there was still room enough for the task of undoing a single union joint that connected two sections of brake pipe. The two shaped ends - one male, one female - sprang apart. Immediately, an oily fluid began dripping to the floor. With this, the deed was only partially done. If left as it was, accident investigators would conclude someone had deliberately tampered with the brakes and would open a murder enquiry. However, with a little further work, Ian considered that scenario might be avoided.

Having wriggled to freedom with as much stealth as he could manage, Ian then crossed the road to the hawthorn hedge, before returning to the tampered with car, carrying a sizeable chunk of dead wood, fallen from an ageing tree.

Shuffling beneath the vehicle for the second time, Ian bent the rear section of the brake pipe back upon itself and jammed the piece of wood between it and the bodywork, in such a way there was little chance of it becoming dislodged. Ian hoped such a device might bring investigators to a different conclusion; that Summerbee had driven over the branch, wrenching the joint apart, causing a loss of brake fluid, leading to a tragic, fatal accident. Finally his work was done, although only because he did not possess the means to take one supplementary measure. Aware that if the pipe had genuinely been rent apart, the union nut would have been stripped, his final task would have been to scrape away at the exposed thread with something hard, until the sharp-cut groove was left a series of rounded over ridges. Unfortunately, none of the tools he had to hand were sufficiently small to reach inside the female half of the union, but that could not be helped.

It was not absolutely necessary for Ian to remain in the area. In the morning, Summerbee would get into his car and set off for work. Driving with defective brakes, his journey was sure to end prematurely and Ian suspected the degree to which his operation had been a success would then be announced in the local newspaper.

It was not absolutely necessary for Ian to remain in the area, but on the other hand, first-hand knowledge of the outcome was clearly going to be of advantage – what went right; what went wrong? Having decided further surveillance was needed, Ian returned to his car where he remained until dawn, at which point he walked back along Outward Fleet Road to reoccupy the ditch.

Already, the world was beginning to wake. Lights showed in many upstairs windows; the streetlights had finished their night shift and now stood tall but lifeless. Early risers walked their dogs along the pavement, and more worryingly, along the public footpath that ran close by to Ian's covert observation point. A paperboy and a postman visited doors randomly, backtracking as they reached the very last property in the terrace. The volume of traffic increased steadily until a constant stream headed out of town, seemingly part of a mass exodus.

Finally, after a long, unsettled wait, Summerbee emerged from his front door.

Ian checked about him for potential onlookers. Satisfied himself there were none, he remained with his head above the parapet, peering through a gap between the hawthorns. The view from the ditch was not ideal, made worse by the stroboscopic effect of traffic speeding by.

Summerbee was at his door. Then he was briefly to be seen re-entering the house. Then he was outside again, troubled by the door that appeared to be sticking. The length of each snapshot varied: a longer gap with the passing of an articulated lorry; a shorter one as the traffic slowed briefly; a flash as it sped up again.

Summerbee was at the car, the driver's door wide open. The door was shut again with Summerbee inside at the wheel. A puff of pale blue smoke shot from the exhaust pipe, dissipating quickly in the breeze.

Ian could only guess what Summerbee was doing. It was likely he had started the car in neutral, handbrake applied. He would depress the clutch with his left foot and select reverse gear with his left hand. His right foot would be covering the accelerator pedal, his right hand controlling the steering wheel. His left hand would move to close around the handbrake, his thumb resting on the ratchet release. Then, with one smooth, automated movement, his left foot would lift off the clutch, his right foot would ease down on the accelerator and his left hand would lower the handbrake to the floor. The car would begin to move backwards.

It did so, right on cue, just as Ian's imagined procedure predicted.

The slope of the drive meant Summerbee had only to supply sufficient power from the engine to start the car rolling, for the gradient and gravity to do the rest. Left unchecked, the speed of the car would increase rapidly, undesirable when negotiating a vehicle out onto a busy road.

From his vantage point in the ditch, Ian could see the brake lights illuminate, strong and constant. The car continued to roll backwards down the slope, its rate of descent apparently unchanged. Then the lights began to flash rapidly, evidence of Summerbee pumping the brake pedal, desperately trying to induce pressure into the system.

Panic must have overtaken the driver. The handbrake would not be as effective as the foot brake, but it would nonetheless slow the vehicle if it were being used.

Miraculously, the rear end of the car emerged from between the gateposts, out onto the carriageway, just as there was a lull in traffic. The lead oncoming vehicle was able to swerve violently around the hazard that moved across in front of it, the driver sounding his horn angrily as soon as he had regained control. The next had sufficient warning to brake hard and come to rest without collision. Then there followed multiple screeches as tyres bit deep into the road surface.

Above the frantic sounds of shedding rubber could be heard another - a sickening crunch as the rear of Summerbee's car stove in against the telegraph pole that stood firmly planted in the verge opposite his house.

Seeing the action from ground level, Ian's view of the incident was unique. His intended victim's car had glided towards his position, unstoppable yet sedate. The collision had taken place only a metre or two from where he was hidden. Primeval reactions of self-preservation forecast the stricken vehicle's immediate future, causing him to scramble from the ditch, throw himself onto his back and kick himself away from danger, continuing to do so, even after the car had come to rest. Another car, having taken evasive action, ended its journey perpendicular to its intended direction, the bonnet penetrating the hawthorn, directly above Ian's observation point.

For a short time, all was quiet. Then, as Summerbee emerged from his car - ashen and visibly shaken - there began a cacophony of noise. Drivers descended upon the scene, some angry, some anxious to help, others desiring to satiate their curiosity, all adding to a babble of voices.

Ian's attempt to kill his adversary had failed. Not only that, it was clear even a major revamp of the basic plan would never prove satisfactory. He could see how he might somehow alter the timing of the incident so that Summerbee rolled into the heaviest of traffic, but even that was unlikely. To affect any real improvement – for there to be any real increase in the chance the operation would end in success – Ian knew he must continue to remain elusive while maintaining influence over the split-second timing of Summerbee's movements. Having seen the chasm between idea and outcome, the would-be murderer accepted this was unachievable. He needed an entirely new approach.

15

The recollection of the librarian's smile had been sufficiently etched into the folds of Ian's brain to provide a point of reference that enabled the deletion of time to be both swift and accurate. However, the memory did not do justice to the disarming power of the genuine article. The bearer was not beautiful, but her smile most definitely was.

Having finally found the strength to avert his gaze, Ian realised, to his relief, he had not forgotten the details of the events he had just wiped clean. He still knew the whereabouts of his adversary, remembering details of the house, from its number and general character, right down to the problem of the sticking front door. He remembered the time at which Summerbee would leave his house, and the direction in which he would travel. Previously, the effectiveness of his memory regarding such things had been hit and miss, but now it seemed his powers of recall were total; the only explanation being that either time, or practice, was improving his ability, just as Summerbee had predicted.

Aware of the possibility he might be spotted and later connected with the scene of the intended murder, Ian spent the remainder of the afternoon and early evening away from the area, parking in a number of lay-bys, staying at each for only a short while. Then, as the time of Summerbee's departure drew near, he made his way to the now familiar side road in which he had previously parked, a mile from the scene of the failed car crash. There he remained in his vehicle, eyes flicking between his wristwatch and the traffic that sped across his path, along Outward Fleet Road.

Pin-point timing being key to his new plan, Ian made a quick calculation. Summerbee had emerged from his front door at exactly twenty minutes to eight. Allowing time for the target to get in his car, reverse off the drive and pull off, Ian judged he should aim to reach Summerbee's house at seven-forty-two. Taking into account the distance from side road to rendezvous, the potential for delay caused by the need to first pull out into traffic, and believing it prudent to factor in a redundant minute to account for unforeseen errors, Ian determined the Escort's engine should spring into life at precisely seven-thirty-nine. This it did. Moments later, the vehicle drew up at the mouth of the junction and stopped, further progress being left to the mercy of a stream of cars that seemed to have made a pact, determined to prevent Ian's Escort joining the flow.

A gap appeared, but not a large one. To fill it would mean having to pull out violently from the side road, inevitably causing the car next in line to brake heavily. It was not in Ian's nature to upset other road users, and even if it was, he feared such driving might draw unwanted attention. He let it pass. Another batch of cars sped by, bumper to bumper. The delay seemed endless, forcing Ian to act, whether or not he was ready. As soon as a second gap presented itself – although equally small as the first - Ian pressed down hard on the accelerator, causing the rear wheels to spin as they directed the vehicle into the flow, and continue to spin until he was able to straighten up.

A reversed image of a car immediately filled the frame of the rear view mirror, but the absence of flashing lights, or an angry horn, indicated the driver had taken the incident in his stride.

Within two minutes, the annoying consequence of his delay was revealed. Summerbee's car was gone.

Hoping to catch it up, Ian continued on the same road for several miles, but the scent had grown cold, leaving only one course of action. Following a brief buzzing sensation, Ian once again sat facing the traffic as it roared past in front of him. The first gap presented itself. This time, Ian took his chance.

The bonnet of the following car dipped as it braked hard, and the driver's head could be seen shaking in disbelief, but still no horn; no flashing lights.

A short while later, the moving line of traffic slowed to a halt. Ahead, Summerbee's car had reversed from his drive to sever the line. The situation could not have been more perfect. Ian had his intended victim in his sights, but was far enough back so as not to be suspected of following him.

Having passed beyond the town limits, Summerbee's car pulled off the main road into a winding lane. Ian recognised the junction as the one in which he had previously performed a U-turn, on the occasion he had overshot the Summerbee home.

Hedges grew tall on either side, obscuring all but the roof of Summerbee's Chrysler as it negotiated the bends several hundred metres ahead of its pursuer. The gap between the two vehicles shortened briefly as Summerbee turned left at the next junction. A road of even lesser importance continued through the countryside, narrowing in parts to one lane, the available space limited by the presence of ancient trees that had sprung from the earth long before a tarmacadam surface had been dreamt of. The lane ended, bursting into the open. Here it met another road; a broad stretch of concrete running east to west. By the time the Escort reached this point, Summerbee had already indicated, turned right and progressed some way into the distance. Unhindered by traffic, Ian increased his pace, concerned he was about to lose sight of the target. The road continued through a tunnel, beneath a substantial bridge and ended at another junction, illuminated and littered with street furniture: bollards; signs; crash fences. A left turn, a short drive and the road terminated at a roundabout.

The first exit led down onto a dual carriageway, heading west. The second passed a petrol station en route to the next small town. The third exit lead onto the same dual carriageway as did the first, but in the opposite direction. It was this road Summerbee had chosen.

The sight of the filling station prompted Ian to glance down at the fuel gauge. To his annoyance, the needle was as low as it was possible to get, resting on a pin that protruded from the face of the dial, indicating the tank was technically empty. The car could roll to a halt at any moment and the pursuit would be off. Now was not the time to stop for fuel, though. If he did, he was certain to lose his prey. It might only be an inconvenience to do so, but it was one he hoped to avoid.

Several minutes passed, all the while Ian maintaining a steady speed, the sole of his shoe keeping only the most delicate contact between it and the accelerator.

Summerbee's car was visible in the near distance. Few other vehicles shared the road. Every steep embankment they passed was a potential point at which the hunter's car might force the target vehicle onto a new and fatal trajectory. However, each opportunity was summarily dismissed, and for the same reason: Ian would be personally involved in the accident; he would be liable to prosecution, and there was no guarantee Summerbee would be killed.

The Chrysler passed beneath a high bridge that connected two tracts of farmer's land, cleaved in two when the by-pass had been laid. It was now the sole means of moving cattle from pastures on the north side to those on the south.

Ian felt suddenly inspired.

A quick check of the time revealed it was exactly two minutes past eight o'clock. Remembering this would be vital.

The bridge was no ordinary crossing. Sharply rising slip roads led to the top and down again the other side. Access to the fields was by way of a gate at each end. Signs prohibited use of the structure by anyone other than the farmer and those who had been given his permission. Ian had no intention of driving up onto the bridge, or even parking at its base. What he did want was the opportunity to stand undisturbed above the eastbound carriageway at exactly two minutes past eight. From there he could drop a suitably large piece of concrete through the windscreen of his enemy's car, killing him outright. The plan excited him. With sufficient preparation, and providing nothing out of his control went wrong, the purpose of Ian returning to his past would be fulfilled, and the blame would be levelled at vandals.

No longer interested in Summerbee's destination, Ian let the gap between the two vehicles lengthen.

A short distance further, a minor slip road led to a small country lane. Having turned in, a gap in a high hedge then gave access to an unmade car park in which Ian stopped his car, pulling up tight in one corner. His was the only vehicle there. At this location, foliage shielded him from view, both from the lane and from the dual carriageway. A log barrier prevented vehicles from straying into the grassy fields beyond, but left a small gap through which pedestrians and bicycles could pass. An information board declared the area to be a country park, mapped the network of footpaths that criss-crossed the land, and listed wildlife its users might expect to encounter. This meant the only likely visitors to the car park during his stay would be owners walking their dogs, or young couples keen to find a discreet location. Neither would present a problem. If they did happen upon his car, they would assume he too had taken a dog for a walk. In any event, it was probably getting too dark for most pet owners while still not yet dark enough for amorous young couples.

A dry run was the obvious next step.

The land on the opposite side of the lane clearly belonged to the farmer. Here, the fields had been planted, but around their edges, footpaths remained navigable. Mapping his route was easy. All that was required was to remain in view of the dual carriageway, not worrying about who might see him as his every footfall was destined to be wiped from their memory, along with the rest of their day.

Half an hour was needed to retrace the journey that had taken only a few minutes by car, but being a hiker by choice, the trek was an easy one; the target location proving to be worth the effort. The choice of bridges could not have been better, it being possible to approach the end of it while remaining at all times out of sight of the motorists that swept beneath. Conveniently placed bushes would allow him to arrive ahead of time, remaining unseen until the very moment of Summerbee's approach.

All he needed to do now was to rewind time, ensure he had enough fuel in the car, and source a suitably heavy object to drop on his enemy. Discovering a lump of concrete at the bridgehead would have been ideal, but a search provided nothing.

At least now Ian knew he would have to bring a bag capable of transporting the projectile and had a clear idea how much ahead of time he would need to arrive at the car park, taking into account how much the load was likely to slow him down.

When considering how far he should rewind, it seemed appropriate to begin the day from its very beginning. This time, though, he would go to work, despite the prospect of having to face an interview he could not possibly pass, believing the closer his movements mirrored the original timeline, the less chance there was of suspicion falling upon him once the deed was done.

To delete any more than five minutes, with any degree of accuracy, Ian knew he needed to fix upon an event he could recall as though it had just happened. Unfortunately, there seemed nothing obvious to which he could pin his thoughts. There was the sound of the alarm clock, but that went off every day, so there was no guarantee when that might take him to. Everything after that point was for deletion anyway: his being late for work; his calling in sick. On reflection, it seemed better to go back further, if only to find something more definite, something he wanted to keep. The answer was obvious: the call with Debbie, during which conversation she agreed to their meeting on Wednesday evening.

Ian closed his eyes and concentrated. Effort was no longer required; he just thought and he was there, holding the receiver to his ear.

'Debbie?'

'Yes, we've already established that.'

Ian felt foolish.

'Sorry, I'm a bit nervous. Have we fixed upon a date when we can meet yet?'

'You're forward aren't you,' Debbie responded, simulating effrontery.

'Sorry,' Ian apologised for a second time. 'I...I...'

'I'm free on Wednesday.'

'Wednesday would be fine,' Ian responded, breathing a sigh of relief. 'I'll pick you up at eight.'

There followed an exchange of details, a few pleasantries, and the call was done. It had not gone as smoothly as the first time, but the end result was the same and that was all that mattered.

The day drew to a close in much the same way as it had before, but this time many of the pressures that had previously accompanied him to bed had evaporated. He could sleep, comforted by the thought he knew exactly when and where to find his victim. He had a plan to kill the man; one that had every chance of success. Best of all, he had fixed a date to meet his future wife, in three days' time; the point from which he would begin his journey back to normality. His job of yesteryear was of no consequence; failing the interview was of no concern, no matter how humiliating the experience might prove to be. Once he had cemented his relationship with Debbie, his next task would be to change his career path; to what, he knew not, but he was confident it would not be built on his knowledge of export shipping.

The alarm clock sounded as harshly as before. This time though, Ian swung out of bed without delay. Having spent a short time in the bathroom, he dressed, before descending the stairs with time to spare in which to have his breakfast and find a sturdy bag; one capable of carrying whatever lump of concrete he was able to procure during the remainder of the day. Without too much difficulty, he found a small, heavy, canvas, army surplus backpack that he once used to carry his books to school. It seemed ideally suited.

At half past eight, Ian reversed off the drive and headed for the office. The journey was both simple and familiar. Back lanes avoided the majority of commuter traffic and the need to drive through the centre of town. At the mid-point, the road passed through a row of outlying houses. The council must have decided they needed a pavement, one that stretched twenty metres further than the line of properties in each direction. The project was only half complete, leaving a row of illuminated cones, a length of striped tape, a line of kerbstones, waiting to be fixed in place, and a small stack of spares.

Conveniently, nobody else was around.

There was no time for planning. Instinctively, Ian pulled over where the cones ended; at a point he judged he was not overlooked by a single window. The door of the car flew open and closed again, but remained ajar. With a quarter turn of the key, the boot lid sprung open. From the stack of spare kerbstones, pressing into the verge, Ian selected the uppermost, heaving the great weight into the back of the car. The boot lid shut, as did the driver's door, and immediately afterwards the Ford Escort was once again under way; phase one of his plan complete.

It was a strange feeling to be parking outside an office he had not visited, or even seen, in many years. Butterflies of many varieties fluttered in his stomach: those that became active on the first day of a new job; those that accompanied an interview; those that took flight when a man was planning to kill with malice aforethought.

As he locked the car door, a man approached across the car park. It was a younger version of his friend, Roland; his boss.

'Ready for the big day?' Roland asked, an encouraging smile dominating his face.

'Not entirely,' replied Ian, thinking just how little his friend appreciated the truth of what he was saying.

'You'll be fine.'

The two men made their way upstairs to their desks. It was a shock. The company had been slow to modernise, but by the time Ian had moved on to pastures new, computers had been introduced. That modernisation was yet to come. As it stood, ancient typewriters sat on equally ancient shiny black melamine desks. A huge, dated, communal telephone perched on a shelf in the middle. Next to it, a bottle of correction fluid, something that Ian had not used since the advent of the printer.

'I'll get the coffees,' Roland said, grabbing a tray from the top of a filing cabinet before heading towards the door. 'I'll get Paul one too; he'll be in in a minute.'

The temporary absence of anyone else on the section gave the interviewee time to acclimatise. He knew which desk was his and sat down, noting the swivel chair, although nearing the end of its life, was set at the perfect height for his stature.

The single drawer contained his possessions. It was as though someone else had placed them there - to make the new boy feel settled. Among the items to be found were a number of lengths of wire, bent and twisted into interesting shapes, some even linked together. These were the result of an ongoing competition between Ian and Roland, taking the art of paper clip bending to the extreme. Whatever innovation Roland had devised, Ian had always responded with something more ingenious, proving, even in those days, his artistic talents had fought for recognition.

An in-tray contained a number of orders. Roland had used a highlighter to draw attention to the most important points: who wanted what, how much and when. Piles of various shipping documents lay accessible to all three members of the section. Each form consisted of a number of titled boxes, the completion of which was self-explanatory. To make things easier, Ian remembered it was normal practice to retrieve the customer's last order and copy the details, one from the other, altering quantities as necessary. He wondered what could be easier, being reminded what it was about the job he had found so boring as to consider jumping from the window ledge.

The main form was printed in light blue ink - another reminder. The form was in fact a template, allowing various documents to be produced via a specialised photocopier, operated by a girl employed solely for that purpose. All she needed from the clerks was the template, the number of copies they required, and a list of finished documents to produce. This too was easy. Each document had a code; a simple one or two digit number. These numbers would be typed at the bottom of every template, making the task of supplying the information as simple as copying the numbers from the customer's previous form.

With the realisation he might, after all, be able to perform his tasks as he had done before, Ian's confidence grew rapidly. Such was the improvement in his mood, he even dared to imagine he could pull the rabbit from the hat and achieve the promotion he had previously written off as a hopeless cause. Whatever the case, he had less than an hour before he would find out; a thought that prompted his bladder to send signals to his brain suggesting he should pay a visit to the men's room.

Ian stepped from the main office into the corridor. Approaching from the opposite direction was a young, dark-haired female whose face was familiar, although much younger than he was used to.

'Hello Faye,' he called, cheerfully. 'How are you?'

Faye looked surprised.

'How do you know my name?' She asked, looking upon her inquisitor with suspicion.

At this point, Ian would like to have said it was because he had known her for twenty years and that he had seen her naked. However, he managed to stop himself, it being clear the two had not yet met; an easy mistake to make under the circumstances.

Just as he was about to offer an explanation, a door burst open beside them and a man swung his upper body into the corridor, his hand gripping the doorframe tightly.

'Ah, Mr Bradshaw. I thought we might do the interview a little early, if you're ready.'

The man spoke loudly; confidently.

Thoughts of needing the toilet evaporated.

'Certainly sir. Ready when you are.'

Faye's face remained a picture of surprise, even after the manager's door had shut.

'Take a seat,' directed the manager, settling himself down into a large, comfortable, leather chair situated behind a substantial, important-looking desk.

Mr Gray did not bother to introduce two other men who occupied lesser chairs, one either side of him. The company's workforce was not large and so it was accepted every employee knew everyone else, especially those in management.

Mr Pearce, to Mr Gray's left, and Mr Gainsborough, to Gray's right, both looked as though they were thoroughly enjoying the experience. Having the power to affect the future of men clearly appealed to their nature, both managers looking particularly smug; overflowing with a sense of their own self-importance.

'Tell me, why should we give you the job?' Mr Gray asked, bluntly, leading the attack.

However hard they tried, the darkly-suited trio were not going to intimidate their interviewee, who had the body of a man in his early twenties, but the maturity of someone nearly twice that age. Years of experience had taught him how to behave: to sit at the back of the chair, not perched on the front edge; to keep his hands resting on his thighs to prevent the shakes; to look into the eyes of the man who had put the question. Employing these simple techniques, Ian appeared relaxed, confident, a man who could cope with the increased responsibility the new position would bring.

'For the most part, the job of the section head is exactly the same as that of the clerk. I currently do a competent job as a clerk and I assume you accept that, otherwise I wouldn't be sitting here.'

All three interviewers looked lost for words, surprised at such candour. After a few moments of involuntary head twitching and more than one grimace, Mr Gray had to agree.

'In addition to the work I already do, as a Section Head I would be responsible for compiling the monthly figures – something I have done on numerous occasions when the Section Head has been unavailable.'

Ian delivered the statement with conviction, although he had no recollection of whether or not it was true. There being no appeal to the contrary, the interviewee assumed it was and moved on, the general principles of the role returning to him, piecemeal.

'Where the two jobs differ most is in the need for the section head to coordinate the work and drive the figures. I know how to prioritise. Were you to promote me, I'd ensure orders were dealt with in an efficient manner. I'd be a source of information and inspiration for my staff. I'm never late for work and I rarely go sick. In short, I'm reliable, I communicate well with others, staff respect my ability, and I believe I am the man for the job.'

The passion with which Ian's impromptu speech was delivered had an effect on those who sat in judgement, the trio independently coming to the same conclusion – that they had perhaps underestimated the young man who sat friendly but defiant before them.

Mr Gray spoke for the panel.

'Well, thank you Mr Bradshaw. If there's nothing else you wish to say, then you may send in the next man. Mr French I believe.'

Ian gave the next candidate the thumbs up and wished him good luck, passing him at speed as he headed for the toilet at the far end of the corridor. Ian then returned to his desk to be interrogated by Roland who wanted to hear every detail of his friend's ordeal. Lunchtime came and went, after which Ian struggled silently through an order. Thankfully nobody expected much of him, this being the day of the interview. Had they known the truth behind his anxiety, they would not have been so charitable. Although it was likely they would comprehend how traumatic the prospect of murdering someone would be, they could hardly be expected to offer sympathy.

At half past four, Roland received a brief phone call. Even as he was replacing the receiver, he turned to Ian.

'The boss wants you in his office,' he said, his face screwed up in mock pain, his acknowledgement that this was the moment of truth.

Ian rose from his chair and walked the short distance to the door of Mr Gray's inner sanctum, hoping his gait had not been too affected by nerves to be obvious.

'Come in. Take a seat.'

The manager was alone. His voice sounded warmer. Whether this was because he had good news, was trying to break bad news gently, or because he did not have to perform in front of his colleagues, the jury was still out.

'I won't beat about the bush,' he said, leaning forward, arms folded, elbows resting on the desk. 'We're giving you the job.'

The rest was waffle. Having spoken the only words Ian wanted to hear, his boss' reasons behind the decision were irrelevant.

As Ian returned to his desk, the smile upon his face told Roland all he needed to know.

'Excellent. Do you want to go for a drink after work to celebrate?' he asked, genuinely pleased for his friend.

'I'd love to, but I've got to get home. Maybe some other time.'

16

The drive to the country park went without a hitch, Ian's car passing beneath the farmer's bridge with almost an hour to spare before he was due to perform the act. He found the turn-off easily and was grateful to discover the car park was empty – no cars and no sign of dog walkers, joggers or kids on bikes.

The canvas bag chosen for the mission was strong, but Ian doubted it would survive the overland trip if it were used as a backpack in the normal way, the kerbstone being many times heavier than he would ever have imagined one to be. The bag was also rather small, the flap being too short to stretch over the concrete and fasten shut. It did, however, disguise its content. Besides, with the cargo being so heavy, the only way to bear the load was to cradle the bag in folded arms, pressed against the chest as though it were an extremely weighty baby. The canvas swaddling at least prevented sharp edges slicing and scrapping his forearms.

On the first occasion Ian had walked the route from the car park to the bridge, it had taken him half an hour. This time it took a good fifteen minutes longer, his steps being shortened by the weight of his load, and there being the need for a rest every twenty metres or so. This left only five minutes before the drop.

The plan was to loiter out of sight in nearby bushes, walk out at the last moment, to a position above the appropriate lane and drop the load on Summerbee's car as it passed below.

At eight o'clock, with ninety seconds to go and a dozen paces to cover, Ian readied himself.

Squatting on his haunches, he peeled the canvas from the kerbstone and glanced at his watch. With thirty seconds to go, he took the strain, stood tall and walked purposefully into view, counting down the last remaining seconds in his head.

'Ten elephant. Nine elephant...'

At 'five', he lifted the heavy weight onto the railing, expecting his eyes to lock immediately on to the approaching target, but instead was frustrated to catch its back end, the vehicle already passing beneath the bridge at speed. There was nothing to be done but try again.

Ian closed his eyes, rewinding the last few minutes, obliterating them from history. Again, he squatted over the stone, removed the canvas bag, took the strain and stood up. This time though, he set off ten seconds earlier than before. The movement was conducted smoothly, purposefully, bringing the heavy lump of concrete to a state of readiness, teetering on top of the railing. This time his eyes met Summerbee's vehicle, heading in his direction. There was a mark in the road; a thin line of bitumen sealing a crack that spanned almost the entire width of both lanes. As the Chrysler's front bumper reached the mark, Ian nudged the stone forward.

The moulded kerb fell, gracefully performing a half summersault before impacting heavily towards the rear of the car's sheet metal roof. Although the damage was substantial, it was nevertheless a metre behind the bull. Summerbee had not received a direct hit, nor had the impact affected control of the vehicle sufficiently to cause it to crash. It was plain to see, Ian had failed for a second time. However, his patience untested, he simply rewound again, prepared to carry out the task many times over until his goal was finally achieved. As it happened, he needed no more than a third attempt. Sending the stone on its downward journey shortly before the car reached the bitumen mark, Ian's eyes followed with satisfaction as it plunged through the windscreen on the driver's side, the resulting sound confirming a devastating impact. There was no need to watch the car's new trajectory, or to see its final resting place; the job had been done. Ian's priority was to distance himself from the scene and rely on the media to report the level of his success. In the unlikely event he had failed, he knew he could always return and try again.

His bloodstream awash with adrenalin, Ian grabbed the empty backpack and ran along the dirt track to his vehicle, not stopping once to catch his breath. There he found the car park and surrounding countryside deserted, although his tunnelled vision would have prevented him seeing anything not directly in his path, even if it had been a man waving him down. The act of getting underway was performed clumsily, overuse of the accelerator causing the Escort's spinning rear tyres to bite into the surface, sending a spray of gravel into the air, leaving the tell-tale tracks of a fast getaway. The car laid down further marks – streaks of black rubber – as the driver pulled out from the junction, onto the main road. Still breathing heavily, as though he had just collapsed over the finish line of the London marathon, the car continued at speed, away from the crash site.

The bicycle should not have been there, but it was. The driver should not have hit it, but he did, Ian's speed being far too high, his reactions far too slow. The windscreen shattered, the Escort slewed to a halt, the engine dying abruptly, producing a bubble of silence, marred only by the swish of vehicles passing at speed in the opposite direction, on the far side of the central reservation. Another vehicle stopped, the driver opening Ian's door after a long pause to ask if he was all right.

'I'm fine. What about the cyclist?'

'I think he's dead.'

The man in his forties appeared to be playing down the truth.

'You sure? Maybe I should take a look.'

'No, don't. Nobody should see that.'

Ian ignored the advice and discovered for himself the victim's head was missing, leaving no doubt as to the prognosis. Much to the surprise of the other driver, rather than experiencing shock, Ian appeared to derive comfort. What the other driver was not to know was that the youngster experienced the event as a much needed virtual slap to the face, commanding him to pull himself together. He had gone to a lot of trouble to blame Summerbee's death on a mindless act of vandalism. The plan had been executed to perfection, only to become unravelled because he had failed to remain calm post mortem.

'Weird. This is normally a busy road, yet you and I appear to be the only people on it.'

The youngster was apparently ignoring the elephant in the room. What interest was traffic when a man lay dead at his feet? The other driver was no psychiatrist but thought it best not to refocus what he assumed was a deeply traumatised mind.

'By the way the traffic is slowing up on the other carriageway, I reckon something must have happened back there.'

An erect thumb indicated the direction of Summerbee's sudden exit from the world.

'I do believe you might be right in your assumption. Now, do you think you could find a phone and call the police? I'm not sure I'm in any fit state to do so myself.'

The young man spoke like someone many years his senior. The man to whom he spoke dismissed it as further evidence of shock.

'No problem. I'll be as quick as I can. You going to be all right?'

Ian managed a smile.

'Take your time. I'm going to sit in my car for a while.'

There was no denying the cyclist was dead, but Ian knew that was not going to remain the case for long. As soon as the effects of adrenalin had subsided, he would perform a miracle, resurrecting the headless torso, leaving it for someone else to mow him down as a penalty for his stupidity. Even if it meant surrendering to the police, Ian was prepared to sit in a cell for the night if needed. From the comfort of the Escort, Ian watched as rubberneckers came to realise the item they had assumed fell of the back of a lorry was in fact a corpse. He was amused to see their reactions and the minor collisions that followed.

'Hmm.'

The dismissive note preceded the closing of his eyes and the return of the familiar buzzing sensation at the centre of his head. All of a sudden, the block of concrete was punching through Summerbee's windscreen, at which point Ian ducked out of sight before walking with purpose back to his own vehicle. On this occasion he was certain no one else was in the vicinity as he took the time to check thoroughly. The Escort left no marks in the gravel, or on the tarmac leading onto the main road. A short while later, the man who had witnessed the decapitation of a pedal cyclist drove by at a respectable speed, untroubled by ugly memories that had been sucked from his mind. Further on, there were no dead bodies littering the road, and no work for recovery vehicles on the opposite side of the crash barrier. All was good.

'You're late,' Ian's mum commented, looking up from the TV listings.

'I got that promotion,' Ian replied, cheerily. 'I've been out for a quick pint of coke to celebrate.'

'That's marvellous,' his mum responded, surreptitiously smelling her son's breath for evidence he had been driving while under the influence of something stronger than fizzy pop.

Satisfied her son was not drunk, she offered to put the kettle on and break open a fresh packet of his favourite biscuits. Ian said he thought it a great idea, but he needed a bath and would probably then go straight to bed. Pre-interview nerves had given him a sleepless night and he was now desperate to catch up.

The bath did not help. In truth, pre-interview nerves had done little to prevent him sleeping; post murder recollection did a much better job. The only thing to do with an overactive mind in a darkened room, hour after hour, was to try to convince himself what he had done had been necessary and proportionate to the danger Summerbee had posed. However legitimate the act had been – however much his hands had been forced – he had killed a man. He was a murderer – a fact that would remain with him - be a part of him - for the rest of his life.

At work the next morning, Ian appeared distant, prompting several of his colleagues to ask whether he was all right. His stock answer blamed the interview of the previous day; how it had prevented him switching off when the time came for him to go to bed. He assured all concerned he would be back to his old self in the morning, although that seemed unlikely, given his mind was out of synch with his body and he had now murdered twice, it mattering not that the victim was the same in both cases.

In truth, insomnia was only partially to blame. There was guilt too, but perhaps the greatest factor was the waiting; waiting to get his hands on the evening edition of the local paper. Only then would he know for certain that Summerbee was dead.

Ian was the first to leave work, turning left out of the gate, not right, steering his vehicle in the direction of a lone newsagent – a keen spot for pilfering children on their way to and from school. Despite Belgrove having turned out more than an hour before, several groups of small people remained outside, each with a nucleus of a boy on a bike, leaning against a convenient metal pillar or a lamppost.

The Gazette lay on the bottom shelf, its front page dominated by a single picture beneath a striking headline, both confirming Summerbee's life had been cut short. The image showed the twisted wreckage of a car that had sustained considerable damage, having first been hit by a falling lump of concrete and then been involved in a collision with something solid, and that was before firemen had set to work with various cutting tools. The photographer had caught the scene in great detail but Ian was not interested in any part of it, the headline stealing his attention.

Two Die, One Injured in Act of Vandalism

Ian's heart missed a beat. He felt sick.

It was only as he read the accompanying print that he discovered the true horror of what he had done. The article did not refer to the death of just one young man, but also to that of an entirely innocent woman, and to the serious injury of a third person who had been travelling with the unscheduled victim.

'Are you going to buy that?'

Losing much of his profit to wayward school kids, the shopkeeper was not going to entertain further loss, allowing members of the public to use his shop as a library.

'Sorry.'

Having paid for the paper, Ian stepped out in to the evening sunshine, keen to finish reading the article. Aware the environment was not ideal, he waited until he was once again cocooned inside his vehicle. Even then he felt exposed – as though someone would see what he was reading and guess he had something to do with it.

The article reported details already known to him and those he had not witnessed. The account was certain to evoke trauma in anyone who read the article – more so in the man whose actions resulted in its writing.

'...The driver, Mr Michael Summerbee, 24, was killed instantly when a kerbstone, thrown from an overhead bridge, ploughed through the windscreen of his car...The stricken vehicle was in collision with a second car, the driver of which, Mrs Eileen Cole, 47, died in hospital last night from her injuries. Her daughter and sole passenger, Mrs Sarah Benson, 25, received multiple injuries and had to be cut free by the fire service. She is now in intensive care and her condition is said to be critical...Mrs Cole leaves a husband and one further child...The death appears to have been the act of vandals. Police are appealing for witnesses.'

Ian's immediate thought was to return to the bridge and there keep hold of the kerbstone, thus ensuring the Coles and Bensons did not become accidental victims. However, there were counter-arguments.

As it stood, Summerbee was dead and no longer presented a threat to either Ian or to the family that would one day be restored to him. It was regrettable that in securing this degree of personal safety, his actions had resulted in their being two unanticipated casualties. Of course, there was always the option of him going back and trying again, but it was hard to see what modifications he could make, given the same situation, that might prevent unnecessary injury. There was the option of a different venue, but there were no guarantees he would find a better opportunity, or that in doing so, he would avoid killing other innocent people. On the other hand, how could he ever justify not restoring the lives of Mrs Cole and her daughter? At least two families would be devastated by what had happened – there would be a widow, possibly children without a grandparent, and certainly a woman with mental and physical scars to bear for the rest of her life.

The decision was his alone to make. It would have been nice to talk it over with someone first, but with whom: his best friend; his work colleagues; his mum? The truth was that none of them would believe he had the gift to turn back time and they would be horrified on hearing his confession he had murdered Summerbee, never mind that he had been the cause of a second death and a critical injury.

Ian knew in his heart that the deceased woman had to live again, but on the other hand, there was no need to be hasty; no reason not to give himself time to consider other ways he might be able to rid the world of Mike Summerbee – ways that brought about only one unfortunate death and allowed Ian to escape a sentence of life imprisonment. Yes, the families would be left to suffer, but after a time they would not and would never have been.

Sitting alone in his car, the voice of inspiration remained silent; no hints or tips that might form the seed of an idea. The enormity of the situation he had caused blanked all other thought. What he needed was to change the subject and hope that something popped into his mind when he least expected it. A drink with his future wife in an out-of-the-way pub would have been ideal for the purpose, but she was unavailable until the following evening. Looking for an alternative, Ian's thoughts turned to Nicola, the girl he had admired from a distance during his school years and whose telephone number he had in his wallet. He knew how this might look to Debbie – that she could never be convinced he was not seeking to be unfaithful – but his desires were innocent, regardless of what she would say if she knew. The only reason he considered such behaviour at all was the knowledge the event would be deleted, along with the recent deaths, as soon as he had his solution. No harm could come of it, of that he was sure.

17

There seemed an eternity between the ring tone being answered and the coins being accepted, connecting the call.

'Nicola?' Ian asked, pumping a second coin in to the slot.

'Yes.'

'It's Ian – Ian Bradshaw; from the school reunion.'

He felt foolish having to explain who he was; inviting the possibility she would reply with an awkward 'no' – either because he had genuinely gone from her mind, or she had sobered up and come to her senses. At least he had a trick up his sleeve, being able to delete the call and save his money at the first hint of denial. However, he need not have worried, his self-doubt being quashed within less than a second.

'Ian,' Nicola responded, brightly. 'I'm so glad you called. What can I do for you?'

There was quite a lot that Ian would like her to do for him - do to him - have him do to her, but none of that was going to happen.

'I wondered if you would like to go out for a drink this evening. No ulterior motive. I just need to unwind.'

'Great! What time?'

'Eight-thirty?'

'Excellent. There's a little pub down the road from me called 'The Bell'. How about we meet there?'

'Sounds good, but I don't know where you live.'

'Oh, sorry, I wasn't thinking.'

She was extremely good at giving directions; so good that Ian could almost picture the journey in his mind.

'Great, I'll see you soon.'

If at all possible, Nicola looked more attractive when they met at the bar than when he had chanced upon her at the school reunion, and in all the years he had leched over her quietly in the classroom. She lowered herself onto a seat in a quiet corner of the pub, keeping her knees locked firmly together to maintain her modesty, her skirt being so very short; so very tight. Ian could not help but steal a glimpse of the exposed thigh on display beside him. It was sufficiently distracting that he almost missed his companion's first question. Thankfully his ears worked independently of the lust centre of his brain.

'Did you hear the news?'

'What news?'

'It was on the radio. Michael Summerbee was killed last night. Some vandals dropped a lump of concrete from a bridge onto his car.'

Ian did well to reply without giving anything away, either by word or body language.

'Who's Michael Summerbee?' he asked, innocently, concentrating hard on a beer mat that lay on the table in front of him, trying to fight the emotions that suddenly churned his stomach.

'He was at the reunion the other night. Didn't you know him?'

'No.'

Ian hoped he sounded convincing, but was all too aware his voice suffered a slight tremble. 'Anyway, how do you know the man in the news was your chap?'

'He's not my chap, as you call him.'

'Sorry.'

'There can't be many people around with a name like that; not aged twenty-four anyway. And they described his car.'

Ian found himself lost for words, but managed to cover the moment with a stock expression of solemnity. Inwardly, he was wishing she would change the subject, but she did not.

'Someone else died as well.'

Ian did not need reminding of the fact. The very reason he had arranged to meet Nicola was so he might forget, at least for the duration of the evening, that another person had died and another had been seriously injured, thanks to his actions.

'Vandals eh?' he said, shaking his head subtly in mock disbelief.

'That's what the police think. Probably youngsters who don't realise it's not a game.'

'Probably.'

He paused for a moment.

'Terrible though, even if I didn't know him.'

'I knew him a bit. I was talking to him at the reunion. He seemed a little weirder than I remembered. Kept on about déjà vu. Said he'd been experiencing it a lot lately. Said it was not like normal déjà vu when you think you've done the exact same thing already. He said it was as though he was about to do something, remembered he'd done it before, and stopped himself doing it again.'

Ian's eyes widened. The words she spoke echoed his own experience when the first signs of his emerging gift had appeared. Summerbee had been far closer to becoming a danger than he had realised. It made the situation far clearer. Ideally, over the coming days, he would find a better way of despatching his enemy, but if he could not, the man would have to stay dead, regardless of the consequences for the Coles and the Bensons.

The remainder of the evening passed quickly. Nicola was good company, the conversation being helped along by several more drinks than Ian could afford to buy.

Walking from the stale atmosphere of the pub, back into the fresh air, both he and Nicola instantly became aware just how much their alcohol consumption had affected them.

'We should get taxis, Nicola suggested, slurring her words slightly.

'No, I'll be all right,' Ian replied, not wanting the inconvenience of having to fetch his car in the morning, or the expense of a cab he could ill afford.

Besides, he had to get home. It was a weekday and he would have to get up early for work.

'You've had far too much to drive,' Nicola said, trying to talk sense into him.

'I'll tell you what,' Ian reasoned. 'I'll take you home so you don't have to drive. If we crash or I get stopped by the police, we'll take a taxi instead.'

Even under the influence, Nicola saw Ian's cryptic offer as a reference to the conversation she reported having with Michael Summerbee at the reunion. Bearing in mind the man had died only hours earlier, she took it as a comment made in the worst possible taste.

'Are you taking the piss out of Michael?'

'No, I am not,' Ian replied, surprised and confused by her interpretation of his suggestion. 'I think you're right though, I am too drunk to drive.'

Excesses of alcohol prevented Nicola from giving proper consideration to his response, leaving her mind blank, unable to fix on anything specific. Ian took the opportunity to distract her further.

'Maybe we could get a taxi back to your place. If I get up early enough I can pick my car up in the morning and still make it into work.'

'That sounds like a really bad chat-up line if you ask me,' Nicola said, having entirely forgotten her outrage. 'As it happens, I was going to ask if you wanted to stay. I do hope that you're not too drunk.'

Ian could not believe what he had just heard. The girl that had been unobtainable for so many years had laid it to him on a plate.

Having experienced a pleasant evening, successfully distracting himself from the revelations, printed across the front page of the local newspaper, there was one course of action Ian knew he should take. Nevertheless, one part of him urged the other to let this particular chain of events continue. If necessary he could be sober at a moment's notice, sitting in his car outside the newsagent's with a valuable new piece of information about Summerbee, one that would spur him on to seek an alternative solution – and fast. In the meantime, there was the possibility he might have a nightcap with Nicola, bed down on the sofa, and in his relaxed state, realise the solution as he drifted off to sleep.

The taxi drew up outside a modest two-up, two-down, mid-terraced property, probably built in the seventies. Large enough for one person, or perhaps a couple, it did not seem big enough to house a mature family with a twenty-four year old daughter. There could be only one conclusion.

'Is this your place?'

'Yep, all mine. Well, at least one-three-hundredth is mine. The rest belongs to the mortgage company. I've only had it a month,' Nicola replied, a proud confidence banishing any hint of an alcohol-induced slur.

Ian was impressed by Nicola's spending power. The house was not at all grand, but she could at least afford to fly the nest.

She led the way through the front door to an open-plan living room; stairs to one side; no hallway.

'Sit down,' she said. 'I'll make us a drink.'

Left alone on the settee, Ian felt slightly awkward.

'You can put the tele on if you like, but it's all repeats these days,' Nicola called from the kitchen, the sound of the kettle being filled clearly audible in the background.

'Don't I know it,' Ian replied ironically.

The television remained switched off.

'Tea or coffee?'

A few minutes passed before Nicola re-entered the room holding two steaming cups. Placing them on a small table, convenient to both of them, she settled herself down, choosing to sit tight up against her guest.

'Do you remember Physics lessons?' she asked. 'And the way I used to rub my chest into your back while we were all gathered round to watch an experiment.'

Ian nodded.

'I thought that was a happy accident,' he said, innocently.

'It was my way of trying to get you to notice me, but it was obviously too subtle for you.'

'Subtle? You terrified me. I never dreamt someone of your calibre would be interested in me.'

'Well, I was.'

She oozed self-confidence. By the way she looked and by the fact she could afford a mortgage at the age of twenty-four, evidently she had the right to. Ian was not nearly so self-assured, even though he had lived for getting on twice her years.

'Would it be all right if I crashed on your sofa tonight?' he asked, hoping she would simply agree, saving him from any moral dilemma.

'No,' Nicola said firmly. 'I've got other plans for you. Drink up.'

With this, she stood up, making it clear her guest should do the same. He had no choice but to comply. She moved closer, looked meaningfully into his eyes and then slipped her hand into the waistband of his trousers. Then, gripping his belt tightly, she led him towards the stairs.

An hour later, Ian was lying on his back, more relaxed than he could remember ever having been before. He stared at the ceiling, his fingers interlocked on his bare chest, a self-satisfied smile etched onto his face.

'Wow,' Nicola exclaimed. 'We're going to do that again.'

Even if he said so himself, Ian had performed brilliantly. Surprisingly so, considering how much alcohol he had consumed during the course of the evening. He could only conclude that the restored fitness of his youth, coupled with the experience his true age had given him, was to thank for what he had just achieved.

'You bet,' Ian replied enthusiastically. 'But give me a minute to recover.'

'A minute?' Nicola looked doubtful.

'Twenty then.'

'Okay, I think you've earned it. In the meantime, I'm going to get a drink of water. All this has made me really thirsty.'

She climbed off the bed and walked unashamed by her nakedness across the bedroom towards the door. Ian's eyes followed her all the way, studying each blemish-free curve of her body.

As soon as Nicola was out of sight, the realisation of what he had done burst into Ian's thoughts. For the very first time in his life he had been unfaithful to the only woman he had ever loved. The fact they had not yet gone on their first date was merely a technicality. Even though no one else knew, in his mind, he was still a happily married man. Even if he tried to ease his conscience by falling back on the fact he and Debbie were not yet officially an item, he knew how it would make her feel if she were to discover he had fitted in a night of passion with another woman while he waited for their first date. Rewinding the evening would remove any danger she would ever find out, but it would do nothing to wipe the guilt from his mind. That said, before he could act, Nicola returned to the bedroom, at which point Ian's subconscious took control of his groin, raising it to attention, dispelling any thoughts of his wife-to-be.

'So, how's life treating you?' she asked casually, rolling onto her side to face him.

Ian jerked involuntarily in response to her hand taking hold of him gently, massaging him back to full strength. Her eyes bade him to answer, despite the distraction.

Ian gathered his thoughts, it being hard to get beyond the fact he had become a murderer.

'I did pass an interview for promotion this morning.'

'That's good,' Nicola said cheerily, her eyes temporarily diverting towards her moving hand.

'Not really,' he countered, his voice broken with pleasure. 'It won't lead to anything. I'll still be stuck in a dead-end office job for the rest of my life.'

'You don't know that. Nobody knows what the future has in store for them.'

'Don't they? My only consolation is that I'll land up having a beautiful wife, two children - a boy and a girl - and they'll both go to university and make me proud.'

'Well, there you go then,' Nicola said, not sure how to take her lover's ramblings.

'The thing is,' Ian continued, 'I'm already beginning to forget what they look like and I haven't even got a photo to remember them by.'

Thankfully, Nicola missed what he was saying as she chose that moment to massage herself with the tip of his erection.

'Anyway, what have you been doing since leaving school?'

Nicola's response was spoken on a wave of underlying pleasure, her response punctuated with a series of escaping breaths.

'I've been very lucky really. I own my own business.'

'Really,' Ian was clearly both surprised and impressed.

His single-word answer, delivered with a feeble grunt, implied he wanted to know more.

'Yep. We make displays. You know, when a museum wants a model of a castle, we make it – the model, the information boards, even the display case if they want.'

'I'm impressed, but is there much call for it?'

'You'd be surprised. We bring proposed building developments to life; we produce railway layouts for toy shops; we've even made a model of a prison.'

'That sounds a bit dodgy doesn't it?'

'It's not for the criminals you fool; it was for the prison - to show people where things are in an emergency.'

'Oh, I see. Sounds like a brilliant way to earn a living.'

'It is.'

Judging by the way she spoke, even though she was well on her way to a second orgasm, it was clear her business was what made her tick. It was lovely to see a person so enthused, and her feelings were proving infectious.

'Hey, you were good at art at school weren't you? I remember how jealous I was that you were better than me.'

'I was better than everyone – top of the year, every year.'

'Yes, I remember. So, why didn't you go into design or something?'

Ian shrugged his shoulders, simultaneously partially closing his eyes, issuing two further grunts, this time more powerful.

'Maybe you should come and work for me.'

Ian's inability to speak was taken mistakenly as an indication he was not sold on the idea.

'I'd pay more than you're probably getting doing office work,' Nicola continued, feeling the need to make her offer sound more attractive, but she had misjudged the moment. Ian would have gladly worked for nothing just to be given a chance like this. It was a fact he had been good at art during his schooldays - exceptionally good - and he still was. Only the drudgery of office life had kept his talents subdued. Even so, he still liked to draw and scratch-build models from time to time.

'I'd like that. Aaagh.'

'That's a deal then. You must come to my workshops and show me what you can do, and then you'll work for me.'

'Trrr-y and stop me.'

'I think we should celebrate,' she said, wrapping her legs around his. 'What do you say?'

Here was a complication Ian had not foreseen. He wanted the job. He wanted it badly. The fact he felt suddenly more alive than he had done in many, many years told him that. On the other hand, it had been his intention to rewind time so the events of the evening – the murder and the affair - had never happened. If he did so now, Nicola's offer would cease to exist too.

'Look, Nicola. I've really enjoyed tonight and I really want to come and work for you but…' He searched for the right words. 'But, I'm going out on a date with Debbie tomorrow night and I have the feeling it's going to be the real thing. If she ever found out about us, it would be over between Debbie and me before it even started.'

There was a pause during which time Ian waited nervously. There was the very real chance Nicola would take the news badly, having thought their relationship was going to be 'the real thing'. She might be the spiteful type. Worse, she might be the moral kind who would feel it her duty to tell Debbie everything. Finally, Nicola put Ian out of his misery.

'Don't worry,' she said. 'We're both adults. I won't tell anyone if you don't.'

She sounded sincere, although Ian was not sure how good a judge of character he was under the circumstances. He knew the offer of a new career might be clouding his judgement, or the fact an extremely attractive and naked young woman was about to have sex with him for a second time.

He smiled.

'It'll be our little secret.'

She guided him inside.

'Your Debbie's a lucky girl. You're a great fuck.'
***

Ian woke from a restful sleep with a fresh plan of action on his mind.

'Ahem, Roland Marsh speaking.'

'Roland, it's Ian,' he spoke weakly, his mind adopting the part of a man who was on his death bed. 'I'm not coming in today. I must have eaten something that didn't agree with me. I've been on the toilet all night.'

'Nasty.'

'I'll probably be back tomorrow. With any luck, I'll be better by then.'

'Okay, mate. Take it easy.'

'I will.'

Having returned the receiver to its rest, Ian lay back on the bed, slapped both his outstretched arms on top of the duvet, turned his head to one side and smiled.

'Done.'

'You've got the day off?'

'Yep.'

'Good,' Nicola spoke seductively. 'Now that's sorted, you can poke me one last time and then we must be leaving for the office.'

Playfully, Ian took Nicola at her word. With an exaggerated movement, he extended his index finger and prodded the flesh of her upper arm.

'Like that, do you mean, boss?' he asked jokingly, feigning submissiveness.

'Don't you go giving me that 'boss' bit just yet. A lot depends on how well you perform today.'

'Do you mean today, or just the next twenty minutes?'

'Cheeky.'

'Seriously though, we are agreed this is a one off.' Ian's tone had changed, indicating his concerns were genuine. 'After today you've got to forget any of this ever happened.'

Nicola looked her bedfellow in the eye and replied with a degree of sobriety to match.

'The only way I'm likely to forget anything is if you bonk my brains out.'

A wry smile twisted one corner of her mouth.

'Very funny. Seriously though, I don't want to mess things up with Debbie.'

'Don't worry lover boy, I won't tell a soul.'

Having showered, there was no time to retrieve Ian's vehicle. Instead, he and his potential new boss travelled together in hers. It was small, but nearly new and top of the range, boasting optional-extra metallic paintwork and a stripe down the side.

Ian did not feel at all uncomfortable now his one-night stand was at an end. As for his short-term lover, she seemed even more relaxed about the situation; as though she was no stranger to the morning after.

Nicola's business premises were one of many almost identical units to occupy the industrial estate. Constructed from variously formed sheets of corrugated steel, painted blue, it looked as though it had been erected overnight and inspired little confidence it would still be around in another fifty years. It was, however, clean and modern, giving the right first impression to customers who called there.

A large shuttered door dominated the front of the building. To its left, a conventional entrance provided access to visitors, clearly signposted, making it clear where they should go.

Inside, the reception was small but welcoming.

Off to one side was a comfortably appointed room where clients could discuss their needs over a cup of freshly percolated coffee. Between this room and the receptionist's desk, a door led through to the main workshop where a small team beavered away, turning two-dimensional drawings into three-dimensional representations of buildings and landscapes. Another area played host to a second team who worked to produce the stands on which the finished product would be displayed, and cabinets if the model was destined for a less 'hands-on' use. A third team worked to produce information boards, describing in words and photographs what the models depicted.

The workforce was not chatting excitedly, nor were they smiling uncontrollably, yet it was somehow evident they loved what they were doing. Perhaps it was Ian's own desires to join them that influenced how he perceived their morale, but he thought not.

A flight of stairs - industrial in appearance - led to the first floor where further rooms provided an area for accounts, sales and purchasing, and for Nicola's own office. Finally, at the far end of the building, there was a small kitchen, toilet facilities, and a cleaning cupboard. All in all, Nicola had herself a small but impressive operation.

Throughout the guided tour, Ian had been introduced to many of the workers. He should have been nervous – the potential new boy being shown where he might work if his interview was successful - but he was not. Knowing the boss made all the difference, making him feel more like an invited guest than a potential employee.

The tour ended back in the reception area.

'So, what do you think?' Nicola asked, proudly.

'Very nice,' Ian replied, always one for understatement.

'Well, you got through the sift last night. Now let's see if you're good enough for the job.'

Ian gulped almost audibly as she spoke and again as she led him through to the confines of the consultation room. Here she offered him a chair. He took it and sat perched nervously on the edge, his knotted hands resting on the table in front of him, his eyes fixed upon the jumble of fingers.

She offered him a drink. His mind felt slow, as though it were translating her words from a different language. This caused there to be a delay where it was not natural for one to exist. The question had been simple and the answer should not have required much consideration. He either wanted a coffee, or he did not; it was as simple as that. In the end, he declined. Saying yes would have meant further questions: black or white; with or without sugar; was it too dark for him? Each question resulting in another delay; another sign that perhaps he was naturally slow witted.

She moved away, giving no indication she had noticed the pause. Ian could hear her rifling through a four-drawer cabinet in the corner of the room behind where he sat. He could hear the click, click of suspension files knocking, one against another. Then he could hear the sound of one such file being pulled from its resting place and the drawer being slid shut, ending with a decisive 'clonk'.

'Yes, this will do,' she said, without offering explanation or comment regarding the particular file she had chosen.

She led Ian back into the workshop, to a secondary, but none-the-less well-equipped workbench. Here she beckoned Ian to sit down, this time on a stool.

'I want you to interpret these photographs into a white-card scale model of the building they depict,' she spoke in a suddenly business-like manner. 'It is to remain unpainted. I'll be looking at the quality of finish, what details you find necessary to include to achieve the overall finished effect, and how much you can do in the allotted time.'

He felt nervous. He was no longer the friend of the boss. He was an interviewee for a job; one he desperately wanted, but also one he was not at all sure he was qualified to do.

When the time was up, Nicola returned, hoping above all things that Ian had made the grade. She was not disappointed.

'Exquisite,' she said, simply, holding within the tips of her fingers the flawless representation of a photograph-brought-to-life. 'You have many talents Mr Bradshaw. It seems you model every bit as well as you shag.'

'Thank you,' Ian responded, accepting the double compliment with a slight reddening of his cheeks.

'Can you start on Monday?'

'Try and stop me.'

18

Debbie lived with her parents. She could be seen waving them goodbye as she stepped from the front door, heading for Ian's car before he even had the chance to turn off the ignition.

Leaning over to open the passenger side, Ian greeted his date with a smile so alive it could only be genuine. Debbie matched it and swung herself down onto the seat beside him.

'Evening,' Ian said, smoothly.

'Evening,' Debbie reciprocated. 'I'm glad you were so punctual. I was nervous enough, wondering whether or not you'd turn up. If you'd made me wait even a minute, I'd have been a gibbering wreck.'

'Why on Earth would you think I wouldn't show up?' Ian asked, there being a note of disbelief in his voice.

'I don't know,' Debbie answered innocently. 'It seemed too good to be true.'

Ian had forgotten how she had always harboured such a low opinion of herself, an attitude he had never understood. The way she looked, the way she thought, the way she was - how could the whole world not want her?

'Listen Debbie; let's get things straight right from the word go. I'd have cut off my leg with a blunt picnic fork if that is what it took to make this date. Believe me, you'd be worth it.'

Debbie smiled again. It was a lovely smile, one that would make the evening a success even if she were to do nothing else.

'So, what have you been up to?' she asked, trying to detract attention from the damaging first impression she believed herself to have given. The question, simple as it was, brought suddenly to Ian's mind the events of the hours preceding their meeting.

'I have had the most fantastic day,' he enthused, pointing at her with a limp hand.

Debbie's ears pricked up, her every atom genuinely interested to know what had happened to make the day so memorable.

'When we went to the reunion the other evening, I met a woman called Nicola Appelby. You won't have met her, but she was a girl in my form. It turns out that she runs her own business, and she's given me a job. I start Monday. I can't believe my luck. It's the sort of break I've only ever dreamt of.'

Ian spoke without pause, fired up by his news.

'That's excellent,' Debbie congratulated as he finished.

It was clear she was as happy at hearing the news as if it had been coming direct from the mouth of one of her closest family members. The fact she was so pleased for a man she had met only twice went some way to demonstrate her true nature.

She asked for more details. Ian was glad to furnish them, confident she was not just saying it to be polite. The more he spoke of his new career path, the more excited he became. Monday would not come soon enough.

'Do you know what I am going to do?' Ian asked, rhetorically. 'When I get into work tomorrow, I'm going to tell my boss just where he can stick his job.'

Debbie looked worried.

'Sounds like fun, but you should be careful,' she warned. 'I mean, you might be burning your bridges, mightn't you?'

'Just recently, I find people tend to forgive and forget the things I say. Well, forget anyway,' he said, amusing himself.

Neither his expression nor his words managed to impress.

'I don't understand,' his date responded, simply.

Ian noted the look of innocent puzzlement on her face and felt instantly ashamed he had been unfaithful to her, albeit technically.

'Sorry,' he said. 'I get nervous at times like this. It makes me come out with all sorts of rubbish.'

'I know what you mean,' Debbie responded, brightly. 'I'm always wishing I could take back something I've said. That way people wouldn't think I'm an idiot.'

'You're no idiot - you're lovely - but I agree it might be nice to be able to take things back. On the other hand, even if you could – things you'd said; things you'd done – you'd know that you had said and done those things. The person who had been wronged would be spared, but the person who had done wrong would continue to feel the guilt. I suppose it's only right that he should continue to suffer; as punishment, and to make sure he didn't do it again.'

Debbie looked at him curiously.

'Boy, you must be nervous,' she said, her words superimposed over a feeble laugh. 'You're not making any sense at all.'

Ian dismissed his comments with an apologetic smile.

There followed a lull in the conversation during which he studied Debbie's face with great interest. He found he no longer wished to discuss his job. Instead he wanted to make love to her with as much tenderness and devotion as he had only days before, but years in the future. His desires, however, were not possible to fulfil. The memory of their dating was fogged by the passing of twenty plus years of married life, but some details remained. She had not been quite so ready to give herself up to him as had been the case with Nicola. He wanted her then and there, but knew he would have to wait. Given time and patience, everything would come to him and then he would satisfy her as he had done Nicola. Together with this thought came another - Nicola might already have developed an insatiable appetite; the younger version of his wife, on the other hand, had not. She had taken years of gentle persuasion and encouragement to reach her full repertoire. If he went in now, both guns blazing, she was sure to be shocked, perhaps sufficiently so to kill their relationship dead.

The evening came to a close, ending with a kiss and a promise to meet again after work on Monday. Both parties would have preferred their next liaison to be sooner, but Debbie had long-standing commitments she would find difficult to break. Realising the pressure she was under to do so, Ian immediately put her mind at ease. He knew they would have the rest of their lives together. Taken in the context of the bigger picture, a weekend would make no difference at all. He knew this as fact, yet he could not tell her. Instead, he stressed it was wrong to let people down, reassuring words Debbie was both relieved and pleased to accept.

The night brought restful, rejuvenating sleep. On waking, Ian left for the office, a spring of purpose in his step, a permanent smile distorting his face. The task before him was a rare pleasure indeed. There was the satisfaction of leaving a job he hated, of seeing the shock on his manager's face when he realised his employee was not only snubbing his nose at the company, but also at the promotion he had so graciously awarded him. In the future, Ian had practised this moment, unleashing a torrent of abuse upon his boss only to have his sense of regret trigger the rewinding process, retracting his statement so it had never happened. This time though, whatever he chose to say would be allowed to stick.

'Morning,' he said, on seeing his friend Roland, who was already seated at his desk.

'Feeling better?' Roland asked, pleased Ian had returned before too much damage had been done with regard to his new position.

'Much better thank you.'

The first surprise of the morning was the fact that, having settled himself at his desk, Ian then failed to do a single stroke of work, choosing instead to swivel in his chair; to bend paper clip after paper clip, forming them into ever more elaborate and interesting shapes; and doodle works of art on the backs customers' pending orders.

The second surprise of the morning came when, without comment or warning, the distracted employee rose from his desk, made his way to the manager's office and entered without knocking. The door opened again a few minutes later, Ian emerging wearing the same unnaturally wide grin that had been fixed on his face since his bedside alarm marked the start of a new day. The door closer did its job. As it did so, Mr Gray's apoplectic voice could be heard launching gobbets of spittle across the room.

'He didn't take that very well,' Ian said, answering the enquiring expression of the secretary who rushed in to see what on Earth was wrong.

When Ian returned to his desk, it was with a round of hot drinks and the disposition of a true sociopath, seemingly without the slightest care for what he had just done.

'What was all that about?' Roland asked quietly, his eyes wide, his face twitching.

'I resigned,' Ian answered coyly, 'and I may also have told him a few home truths. I don't think he liked it.'

Just how much Mr Gray disliked it was revealed moments later when the door to the main office flew open. The manager's face, purple in colour, carried two angry eyes that glared directly at the man responsible for such a rapid rise in his blood pressure.

'I want you gone from this building within fifteen minutes. You are never to set foot in it again and don't expect a reference,' he said venomously, before leaving just as violently as he had come.

The weekend came and went. Unable to spend any part of it in the company of his girlfriend - a term that would take some getting used to - there were limited alternative ways of passing the time. As he grew older, television had become of less and less importance to him. Now that every programme, including the news, was a repeat, his desire to watch it had almost totally vanished. Thus, he spent much of the day walking alone, being reminded of the countryside as it had looked before housing developers built on it to its destruction. Already there were signs of the unceasing creep of civilisation into the untamed wilderness. There had always been progress, but it was at this time the land immediately surrounding his neighbourhood had begun to fall victim. It made him sad.

Ian's state of melancholy was no longer apparent when he woke on Monday morning. Nicola had asked him to go in at ten o'clock on his first day to ensure she was there to settle him in. He was up and ready to go far ahead of time.

On his arrival, a quarter of an hour early, he reported to the receptionist; a friendly and well-groomed woman in her mid-thirties. She offered him a seat, a coffee and a newspaper. He declined all but the chair, it seeming wrong that a fellow employee should pamper him.

Nicola's appearance, shortly afterwards, dispensed with the need for idle conversation, something for which Ian was eternally grateful, that ability having always featured high on his list of shortcomings. She took him directly to her office upstairs and ushered him inside. Following close behind, she closed the door, remaining just inside the room, her fingers still gripping the handle.

'Help yourself to coffee,' she offered in a friendly tone, indicating the makings on a tray, set on a low filing cabinet behind him.

Ian noted she did not move from the door. Either she felt the need to demonstrate their respective positions within the company by getting him to do something subservient, or she was simply keen to maintain her control over the only means of egress. He preferred to believe it to be the former.

Ian felt the weight and momentum of the kettle. It was full. He flicked the switch, picked up the jar of coffee, removed the lid, plunged the teaspoon into the granules and measured a portion into his cup. Then, with jar and spoon hovering over a second cup, he turned his head to face his new boss.

'Would you like one?' he asked politely.

He felt infinitely more relaxed than he had done at the interview five days before. Being a businesswoman first and foremost, it was understandable that Nicola had shown no favour when it came to determining whether or not he was the man for the job. With that unpleasantness now in the past, it seemed their special relationship had been restored.

'Thank you,' she answered simply, not moving from the door.

'Milk?'

'Please.'

Ian poured from a carton into both cups. It was plain these facilities were never meant to be seen by anyone other than employees. A jar and a carton would not maintain the image that the percolator in the consultation room downstairs had set out to achieve.

'Sugar?'

'One.'

The kettle must have been recently used as steam began to billow from the spout just as the cups were ready to receive water. All was silent save for the sound of pouring and of hissing as water splashed back on the bared hot internal surfaces.

The teaspoon clinked twice against the rim of each of the cups before being placed down with a small clatter on the plastic tray. Ian picked up his cup by the handle, Nicola's by the body, his fingertips bearing the pain of heat long enough to hand it to her.

'Thank you.'

It was clear, Nicola was not as relaxed as her new employee.

'Is something troubling you?' Ian asked, his ability to detect emotions being far more attuned now than when he had first experienced the age of twenty-four.

'No,' she replied, but her body language spoke differently. 'Did you enjoy your date?'

Unrelated to anything that had gone before, this obviously went to the heart of what Nicola was truly thinking. Immediately Ian assumed the worst, anticipating her announcement that their unwritten agreement to forget their one-night-stand was about to fall within the first hour of him starting work.

'Yes, thank you,' he replied, coyly, certain in his own mind what was to come next.

'You'll be seeing her again?'

Nicola was painfully slow getting to the point.

'Yes. It appears we were meant for each other. I'm sure of it,' Ian said, declaring his position.

'Did you sleep with her?' Nicola spoke casually, her voice failing to disguise an undercurrent of something approaching awkwardness.

'I really shouldn't answer that, and you really shouldn't be asking it,' Ian said as tactfully as possible, hoping she could be persuaded to change the subject.

'No, of course not,' she responded. 'It's just that if you had, I imagine she'd have enjoyed it as much as I did.'

Tact had not worked, but what else was there? If he became abrupt, she might take offence and that might lead to him losing his dream job even before he had begun.

'Nicola,' he began, trying to sound concurrently sympathetic, serious and mature. 'This is making me feel really awkward. I've just jacked my job in, I've given up promotion and as a result, I'm feeling more than a tad vulnerable right now. Believe me, I want to work for you. It could be great for both of us, but you're beginning to make me wonder if I've done the right thing.'

There was a short pause while Nicola took in what had been said. Then she smiled - an embarrassed, humble smile.

'I'm sorry. You're just too damn good. I guess I'm a little jealous. I promise I won't say another word. Will you forgive me?'

Their one night of passion had meant something to her. More so since Ian had made it clear it meant less to him by immediately having gone on a date with another woman. In hindsight, it was amazing she was not more upset; more amazing still that she had apologised for reactions most might consider quite reasonable. It was true she had broken her promise never to mention the subject again, but she seemed genuinely to regret her display of jealousy and there was no reason to believe there would be a reoccurrence.

'No harm done,' Ian responded graciously. 'Shall we drink our coffee and then you can show me what you want me to do.'

During the afternoon, Ian experienced something he had never associated with work before. So engrossed had he become in what he was doing that he failed to realise it was time to go home. In all probability, he would have remained oblivious to the fact had it not been for one of his new co-workers tapping him on the shoulder as he gathered his coat on his way out of the door.

An almost perfect day ended perfectly, his embryonic relationship with Debbie continuing to grow exponentially. He had feared their true age difference might have been a problem – that they might no longer have anything in common. He need not have worried. She was the same person – infectiously full of life, kind, thoughtful and beautiful. With regards to how she perceived him, she could only see how 'right' things were. They had clicked from the first. The way he spoke to her, acted with her, it was as though they had always known each other.

There was no need to mention Nicola at all, but in Debbie's presence, Ian felt compelled to tell the truth, or as much of it as he thought prudent. In answer to her question as to how his first day had gone, he had to mention the events of the morning.

'It turns out my new boss used to have a bit of a thing for me back when we were at school together, and I never realised.'

Debbie shifted uncomfortably in her seat, but remained silent and attentive.

'Anyway, when she wanted to go out for a drink with me the other night, I just thought it was to catch up on old times. We talked about what we had done since leaving school and she landed up offering me a job. I was over the moon.

'Then we talked about me for a bit and I told her I had a date with you. I thought nothing more about what I'd said until ten o'clock this morning when she told me how jealous you had made her for going out with me. I put her straight and she apologised. I thought for a moment it was going to get ugly, but when I explained the situation she agreed to back off and that was that. After that, the day went splendidly. In fact, so well I still can't believe my luck. The job's just fantastic.'

Having finished, Ian looked to his girlfriend for her reaction.

'I can't say I'm happy you're working for a woman who has fancied you for the past decade, but I am pleased you like your new job so much. It's important.'

Ian reached for her hand and held it gently.

'It must be hard for you. I wouldn't like to hear that your boss had come on to you. I'd probably want to meet him and plant one squarely on his chin.'

Debbie smiled. 'I don't really see you as the violent type.'

Ian's face became serious for a fraction of a second before he was able to recover, shrugging off the idea with a smile that matched hers.

'No, I suppose you're right. The point is, though, that I wanted there to be no secrets between us.'

'Me too.'

By the end of the week, Ian felt as though he had his feet firmly under the table at work; every day filling his head with more happy memories than he had accumulated in half a lifetime toiling in drab offices. His social life improved too. Already he had met many of Debbie's friends. Although he knew they were destined to drift apart, for now they made good company.

As for progress with regards to Debbie herself, she had always been a keen kisser and had been happy to plunge her tongue into his mouth from the outset. At first, his hands had been content to hold her waist, shifting to new positions defined by the area of her back, but this show of restraint did not last long. As the length of their relationship grew day by day, his hands drifted downwards to her buttocks and soon after, upwards to her chest, eagerly groping her breasts through her top. The result had not been a slap to his face; rather she took to kissing him with even more passion.

Friday marked the last working day of the month – payday.

Although he had worked for Nicola for only one week, Ian's take home salary, combined with the final payment from his previous employer, showed a definite increase. It was fortunate it did. Entertaining his girlfriend, plying her with drinks night after night, was an expensive way to live.

Despite the fact he was now relatively affluent, with the prospect of being more so once he had completed a full month, Ian thought it sensible to tighten his purse strings over the weekend. Feeling he and Debbie had seen the inside of a pub once too often, he instead suggested she accompany him on one of his country walks. She agreed.

On Saturday, the couple went shopping together, she spending her hard earned wages on beauty products, he on items to make the walk, planned for the following day, take place without a hitch.

The walk was taken at an easy pace, the goal not being to cover as much distance as possible, or to conquer the most difficult terrain. For Ian, it combined the romance of being with the one he loved and the opportunity to reminisce.

The footpath began on the opposite side of a drainage ditch that ran round the edge of a triangular-shaped field, trapped between a busy road and an unmade lane. In truth, the road was not yet as busy as it would become when the changes of the future began to leave their scars. In less than ten years it would become a victim to modern traffic, a continuous stream rumbling by for much of the day. The unmade lane would suffocate under a layer of tarmac. The field would be seeded with a crop of houses. The ancient oak, with its preservation order to protect it, would fall to an 'accident' carried out on the orders of the property developers that had a driveway planned for the spot it occupied.

The leap across the ditch was an opportunity for physical contact, Ian holding Debbie's outstretched fingers for support. She giggled sweetly as she made the jump, aware of her lack of prowess.

Along the path, the couple reached a pond – stagnant, black and lifeless; hardly the place to loiter, but Ian found happy memories there; ones he wished to share.

'This pond has been around for as long as I can remember. When I was little, my parents would bring me on this very same walk. We'd always stop here and I'd throw a stone in and watch bubbles of methane rise to the surface.'

As he spoke, he grubbed around at the edge of the pond, idly searching for a suitable projectile with which he could re-run the experiment.

'You had to be quick though to avoid being spattered.'

With this, a small stone, released from Ian's grip, swung in a high, slow, arc towards the centre of the pond. It plopped beneath the surface, sending a gobbet of foul-smelling, inky black water back along the arc towards the source of the stone that had given it life. Ian leapt back just in time for it to miss him, landing instead in the grass only centimetres from his feet.

'There, see!' he said excitedly, pointing to bubbles breaking free from the murky depths.

'Oh, yes,' Debbie reacted with fascination, having witnessed something she had never seen before.

The next point of interest was a bridge. It was not picturesque like the stone structures of the Yorkshire Dales. Rather, it looked as though it had been hastily constructed from galvanised scaffold poles, boarded over to provide a level surface on which to walk. No graceful arches or aesthetically pleasing textures, but it did make the perfect platform from which to throw sticks, racing them from upstream to down. Pooh Bear himself would have felt at home.

Debbie had not played such games since her childhood, but soon rediscovered her natural skill, taking delight in beating Ian in a 'best of three' that quickly became a 'best of five'. Eventually, Ian had to admit defeat, crowning her victorious with a kiss.

Eventually, the walk reached its furthermost point – an isolated church that sat in the middle of nowhere, still used by parishioners who, no doubt, made their way by car. The well-tended cemetery lay peacefully surrounding the flint structure of the church. A bench had been placed in a sheltered corner, donated by a widow who wished to remember her 'beloved' dead husband to all who sat there.

'This'll do,' Ian announced, settling himself down on the wooden slats.

Debbie sat close beside him, but moved along a little when she realised Ian intended to lay a table between them. Reaching into his rucksack, he first produced two wine glasses, wrapped in a tea towel for protection. This he used as the tablecloth, defining the small area between them on which he could set out the rest of the picnic. Next came a bottle of wine, red and more expensive than even his new found wealth could afford. Another tea towel protected two plates. Then came a succession of small boxes containing two chicken breasts, cheese and a mixture of shredded lettuce, green and red peppers and spring onion. One final box contained ham slices, smothered with cream cheese, rolled around spring onions and sliced in to bite-sized pieces. Two rustic rolls completed the main course. All that remained were two cartons of caramel dessert, two cutlery settings, salt, pepper and a corkscrew. The whole had been kept cool by the addition of a number of ice blocks, taken direct from the freezer compartment of his mum's refrigerator.

'How on Earth did you know what my favourite food was?' Debbie asked, merely as a way of expressing her appreciation for her boyfriend's efforts.

Ian took her comment to have more gravity than she had intended, being all too aware he had a secret waiting to be discovered. At this stage of their relationship he should not yet know her likes so well. In order to counter this subtle clue to the truth, he felt obliged to come up with an excuse.

'Your star sign,' he said, thinking quickly. 'It's a well-known fact that Aries like red wine, chicken salad and caramel.'

'I've never heard that before,' Debbie said, smiling. 'What does your star sign like?'

Ian realised he had inadvertently begun the sort of dialogue typical of young people in love. Of course his explanation had been ridiculous, but in these circumstances it was acceptable. In fact, the sillier their banter became the better.

'It's another well-known fact that Capricorns love real ale and curries that make you beg for mercy,' he replied with firm conviction. 'Not really the right stuff for a picnic, I think you'll agree.'

'No, not really,' Debbie laughed.

That was the way Sunday went – two romantics sharing a walk and a meal together, each making the other happy just by their being there.

19

Monday morning started as well as the weekend had ended. Ian found no difficulty getting up for work. Indeed, he had to hold himself back from leaving the house too early, so keen was he to continue with the project he had been forced temporarily to abandon.

During the morning, he found himself alongside a colleague putting the finishing touches to an extensive diorama. Such was his level of concentration he did not see Nicola coming. The first he knew of her presence was her chin close to his shoulder and the pressure of her chest against the middle of his back. He froze for a moment, not knowing how best to handle the situation, before deciding to continue with his work as though nothing untoward was happening. She slid across behind him - maintaining contact - to his other shoulder, furthest from Ian's colleague.

'Remember Physics lessons?' she whispered.

Ian stared across the diorama, not knowing where to look, or how to react. The discomfort of the moment seemed to stretch to infinity, but in reality, it was so brief, so subtle, as to go totally unnoticed by any other member of staff.

'That looks excellent,' she said aloud, stepping back. 'Our customers are bound to be pleased. Well done.'

She then drifted away without saying another word.

The second full week in his new job continued following much the same pattern as the first. Five days of doing something he loved; five evenings of being with someone he loved.

He chose to keep Nicola's harassment to himself, not wishing to worry Debbie unnecessarily, in doing so avoiding the prospect his girlfriend might demand he took action. Confrontation was not his way and he would do anything to avoid it. Things might be different if he was complaining to his manager about a co-worker, but there was no one in higher authority than Nicola, save for the police. Seeking their advice would clearly not be the best career choice he had ever made and the notion was dismissed out of hand.

Monday came round again. No sooner had Ian walked through the main door to reception, was he summonsed upstairs to Nicola's office.

'Ian,' she said brightly. 'Come in and take a seat.'

It was as though the incident down on the workshop floor had never happened. He sat down, filled with suspicion for what she was to say next.

'I'm going away for a couple of days to meet a potentially important new client and I want you to come with me.'

The concern written across his face spoke a thousand words.

'Don't worry, I remember my little promise. Nothing is going to happen. I just need you to help me win the contract. It'll only mean staying over for one night and then you'll be back with your precious Debbie.'

Ian did not take kindly to the hint of sarcasm in her voice, but he realised how foolish Nicola could make him feel if he declined to go. Any refusal would mean having to express to her his fear she would attempt to seduce him and that he was not man enough to fend her off. There was nothing to do but accept now and placate his girlfriend later when he broke the news.

As anticipated, Debbie was not at all happy with the idea of her boyfriend going away with a woman who had expressed her jealousy over the fact he could not be hers. She was not happy, but at the same time she could see the predicament Ian was in and demonstrated her trust by accepting he had to go.

A guilty man who had successfully fooled his partner could not have felt happier at her decision. In Ian's case, it was not the fact he had fooled her; he had not. He felt relieved and elated because Debbie had shown how strong their relationship had become. He could now begin to believe that all would be right between them; that they would marry and, in time, go on to produce the two children he so sorely missed.

The meeting was not until the afternoon of the following day. In the morning, Ian was instructed he would be acting as chauffeur and to put his overnight bag in the boot of the executive car Nicola had hired for the trip. She obviously wanted to create the right impression.

Setting off before lunch, Ian was quick to put a question he had been bottling up since being told of the meeting.

'So, why me?' he asked, candidly.

'Why?'

'You know. Why choose me to come on this trip with you?'

Nicola mused for a moment.

'For two reasons: firstly, it seemed logical to leave the business in the hands of the most experienced; I mean, you're good, but let's face it, you've only been with us a couple of weeks.'

Ian felt foolish. Perhaps he had jumped to conclusions that had exposed a conceit he did not know he possessed. Perhaps the reason Nicola had not mentioned the incident with her breasts was because it had meant far more to him than it had to her.

'And secondly...' he prompted, wanting to hear the rest of the horrible truth before he could bear it no longer.

'And secondly: because I like you; we make a good team. You can't blame me for wanting to be with you. I'm just sorry you made me promise to forget what happened between us.'

On the other hand, he had every reason to believe the worst of her motives. The woman had an agenda and Ian had the sneaking suspicion they had only reached item one.

Following a stop for an unpleasant meal in a motorway service station, the delegation arrived at their destination in good time. The meeting went well, during which Ian saw another side of Nicola – the astutely professional businesswoman. She had won the contract even before making her formal presentation; such was her charm, working its magic with the directors.

'Time to celebrate,' she said, once the car was clear of the premises. 'We should drink to our success.'

'I shouldn't,' Ian said. 'Not when I'm driving.'

'Then we shall wait until we've booked in at the hotel. They're bound to have a bar.'

The motel was intricately woven between and beneath the convergence of a number of major roads. If it was expensive, Ian wanted to know why. In all likelihood, Nicola had chosen this spot for the opposite reason; because it was cheap and she was trying to keep a tight grip on her overheads.

'Stay here with the bags,' she instructed. 'I'll book us in.'

Five minutes later, Nicola returned, her finger through a single key ring; a single, large wooden fob hanging down from the clutches of her hand.

'We're in 324,' she said efficiently.

'We're in 324?' Ian repeated, transforming the statement into a question, one suggesting he did not know if he had heard correctly.

'Yes. Look, can we wait until we get to the room. I don't want to talk about it here?'

Ian, always one to avoid embarrassing confrontation in public, agreed without further ado. Once behind the door of the room, though, he remained silent, but demanded an explanation by way of an enquiring look any interrogator would be proud of.

'I know how it must look, but I only booked one room to save money. We're a small company and there was no guarantee we would get the contract. I have to think of the purse strings.'

'If you wanted to save money, why did you hire that bloody great car?'

'To give the right impression. Don't you see? It's all about giving the right impression. They judge our company on what they see – us and our vehicle. They don't see where we're staying.'

Her impassioned plea for him to see reason resulted in just that, but it still left doubts as to her true intentions.

'What about the sleeping arrangements? We may have been naked together once, but that's all in the past. I've got Debbie to think about now.'

'Don't worry. You know how I feel about you, but this is business. If you would just open your eyes for a second rather than spend all your time having a go at me, you'll see that there is a sofa-bed over there in the corner. The bathroom door has a lock on it and I've packed pyjamas.'

She had truly knocked the wind from his sails. Becalmed, he had not the faintest idea what to say next. Seeing him struggling for words, Nicola chose the moment to diffuse the situation.

'Come to the bar with me. I think the company budget can stretch to a few drinks.'

Ian smiled, glad at being offered a way out of such unpleasantness.

After three rounds, both Ian and Nicola were getting peckish. Sharing a basket of salted chips served to quell their hunger and line their stomachs for more alcohol. By the time they had finished, they had been drinking steadily for four hours, leaving both heavily under the influence.

Back in the room, Ian flopped down, slumped on the edge of the bed.

'I wish I'd made up the sofa before we went to the bar,' he slurred, his body slowly crumpling, unable to support its own weight. 'I'm not sure I can do it now.'

'Don't then,' Nicola suggested, managing to sound as if consideration for his welfare was her only concern. 'It seems daft you sleeping on a sofa when there's a perfectly good bed available.'

'You're probably right.'

Ian did not have the energy to fight. Instead he chose to lie back, fully clothed, on top of the bedding.

'I hate it when the room starts spinning every time I close my eyes,' he said, staring at the ceiling, trying desperately to focus.

'Don't close your eyes then,' Nicola said smoothly, standing close to where he lay.

She looked down her front and began unbuttoning her blouse. The seductiveness was lost until the garment, dropping to the ground, caught his attention. He looked in her direction, trying to make sense of what she was doing. Her intention became that much clearer as she unfastened the waistband of her skirt, undid the zip, and dropped it to the floor. She stepped clear of her discarded clothing, bringing her closer to where Ian lay. She had nothing on except for a matching set of lacy white bra and panties, and she was massaging her body.

'What are you doing?' Ian sounded forceful, despite the alcohol poisoning.

'What's wrong? You've seen me before. Hell, you've been inside me three times.'

'Listen Nicola; let's get this straight once and for all; I may be drunk; you may have a fantastic body and yes, you're a pretty damn good shag, but I am with Debbie now and this is not going to happen.'

The message was not getting through. Nicola ignored him, removing her bra before draping it across his face. Ian swept it away with a number of movements as though he was fighting off an annoying fly. Still she thought she could break his will. Oblivious to his words and actions, she placed the flat of her hands inside the waistband of her panties, and slid them slowly past her thighs and on down to her ankles. Again, she stepped free, maintaining a hold of them so that she stood, entirely naked, stroking his face with her underwear, before letting them fall to land on his groin.

Ian fought to sit up. As he did so, Nicola slid her hand the length of her firm abdomen and on down between the tops of her thighs.

'You know you want to. Debbie need never know. Just one last time and I promise never to bother you again.'

'No, no, no!' The slur had gone, replaced by a voice driven from the pit of his stomach by a sudden burst of anger.

Ian managed to lumber from the bed, bouncing gently off two walls before ending up within the sanctuary of the bathroom, complete with its lockable door. Here he had in mind taking a very long time in preparing for bed: at least ten minutes on the toilet; a lengthy shower; a good five minutes buffing his teeth. When he emerged, hopefully Nicola would be asleep and he would then be in a fit state to unfold and make up the sofa bed. His plan, however, proved unrealistic from the outset.

The rejection embarrassed Nicola more deeply than she had ever experienced before. Her intentions upon him had been so clear there existed no escape route. Pretending there had merely been a misunderstanding would be futile. The only remaining option was to attack the man who had snubbed her.

'How dare you turn me down,' she shouted, releasing the first volley at the door, penetrating it with ease.

Her outburst continued without pause for breath, or without thought as to what she was saying. The embarrassment she felt this evening would be nothing to that which she would feel in the morning when the memory of her diatribe floated to the surface of her sobering mind.

Only weeks before, Ian had believed her to have many qualities: her looks; her sexual appetite; her sexual prowess; her ownership of both house and business. Now, he could see beyond them all. Everything Debbie was, Nicola was not. If ever there had been the need to prove he had made the right decision, her current behaviour was more than enough to demonstrate he had.

Her fury could not last forever, and even when it had died down, Ian would wait a little longer. Emerging back into the room while it was still occupied by a woman scorned - a drunken one at that - was something not to be done in haste.

Eventually, hearing nothing more than sobbing, stifled by the density of a hotel pillow, Ian judged the time right to re-join her. Further criticism of her behaviour at this stage would serve only to make matters worse. Words of reconciliation, however, would quicken their journey to much needed sleep and would be sure to make the morning more bearable for both parties.

'Nicola,' Ian spoke gently, laying one hand upon her still naked shoulder. 'I can see that I've hurt your feelings, and I'm sorry for that. We've both had far too much to drink this evening.'

Nicola's sobbing subsided, but she offered no further confirmation she was listening to a word he was saying. Undaunted, Ian continued.

'I think we should go to bed – in separate beds – and talk about this in the morning. What do you say?'

She had stopped crying altogether, but still she said nothing.

'I hate to think I have hurt you after all you've done for me, and the good times we've shared.'

Again, she said nothing. Ian raised himself to his feet, allowing his hand to rub her shoulder tenderly. Then he moved away towards the sofa.

'Sorry,' Nicola said, shakily.

Ian smiled, reflecting his expression in the way he spoke.

'Don't worry, we'll talk it over in the morning and everything will be all right.'

Nothing more was said.

Soon after, the lights went out and all was dark and silent.

Blackout curtains maintained a false night until they were opened at nine o'clock the following morning. This, and the absence of an alarm, gave the two sleeping drunks the lie in they needed.

Having managed to dress without either roommate seeing a centimetre of the other's bare flesh, they went to the restaurant area, ate a Spartan breakfast and got back on the road without delay. Conversation remained civil, but infrequent, creating an atmosphere so uncomfortable something, or someone, had to break. That someone was Nicola.

'Look Ian, I'm really sorry for the way I behaved last night. I tried to control my jealousy but I couldn't. I know I've said it before, but this time I mean it. If you can forgive me, I promise nothing like this will ever happen again.'

Ian was grateful for the apology, but things had been said he doubted he would ever be able to forget.

'Let's just forget it,' Ian suggested graciously. 'We should concentrate on the positive side of all this – you've just landed a new client, remember?'

Never was any man more grateful to see his girlfriend than was Ian on seeing Debbie that evening. Without hesitation, he told her much of what had transpired, ever wishing to demonstrate his honesty. She was shocked, but nevertheless accepted Nicola's latest apology was genuine. The views of all parties had now been aired, with the result that Ian felt confident he could continue working for his new employer, at least while nothing else happened.

The following day saw Nicola keeping her distance. She would come to the workshop floor, but she would neither talk directly with Ian nor enter his personal space.

Friday dawned. Ian longed for it to come to an end so the weekend could put a wedge between the mistakes of one week and the new beginning of another. His wish lasted half an hour, after which time he was again summoned to Nicola's office.

On entering the inner sanctum, he found her standing behind the protection of her desk, her hands clenched at the ends of arms that protected her torso. Everything about her body language spoke of defence and ill ease.

With the click of the door closing, and even before Ian had the chance to take a seat, she began, unable to wait a single second longer.

'I think that maybe you should reconsider our relationship,' she said, the words bursting from within.

'Nicola,' Ian reacted to her slippage into her old ways with an exasperated voice that continued firmly. 'There is no relationship. Don't you get it?'

She had anticipated his every word, but he had not foreseen the trump card she was about to play.

'Perhaps the fact I'm carrying your child will sway you.'

Her news was delivered in such a tone, all thoughts of it being meant as a joke were banished.

Ian sank into a chair, stunned into silence. The delay, brief though it may have been, was sufficient to induce an atmosphere so unpleasant as to deprive Nicola of at least two breaths. Eventually though, he spoke, addressing the surface of the table on which his elbow now rested.

'Some time ago…'

Having delivered a mere three words, Ian paused, interrupting his own flow with another train of thought.

'Do you know,' he said, lifting his head so that he looked directly into Nicola's eyes, 'I can't even begin to describe when. I mean, do I count deleted days? Do I include the many versions of the same event I have lived through, even though they no longer exist?'

Nicola had anticipated anger, shock, or even the faintest possibility of pleasure, but not this. Here was a man that shared her mastery of the English language, but who was making no sense at all. The situation was one she had not experienced before, and the only response she could give was to stand silently motionless, reluctant to say or do anything that might provoke a violent response.

'I was living my life,' Ian continued, either blind to the effect he had produced, or not interested in the fact he had produced it. 'I admit I was not happy, but another seventeen years would have seen me drawing a reasonable pension, retired, with time on my hands to do whatever I wanted. Then I was given a 'gift' - if that is what you can call it - and it poisoned my life.

'I have murdered twice. I have killed an innocent person, and ruined the lives of many others. I came to you during my darkest hour, and you gave me hope. You gave me a taste of the job I have always wanted: creative; challenging. Now you have poisoned that too and with something that causes more pain than death itself. I shall never forgive you for what you are forcing me to do.'

Suddenly Nicola was worried. Ian was quite clearly mad and had indicated his intention to exact his revenge. By his own admission, he had killed before and now he intended to strike again. Despite the fear that ran cold through her veins, Nicola remained motionless, unable to twitch the smallest of muscles; unable to utter a single sound.

'I have won great sums on the National Lottery, and been robbed. I have been given a career I had previously only dreamt of, only to have that taken from me too. How do you think that makes me feel?'

Ian's mad, desperate eyes pleaded for an explanation; dared Nicola to offer an excuse. She gave neither. Instead she began to tremble.

'What are you going to do?' she asked quietly, the force of her voice being almost entirely absent.

'I don't know exactly what I intend to do, but by the time I am done, I will never have worked for you, you will not be having my child and memories of our night together will reside solely in my mind for me to forget over time.'

He spoke the truth, choosing his words deliberately, knowing his cryptic phrase could be interpreted as a mortal threat. He knew the effect he was having and relished it. Nicola needed to suffer for what she had done.

'Listen Ian, I didn't steal from you to make a baby. You put it there. You can't blame it all on me.'

'Baby or no baby, you promised it would remain in the past. You knew I wanted Debbie and still you have been trying every tactic known to womankind to end our relationship. That was your decision and for that I cannot forgive you.'

Nicola, a broken woman, slid down the wall, landing crumpled and sobbing in the corner of her office. Satisfied he had extracted from her at least some payment towards the damage she had done, he turned his attention to other matters.

There was only one place to which he should return; one moment both convenient to his plans and easy to fix in his memory. He would never forget the moment he learned of the death of the second victim of the car crash he alone had caused. The content of the newspaper article was etched in his mind.

Closing his eyes, Ian could see the font; the texture of the paper; the stand on which the newspaper was displayed. He could still feel the deluge of emotions that had threatened to drown him.

The core of his mind buzzed for a moment and in a fraction of a second he was there.

20

In front of Ian stood a rack of shelving, laden with newsprint: tabloid and broadsheet; national and local. Adjacent to the shelving, a separate wire rack held three further editions. Ian immediately focussed on one in particular, its front page devoted almost entirely to its headline and accompanying photograph – the twisted remains of a car.

Buying a copy was unnecessary; reading the lead story was unnecessary. The article made the paper; Ian Bradshaw had made the article. He knew what it contained and it made him shudder every time he let the words bob to the surface of his mind. He wanted to undo what he had done, but it was still too soon. The fated career opportunity had been a distraction, leaving vital decisions yet to be considered and made.

If he carried on regardless, what would he do? He had no longer resigned from his job, and therefore still had his promotion, but he knew just how far that avenue would lead him. As an alternative, he might consider starting his own business, but possessing the ability to turn back the clock would not make him an entrepreneur. On the face of it, there seemed little to persuade him not to go back, other than keeping Summerbee in the ground.

On the other hand, if he did reclaim the last twenty-four hours, he would restore the lives of Eileen Cole, 47; her daughter, Sarah Benson, 25, and the lives of their families who were currently grieving for one; worrying for the future of the other. It was the right thing to do.

Ian had at least reached one decision – to go back, restore the innocent, and kill Summerbee for a third time. Regardless of the potential difficulty he might experience finding the right method and opportunity, the act itself could only become easier. Frustration born of the fact Summerbee refused to stay dead was enough to overcome many of the mental barriers that should have stood in his way.

Still Ian was not ready to make the jump. He had acted, retracted, and acted again, and for all the progress he had made, he might as well have let Summerbee kill him in the future. So far, the only ticks against his to-do list were: killing the bad man; arranging a first date with his wife to be; securing a promotion that would simply maintain the unbearable career path he had originally suffered, and even these were about to be erased.

Before deciding upon his next step it seemed prudent to seek advice, but asking any sane human being whether they believed he should continue forward with his life, or go backwards, was certain to invite ridicule. However, if the question was posed as hypothetical, he might get away with it.

The first person to whom the question could be put was his mum. Having returned home, changed out of his suit and eaten, Ian made them both a cup of tea and settled down in front of the television. Even if his mum was enjoying the current programme twice as much as himself, she would no doubt welcome the distraction his conversation would bring, the choice of viewing being so dire. He was correct.

Keen to get to the point, Ian avoided the preliminaries.

'If you had your time again,' he said casually, without forewarning, 'what would you do differently?'

Judging by the speed with which she answered, his mum had already given the matter consideration.

'I would have travelled the world before I settled down and I wouldn't have married your father.'

'Charming,' Ian said, instantly seeing the implication of his parents not having joined in holy matrimony.

'I don't mean I wish I hadn't had you,' she qualified hastily. 'I just wish your father had been someone else.'

This was hardly advice that could be applied, or even adapted to his particular situation.

'Would you go back and stick with any of the jobs you've had?' he asked, trying a different tack.

'The only proper job I ever had was with the bank, and I hated it. That's probably one of the reasons I married your father in the first place - to get away from it. Then he left me to bring you up on my own and from then on I had to dress us in hand-me-downs and manage on the charity of the state.'

Ian was doubtful whether further debate would yield anything useful and decided to drop the subject.

Plan B would be to ask Roland for his views.

Ian drove to work the following morning fully aware that on the flip side of this day he had attended and passed an interview for the best job he was ever likely to land – the position given to him by Nicola. That option now closed to him, he would accept a return to his original job until he could figure out what to do next: to go forward; to dip backwards; to go further back and make fundamental changes.

So far, the experience associated with revisiting this particular place of work had not been typical of that time. He had reported sick to avoid an interview, had then sat the interview and had reported sick again to facilitate undergoing an entirely different interview. This would be the first day on which work would be carried out as normal.

The pay was poor, even when taking inflation into account. The work was dull and repetitive. The management, each and every one of them, was both ineffectual and devoid of ability. On the other hand, by mid-morning, Ian was reminded just how little work he had to do; just how little work any of them had to do. Between the tea breaks, endless conversations, playful diversions, and the making of personal telephone calls, it was surprising the business had not simply collapsed – but of course, it had. Within a year of him leaving for an equally dull, but slightly better paid job, the first of his ex-workmates had been made redundant. More had followed until the company had been forced to relocate to Ireland, leaving Ian thankful he had got out at the right time. On reflection, that was a small mercy. He had retained employment, but had been even more miserable ever since.

Bearing in mind the crucial decision he now faced - to go back, or to go forward - this memory at first swung in favour of him turning away from the future. On the other hand, accepting he would leave the company as before, the direction in which he then headed did not have to be the same. Promotion at this company had secured him a new job at another. He might apply for other positions instead, ones that he had not felt capable of doing the first time round, and he was ignoring the possibility Roland would come up with a suggestion for an entirely new career.

If the decision was to go forward, Ian would simply go back, undo the wrong he had done, pass the interview again and then head for pastures new. He would have to dispose of Summerbee again, and do it quickly, the signs pointing to the fact his enemy was on the cusp of discovering a new talent. Alternatively, he could go back further and kill Summerbee before he re-took the interview. The rest of the plan would be the same.

If the decision was to go back, it was not immediately clear how far he should go: a day; a week; a month.

During one of the many lulls in activity, Ian posed his questions to his friend.

'If you left this job...I don't know, if you were made redundant or something, what would you do?'

Roland liked the hypothetical and pondered a while before answering.

'I'm not sure. I could try and get the same job with another company I suppose - maybe in the city. At least then I'd be on more money,' he said, uncertainly. 'I'd like to do something different though, but I don't have any skills.'

'Ever thought of retraining?'

'No, it's too late for me,' Roland answered, resignation permeating his voice. 'I can't drop out of work now; I've got too many commitments, including a whomping great car loan. Besides, even if I could afford to manage until I'd finished training, I wouldn't start my new career on top dollar would I? I'd have to work my way up like everyone else. It might be years before I got myself straight.'

He had a point. Ian had abilities - artistic, communicative, and many more besides - but nothing in writing he could present to a potential employer. He did have a handful of G.C.E. 'O' levels, but those qualifications were only sufficient to start him on the career path he had already taken. Like Roland, he too had commitments. They were far fewer than they would be at any time hence, but he had them nonetheless.

The common theme presented by both Roland and Ian's mum, and the preliminary conclusion he himself had drawn, was that if change were to be effected, it would have to be done in the past. Before making his final decision though, there was one other person Ian wished to consult.

Debbie could be seen waving goodbye to her parents as she stepped from her front door, heading for Ian's car before he had even had the chance to turn off the ignition. Ian leant over to open the passenger door as she approached and greeted her with a smile.

'Evening,' Ian said, as she sat down beside him.

'Evening,' Debbie responded pleasantly. 'I'm glad you were so punctual. I was nervous enough, wondering whether or not you'd turn up. If you'd made me wait even a minute, I'd have been a gibbering wreck.'

Ian had been here before and wanted to move on as quickly as possible.

'Don't be daft,' he said, making light of her concerns. 'If anyone has the right to be nervous, it's me. For all I know, when you agreed to come out with me, it might have been the drink talking.'

Debbie smiled a relieved smile, and it was lovely.

'So, what have you been up to?' she asked, making small talk.

There was so much Ian could say, but it would be pointless, confusing and probably unnerving.

'Not a lot. I did get promoted on Monday, but otherwise it has been quite boring.'

'Promotion. That's great,' Debbie said excitedly, genuinely pleased at the news.

Ian held back putting the questions he truly wanted to ask until they had each consumed at least two drinks. Then, judging the moment to perfection, he slipped the first into the conversation.

'If you had your time again, what would you do differently?'

'Oh, you should never look back,' she said, earnestly.

'Why's that?' Ian was genuinely keen to know her reasoning.

'If you left your job for a new one and the new one didn't work out, you should find something new,' she answered as though her argument was well rehearsed. 'I mean, you left your old job for a reason. Why would those reasons be any different now?'

'But what if going forward was really going back?'

The moment the words left Ian's lips, he realised further explanation was needed.

'Okay, you go back in time. If you lived your life the same as before, in effect, you would be looking back.'

'Then you would have to do things differently. Like I said, there must have been something about now that you didn't like for you to leave it. Why would things be different the second time round if you lived your life exactly the same?'

'Sorry,' Ian apologised. 'All this is a bit deep for a first date.'

'Don't be sorry. I like it. It's different.'

'Okay then, if you went back in time, how would you do things differently?'

'I'd have to make fundamental changes – take a completely different career path or something.'

'That's all very well, but if I went back to when I was looking for my first job, my qualifications would always limit me as to what I could do.'

'There's your answer then. You would have to go back further and get better exam results.'

It was easy for her to come to such conclusions as she did so believing the debate to be a purely intellectual exercise. For Ian though, it was the last piece of the jigsaw. Three people had been questioned. All agreed the solution was to return to the perceived source of their current situation. Debbie had gone one stage further and offered a suggestion as to what that source might be.

He had to return to the time of his exams, in the final year of secondary school. Obtaining better results would open the options available to him; obtaining a better job on those merits alone, or using them as a stepping stone towards 'A' levels, and university.

Now he had his answer, there was little point in continuing with the remainder of his first date. Regardless of how much he loved Debbie, there would still be much repetition, and besides, he had a lot to consider.

Fixing his thoughts on the news of Summerbee's demise, Ian returned in an instant to the floor of the corner shop, with its displays of daily newspapers. From there, he drove home, making straight for the solitude of his bedroom.

Having already rewound twenty-four years of his life, the decision to go back further was not an easy one to make, but it was a necessary one. Comforting him was the knowledge that whatever he did to change the future, he would always be able to attend the school reunion, and therefore meet his wife, and eventually be reunited with his children. As for obtaining better results, he was confident his maturity would allow him to pass examinations where before there had been failure, and to get grade 'As' where before he had achieved only 'Bs' and 'Cs'.

Accepting this course of action, the next step was to find a way of getting back to the time of his exams safely. As try as he might, he could think of no one incident that would allow him to lock on with any certainty. He remembered faces, pencil cases; insignificant moments from his school days, but none of them were of use.

When he had made his first big jump, he had needed to go from point 'B' to point 'A' in one leap, thus avoiding bringing Summerbee back to life as a man with the ability to rewind time. Now it was no longer an issue, Ian could afford to use an alternative method. He could activate the rewinding process, waiting until the high frequency noise kicked in, and then count to a specified number. He would then open his eyes to terminate the process, check on his progress, and adjust the length of the next rewind accordingly. In this way, he hoped to complete the minus eight years journey in as little as three large jumps, followed by a few lesser ones, necessary to achieve the required fine-tuning.

On the first occasion Ian had experienced the high pitched buzzing sensation, he had travelled back three days before opening his eyes in panic. Time elapsed: less than a second. By extrapolation, a full second would rewind a week, and an entire year would pass in fifty-two seconds. Two years, his chosen jump, would therefore take one minute and forty-four seconds. Knowing the crude nature of his calculation, and the possible fluctuation in the variables, it seemed prudent to activate the rewinding process for less than that, especially when conducting the first stage of his plan. His concern he might have got his sums wrong was real, but somewhat allayed by the knowledge there was plenty of room for error. Overrunning by two, or even three years would ultimately only serve to reduce the number of stages that had to be performed. There was nothing more to do now than have faith and get on with it.

As far as technique mattered, there was no reason to lie down and get comfortable before beginning the process, but doing so seemed somehow important. A hard decision had spawned drastic action, an occasion warranting some form of ceremony to mark its significance. In this case, the ceremony amounted to lying on top of the bedclothes with a pillow covering his eyes and forehead.

At the first hint of high frequency buzzing, Ian began to count.

'One elephant. Two elephant…'

By the time the herd had increased to twenty, he was starting to become nervous. He had not done anything like this before. What would happen if he were wrong? He might overshoot by twenty years, and then where would he be? The count continued with Ian resisting the temptation to speed up his delivery. Everything would be all right. The calculations might be wrong, but there was absolutely no way they could be out by more than a year or two. A minute passed by which time the urge to open his eyes was becoming too great to ignore. Only a momentous display of willpower kept the clock ticking.

'Eighty-eight elephant, eighty-nine elephant, ninety elephant.'

Ian opened his eyes to blackness.

***

Ian had begun his journey lying on his bed, on top of the covers. By coincidence, he had ended up lying on the same bed, but beneath the covers. Other than that, the two most noticeable differences were that it was now some time during the middle of the night, and he was now suddenly extremely tired. The effect was so swift, and so great, it was as if he had been the unknowing victim of a most powerful soporific. Fighting the desire to turn over and go back to sleep, Ian threw back the bedding and heaved himself up and round to the sitting position, the soles of his bare feet firmly in contact with the carpet. Here he stayed, his body convinced it had been disturbed enough. It was mistaken.

One vital element, central to each stage of the trip back to his schooldays, was the determination of how far back he had gone. It was difficult to see how this might be achieved, perched as he was on the edge of a bed, in an unlit room, during the early hours of the morning – the display of the clock radio telling him at least that much. He had to summon the strength to go and investigate.

Thinking drowsily where he might find the information he desired, Ian soon hit upon the idea of reading the TV paper. It would be downstairs in the lounge.

Not wishing to wake his mum, he padded quietly out onto the landing. Gently shifting his weight onto each step in turn, he tried to reach the bottom in silence. The sleeve of his dressing gown rubbed harshly against the wallpaper, the sound amplified by the still of the night. Every alternate step creaked or squeaked as weight was applied and then lifted. To Ian's ears, he might as well have been playing in a brass band. Thankfully, his mum continued to sleep soundly.

With the flicking on of the living room light, a searing pain struck at the very centre of Ian's retinas. Automotive responses kicked in, the muscles around his eyes scrunching up, his head turning away from the source of discomfort, and all within a fraction of a second. Slowly he became acclimatised, at first blinking wildly before gradually being able to keep his eyes open as two narrow slits.

The magazine he sought was easy to spot, it lying over the arm of the settee. A quick glance at the cover showed it to be June 1981; two years further back than he had calculated; the process must have stepped up a gear having been applied for so long. This was no disaster - he merely had to make adjustments for the next jump - however, it did act as a reminder for him to be more cautious in future. Already going back further than he would have liked, the consequences of mistakenly going back an additional two years did not bear thinking.

Ian was now twenty years old and had already been in employment for several years. Catching sight of himself in a mirror, hung on the chimney breast, he was shocked by how young he looked; how unkempt. He recalled a non-specific moment when he was only nineteen, when he felt he was a fully-fledged adult, but now he saw only the face of a child; a spotty, downy youth with no self-respect. At that moment a decision was made; a vow to himself. Not only would he work to improve his grades and employment history, he would pay closer attention to his appearance, taking a holistic approach. He would make the most of the mess he found himself in. He would be a better man.

Having settled into the moment, it occurred to Ian his mouth was parched, causing him to consider making a cup of tea before continuing on his journey, but he quickly realised there was little point. On completion of stage B, he might open his eyes to find he had just finished a beverage of some description, or equally likely, that he was thirsty again. Either way, whether he chose to drink now, or not, it would make no difference to his past. However, two factors persuaded him he should succumb to his mouth's demands. Firstly, he felt tired and muggy and needed waking up properly before he was ready to concentrate sufficiently on the next jump. Secondly, although his thirst might well return within a moment of him satiating it, the comforting memory of drinking the tea would nevertheless remain.

Just as he poured the hot water onto a tea bag that lay helplessly at the bottom of a mug, decorated with a likeness of the family dog, his mum appeared at the door to the kitchen, bleary eyed.

'I couldn't sleep,' he offered by way of explanation. 'Would you like a cup?'

Mother and son sat for a while, exchanging the occasional sentence until their cups were dry. Her considerable ability to make conversation was dulled almost to extinction by fatigue, but it was nice she had been willing to forego part of a good night's sleep to keep him company. Her stamina lasted only as long as it took to drain her cup, before she went back upstairs with a warning he should follow soon or find it difficult to get up for work in the morning.

With his mum out of the way, and his thirst at least temporarily satiated, it was time to take the second step, but before doing so Ian recalibrated his calculation. Ninety seconds had brought him back three years, eleven months – approximately two seconds for every one month. A further forty-four seconds should equate to approximately two years, allowing for a little wriggle room.

The low frequency buzzing began afresh, and again Ian was ready for the sudden alteration in pitch.

'One elephant, two elephant, three elephant...'

With the confidence of a man who had done it all before, Ian continued to count slowly and consistently.

'Forty-two elephant, forty-three elephant, forty-four elephant.'

***

Ian's eyes opened abruptly; not only to end the process; not only to discover where he was and how far back he had come, but also in reaction to finding someone else's tongue writhing about inside his mouth. Not only that, but the owner of the tongue was seated, while he was standing, bent over, one hand tucked in his jeans pocket, the other holding a plastic beaker half filled with lager. Breaking free, he stood up sharply, instantly regretting the sudden movement. The room moved out of synch with his body; his eyes were slightly out of focus; the music that played and the voices that competed to be heard over it, all lacked clarity. He was drunk; very drunk.

Without a word of apology to whomever it was he had just broken away from, Ian walked unsteadily away from her, towards the door of the room he now found himself in. The anonymous girl made no fuss. Instead, she simply grabbed the next young man that sat down beside her and found a new home for her tongue, buried deep inside his mouth.

Despite his inebriated state, Ian retained a sense of what it was that had brought him here: to determine the date; adjust his calculations, then make the next and hopefully final big jump. His first shifting thought was to find a TV paper. However, the likelihood of finding one seemed improbable. In preparation for the party, the whole ground floor of the building had been cleared of anything moveable. That being the case, with great effort, his next thought was to seek out a calendar. If there were one, he guessed it would be located in the kitchen and set off to find it, bouncing off the walls of a long, narrow, Victorian hallway as he went.

Squeezing across the threshold, it appeared, as with many parties he had been to, that the kitchen had been taken over as the nerve centre. Faces - many familiar; some not - filled the room, their bodies leaning against the edge of work surfaces for support. Most of those invited were known to him as past co-workers - or was that present?

'All right Ian?' one said jovially, the volume of his voice increased to an inappropriate level by the consumption of alcohol. 'Cradle snatcher.'

Ian looked bemused.

'I saw you in there with Karen's sister. She's only just turned fifteen you know.'

Ian remembered the incident, and the memo written by a co-worker; photocopied for distribution to all departments the very next day he had been at work. Despite the fact the indiscretion had progressed no further than writhing tongues – on both occasions - the unofficial publication told of Ian's conquest and suggested marriage might be in order. Originally, Ian had accepted his colleague's stunt with feigned embarrassment, believing such antics could only serve to improve his image. To a young person who normally froze merely at the prospect of saying 'good morning' to an attractive female, it felt good to share the notoriety normally reserved for other men. Now though, his feelings of embarrassment were genuine. In all but looks, he was a forty-eight year old man who had been caught seducing a minor, one young enough to be his own daughter.

Smiling dismissively at his antagonist, Ian turned away, his eyes scanning the walls, where they were visible. Catching sight of a calendar, partially obscured by half a dozen drunken partygoers, he pushed forward until the displayed month was visible - March 1979. The sum was not difficult, but the answer was slow in coming. Forty-five seconds had brought him back a further two years and three months, slightly longer than before. He was now a very young man of eighteen.

His ultimate aim was to return to May 1977. Given the innate level of inaccuracy caused by the varying speed with which he repeatedly delivered the word elephant, Ian made further adjustments to his calculations before leaning back, eyes closed, ready for the final push. But then he discovered a problem. Try as he might, he found himself unable to concentrate on anything; unable to trigger a buzzing sensation of any kind; unable to rewind and so remove the blanket of cotton wool that shrouded his brain.

'Damn,' he said aloud, the expletive being lost among the ambient noise.

Believing solitude might help, he crept upstairs unnoticed, partially opened the first door that came into view and slipped through the gap into the darkened bedroom that lay behind it. Low levels of light, born of street lamps standing close by the property, penetrated drawn curtains, faintly illuminating a number of features within the room.

Ian slumped down on to a single bed that consumed almost half the floor space, rolled over onto his back and folded his hands neatly across his chest. He felt awful. Closing his eyes only served to make matters worse. The room began to move uneasily, forcing him to open them again and stare fixedly at the ceiling until the room stopped spinning. All further attempts to close his eyes met with the same fate.

The longer his eyes remained closed, the faster the room would spin. While he continued to feel this way, there was absolutely no possibility of conducting any further regressive trips into his past. Ironically, if he were able, the feelings that now plagued him would no longer be there to stop him. As it stood, further movement would have to wait until morning.

Frustrated by his lack of success, Ian returned to the party, cussing beneath his breath with each downward step.

Ill informed as to how he had got to the party, or what arrangements he had made for the journey home, Ian was reluctant to leave. Gradually the crowd dissipated, staggering down the garden path in ones and twos, giggling loudly. None of them prompted Ian to go with them, although a few did make a point of saying 'night' to him in person.

Just as it was becoming clear he would have to be making a move too, Karen approached. As the host of the party, she was ultimately responsible for his condition. Her invitation had encouraged him to drink. Had she not involved him in her little get-together, he would by now have been long gone – several years to be more accurate. If anyone deserved a piece of his dulled mind, she did.

'You're sleeping on the sofa aren't you?' she asked in a cheery tone.

Her manner was disarming, a talent that would be of the greatest value as a front-line, meet-the-public employee of any large institution. Ian melted.

'If that's all right with you,' he replied gratefully, forgetting in an instant his desire to vent his annoyance upon her.

'Sure,' Karen added, a mischievous look on her face. 'If you're lucky, my sister might even make a space for you in her room.'

It was clear she had seen for herself, or had at least heard of Ian's earlier misdemeanour.

'Ha, ha, very funny,' he laughed, sarcastically. 'The sofa will be just fine.'

Too tired and too drunk to move, he curled up at one end of the settee, a female, whose name eluded him, claiming the other end. Their feet met in the middle, but neither was in a fit state to care. A lamp had been left on; so too, the stereo. Someone had thought it amusing to put a classical record on before retiring to bed. Ian remembered the incident from the first time: how the music had annoyed him and how neither he nor his sofa-partner had been in any condition to mute the sound, or to douse the light. The quiet melody had continued for what seemed like hours, stealing any opportunity there was for a quick passage to sleep. This time around, the gentle notes acting upon his unsettled mind had quite the opposite effect, soothing away consciousness, helping him to drift off.

Morning came early, the first hint of daylight being sufficient to rouse Ian from a restless slumber, one filled with disturbing dreams. His neck, released from several hours bent into a succession of awkward positions, ached mercilessly. Thirst clawed at an arid, swollen, tongue. His muscles quivered, his stomach churned, his head pounded. It was occasions such as this that had taught him to moderate his drinking. He had learned the lesson, suffering the effects of alcohol poisoning less and less over the years until he was able to judge to the nearest centilitre exactly when he should stop. It seemed harsh therefore that his sober mind should be punished for the excesses of the younger body it now occupied.

Despite the number of hours that had passed since imbibing his last unit of alcohol, too many unpleasant sensations remained, continuing to make it impossible to affect the rewind that would relieve him of such misery. All he could do was to ease each symptom in turn until he was recovered.

Shuffling from the settee into the hall, he turned away from the front door and headed for the kitchen. Much of what he was feeling - the dryness of mouth and the thumping headache - was caused by dehydration; he knew that. His brain had shrunk. Replacing the lost body fluid would be a start. Ironically, despite the need for water, he had first to expel the same to relieve another distraction. Thankfully, a toilet occupied a small room, tucked away under the hall stairs.

Karen was already in the kitchen making a drink. On hearing the cistern flush, she automatically took a second cup and filled that too. Whoever was up had been a guest at her party. Everyone there had drunk to excess and would no doubt be feeling as bad as she was.

Ian walked slowly through the door to have a hot coffee thrust into his hand. Fortuitously, the drink had been poured shy of the cup's rim. His hands shook so much that had there been a greater volume, it would have spilt; not only that, but Ian very much doubted whether he could have coped with the extra weight.

'Thanks,' Ian mumbled, feebly.

'I haven't put any sugar in it,' Karen said, much brighter than he.

'It's all right, I don't.'

He blew and sipped.

'That's just what I needed. I'm never going to drink this much again.'

'We all say that,' Karen said, smiling knowingly.

The two sat on stools at the breakfast bar. Each forced down a slice of dry toast, nibble by nibble, to help calm their stomachs. A dose of paracetamol took care of their headaches. Only time would stop the shaking.

'Good party, wasn't it?' Karen proposed.

'I wish I could remember more about it. It was so long ago,' Ian replied honestly. 'I seem to remember me setting light to someone's shoe laces and someone else throwing frozen chicks about, but the years have fogged the rest.'

Karen missed the reference to time.

'That'll be my ferret's food,' she said, matter-of-factly. 'Do you want to see him?'

'No thanks,' Ian said, shaking his head slightly.

An hour past in idle conversation, Karen and Ian's words exchanged over a number of coffee refills and half the contents of the biscuit barrel. All the while, Ian felt nothing but frustration and annoyance at being trapped inside an ailing body when he had more important things to be doing. All he needed was to be well enough to cause the core of his mind to buzz for one single second. That would take him back well before he took his first swig of whatever had got him into this state. From there, he could count another thirty-five seconds to complete the last of the major jumps back through his life.

Another hour passed while Ian convalesced on the sofa, sitting between Karen and the now conscious girl he had spent the night with, her name still eluding him.

Testing the degree to which he had recovered, Ian sunk into the backrest and closed his eyes. No one would think it strange. To one degree or another, each of them was experiencing the same effects of sleep deprivation and alcohol abuse. He began to concentrate, trying to suck the world in through his ears. The reward for his effort came with the return of the low frequency noise that had been absent for longer than he cared to tolerate. Elated, he pushed on, the low level buzzing sensation quickly giving way to a higher frequency. He began to count.

'One elephant…'

While one portion of his mind counted without missing a beat, the majority of the rest revelled in the sense of escape.

'…Thirty-six elephant.'

21

With the procedure complete, Ian opened his eyes to find himself at home, sitting motionless on his mum's settee in much the same position as he had left Karen's. The major difference being that, far from feeling better, he now felt at least one hundred times worse.

His head was tilted back, apparently his neck being unable to support it. He could feel heat radiating from his flushed skin. His body ached right down to the marrow-filled cavities within his bones. He possessed no energy: not enough to raise his arms; not enough to fully lift his eyelids; not enough even to bring his cracked lips together.

Unwittingly, he had returned to an illness and the sense of despair and misery that accompanied it. If he had been able, he would have cried.

'I'm dying,' he said in a croaking whisper.

'Don't be silly. You're not dying,' a female voice said reassuringly. It was not his mum. 'Here, take these. They'll help.'

With the greatest of effort, Ian raised his head, placed two tablets in his mouth, and sipped from a glass of water. The young woman who handed it to him was another name from the past; one who he was fated to lose contact with over the coming years. For now though, she was his Florence Nightingale.

'I remember this. Mum was in Amsterdam with her friend. You came round to look after me.'

Jane was not sure why her patient should be talking in the past tense, but decided not to enquire upon the matter as he was obviously in no fit state to be answering questions.

'Can you pass me the TV paper,' Ian requested pitifully, his head lolling about, his breaths shallow and laboured.

Jane dutifully handed him the magazine, wondering of what use such a publication might be to someone who was experiencing difficulty simply holding his head still, never mind watching television. He studied the front cover for a moment before dropping the paper onto his lap, allowing his head to fall back into the rest position. The sudden movement was clearly painful as could be seen by the wince that exploded across his face, contorting his features such that it was unbearable to watch.

'August, nineteen-seventy-seven,' he said.

Jane had never seen someone this ill before.

'You're beginning to worry me,' she said, her brave exterior on the verge of crumbling. 'Of course it's nineteen-seventy-seven. You don't need a magazine to tell you that.'

Even feeling the way he did, Ian was conscious of the fact his erstwhile friend was becoming spooked and sought to put her at ease.

'It's all right. I'll be fine in a day or two. I seem to remember this being German measles, but I might be wrong.'

It was not helping that he continued to talk as though all this had been in the past.

'Whatever it was, I lived long enough to forget it,' he continued.

'I wish I knew what to do. I've got to be getting back to work, but maybe I should stay and call the doctor.'

'No need. I'll be fine. I just wish that every time I opened my eyes, I didn't feel like shit. It's really beginning to get me down.'

Taking his statement at face value, entirely missing another of his cryptic messages, Jane suggested he might feel better if he went for a lie down.

'I'll do that. You must get back to work before you get into trouble. Thanks for everything.'

She left, promising to call by later. If the lights were still on, she would knock.

With the house to himself, Ian could devote all his efforts to calculating how many months he had stolen back from the universe - March 1979 to August 1977. Several attempts at determining the difference failed half way through, Ian's aching mind wandering hopelessly off at a tangent. Even when the answer finally came to him, with some degree of certainty, there was then the matter of calculating how many seconds equated to each month. He had made three jumps from 1985 and each time his estimate had proved wrong, leading him to conclude there were too many variables, some of which he might not even be aware of. Much depended on his ability to count consistently with the same cadence. Then there was the possibility a younger mind sped up the process. Of course, it did not help that he had to commit to memory the months travelled against however many seconds it took to do so, but alas, written notes remained in the future.

All he could say with certainty was he still needed to go back another three months. Four seconds seemed a prudent figure.

Ian made sure no lights were showing that evening, not wishing to experience a repeat of the type of conversation he and Jane had exchanged at lunchtime. He felt too ill to talk and when he did, she felt scared.

Unable to enjoy watching the television, listening to the radio, reading a book, penning a missive, or even flicking through a picture magazine, the afternoon passed as tortuously as if a leaking tap were dripping water onto the centre of his forehead. Pain amplified boredom; frustration amplified boredom; virtual paralysis amplified boredom. He could not walk; he could not talk; he was an abandoned baby longing to pass into unconsciousness to relieve his torment.

At the first respectable opportunity, when the room was dim enough to warrant the use of artificial light, Ian made his way unsteadily to the foot of the stairs. From there, he hauled himself, one step at a time up to the first floor, pausing frequently to muster sufficient strength to make the next assault. Despite the pain and near total absence of energy, Ian made full preparations for bed. Brushing his teeth would not prolong their useful life - if all went well, he would soon regress to a point before they had become unclean in the first place. However, it helped make him feel as fresh as possible; a state that might help him sleep; a sleep from which he might wake feeling sufficiently recovered to be able to rewind out of his nightmare.

Sure enough, in the morning, following a fitful slumber, Ian woke feeling much improved. Following a top-up of paracetamol, a cup of tea and a change of clothing, he returned to bed and slept on until mid-afternoon. When eventually he woke, the world looked a sunnier place. He was still unwell. If he had any intention of staying, he would most certainly not be going to work. However, his state of fitness had recovered sufficiently that he was sure he could make the first of what he expected to be many smaller jumps, fine-tuning the time frame until he reached his school exams.

This time, Ian opened his eyes to a huge projector screen, filled with closing credits that scrolled slowly upwards, accompanied by an entirely forgettable music score, perfectly suited to the post-movie drift towards the fire exits.

Next to him sat a girl he recognised as a blind date, introduced to him by a mutual friend of theirs by the name of Zena. As for the name of the date herself, it had long since been forgotten. All he could remember of her was that she liked to purchase a brand new toothbrush every Saturday morning – every week - without fail. It was true she had remarkably clean teeth, but this was eclipsed by the fact she always smelled heavily of chip fat, as she did now. Her unparalleled lack of intelligence also left a lasting impression.

Passing through the doors to the open air, the anonymous date was bursting with excitement.

'Well, what did you think? Wasn't it great?'

'To be honest, I have no idea what it was we were watching,' Ian replied with brutal honesty.

'Eh?'

'I've seen it all before,' he said, enjoying baiting his forgotten companion with clues she could not possibly hope to solve. 'I'm afraid that for the entire duration of the film, my mind was elsewhere.'

Shamefully, Ian found himself enjoying watching her fail to understand a single word he said.

Her reaction was automated. Evolution had denied her brains, but had compensated by endowing her with an unsophisticated, yet effective, defence mechanism. Faced with something she did not understand, her expression would become blank, her eyes would stray to one side, and when the person had finished speaking, she would simply change the subject. No hint of subtlety, or sign of an apology.

'Do you want to go shopping with me tomorrow morning?' she asked, clearly smitten with her partner, but only because he had agreed to go out with her.

Not prepared to start down the road of exchanging small talk with an unattractive dullard, Ian decided to get straight to the point.

'Tell me...' Ian began, before realising he still did not recall her name. 'Tell me, would you like to hear a trick?'

'Okay.'

'What day is it?'

'Friday.'

'What date is it?'

'The sixth.'

'The month?'

'May.'

'And the year?'

'Nineteen-seventy-seven.'

Bingo.

The girl's anticipation could be seen growing with every correct answer.

'Well?' she said, unable to contain her curiosity any longer.

'Sorry, I've forgotten how it works. Never was very good at doing tricks.'

The date concluded at the end of a twenty-minute bus journey, when the girl-with-no-name stepped from the lit interior in to the chill night air, one stop short of her boyfriend's destination. Conversation had been sparse and there had been no indication he wished to see her again, but none of that mattered. He had said more in deeds than could ever be put into words. Turning to walk towards home, her hand touched her cheek on the very spot where he had placed a kiss, causing a warm glow to engulf her entire body.

Ian arrived home and went straight up to his room, avoiding questions from his mum as to how the evening had gone. In truth, he had no idea with regard to the majority of it and even if he had, he would not want to discuss it. Whoever he had been out with, he would not be making the same mistake again.

At the foot of his bed sat a sports bag, every square centimetre of its yellow vinyl surface covered with layers of doodles, fresh pen-work covering the faded old; the result of countless boring journeys on the school coach, driven by an old, balding lecher with a fag perpetually hanging from his lip. Inside the bag were textbooks, workbooks, an oversized ink-stained denim pencil case and a class timetable. Tucked within the pages of this last item, a folded supplementary A4 sheet detailed the times and dates of the exams he had journeyed back to re-sit. Studying the page, it transpired he had sat an English Literature test paper that very morning. Whereas his classmates would have to wait several months for their results, Ian knew he had achieved a 'C'; a low pass.

'I think I can do better than that,' he said confidently, under his breath.

To do so would need a rewind of something in the region of just twelve hours, but to retake all his exams would require him to retract a few days. This presented a quandary. The period he needed to retract was probably too short to use the high frequency technique, and probably too long to use the safer, lower frequency method, going back twenty minutes at a time. Each had its advantages and disadvantages. Ideally, the best solution would have been for him to remember taking the exam in so great a detail he was able to lock onto those thoughts and travel straight there, but he could not. Not a single trace memory of that time remained.

Weighing up the options, Ian was initially swayed towards taking the safe route; rewinding the universe twenty minutes at a time; speeding up the process a little by first fixing on the vivid memory of the girl with whom he had spent the entire evening, returning directly to the point in the cinema at which the credits had started rolling.

Her face bore features that would not have been out of place during the late Palaeolithic period; a catch for any self-respecting Neanderthal man. Unfortunately for her, Homo sapiens had won the battle of evolution, and to them, she was plain ugly - unfortunate for her, but a blessing for someone with Ian's gift.

In the end, though, he settled for the briefest high frequency shift he was able to perform, hoping not to overshoot too far. At worst, he would probably be a few days out; something he could cope with.

Closing his eyes, he activated the process, ceasing again immediately upon detecting the cusp between low and high frequencies. He found himself sitting on the edge of a table in a place he recognised as the fifth form common room, surrounded by students, including a circle of his closest friends. A mixed-sex group of half a dozen familiar faces was staring at him. Ian stared back.

'Well,' a younger David Utteridge asked, following an awkward silence.

Ian looked back at him in puzzlement.

'Are you going to tell us the end of the joke, or what?'

'Sorry, I've forgotten it,' Ian said lamely. 'I never was very good at telling jokes.'

The group groaned en masse, a few of its number shaking their heads in mock disbelief. Then someone sparked off a new line of trivial conversation and the matter was closed.

Ian sat quietly, studying each of his former friends in turn. One or two maintained a clear complexion, the remainder suffering from varying degrees of acne. Some were scruffy; their neckties knotted fat and ludicrously short. Others - the girls - sat in serene elegance. Clearly there were differences between each of them, but still the common ground remained by far the most predominant – they all looked so very young. Faces devoid of wrinkles; bodies without mass; conversation without substance. Logic dictated his external appearance must be the same as the rest of the youths with whom he shared the room. To the casual observer, it would also be assumed he was the same on the inside too, but he was not. He felt old; older than at any other point in his life. Far from being their friend, he was their father.

This was not the first time he had opened his eyes to 'Ian the younger', having to come to terms with a version of himself he had long since left behind. On completing his first major jump, returning to the age of twenty-four, he had been instantly aware of the changes; some good; some not. On that occasion, he had surrendered a sizeable chunk of his life, just as he had done now, but there had remained tangible connections with all that had been erased. He still went to work, he still drove a car and most significantly, he still had his wife, albeit an un-ripened version.

As a student, there was nothing to link him to his future; there was nothing at this age that could even be described as a less developed version of what he had given up. He felt disorientated, as though he was acting outside his immediate surroundings. He had reached his goal, the point from which he would begin to rebuild his life, only to discover he had absolutely nothing in common with anything or anyone. There being no correlation between his apparent age and his genuine needs and desires, fitting in was going to be challenging.

Without decisive, positive action, there was a distinct danger he might remain in a state of self-pity for a very long time.

Ian gave himself a mental kick.

With renewed determination to maintain the impetus he had created in the future, he quickly fixed upon the need to find out exactly how far back he had gone. At least his wristwatch would tell him the time of day, although, without making reference to it, he already suspected it to be lunch, his stomach feeling full, and there remaining the taint of food on his tongue.

Shooting his cuff revealed the same chromed digital watch he had been wearing on the night of the blind date. He had referred to it at the bus station, but had overlooked its full capabilities. In addition to displaying the time, it could be used as a stopwatch, an alarm clock, or a day-date-month calendar. If only he had remembered that earlier, he could have avoided the need to conjure up a spurious magic trick for the sole purpose of teasing the day's date from the chip-fat girl.

With a single press of the 'mode' button, the date was revealed.

Keen to determine the significance of that particular day, Ian scanned the surrounding area for his bag. It lay by the foot of one of the table legs that shared the burden of his weight. Consulting the timetable that rarely left the confines of the bag for more than a few minutes, he found his luck had finally changed for the good. He had returned to the first day of his exams – no more rewinds would be necessary.

It was a fact in his life that everything silver-lined tended to be a cloud. This was no exception. Not only had he returned to the day of the first test, he had managed to get to within fifteen minutes of its commencement. Effectively, following the necessary preliminaries, the instruction to turn over the Maths paper would occur immediately after the lunchtime break.

The supplement to the lesson timetable detailed what was being sat, where he should be to sit it, and at what time he should get there. It was scribed in an untidy hand; an immature version of his own; one he could not hope to imitate. Thankfully, it would not be his own teachers marking the papers as they might suspect foul play, ruining his plans to forge a better life.

This thought did not help. As the situation stood, his emotions aped those he imagined a covert operative to possess, one in danger of being discovered as an impostor: overwhelmed by the need to be immersed in another's personality; constantly scared at the thought of being exposed.

The maths exam was to take place in the main assembly hall. Even after so many years of absence, he could still remember the route from the common room, and through which of the many doors he should enter when he got there. Many pupils milled about the entrance, few conversing with each other, preferring instead to concentrate on fruitless, last minute, revision.

Ian sat alone at one of the many isolated desks, his being adjacent to the windowed wall on the opposite side to the main doors. Hanging his blazer over the back of his chair, he made himself comfortable. Tensions grew as a teacher placed a question paper, face down, one in front of each expectant pupil. Finally, the instruction came.

'You may now turn over your papers.'

The voice reflected the seriousness of the occasion and the vigorous professionalism under which the test was to be conducted.

Ian duly followed the instruction, in unison with all others present. Papers flapped, followed by a short pause, and then a wave of groans as eyes met what was expected of them. Many pens began to scribble, but not Ian's. He was mature enough, experienced and wise enough, to study the written instructions carefully, reading them twice over before moving on to the heart of the paper – the questions themselves. These he scanned briefly for an overview, confident this methodical approach alone would guarantee an 'A'. His hopes were short lived. Words such as 'differentiation' leapt from the page to evoke a rapidly growing sense of panic. He knew maths. He used it every day, but not this.

Despite his superior knowledge, maturity and life experience, Ian found himself suffering the same sense of despair as were the majority of the pupils who filled the hall. Perversely, even the most unintelligent of them would probably fare better, having been exposed to these obscure recesses of the mathematics curriculum within their recent memory.

Maths was a core subject. He needed to do well.

In order to boost his morale, Ian's original aim had been to tackle the easiest question first, before attempting something a little trickier. However, the initial sift having drawn a blank, he was now forced to reassess the situation, eventually starting with the least-worst. Even so, it was clear that despite settling upon such a low target, he was sure to fail. More worrying was the fact the same conclusion could be applied to most, if not all, of his subjects. English Literature sprang instantly to mind. How could he successfully analyse books he had not read in more than thirty years?

Without even having appended the paper with his personal details, he gave up. His pen dropped noisily onto the desk; his head dropped silently into his waiting hands.

There were now two alternatives, but only one solution: he could let things lie and leave school in a worse state, without a qualification to his name; or he could go back still further and study to pass each and every one of his exams, preferably attaining top marks.

Putting to the back of his mind for the moment the course of action he knew he would have to take, Ian deliberately missed the bus home. Then, without first ringing his mum to inform her of his intentions, he took the number 16 to Lakely, the one-time hometown of his future wife. As a middle aged couple they had driven past the home of her childhood on a number of occasions, to see how the old place had stood the test of time, and to reminisce. She had told him how she and the many neighbouring children would play together in the cul-de-sac until loss of daylight forced them in for tea. Those had been happy times.

Ian arrived at his destination sometime after the schools of Lakely had disgorged their pupils onto the streets, and already they were to be seen, having changed into civilian clothing with the efficiency of Superman, running about in the turning point at the end of the dead-end road. Debbie was among their number, wearing roller skates, weaving in and out of her friends, smiling and loving life.

Ian stood to one side, absorbing the view, forming new memories. He wanted to join in, but knew it was impossible. Eventually, the inevitable happened.

'What you lookin' at?'

Ian did not answer, but instead reluctantly closed his eyes.

Six months would be enough. Any longer would be unbearable; a shorter period would be insufficient to bone up on so many subjects.

Promising himself this would positively be the last time he would ever regress again, Ian felt the cusp, and began to count.

22

On the count of ten, Ian halted the regression, immediately exposing himself to the unpleasant sensation of falling backwards while seated. En masse, the remainder of the class - some thirty pupils - instantly flicked their attention from Mr Gimble, facing them at the front, to the back row where Ian was performing an extraordinary manoeuvre, trying desperately to recover his balance.

'Bradshaw!' the teacher bellowed as the target of his wrath shot his arms out, both hands grabbing for the edge of the desk.

Ian, now recovered, all four chair legs firmly back in contact with the floor, could do nothing but look sheepish.

To perform such an act in front of any teacher was inviting trouble; doing so in front of Mr Gimble, the Deputy Head, and a man unquestionably of 'old school' mentality, was tantamount to committing suicide.

'You could have broken your back, you foolish boy,' the teacher continued, barking his words with such ferocity the entire class cowered despite being entirely blameless.

'Sorry Sir,' Ian offered, apologetically.

Without knowing the thought processes of his tutor, by accepting the reprimand without question or excuse, Ian had done the only thing that could save him from formal punishment. There would be no detention on this occasion.

The bell, marking the end of the lesson, rang out in the corridor. Desktops were cleared away swiftly and in silence, but not a soul moved until Mr Gimble had spoken, giving them the authority to do so.

Right up until the point of exiting the room, Ian fully expected to be pulled to one side, the teacher having changed his mind, but he had not.

Once out of earshot, several classmates patted him on the shoulder, reminding him how lucky he had been.

'That was close. I thought we'd all be staying behind,' Gary Roberts said, speaking in a low tone through gritted teeth, his head fixed rigidly ahead of him, his feet carrying him along at an exaggerated pace away from danger.

By the stairwell, the urgency of the fleeing pupils to put distance between themselves and the Deputy Head had subsided. Only then was there an opportunity to reflect upon what had happened.

The situation had been unpleasant and extremely embarrassing for Ian, but at least the date written and underlined in the top left-hand corner of the blackboard had shown the regression had been fairly accurate, overshooting by less than two weeks. At worst, he now had an additional eleven days in which to revise.

Whether brought on by fear, or a recent history of drinking he was unaware of, Ian found he was in need of a toilet. Memories of the layout of the school did not run to such detail as the location of the boys' room, but, there being several dotted about the estate, finding one without the need for detour proved an easy task.

Reassured by the fact he had friends who were prepared to wait for him, Ian stepped through two sprung doors, chose a urinal, and quickly restored a little comfort to his life. Turning to wash his hands, an image of a young, scruffy, teenager looked back at him from a bank of mirrors mounted on the wall above a row of white porcelain sinks. The young man sported hair that was too thick and too long; longer than that of any his friends, including the girls. Not only that, but it looked unwashed. It was neither a fashion statement nor an indication he was a follower of heavy metal music; rather a symptom of the fact that, at an early age, he had developed a dislike - bordering on a fear - of barbers. To make matters worse, the mirrors also showed a downy growth across his top lip that should have been removed when first it became apparent, and a severe outbreak of acne: white-heads; black-heads; vicious-looking red pimples.

So greatly was Ian disturbed by his appearance that he was reluctant to emerge from the toilets without wearing a bag over his head. Not being in possession of a suitable mask, or the means to do anything about the length and cleanliness of his hair, his moustache or his spots, there was nothing to do but re-join his company, vowing to take remedial action as soon as humanly possible. In the meantime, the very least he could do was remove his ridiculously knotted tie and reapply it with a full Windsor.

Stepping back into the corridor, Ian felt all eyes were upon him, judging him to be the dirtiest individual in the school, anticipating a string of derogatory comments at every turn. Ironically, the only remark made was on the state of his tie.

Mr Gimble's lesson had been the last before lunch. Ian and his friends joined the queue for the dinner hall, shuffling forwards slowly as directed by the dinner lady.

Towards the end of his schooling, set meals of a hot, healthy main course, followed by a pudding, had been phased out in favour of a commercial cafeteria-style operation. There was undoubtedly more choice, but in many cases this had led to the quality and variety of individual diets taking a tumble. In Ian's case, he had liked burgers and chips so that is what he had eaten, each and every day of his school life. Little wonder then his complexion was so poor.

Tastes had changed over the years and now Ian passed by the plated burger in a bun, heading instead for a simple salad; a decision that came as a shock to all who knew him. Originally he had not let a single vegetable pass his lips until as late as his early twenties; other than the humble potato or the odd carrot – peas had been a step too far.

The queue moved on towards the till - a concept that had arisen with advent of the cafeteria. Prior to that, money had been collected weekly by the form tutor. It had disguised the situation that happened next.

As each tray-laden pupil reached the point of paying, they would take a variety of wallets and purses from their pockets and bags, each bursting with excesses of change, sufficient to cover the expense of the mid-morning tuck shop, the newsagent on the way to and from school, and to settle the lunchtime bill in cash. Ian had no such wallet. Nor did he have any money. Instead, reaching into his pocket, he found a small booklet filled with numbered buff tickets in blocks of five. The state was picking up the tab for his food and everyone knew it.

Paying for his meal with a voucher was a reminder of what it was like to rely on handouts; to be labelled as coming from a poor family. The uniform he was wearing had been provided for with a grant. His school trips abroad had been paid from the taxpayers' purse, attracting snide comments from the children of the better off. Being longhaired, unshaven, spotty and generally scruffy, reinforced the stereotype. He might not be able to improve his mum's finances, but he could certainly do something about his personal hygiene and appearance – a priority that would be receiving attention at the earliest possible opportunity.

Following lunch, inclement weather prevented the school from exercising in the fresh air. Even if it had not been raining, the fifth form had standing permission to remain in their common room whereas the lower years did not.

Feeling unable to join in, Ian sat back from his group of friends, staring at each in turn – the only person alive who could reminisce about their future.

'You seem distant today. Are you all right?' Ann Sharples asked, her gender endowing her with more empathy than the boys.

'I'm fine,' Ian replied. 'It's just that it occurred to me we'll be taking our exams soon and then we'll all drift apart. We may only ever see each other again at the occasional school reunion.'

'I'm sure we'll see each other more often than that.'

'Don't be so sure. Some of us will continue with our education; others won't. Some will move up the country; others will move abroad. It's just the way of things.'

'No one knows what will happen in the future; all except for Jim maybe. He's known what he wants to do since he was born.'

Ian held back a lump in his throat at the mere mention of Jim's name.

'I can see things,' Ian said, simply. 'I know the future.'

'Yeah, course you can,' David Utteridge said, mockingly.

Ian maintained an air of serious matter-of-factness that was hard to ignore.

'Go on then. What will I do when I leave school?' David asked, laying down the gauntlet.

Without hesitation, Ian answered.

'You my friend will have your own roofing company. You're going to do well for yourself. You'll also enjoy hiking, and a nice Irish stew. '

If Ian were making it up, he was proving to be a consummate liar, giving himself no time to fabricate a story, delivering his prediction with the utmost confidence.

'And me?' Ann asked.

'You will land up being a solicitor, living in an idyllic little village in Yorkshire.'

'What about me?'

It was Gary Roberts' turn to ask.

'Bizarrely, you'll end up in Bavaria, selling car exhausts.'

'Where's Bavaria?' Gary asked, his head jerking about as would a chicken's, having been given the same news.

Who could make up such a thing on the spur of the moment?

Next to ask, and the last in the group, was Jim Bedford. The man who stood before Ian was full of life, the only one of them who had always known exactly what he wanted to do. Ian could hardly tell him the truth, knowing he would never see his plans come to fruition, it being his destiny to die of cancer at the appallingly meagre age of twenty-three.

'You'll do what we've always known what you'll do. You'll go into wildlife conservation and make a real difference.'

One more voice posed the same question. Nicola Appleby had been standing, unnoticed, behind Ian for the duration of the sitting. Ian recognised her voice immediately and swung round to face her.

'You!' he began firmly, trying unsuccessfully to contain his emotions. 'Don't worry, you'll end up with a successful business; you'll have a house and a new car before the rest of us; you'll be interesting in bed, but most of all you'll do anything, however underhanded, to get what you want. You evil, selfish, bitch!'

Nicola undoubtedly looked the most shocked, but she was by no means alone.

'I don't understand. What have I done?' she pleaded, close to tears.

'What have you done? You've ruined my life! Building me up only to smash me down again.'

The bitterness with which Ian announced the charge cut the atmosphere within the room.

'I haven't done anything to you,' Nicola implored.

'No, but you will,' Ian said, pausing to correct himself. 'You would have done, if I'd left things as they might have been.'

Nicola stormed off crying, closely followed by Ann who threw a scathing glance at Ian as she left. The remainder of the small group, together with every other person in the common room, all stared at the person responsible for such an outburst.

Unwilling to address the whole congregation, Ian looked to his friends.

'I don't think I have experienced a decent night's sleep, or a really good meal, in a very long time,' he said. 'Thirty-two years to be precise.'

The staring continued.

'Look, I'll apologise to her before the end of school. I promise.'

'Spooky', a voice piped up from somewhere at the back.

Angrily, Ian closed his eyes. When he opened them again, outwardly he was staring; inwardly he was still annoyed.

'You seem distant today. Are you all right?' Ann Sharples asked kindly.

'I'm fine. I was just thinking.'

'Thinking about what?'

'If you must know, I was thinking that nobody should know their own future. You'd land up wishing your life away; keen to get to the good bits. So much so that it could make you want to cry. On the other hand, knowing the bad bits you would be destined to endure would make you want to cry too. A no win situation really.'

Ann listened and then stared, a peculiar expression of puzzlement on her face.

'That still sounds a bit weird doesn't it? Oh well, I just hope there's no one else around who can turn back time.'

With that, a brief buzzing sensation resulted in Ann asking the same question for a third time.

'You seem distant today. Are you all right?'

'I'm fine,' Ian replied, careful to avoid using any inflexion that might hint at a deeper message. 'I'm just a bit tired. I really must try and get some sleep tonight.'

Ann was happy with the reply; he had said nothing to rouse the interest of any other party in the room; even Nicola's arrival prompted no comment, action, or suspicion that something was wrong between her and the man she would have destroyed in the future had he let her.

The remainder of the dinner hour passed without event.

Following his lesson timetable, at the sound of the bell, Ian made his way to geography.

Despite his desire not to use his ability, and so avoid drawing the attention of any pre-Summerbee adversary that might potentially exist, after only half an hour with Mr French, Ian had no choice but to retract time once again.

In Ian's experience, the general populous spoke about teachers without criticism; as upstanding members of the community who could do no wrong. However, he knew, as in all walks of life, there were those who did a good job, those who were adequately skilled and those who were utterly incapable. Mr French fell into the latter group; his method of teaching being limited to copying tracts from a text book onto the blackboard, and then asking his pupils to copy the chalk notes and diagrams into their exercise books. It taught nothing.

'You, sir, are a terrible teacher,' Ian said with passion, and then did not say, instead biting his lip, reluctantly letting the demonstration of incompetence pass without comment.

So far as geography was concerned, it was clear Ian would be better off relying on himself to learn the subject.

The last lesson was English Literature, in 'A block'. Ian managed to look natural, as though familiarity with his surroundings would allow him to conduct the journey blindfold. In truth though, his residual knowledge of the building was sufficient only to save himself the embarrassment of becoming hopelessly lost, but that was as far as it went; each new turn in the corridor being a re-discovery of his old world. Guided by a faded map of long-abandoned memories, he was almost surprised when his skills in covert navigation brought him to the right door.

Adopting the actions of others, Ian went inside and sat down, taking the first available chair. His chosen desk formed part of the front row, offset to the left of centre, fully exposed to the teacher's domain. Two of his school days' desires, to hunt out a best friend to sit next to, and to choose as preference the back row, failed to influence him. All that mattered was to sit, and to do so without drawing attention.

No sooner had he placed his bag down by his ankle, Miss Antrim walked in, taking up position behind her desk. She turned towards the board and began sweeping a heavy wooden-backed chalk eraser across the morning's lesson. Her buttocks and thighs, clothed in tightly-fitting corduroy, drew Ian's attention with such force he found it difficult to divert his gaze.

She looked substantially younger than he remembered; bordering on being too young to teach. The first time round, he had appreciated she was attractive, but the age gap had dampened the effect. Now, from the perspective of one who was mentally many years older than her, her youthful, perfectly formed figure was enough to set his pulse racing. She finished cleaning the blackboard all too soon, but the images endured in Ian's mind, causing an awakening in his trousers.

Praying the class was not obliged to stand up as a sign of respect to their teacher, Ian remained seated; puzzled as to why this should happen to him now when he had no recollection of it being a problem before. The only similar situation to this had been a regular one. Almost daily on the school bus he had become inexplicably aroused within five minutes of approaching his stop – possibly something to do with vibration caused by the road passing through the bodywork of the coach, stimulating the base of his groin. In an attempt to counter it, he had filled his head with nothing but anti-erotic thoughts. Invariably, his imagination had proven not to be up to the job, forcing him to shuffle along the aisle from the back of the bus with his bag pressed firmly against the tell-tale bulge in his trousers. Thankfully, by the time he had stepped off onto the pavement, his embarrassment had always disappeared. To his knowledge, no one had ever suspected a thing.

'Right, class; homework.'

In unison, each and every pupil placed a workbook, with uniform pink cover, in front of them, opening the pages to the last entry. Ian followed suit. There, he found a paragraph heading the page, detailing the set task, but of the character study it alluded to, there was no sign.

'Ian Bradshaw, I think we shall start with you.'

Was this bad luck, had she detected a look of surprise or guilt on his face, or was she picking on him because of previous behaviour he was unaware of? In any event, it mattered not. With no memory, there was no defence.

'Sorry, but I appear not to have done it,' Ian said honestly; apologetically; no excuses.

The class laughed aloud, but stopped instantly in response to a disapproving look from the teacher that swept the room, daring anyone to continue.

Her authority restored, her full attention turned back to just one pupil.

'You appear not to have done it?' she repeated, calmly, making sure she had not misunderstood his statement. 'Am I to believe it is possible for you to have forgotten whether or not you did your homework?'

Ian remained mute, contorting his face as if to suggest her summation, as strange as it seemed, was nonetheless true.

'Very well, I shall deal with you at the end of the lesson.'

Half a dozen pupils then proceeded, on demand, to read their short passages and so prove they had toiled for at least five minutes during the course of the previous evening. If their work was of sufficient standard to achieve a pass at 'O' level then Ian could feel confident of achieving an 'A'.

'Now we shall read from the text book,' Miss Antrim announced, her lesson proceeding as planned. 'Ian Bradshaw, please begin reading from the top of page one-hundred-and-four.'

This was clearly a reprisal for having not presented his homework. Without thirty odd additional years in which to hone his skills, it would indeed have been punishment. Originally he had hated reading aloud. So too had the rest of the class. The books were uninteresting, made more so by the complete inability of those chosen to put any feeling or meaning into the spoken passages.

What made the difference though, was that he had experienced those years – reading to his wife when she was ill, and to his children throughout their formative years. Beginning with books in which the pictures outnumbered the words, the tradition had continued into their early teens, when Stephen and Ann were quite capable of reading for themselves. Having developed a love of the written word himself, he would try his best to impart his enthusiasm, reading clearly, with rhythm and, most of all, by making the stories interesting.

A short silence followed, the sole noise being caused by the jostling of the many pupils finding the right page and settling down to follow every word with their fingers. The only thing lifting their hearts was the fact that while someone else was reading, they were not being called upon to do the same.

Ian began.

Within the duration it took to deliver the first paragraph, every pair of ears in the room had detected this was something out of the ordinary. No mumbling; no monotone; no stumbling over difficult spellings and words from obscurity. Here was a pupil, trapped somewhere between grown boy and young man, whose ability to read had changed beyond comprehension over the course of just one night. With closed eyes, it would be difficult to tell Ian Bradshaw from a professional narrator. For the first time since undertaking to study the subject to examination standard, the disinterested were discovering why they had been flogging this particular text to death – because the work was great, possessing the ability to evoke emotional responses; to make the reader feel what had been written. So enthralled was Miss Antrim by her pupil's ability to inject new life into a text that she herself had heard once too often, she instructed him to stop only when his voice began to sound dry. Lost for words, she at first failed to pass the burden onto her next victim. A situation the rest of the class secretly hoped would continue indefinitely.

The bell finally marked the end of the lesson. The pupils filed out in an orderly fashion.

Passing Miss Antrim, Ian expected to be given a pink detention slip in recognition of the homework he had not completed. Whatever else he had forgotten, the detention slip remained as clearly in his mind as it had been on the dozens of occasions he had received them when he was first a boy. In his defence, it was a fact that they had never been awarded for disruptive behaviour. Ian had never been a tearaway. All had been as a result of a major character fault – procrastination. The affect had faded by middle age, but when he was younger he had put everything off until the last possible minute and sometimes until it was far too late.

'Ian, well done. That reading was superb. You might even have found your vocation in life,' Miss Antrim said, smiling.

Here was a teacher entitled to issue punishment, but who had the sense to concentrate on the positive, believing it to lead to better results. For a moment, Ian felt as young as he looked; grateful to his elder for having given him a chance.

As pleasant as it had been to feel the appreciation of his fellow peers, and that of a professional, it was more so to be at home, away from the talk of events. In truth, he was no master of the spoken word; above average perhaps, but it would not be a career path he would be pursuing. Miss Antrim had been too kind, impressed more by the sudden change she saw in him than by his actual ability. Only when judged against the woefully inadequate did he shine, and then he was made to feel a freak.

On arriving home, there was no doubt he was exhausted; the mental strain of navigating his past had taken its toll. Nevertheless, he was keen to cook his own tea so his mum might be given a rest. At this time in her life, she undertook daily cleaning jobs, serving a different employer morning and afternoon, Monday to Friday, and all to make ends meet.

Miss Antrim was not the only person that day to experience sudden change. His mum had always waited on her son, pampering to his chauvinistic needs. Not once in her memory had he prepared more than a bowl of cereal for himself and even then, only when circumstances became desperate. Now, he cooked, making enough for two. They ate. He collected the dishes and washed everything he had used, and more besides. He brewed tea, served his mum while she sat watching the television, poured a cup for himself and climbed the stairs to his bedroom.

Ian's approach to taking his exams was to be a methodical one. The first task was to see what resources he had available to him. This entailed scouring his room, gathering together school textbooks on every subject in his personalised curriculum. In doing so, he rediscovered a set of study aid books his mum had bought from her meagre budget and which he had never once opened and read. If nothing else, they would add structure to his revision. This time her money would be well spent.

With the substance of his plan piled about him, the next few hours were spent drawing up a study regime that would fully refresh his mind on every subject by the time the exams came round again. There would be precious opportunity for leisure activities, but it was a price he was prepared to meet. In many respects, his social life would remain unaffected. Originally, lack of money capped the number of evening he spent with his wealthier friends. Instead, he would watch the television, increasing his viewing hours, year on year, until it was the first thing he did when he arrived home in the afternoon, and the last thing he did before going to bed at night. Failing to allocate a slot for the completion of homework often lead to after-school punishment – the only time during the week when he was free from the influence of the small screen.

Next, there was the subject of his appearance. There was nothing he could do before the weekend about the length and style of his hair, or the downy caterpillar that crawled across his upper lip. What he could do was to have a bath, making liberal use of soap, shampoo, and a flannel. First though, he intended to sweat – a light jog followed by a few press-ups, the beginning of a new regimen of exercise, healthy food and the acquisition of knowledge.

Having noted the extent of his exertions in an empty diary, there was still time before his bath to scrub the worst of the dirt and doodles from his bag, leaving only faded images masking earlier faded images. Following his bath, he set about brushing his teeth for a full five minutes, until his gums bled; ironing his clothes for the following day; completing all the tasks his teachers had set; and packing his bag.

By half past ten, it was all that Ian could do to keep his eyes open. Having bid his mum 'good night', he slipped into bed and turned out the lamp. This was the perfect moment to review the day.

There was much to celebrate. He had finally reached the earliest point of his life that it would be necessary to return to. He had successfully completed the first day of his long journey, one that would eventually reunite him with his family. He had begun to live his life again, maximising its potential.

A phrase began repeating itself inside his head.

'I am one day closer to becoming reunited with Debbie and the kids.'

He tried to picture his children, recalling images of them as they were when he had said goodbye to them at university, and in the photographs dotted around his house. Frustration began to mount with the realisation that, even in his mind's eye, he could no longer see them; no longer speak with them. Images of his wife were fading too; confused by recent memories of the way she looked when he had first met her; of the way she looked even before they had originally met. For many years she had been a pillar of strength, supporting Ian whenever he was down, being there to share the experiences of life; a friend and a lover. If only he had a photograph of them now; one he could slip inside his wallet, but none yet existed.

Gradually the pain that had been subdued by the events of the day rose to the surface, bringing with it tears that leaked from closed eyelids. He began to sob quietly, pulling the pillow over his head to dampen the noise, making it undetectable to any person positioned on the far side of the bedroom door. He cried not like an adult, not like a sixteen-year-old youth, but like a young child, lost, alone, without a living person to whom he could turn. The crying stopped only when the need for sleep overtook the need to express his deep sadness.

23

The following morning, on leaving the house for the start of a one-and-a-half mile slog, mostly uphill, to the school bus stop, Ian met with his neighbour who was experiencing problems getting his car started. With the driver's door wide open, Ian could see Mr Dickens was attempting to bully the engine into firing, pumping the accelerator pedal repeatedly while holding the key forward. The starter motor turned the engine - a frenzy that was rapidly dying, the battery showing signs of fatigue.

'You've flooded it,' Ian said plainly, during a brief lull.

Mr Dickens turned to his advisor with a look of contempt that only a grumpy old man can convey.

'Hmm?' he responded, clearly annoyed.

His reaction warranted no further assistance, but experience told Ian he was right, and that his neighbour would do well to heed his advice.

'Press the accelerator to the floor and hold it there. Then turn the key. It should start after a while. When it fires you can take your foot off and give it some encouragement if necessary.'

Mr Dickens looked at Ian blankly as though the instructions were too complicated.

'Would you like me to do it?' Ian offered. 'I've experienced the same problem myself on a number of occasions.'

Mr Dickens' expression turned to one of suspicion, but after a moment, he stepped out of the car and moved aside. This was the closest thing to an invitation Ian was to receive. He took it, settled himself in front of the steering wheel, and followed the procedure just as described. Within thirty seconds the engine was running smoothly. Ian got out of the car, leaving it running, handing control back to its owner. Again, Mr Dickens looked at him suspiciously.

'Thank you,' he said, reluctantly, closing the door with himself in the driving seat.

Then, without further acknowledgement, he reversed past his benefactor and drove off in the direction of the school bus stop. Ian was now late and had to quicken his pace.

'Miserable bastard,' he said, muttering venomously under his breath.

The school day progressed well, Ian managing to refresh his knowledge on further subjects without again drawing the sort of attention that had plagued him only twenty-four hours earlier.

'Two down, two-thousand-nine-hundred-and-ninety-eight days to go', Ian said quietly to himself, slipping his key into the Yale lock.

Approximately three thousand days would see him dating his wife-to-be. By then he should have a degree, possibly a PhD, and a career to support them in their new life together. Three thousand days was not the only plan. Ian had six-month, two-year and five-year plans, but the three-thousand-day was the big one – the light at the end of the tunnel. The others were merely points along the way.

The front door swung open.

'Ian,' his mum said with a note of sincerity in her voice that spelled trouble. 'Mr Dickens knocked earlier. He seems to think you have turned to joy riding in stolen cars.'

'He what?' Ian responded, truly flabbergasted by the allegation.

'He said his car wouldn't start this morning and that you knew what to do.'

'Yes, I did, and for all the thanks I got, I nearly missed my bus.'

'Ian, we don't own a car, you're too young to drive, and your father hasn't been round for some time, so tell me, if you haven't been messing about in cars illegally, how did you know what to do?'

For a moment, the accused found himself lost for words. How could such a selfless act of assistance, offered to a man he did not even like, have led him into yet another awkward situation? Aware any pause in giving an answer would lead to the suspicion he was fabricating a story, his reply had to be delivered soon and it had to be decisive. Before he could speak though, his mum let rip with the second barrel.

'Mr Dickens said you claim to have done it many times before. What do you say to that?' his mum asked, pushing home her accusation.

'On the first count,' Ian replied calmly. 'I've simply picked up a few tips from car magazines over the years. They're very informative about a great many things. As to the other charge, I stupidly told Dickens I had previous experience to promote his confidence in me so I could just get on and do the job. It was bad enough he should drive off and leave me stranded, but I shall never forgive him for telling you I'm a car thief.'

Agnes had always shared her son's dislike for their neighbour, and was pleased to hear Ian refute the allegations so strongly, and with such obvious integrity. She found the way he spoke a little unusual; the way he phrased his argument; it was as though he were older than his years, but his words rung true nonetheless. Perhaps it was time to recognise her son was becoming a man.

Agnes vowed never again to listen to the ravings of Mr Dickens. Ian vowed never to talk to the man again, let alone go to him in his hour of need.

Following tea, Ian went to his room where he completed the homework that had been set for the weekend, in an obsessively meticulous manner. The new work formed an oasis of neatness among pages of scrawl. Again the teachers would be wondering why there had been such a sudden change, and indeed, whether it was actually he who was responsible for the work in the first place. However, after deliberation and despite their suspicions, in the end they would have to accept it as being his. He might be able to fake the entries completed out of school hours, but they had seen and heard the changes for themselves, live, in class.

By the time he was finished, the evening had worn on. There was still time to conduct his new self-imposed nightly hygiene and exercise regime, but afterwards it was late enough to retire to bed. As a means of relaxing his mind, he chose to read a book before turning out the light, not for study this time, but for pleasure.

War and Peace had stood on his mum's bookshelves for as long as he could remember, now and in the future. On many occasions she had boasted reading it from cover to cover, feeling it gave her membership to some elite club. Now he would join that same club.

Three pages into the book, Ian found himself distracted by sounds emanating from his mum's bedroom. She had emptied her purse onto the bed and was in the process of counting her pennies. As powerfully as long forgotten aromas are capable of resurrecting buried memories, the noise of the coins dropping, one by one, back into her purse, evoked unpleasant recollections of insecurity, knowing his mum was struggling to make ends meet. Tomorrow he would be asking her for funds with which to sort out his mop of hair and to smooth his top lip. Saddened, he began questioning the true importance of his personal appearance. Unfortunately, he concluded they were very important as each time he caught sight of himself in the mirror, it caused him psychological trauma, destroying his self-confidence a layer at a time. He would have to ask her for the money, but promised himself he would then look for a Saturday job to ease her burden.

Unable to concentrate further on the book, he placed the heavy tome down on the bedside cabinet, turned out the light, and settled down to sleep.

He woke the following morning feeling far from refreshed.

'How much do you need?' his mum asked, disguising any hint of being troubled by his request.

The fact she could so easily hide her worry begged the question, what else might she be shielding from him?

'Will that be enough?' she asked, unrolling a five-pound note, the only piece of paper in her purse, supplementing it with a handful of change.

Ian had no idea whether or not five pounds would be sufficient. All he had to go on was a quick calculation of how he believed inflation had affected the cost of living over thirty years.

'I'm sure it will,' he replied. 'Hopefully I'll be able to give you some back.'

The High Street, a mile walk from his home, was an entirely different place than he was used to. The fashion of the people that bustled along the pavements had changed. So too had the cars, of which there were noticeably fewer. The shops were busier, out of town stores still being in their infancy. The variety of shops was noticeable too. In the future, it was destined to become merely a row of eateries, banks, building societies, hair salons and estate agents. In contrast, it was now still possible to purchase goods.

With only a handful of essential items to buy, there was plenty of time to browse. The clothes shops were the hardest to fathom out. Not only were the prices unrelated to those of the modern designer outlets, the styles were so very different too. Everything looked awful, making it impossible to know what would look good in the eyes of others if he were to purchase a new wardrobe.

The hairdressers proved to be one of the more pleasant experiences of the morning. Frequenting one of the first unisex salons to open in the area, Ian's hair was to be washed, cut and blow-dried by a pair of young, attractive girls; not the ageing men of the barbers shop who offered their customers the choice of one style and the opportunity to buy 'something for the weekend'.

Angela was responsible for washing Ian's hair, massaging his scalp in such a way it was all he could do to stop himself becoming aroused – not something he would easily be able to hide, lying back as he was with his head resting in a cutaway sink. No matter how badly the remainder of the experience went, he would definitely be back for another wash – probably the following weekend.

As it transpired, the wash was the least erotic part of the process. Despite it being a cold January morning outside, inside Ellen was wearing a bright red cotton top with cutaway sleeves and no bra.

'How would you like it?' she asked, in a chirpy voice.

Ian used to mumble at this point, but that was when he had truly been a sixteen year old young man.

'I shall leave that entirely up to you,' he replied. 'I don't care if you cut it long or short; with hair over or above my ears; on or off my collar; side burns or none. I just want to look averagely fashionable like my peer group and I don't want to spend a fortune. I've got enough hair to play with so you must be able to do something with it.'

This was not the kind of brief Ellen was accustomed to, especially from someone of his age, but she agreed to do her best nonetheless. Immediately, she began to comb and snip, raising her arm in the air, exposing her shaven, pleasantly perfumed, armpit to Ian's sideward gaze. More importantly, he now had a clear view through her sleeve to a perfectly smooth, firm breast. The apron that saved his clothing from the constant fall of hair clippings, thankfully also saved him from humiliation. Ian had not experienced having something akin to a flick knife in his trousers for many years, and put its high degree of sensitivity down to hormones – a lot of hormones.

The cost of the cut, with an appropriate tip, was ludicrously cheap when compared with what he was used to paying, and it was worth every penny. The new style transformed him from a scruffy young man into someone quite desirable. All that aside, it had eaten heavily into his budget and there were still toiletries to buy. If nothing else, he needed razors if he were ever to rid himself of the downy moustache that marred his new image. On the other hand, he desperately wanted to return as much of his mum's money to her as he could. That is when the idea of walking from the shop without paying came to him.

Logically he needed razors and they cost money; not his money, but that of someone who really could not spare it. Acquiring the items without paying would, of course, be illegal, but this was a genuine case of need, not undertaken for any selfish or flippant reason, and if he did get caught, he could always arrange for the theft never to have taken place.

In practice, the theft was simple. Having pocketed a packet of five, mid-range, disposable razors, he walked from the shop and raised the suspicion of no one. Triumphantly, he felt the stolen item in one coat pocket; the money he had saved in the other. The good feelings lasted only a brief moment, before pangs of guilt began to well up from the pit of his stomach, rising quickly to fill his head with doubt.

It was not too late. He had tasted what it was to be a petty thief and he did not like it. A simple act would undo everything, but he could not bring himself to do it. His fingers stroked the soft fur on his lip and the fate of the stolen razors was sealed. They would not be going back.

The final transformation would not cost anything; physically or morally. With age on his side, obtaining a prescription from his doctor for a potent acne-killing lotion came at no charge. The effects were not instant, nor were they total, but over the weeks, the vicious red bumps that ravaged his face faded to mere pastel-coloured blemishes.

Steadily, Ian began to look better and better. Eating a balanced diet, and in moderation, helped his complexion and to control his weight. Exercise helped define his muscles, rewarding him with a six-pack for the first time in his life.

It was difficult to abstain from eating unhealthily; so difficult that Ian contemplated subjecting himself to a uniquely healthy form of bulimia. It would have meant nothing for him to walk into a restaurant and eat to excess, choosing the most expensive items on the menu. Satiated, he would not then run to the toilet and force his fingers to the back of his throat, while fretting over the size of the bill. Instead, he would rewind to a period before entering the establishment, and simply pass it by, retaining the memory of a delicious meal even if his stomach and taste buds were none the wiser for the experience. However, his ability remained something to use only as a last resort. If there was another killer out there, each rewind would be another bread crumb in the trail that might bring him to Ian's door.

In class, the memory of the type of pupil Ian had been was lost. New memories were being built, based on a young, well groomed, well informed man who had an opinion on any given subject, citing evidence to back up his argument. At times, his searching questions would leave his tutors feeling that somehow he was better informed than they.

This was the positive side to Ian's new life. The negatives were just as many.

In general, he no longer had anything in common with his old group of friends. Their tastes in music and clothing were worlds apart. None of the new releases at the cinema interested him – he had seen them all before. He had also become, by the more forgiving of his peers, branded a dreamer; a liar by the rest. The claims of travel to distant lands while eating courtesy of donations from the state did not ring true. He always knew better than everyone else, rarely watched the television, and studied incessantly. In short, no one liked the teacher's pet that he had become.

After three months, Ian had become a good looking, well educated, physically fit, loner. He would have remained so had not his oldest friend, David Utteridge, invited him to a party he was holding while his parents were away.

The downstairs at the Utteridge's was heaving and in near darkness, lit only by lamps, shaded by a throng of youths, drunk on cider, listening to tapes compiled from the weekend's top forty. Half the guests Ian recognised as the group that used to consider him a friend. The remainder were older; friends of David's sister, Caroline. The party was, in fact, hers. Her younger brother had been allowed a fifty percent share in order to stop him telling their parents on their return.

David had always been a good friend of Ian's, sticking by him even now, although the bond between them had clearly been weakened by recent changes. The two spoke for a while, but inevitably David, being co-host, had to move away and circulate, leaving Ian alone in one corner, supping from a can. He stood there awkwardly for a while, wondering how long he should stay before slipping quietly out of the front door, unnoticed. As that time approached, Caroline caught his eye. She looked confused, her eyes scrunched, her head tilted slightly to one side. Ian looked back in much the same way, he himself confused by her reaction towards someone she had known for as long as her brother. Finally, she walked over.

'Ian?' she asked, bewildered. 'What happened to you?'

'What do you mean?' Ian responded, somewhat affronted.

'I mean to say, you look really good.'

'Thank you. You look pretty good yourself.'

Ian was not merely being polite. He meant it. It stood to reason that Caroline had been as attractive the first time round, but Ian must have been blind to the fact, his attention being focused solely on his friendship with her brother.

The girls that shared his life these days were all young enough to be his daughter. Both physically and mentally, none were mature enough to interest him sexually, or otherwise. Caroline was different though. At around eighteen years of age, she was still young enough to be his daughter, yet old enough to have developed the body of a woman. Exposure to the world outside the school gates had also worked to mature her mind.

'Where have you been? You haven't been round here in months,' she continued.

'I've been busy studying,' Ian answered, simplifying an otherwise complex reply.

'I can't believe how different you look – your hair. You've got muscles.'

'I hope that's a complement,' Ian commented, sure that it was.

'It is.'

'Then I ought to say you've changed too. I can't believe how horny you look.'

Caroline smiled coyly.

Being the other co-host, she found herself interrupted continually by her guests, but then quickly returned to Ian to flirt and then flirt some more, lapping up his responses. They talked and drank. Every time she turned away, he would take the opportunity to study the contours of her buttocks more thoroughly, making it inevitable he would be caught.

'What are you looking at?' Caroline asked, hoping he liked the shape of her bottom as much as she herself did.

'You've got a lovely backside,' he said blatantly, slurring his words slightly. 'I know it's wrong, you being David's sister and all, but I'd really love to squeeze it.'

She looked at him for a moment, during which time Ian hoped the sexual tension he perceived there to be between them was not imaginary.

'Okay,' she said, candidly. 'But not here. We should go upstairs.'

At the mere mention of this suggestion, Ian felt a twitch in his loins.

She led the way, Ian keeping a respectable distance between them, invisible to the rest of the partygoers. At the top of the stairs, Caroline pulled a key from her pocket and unlocked the door to a room at one end of the landing. Once inside, she pushed the door partially closed behind her. The gap looked inviting. Checking the coast was clear, Ian took the invitation, slipped inside the room and closed the door behind him. In the darkness he felt Caroline sidle up to him and press her body against his.

'You can feel my bum now if you still want to,' she offered, seductively.

Ian's hands reached round behind her and cupped, pulling her pelvis tightly against his own. They began to kiss. After a short while, Caroline could feel Ian was ready for something more.

'Have you got any protection?' she asked, showing a side of herself Ian had never known existed.

'No,' Ian replied, excited, nervous and amazed.

'Don't worry,' she said, slipping out of the room. 'Stay here. I'll be back in a minute.'

A shaft of light briefly illuminated a strip of Caroline's bedroom as she re-entered.

'Got them,' she said triumphantly, clutching something in the hand.

'They're not your parents' are they,' Ian asked uncomfortably.

'Where else would I get them?'

'Nasty.'

'I know, but you have to wear one.'

'No, I was referring to the fact they belong to your dad.'

'I know. I don't like to think of them doing it either.'

'No, you misunderstand me. I meant its nasty, the thought of my daughter rummaging through my drawers for one of my condoms.'

'You have a daughter?!'

'No, of course I don't. I meant, if I did…'

'Never mind, we've got them now.'

Her intentions were clear. She wanted to have sex, and by the way she was talking, she had made provisions for having it more than once. Ian tried desperately to convince himself there was nothing wrong with proceeding. She was physically of age; she could vote, and she appeared to have been sexually active long before this evening; they were taking precautions, and were in mutual agreement on what they were about to do. Still, mentally, he was many years older, and should know better. On the other hand, he was aroused, had natural male needs, and was in a room with someone who was able to see to them.

'Lock the door,' Caroline instructed. 'Then we can take our time.'

Later, lying back in bed, exhausted, the battle that had been fought inside his head seemed folly. Both had enjoyed the experience immensely. Both now shared a bond that had been absent before.

'Does this mean we're an item?' Caroline asked, sleepily.

'I don't know,' Ian replied. 'I'm not even old enough to go into a pub.'

'More time for having sex then.'

'Seriously, you should see how you feel in the morning. When the alcohol wears off, you might look at me in an entirely new light.'

'Don't you like me?' she said, lazily, her eyes closed, her words trailing off.

'I think I like you too much,' Ian said, not knowing if she heard his voice as anything other than a dream.

By now it was late and Ian was tired, but there would be no sleep just yet. There were things that troubled him - not so much about what he had done, but about the consequences.

Caroline was very attractive; fun to be with; pleasant. In fact, she possessed many of the same qualities as Debbie, and this was the nub of the problem – Debbie.

Sex with Caroline had been great, leaving him desiring much, much more. That in itself was not so bad. Debbie had been fully aware he was not a virgin when they first met. Anything he did between now and the school reunion would therefore be acceptable. What was bad - what he now feared - was that a prolonged relationship might lead to him falling for Caroline in the same way he had his wife. True, Caroline was still young and would probably want many more relationships before she found the right man, but there was the chance she already had. What if they began dating and discovered true love? If he were already married to Caroline, he could not marry Debbie. If he did not marry Debbie, there would be no return for his children. Shivers ran down his spine.

Stephen and Ann did not yet exist in the physical world, but real memories of what they were destined to be were intricately embedded with the vast majority of their dad's stored thoughts. To deny them existence would be to abandon them just as really as if he had walked out of the marital home - something Ian's dad had done to him. Unlike the break-up of Ian's parent's marriage, in this new scenario, no one would be left feeling bitter, but Ian had witnessed his children's zest for life; their achievements.

Ian was destined to marry David's friend; not his sister. He would not see his children for more than a decade. He would not see them as the young adults he remembered them to be for more than three decades. He could not see their faces, but his love for them was still as strong as ever. He would not let them cease to be forever. He would not have done to them what his dad had done to him.

Ian fell asleep without being aware he had done so, thinking about his parents' separation and their eventual divorce - the circumstances under which his dad had left them and how that had made him feel. After all these years, the hurt was still strong.

In his sleep, Ian imagined a brief buzzing sensation, deep in the central core of his head. When it stopped, he opened his eyes to discover he was at home.

24

Bewildered, Ian stood in the hall of his parents' house. From there, he had a clear view into the living room in which his mum could be seen, curled up on the settee, sobbing loudly.

'See what you've done?'

His dad stood in close proximity to him, shouting. There was no doubt, whatever had occurred to reduce his mum to tears; Ian was the one at fault. At this precise moment though, her upset was far from uppermost in his mind.

'Oh God, no!' Ian exclaimed in despair, realising at once what had happened. 'How far back have I gone?'

His dad looked puzzled at his son's reaction, more so as Ian barged past him into the living room. He was not heading to comfort his mum though. What he sought was the date, and the surest way of determining that was via the TV paper.

The news was not good. So competent had he become at rewinding the fabric of time, the concentration his mind had given to the memories of his parent's divorce, even while asleep, had been sufficient to turn back another eleven months of his life. All the dedication he had shown to exercise, healthy eating, and to grooming himself had been for nothing. All the rewards built on months of self-denial had been undone. The benefits of the revision programme still remained, but the need for its completion had been pushed back from having three months to go, to having more than a year.

Unable to cope with his mum's distress, piled on top of this latest in a series of disasters, Ian ran from the house, desperate for seclusion.

'That's right, run away and hide,' his dad called after him, lumbering up the hall, there being no real intention of catching him. 'Bloody child.'

In his haste to get away, Ian had forgotten to grab a coat, regretting this oversight the moment the front door slammed shut behind him. Outside, the ambient temperature was low; the conditions unpleasant. Blown on the breeze, small spots of rain threatened something much heavier. The thought crossed his mind that he should turn back, but to do so after such a melodramatic exit would be like a dog returning to its master, tail between its legs. In any event, he did not have a key. Either it had been left in his coat pocket, or he was not yet of an age when he had been entrusted with one of his own. Knocking on the door, begging entry, was not even worthy of consideration.

Sanctuary was the same field Ian had retreated to on his first major step back in time – a place of continuity in an otherwise manic universe.

Finding a tree stump to sit on, and some degree of shelter in the lee of the hedgerow, he let the elements do their worst. The cold breeze could be ignored - with his eyes closed he could be on any one of the cross-moors walks he had undertaken in his future. The rain that followed, however, was not so easy to dismiss: copious; icy; scalp-numbing – a wintry shower in the middle of April. It was not long before Ian's clothes were as wet as they could become. A bucket of water tipped over his head at this point would not have made matters worse.

All the while, Ian sat and thought with as much clarity as conditions would allow.

There was little to be gained by dwelling on the accident that had brought him here. Rather, he would do better to learn from it. So adept had he become in the use of his ability that further accidents were sure to occur whenever he allowed himself to lose control of his mind. If he were to avoid again experiencing the trauma of accidental slippage back through his life, he would have to abstain from drinking with as much vehemence as a recovering alcoholic. Not one drop would ever be allowed to pass his lips again.

Looking positively on what had happened, the additional eleven months could only lead to higher grades and other people's memories of him as a scruffy, spotty, youth being forgotten all the sooner. More significantly, historically his behaviour at the age of fifteen had led to the breakup of his parent's marriage; his dad having left him in no doubt whose fault it was. From this moment on, he would change. His mum would not be driven to distraction; his dad would not become stressed by her constant fits of crying, to the point of collapse. They would be happy again and history would record they remained husband and wife until parted only by death.

Bolstered by a new sense of purpose, Ian strode home, ready to face the music, knowing this would be the very last time his mum and dad would have cause to complain.

The front door opened; the lecture began - both barrels. Ian accepted every harsh word without once appearing cocky. Having listened and absorbed, he apologised and vowed never to do such a thing again.

The following morning was a Sunday. Ian allowed his parents to lie in, undisturbed, until they felt ready to rise. Then he made them each a cup of tea before he returned to his room to redraw his revision timetable and fitness regime. By the time they saw him again, he had tidied his room, weeding out things that had interested him as a fifteen year old boy, but not as a forty-eight year old man. Once again 'War and Peace' sat next to his bed. This time he would finish it. Adding to the pile, he had brought a copy of the Bible to his room. Having only ever read Genesis and Revelations, he thought it high time he filled the gap in his knowledge.

Back downstairs, he helped prepare lunch. By mid-afternoon, his dad looked restless, as though he was desperately trying to find fault where none was apparent. Perhaps his parents needed time alone together.

Having run the vacuum cleaner over the whole of the ground floor, Ian carried the Hoover upstairs to complete the job, with the intention of remaining there so as to get out from under his parent's feet.

Alone together, Ian's mum and dad had a chance to talk. Whatever they said ended with the living room door slamming shut, his dad declaring he was going out, and his mum curled up on the settee once again, crying into a cushion. Coming to the top of the stairs to see what had happened, Ian observed his dad angrily putting on his coat, grabbing his car keys and making to exit the front door. Seeing his son, he turned towards him.

'See what you've done?' he snapped.

Then, without another word spoken, he stepped outside and was gone.

The incident could be classed as a typical example from this point in Ian's past: his mum crying on the sofa; his dad laying the blame squarely at Ian's feet. The fact it was typical of what had happened then, made it so wrong it should be happening now. Originally, Ian had always been able to connect something he had done, or something he failed to do, with the blame that had been heaped upon him. Now, this was not the case. Why would his dad be fated to repeat the same guilt-laying phrases when clearly the situation had changed? Why would a man deliberately accuse someone else, knowing him to be innocent? There could be only one answer – to deflect the blame.

In hindsight, his dad had been looking for an argument all afternoon, one that would allow him to storm from the house. Ian posed another question – why should his dad wish to do such a thing? Again, the answer came without much searching – to meet someone. A moment passed, allowing for the logic centre of his brain to form new conclusions. His dad was meeting someone all right, but not just anyone, he was slipping out to see Katherine.

Originally Ian had made life so unbearable for his mum she had cried constantly. Understandably, this led to arguments and to his dad, Ron, leaving the house in a fury on more and more occasions. Eventually, Ron had been unable to take his son's disobedience, or his wife's fragile emotional state, anymore and had left for good - on the eve of his birthday, some eight months from now.

Later, Ron had found solace in the guise of Katherine, a woman he met in the workplace long after his departure from the family home. Looking at the scenario with fresh eyes, it now seemed as though things might not have happened in quite that order. More likely, his dad had met Katherine long before the separation and had found an excuse to leave the home to be with her. The excuse he had chosen happened to have been a younger, more impressionable, Ian.

The clues were there on his dad's return. Naively, the son of the past had overlooked the smell of wine upon his dad's breath, mixing with the unmistakable odour of cheap perfume. The new Ian could read the man like a book, confirming his theory his dad had not been a victim after all, but the perpetrator of a most heinous act. To be with his new woman, he had been prepared to consign his wife and his only son to a life of poverty.

'Now I see it,' Ian said, staring accusingly at his dad, anger building within him; anger that was looking for escape. 'It was you who was responsible for mum's suffering. Yes, she broke down whenever I did anything wrong, but that was because you had made her life such a misery. The way you made her feel, anything would have made her cry.'

His dad shifted awkwardly, moving his weight to his back foot, his open hands springing up ready to deflect the blows that seemed likely to be coming in his direction.

'Are you mad? Anyway, why are you talking in the past tense?' he responded, nervously, bewildered by the unexpected accusations, and by his son's sudden change in attitude.

Correcting himself, Ian continued the tirade.

'Let me guess. You are already having an affair with Katherine, aren't you?'

His dad looked shocked. His wife had suspected an affair for some time. That is why she cried so much. She had never challenged him outright though and there was no question of her knowing a name.

Ian continued to lay details of the charges, more certain than ever he was right.

'You intend to leave us, claiming you cannot cope being around someone who cries constantly – that it is a strain no man could bear. You're going to blame her and you're going to blame me for making her that way. And all the time you just wanted an excuse to get away from us to be with another woman; one young enough to be your daughter. How could you do that?'

His dad's lips tried to form words, but failing, he remained in stunned silence. Not only did his son know the name of his mistress, he also knew she was fifteen years his junior.

Ian was far from finished.

'I don't suppose you ever stopped to think what you did to us. You ruined our lives. Mum had to hold down three jobs just to make ends meet. We were poor because of you. I had to suffer the indignity of free school meals; of uniform bought with a grant, and school trips paid for by the state. We couldn't afford holidays; we couldn't afford new clothes; we couldn't afford anything.'

Ian would have continued, unabated, were it not for the appearance of his mum at his side.

'Well, is any of this true?' she demanded.

'Judge for yourself – you, holding down three jobs? Free school meals? He's talking nonsense.'

'I meant is there a woman called Katherine?' she continued, slowly, deliberately, choosing her words with extreme care. 'I meant, is it true she is fifteen years younger than you. I meant, are you screwing her?'

Wilting in the face of accusations that would be difficult, if not impossible to deny on the basis they were true in every respect, her husband looked towards the floor and nodded slowly. For once, Agnes did not cry.

'I hope she's got a place big enough for both of you,' she said, coldly. 'Assuming, of course, she's old enough to have left school.'

Her husband looked up at her, tears welling in his eyes.

'You can pack a suitcase now and come back for the rest at a later date,' his wife responded, any thoughts of forgiveness being completely absent from her mind.

Despite Ian's resolve to prevent the recurrence of his parents' break up, it had nonetheless gone ahead much as before. The fact it had happened sooner had saved months of tension, fighting and sadness. The fact his dad had confessed all had lifted a huge weight from Ian's shoulders, knowing he had not been responsible after all. On the other hand, with the departure of his dad went the family car also, signifying the beginning of years of hardship.

The following morning, Ian attended school against his mum's wishes. She was certain he should first have a chance to come to terms with the sudden loss of his father. The Headmaster would be sure to understand. Ian, on the other hand, felt he had mourned enough. Thirty-three years was more than adequate for even those with the most delicate of constitutions.

It puzzled his mum he should be so keen to go to school when in the past he had found any excuse to stay at home. The fear he was bottling up his emotions - that he was somehow in denial - worried her greatly as her little boy strode off up the road, his newly scrubbed, graffiti-free bag slung over his shoulder.

In the playground, during the free time before the first bell sounded, Ian stuck close by his oldest friend, David Utteridge. There was time enough for David to realise something was not right with his friend.

'What's the matter with you?' he asked, genuinely concerned.

'Dad left last night,' Ian replied bluntly. 'He won't be back.'

'Blimey,' David exclaimed, too shocked to say anything helpful.

David had been there for mates who had experienced their bikes being stolen; he had been, or would be, there for friends whose first love had dumped them, but this was way out of his league.

Addressing an imaginary focal point, somewhere in the distance, Ian added a postscript, delivered resignedly.

'His last words to me were, I hope you're satisfied. All these years, I genuinely thought I was to blame. The bastard ruined my life and I hate him for that.'

There was a pause, a subconscious effort on David's part to avoid the next question sounding flippant.

'Has it been going on a long time then?' he asked, slightly recovered.

Before Ian could answer, the bell went and the matter was closed.

The following days proved tiring. Yet again, Ian found himself avoiding detention only by the skin of his teeth. Yet again did he find himself having to rely on subtle clues to tell him what he was supposed to be doing next.

Exposing his dad for the man he truly was caused Ian to experience wave after wave of bitterness, strengthened by every problem and every inconvenience that presented itself. Bitterness brought with it the desire for revenge; the need to make someone pay for the theft of nearly two thirds of his life. That someone was Michael Summerbee.

The school supported a large population. Conversation at Summerbee's country retreat, many years into the future, had uncovered the fact he and Ian had been pupils together, but had remained unknown to each other for their entire period at Cardle Street Secondary School. Now Ian knew of Summerbee's presence, it was only a matter of time before the two of them met.

Lunch and break recesses seemed the most likely opportunity for Ian to spot his prey, but after three days covertly scanning the faces of every boy in the playground, Summerbee remained stubbornly elusive. Then, as Ian and his friends walked through the corridors of 'C' block, on their way to the dining hall, he suddenly spotted a bespectacled young man entering a large, empty classroom, the crudely painted posters that littered the walls showing it to be the art room. The boy's profile looked very much as though it belonged to a leaner, fresher version of Summerbee. Ian immediately broke loose from his group and followed the suspect inside.

The boy, physically from the same age group as Ian, stood at the back of the classroom looking through the contents of a large, home-made sugar-paper folder. Sight alone was not sufficient to confirm identification.

'Michael Summerbee?' Ian asked across a number of grey melamine desks, grouped together in randomly placed islands.

'Yes,' Summerbee replied suspiciously.

'I wasn't sure,' Ian continued calmly. 'You're obviously a lot younger than when I last saw you, and you're wearing glasses.'

'I've worn glasses for years,' Summerbee replied, puzzled.

Having now confirmed he had the right man, Ian could not hold back his emotions for a second longer.

'I fucking hate you,' he spat, emphasising the beginning of each and every word.

The young Summerbee stepped back from his work, shocked by the unexpected onslaught.

'What?' his voice quivered nervously.

'You've caused me to lose everything. Everything!' Ian screamed through gritted teeth, reiterating the gravity of the accusation.

Summerbee, realising the only way out was past this madman, looked and sounded terrified.

'What have I done?' he implored, certain of his own innocence.

Ian was pleased to see the fear in his enemy's eyes. It could be considered part payment. Now he would collect the balance.

'I'm glad I've found you,' he said, calmness restored to his voice, sounding more sinister than when ranting at full volume. 'I wanted you to know it is my intention to kill you. It has become a bit of a pastime of mine and I'm actually beginning to enjoy it. I was going to wait until you were twenty-four, but seeing as I find myself unexpectedly with eleven months of dead time on my hands, I may as well do it now.'

If Summerbee's judgement of human nature and his interpretation of body language was only half as reliable as he believed it to be, the threats were genuine.

'I don't understand. I don't even know you. What do you mean, kill me?'

'Don't worry Summerbee; I'm not going to kill you right this minute. I haven't yet thought of a way of doing it without me going to jail.'

Summerbee stared at his accuser, fixed to the spot, unable to control the muscle spasms that were shaking his body ever more violently. A certain look spread across his face, causing Ian to look to the boy's feet, around which a puddle of aromatic water was spreading. Ian looked on with satisfaction.

'That will do for now,' he said, closing his eyes, re-joining his group of friends as they approached the art room.

'I'm starving,' he said cheerfully. 'I can't think on an empty stomach.'

25

The school day ended with one final blast of the bell. Ignoring the school bus, Ian instead remained on foot, stalking Summerbee - his prey - at a comfortable distance. At first, the pavement thronged with the outpouring of pupils local to the area, but as they moved further away from the school, the numbers thinned to a trickle. Summerbee walked alone, leading the withered pack towards a housing estate on the far side of a busy main road; one devoid of a pavement.

In front of the remaining few, planners had dipped the carriageway into the ground, at the same time raising the embankment on either side using the spoil. The result was that they achieved sufficient clearance over the road to lay an unsightly, but efficient, footbridge with no requirement for steps that might hamper prams, buggies and cycles. The sides of the bridge were high - a little below shoulder height - and were clad in galvanised steel sheeting, painted blue, decorated with all manner of 'tags' appended by thoughtless youths with spray cans. This would be the venue.

A short buzzing sensation allowed Ian to catch the school bus.

Sat, staring through the window, taking in none of the scenery that swept by, the thought occurred to Ian that detention might be useful to his purpose, permitting him to remain in the area after school hours, long after the rest of the pupils had left for home. How that arrangement might be put to use was not yet clear. If the population of the school had already left the premises, so too would have the young Summerbee.

Over the coming days, another piece of the jigsaw fell into place, when Ian discovered his intended victim stayed after school every Wednesday for drama club. A detention on that evening would put Ian and Summerbee in close proximity, and with few others about to bear witness.

The most important observation though, came later within the same week.

Laying the foundations for the forthcoming murder, Ian had been careful not to stand out from the crowd: putting only minimal effort into his homework; refraining from raising his hand in class; feigning interest in his peers' conversation. Moving with them as a pack, he could observe without being observed, and it was during these manoeuvres Ian spotted something useful.

During morning break, Summerbee was seen penned in by a group of four other pupils: all paid up members of the lower sets; all low in intelligence, but high in brawn. What nobody other than Ian seemed to realise, or care, was that there was a blatant act of bullying being prosecuted right before their very eyes. Despite the identity and nature of the victim, Ian's first reaction was one of outrage. Having put two children of his own through school, from reception class to university, he knew the possible consequences of such actions. Whenever it occurred, someone stood to be emotionally scarred, to have their self-confidence sapped, to have their education ruined. In the worst cases it could even lead to death.

At this point, outrage turned to satisfaction.

The weekend passed with Ian deep in thought; plotting; scheming. For much of the time he sat in front of the television, seeing nothing of what was being broadcast. For the rest, he lay in bed, the quiet darkness appropriate to the task of discovering solutions to the trickier problems. Having formed the framework, he then had to work back from the final act, determining what needed to happen beforehand, and in what order. By Monday morning, every detail had been thoroughly examined; every possible hiccup being supplied with its own contingency. Not a single character of the glorious plan had been committed to paper.

Unseen, Ian slipped into the form room before the first bell. Built into one corner was a stock room: long, narrow, and more importantly, unlocked. From it, he took two items: a lined exercise book with a dark grey-blue cover and an uncut A4 sheet of pink detention slips; four per page. From his bag he took a pair of rubber washing-up gloves; a spare pair borrowed from beneath his mum's sink. Wriggling his fingers inside, he proceeded to remove a single sheet of paper from the exercise book, placing the unused remainder in his bag, together with the detention slips. He then placed the single sheet of lined paper on top of a low cabinet that stood against one wall, close to the last in a row of desks. All was set.

When the bell rang, thirty pupils filed into the room, Ian being among the first. Loitering just inside the door, he waited until the end seat of the second row was occupied before settling himself down on the next chair in. A fidgety murmur filled the room as the class waited for its form tutor. In the meantime, bored minds searched for something to do. Ian, a host to one of them, pulled out his pen and looked about for a scrap of paper on which to write. Pretending to spot the planted sheet lying on top of the furniture close by, he asked Karen - the girl seated between him and the cabinet - if she would mind passing it to him. She did so without hesitation, placing it down on the desk in front of him. Without touching the paper, Ian poised his pen ready for use, but wrote nothing. Instead, his eyes looked up and to the left, as if accessing the imaginative portion of his brain, thinking of what he should put.

'What you doing?' Karen asked, displaying mild interest.

'Oh, I'm just bored. I thought I'd pass the time by listing my top ten most favourite films ever.'

He never got the chance. At that moment, Mrs Darling walked in, dumping a heavy pile of paperwork down on her desk, instantly gaining the attention of all present. She took the register before making a number of announcements, adhering strictly to the regime she followed every morning. As usual, she deemed them to be important, requiring them to be written down so as not to be forgotten. Jotters were hurriedly extracted from every bag and notes were taken, some good, some illegible. Nobody noticed that Ian's rough notebook was nothing of the sort. Having written down the salient points of Mrs Darling's ramblings within the pages of his brand new exercise book - one sporting a grey-blue cover - he returned it to his bag. The single lined sheet of paper that Karen had so helpfully placed before him remained on the desk, untouched. Or at least, its twin did. With sleight of hand comparable to that of the great magicians, Ian had swapped the sheet on the desk for its twin that had remained loose within the exercise book since he stole it, and vandalised it, less than half an hour previously. Not only had he made the switch unnoticed, he had carried out the feat without once touching the sheet that Karen had handled.

All that remained to do was to screw up the blank sheet in full view of Karen.

'No time for that then,' Ian said casually, dropping the crumpled paper to the floor.

Later, alone in his bedroom, once again wearing his mum's rubber gloves, Ian removed the carefully collected page from the protection of the stolen exercise book, placing it on the bedside cabinet on which he occasionally completed his homework. Using a folded length of toilet paper, he then rubbed the page over its entire surface. If tested forensically, it would look suspicious if there were no fingerprints at all. By smudging the blank page though, hopefully traces would remain, but so degraded they would be of no use. In any event, if a set of prints could be lifted, they would not be his.

It was now time to write upon the page. For this, he used a pen taken from the kitchen, not from his own pencil case.

Although his handwriting had changed over the decades, Ian feared an expert might still see sufficient similarities between the two styles to make a connection. To avoid this, he intended keeping the note short, and to disguise it as best he could. Armed with a hazy recollection of what graphologists looked for, Ian wrote in a fabricated hand: italicising letters; rounding characters; altering normal spacing; changing the margins; adding small circles over every occurrence of the letter 'I'; misspelling words; neglecting grammar. The result was a note that appeared to have been written by an illiterate young female, not a worldly wise forty-eight year old man, nor his fifteen year old alter-ego.

It read:

Im woried about Michael Summerbee

Hes being bullied
I think he might do somthing
Please help him

Too many spelling mistakes and it would look as though it had been penned by a Victorian street urchin.

The note was folded and placed back between the pages of the stolen exercise book, ready for delivery.

The next task was another forgery – a detention slip, authorising the school to keep Ian back after hours on Wednesday evening. This required less effort than the note. There were few details to add: a name, a class, a 'delete as appropriate', a date and a signature, all to be written in an adult hand. Nothing could be simpler.

Tuesday passed slowly, Ian being frustrated, keen to put into action what he had so carefully planned. The evening brought the first move when he sheepishly handed his mum the forged detention slip.

'Oh Ian,' she said, disappointedly. 'What is it this time?'

'I did do my homework. It's just that I forgot to hand it in.'

'Didn't you explain to your teacher?'

'Yes and she said she wanted it by the next lesson.'

'And?'

'I forgot two more times.'

His mum looked at him disapprovingly and continued to prepare their evening meal in quiet despair.

On Wednesday morning, Ian left for school a little ahead of schedule, keen not to miss the bus on such an important day. Strapped diagonally across his shoulders hung his bag, the usual contents hiding a number of additional items, folded at the bottom.

At the final bell, Ian loitered just long enough to ensure that Summerbee had stayed behind for drama club, as the plan required. Then, making his way round to the front of the main building, he dropped the forged note into the post box, knowing the secretary would not empty it until the following morning. He then made his way to the footbridge to lie in wait, hidden from view within a bank of well-established shrubs that had been planted in an attempt to suppress the noise produced by the traffic below.

Out of sight, Ian removed the additional contents of his bag and readied himself for the final act.

The footbridge, and its associated network of paths, had been constructed largely to service the needs of the school. Non-pupils were free to use it, but rarely did. In fact, as Ian waited only one old man and his dog, and a blind man with a stick, ventured across it.

After the best part of an hour, almost to the calculated minute, Ian's patience was rewarded by the sight of Summerbee on his last ever walk home. A visual scan of the area confirmed he was alone and there was no one else in the vicinity.

Summerbee was permitted to pass and to continue a short distance on to the bridge before Ian emerged from his hiding place, still wearing his uniform, but with the notable additions of a see-through plastic rain Mac and his mum's bright yellow washing-up gloves. In his right hand, he held a long-bladed carving knife which, although cheap, still managed to glint menacingly.

'Summerbee,' Ian called, with authority.

Michael Summerbee looked back over his shoulder and stopped dead in his tracks. He might have run at this point, but this strangely-attired attacker was standing too close to be sure of a clean getaway.

'I haven't got any money. They took it earlier,' Summerbee spoke with urgency.

'Excellent.'

The fact the knifeman was pleased he should have been robbed once today already confused and panicked Summerbee all the more. What could he want if he did not want money, and why was he dressed in such a peculiar way?

'Walk,' Ian instructed, holding the knife towards his victim; an incentive for him to comply.

As the two young men reached a third of the way across the bridge, Ian barked a second order.

'Stop.'

Ian positioned himself on the centreline of the bridge. From here the occupants of the vehicles that passed below could not see him. Summerbee stood facing his assailant, his back pressing against the painted side panels that filled the gap between bridge deck and handrail.

'Put your bag down,' Ian instructed. 'Take your glasses off and place them on the bag.'

'Why? What are you going to do to me?'

'Nothing, just do it.'

Summerbee complied, shaking visibly.

'Now, turn round, fold your arms across your chest and close your eyes. Don't move a muscle until I tell you, or I'll cut you. If you do as I say, everything will be all right. Have you got that?'

Summerbee nodded, too terrified to speak.

Ian had to act fast. A witness might appear at any second, ruining everything.

As always, if events did not turn out as they ought to, at least he had the option of rewinding and trying again, making modifications where necessary, but that was a scenario to be avoided if at all possible.

Having placed the knife silently on the ground, Ian suddenly thrust his body forward, grabbing Summerbee just below his knees. Then, using the power of his own legs to lift his victim bodily off the floor, he simultaneously thrust upwards and forwards.

With his arms folded, there was not time for Summerbee to save himself - to prevent himself plunging from the bridge, landing unseen with a sickening thump, audible even at this distance. Tyres screeched as several cars fought to avoid impacting one another. Even before the mayhem had ended, Ian had disappeared from sight, first back behind the bushes to transform himself into the normal pupil everyone thought him to be, and then to the bus stop to travel home following his detention.

The school assembly, held the following morning, was a sombre affair. The most senior staff accompanied the head master on stage, several finding it difficult to hold back their tears.

'It is with great sadness that I have to inform you all of the death of one of our pupils last night,' the headmaster said, bravely.

A shocked murmur rose from the congregation. For many, the announcement was confirmation of a rumour that had been circulating since pupils, local to the school first began to merge on the paths leading to the front gate, suddenly dispelling the hope it was just that – a rumour.

'Michael Summerbee was an intelligent boy...'

The revelation of Summerbee's name was met with howling tears from one corner of the hall, providing a good suspect for whichever pupil had written the anonymous note that by now would almost certainly have been found.

So far, the authorities had a boy who had apparently jumped from a bridge; one who had first removed his glasses – a well-known trait associated with those about to commit suicide; something to do with not liking the thought of broken glass getting in the eyes. They would also have the note, indicating the deceased had been a victim of bullying before he died; a note that had arrived too late to prevent a tragedy. Investigation on the strength of it would undoubtedly bring to light a catalogue of terrorism, shamefully executed by a group of pupils on an innocent boy.

Forensic examination of the body would not alter the initial theory that Michael Summerbee had taken his own life, there being no evidence transferred from Ian's body to the victim's, thanks to the raincoat and gloves. There would be no sign of a struggle and, as far as Ian was aware, no witnesses.

As to Ian's whereabouts at the time of the death, the school would assume he had been at home, miles away, and would not think to prove otherwise. His mum, on the other hand, believed her son had stayed behind for detention and had arrived home as expected. She would later receive the news of Summerbee's death – either from Ian's mouth, or from the pages of the local newspaper. She would undoubtedly comment upon it, but would have no suspicion her son had any involvement. In fact, she would not have any reason to believe he had seen anything at all as he had not mentioned it when he arrived home the previous evening, something he surely would have done if he had just witnessed a fellow pupil committing suicide. As far as everyone at the school was concerned, Mike Summerbee and Ian Bradshaw did not even know each other, they being in different forms. The plan could not have been executed more perfectly. Mike Summerbee could not have been executed more perfectly.

'Gotcha. You bastard,' Ian said quietly to himself, as soon as he was alone.

Now, the long haul back to his wife and children could begin in earnest. The pangs of guilt he had carried with him for many years, caused by the break-up of his parents' marriage, were gone. The person that had caused him to rewind so much of his life was gone too, and without any unnecessary loss of life or injury to the innocent. From this point on, Ian could build his body and mind; fitter and healthier than before. In a little over a year, he would sit and pass his exams, getting top grades in all subjects, much to the surprise of his current teachers. Then he would take 'A' levels and from then on everything he did would be new and improved. He would get a degree and a career that made him want to rise from his bed in the mornings. He would attend the reunion and ignore Nicola. He would meet Debbie again as if for the first time. He was already in love with her; she would fall in love with him. They would have children – a boy and a girl; just as before. They would be raised by a dad who worked for a good salary and was content with his life. Ian would meet middle age, not as something to be scared of, but the beginning of an entirely new journey he had not travelled before. Finally, he and Debbie would live together as man and wife until only death itself parted them.

Ian's progress towards that vision warranted celebration.

Sitting in his bedroom, not long after his mum had retired for the night, Ian held a bottle of vermouth in one hand, bequeathed by the previous head of the household, recently departed to be with his mistress. Pouring the beverage, a glass at a time, the bottle was soon empty. Ian wished, more than anything else, that he could share the occasion with those he loved, but there was not another person on Earth who would, or could, understand what caused him to celebrate – the death of a young boy, and the certainty of a future that did not yet exist.

On an occasion such as this, Ian should have found himself in the company of an old friend, sitting and drinking together, reminiscing over the past, pawing old photographs, jogging each other's memories; but there was no one. All those people he would have chosen to be with were not yet in his life, and would remain absent for many years to come. There were no pictures of his family-to-be. The memories of them existed only in his head, waiting for them to catch up with their creation in the physical world.

The one person that remained a constant was David Utteridge, but even he shared only a small part of Ian's recollections. At least where David was concerned, Ian did have pictures of them both together; tangible proof of a decade of friendship; photographs that would still exist in the future, stored alongside those of Debbie and of his children.

Unsteady on his feet, due to the influence of too much alcohol, Ian still managed to retrieve a shoe box full of photographs from the bottom of his wardrobe and place it upon his bed.

The majority of the collection was of small, square, black-and-white snaps. Among them, larger colour portraits of Ian in school uniform marked off his life in increments of one year. There was one group photograph – twelve smiling children arranged on the steps outside a church, commemorating the occasion of their first Holy Communion. Ribbons and a medallion hung from each of their necks.

Wearing shorts and sandals, with grey socks pulled up to their knees, Ian stood in the front row, furthest to the right, with David next to him. On the back of the photograph were the words, 'aged 7', written in blue ink, and the pencilled names of all but two of the children in the group.

Lying on his bed, Ian stared into the picture, through eyes glazed with excesses of alcohol, trying to relate to the face of himself as it appeared, captured on the surface of the glossy, pockmarked paper. Such innocence. How could that boy have become a murderer; a womaniser? How could he have got himself into such a mess?

The hand holding the photograph flopped onto Ian's chest as his eyes rolled upwards in their sockets, and a few seconds later, he began to snore peacefully.

However, no more than a moment later, Ian opened his eyes again in response to hearing an unexpected instruction.

'Say cheese'.

26

'No! Please God, no! Not again!'

The words were delivered in a light voice; one that had not yet broken.

The click of the shutter had the strangest effect.

The camera captured two images in quick succession. The first depicted twelve angelic children, standing to attention, proud to have received their communion medallions - the very image that had acted as a target for Ian's unintended rewind. The second image, captured less than a second later, depicted the heads of eleven startled children turned towards a distraught twelfth, his legs buckled, his body shifted forward of centre, his arms tucked in front of his chest, braced for impact with the ground.

'Please, I want to pass out. I don't want to be here. Please help me. Please.'

Parents, teachers, a priest and a photographer quickly surrounded the fallen child, unable to fathom out what had happened that he should suddenly end up on the floor in the foetal position, crying with the despair of a mother who had just lost her baby.

Gathering him in his arms, Ian's dad carried his son to the car and laid him on the back seat.

'Do you think we should take him to a doctor?' Agnes asked.

'We'll wait and see how he is in the morning,' Ron replied. 'Poor little fellow. I wonder what's caused all this. He was fine just a minute ago.'

The ingrained bitterness that Ian felt towards his father burst to the surface, evoked by the mere sound of his voice, stopping his cries as abruptly as they had begun.

'Stay away from me,' Ian shouted. 'I never want to see you or speak to you ever again.'

Once home, Ian was immediately carried up to his bedroom where he was tucked beneath his blankets, his mum promising as a treat he would be allowed to eat his lunch in bed. Robbed of energy, he offered no resistance and lay quietly, staring fixedly at the blankness of the matt white ceiling.

His mum returned with a tray on which she had placed a plate of re-hydrated instant mashed potato, impaled with half a dozen fish fingers, and beside it, a beaker of orange squash. For afters, there was a plastic pot, fresh from the freezer compartment, containing mint flavoured mousse as solid as a block of ice.

'There, your favourites,' she said, cheerily.

As depressed as he was, Ian could not shun his mum's attempts to raise his spirits. He sat up, placed a pillow on his lap, placed the tray upon the pillow, and began to eat.

'Thanks,' he said, as sorry to have upset her as he was to find himself in this latest predicament.

His mum sat on the edge of the bed, placing a reassuring hand on his blanketed thigh.

'What was all that about,' she asked kindly. 'You had us really worried.'

The temporary lift in his spirits suddenly dipped again as he was reminded how foolish he had been; how simple his error; how devastating his punishment.

'I promised myself never to drink again,' he said.

'You've been drinking?'

'A bottle of Dad's Vermouth,' he confessed. 'It was supposed to be a celebration.'

'Ron!' Agnes called out, projecting her voice downstairs. 'Come up here.'

There would be trouble; trouble on top of trouble. There was never a good time to suffer it; even more so now. Ian's head buzzed casually so that he was suddenly taking his first forkful of mash again: watery, with pockets of starchy powder that had been missed in the mixing process.

His mum sat down again and posed the same question.

'Nothing really. I must have been having a bad daydream,' he replied, lamely.

For a moment, his mum looked curiously at her son. Then, having found no answers, she patted his leg, got up, and went to leave the room.

'Eat it all up,' she said. 'It will make you big and strong.'

The one benefit of being trapped in the body of a seven-year-old was that he suddenly had no responsibility for anything. His mum woke him in the morning; she told him what to wear; she made him breakfast, and made it known when it was time to leave for school. She even walked him to the gate and kissed him goodbye when the bell rang. Conversely, the list of disadvantages contained the self-same points, and many, many more.

His first day back at junior school proceeded in a daze: going through the motions; doing what was required of him, but nothing more. Interaction was kept to a minimum. What was he supposed to say to a rediscovered friend who asked him what he thought of his new pencil rubber? How motivated could he become, answering questions from the teacher on the most basic of subjects? Certainly not enough to raise his hands as did his peers, trying their hardest to attract sir's attention with the addition of a strained 'ooh ooh' sound.

New problems surfaced almost immediately. It was impossible to write an essay of few enough words, in an undeveloped hand, and with sufficient naivety. When the pupils were made to pair off, the intention being they pencil a portrait of their chosen partner, it again proved almost impossible, Ian trying his hardest to suppress his ability in order to avoid being seen as some sort of child prodigy.

In the playground, Ian sat alone, unable to pretend he had a machine gun; unable to join in with a game of British Bulldog that drew in half the school.

A well-meaning, ancient dinner lady noticed the sadness on his face and clutched him to her shrunken bosom, meaning to comfort him. It made matters worse. Not only could he not breathe, it also highlighted the fact that even a woman of such advanced years had the power to restrain him against his will.

There was time enough to think, between the efforts of his friends to snap him out of his torpor. Could he have done anything different? Save for the problem with the alcohol, had he always been destined to return to this misery? The answers were hard to accept.

In hindsight, he need never have returned to six months before his exams. A week would have sufficed. In that time he could have covered all subjects sufficiently. By reliving that week over and over again, he would never have got any younger, but would still have accumulated the knowledge he required.

More disturbingly, he need never have left the age of twenty-four. Before doing so, he had sought advice and had argued he was not an entrepreneur. The truth was he did not need to be. Had he opened a shop, a task that even the most economically inept person could manage, he could have sold the latest fad, whatever it was, whenever it appeared. Even with his knowledge of the future being fogged by the passing of time, he might not be able to remember exactly when each new product became a runaway success, but he would remember it when he saw it and would never have his fingers burnt. On the other hand, he would know when to get into swimming pools, sleds and which toy was going to be indispensable for the perfect Christmas.

At twenty-four, Ian could have found some other way to kill Summerbee, after he had restored the lives of his innocent victims. At twenty-four, Ian would be dating his wife-to-be, planning their marriage, looking forward to starting a family he knew would be a success. At twenty-four, Ian was young enough to follow a new career path, and by the age of forty-eight, when he no longer had the benefit of foresight, he would probably have become an entrepreneur in any event. That or he would be rich enough to retire, never having made a poor business decision in almost twenty years.

Now, he was seven and Summerbee was alive once again. Even taking his exams at ordinary level seemed a distant, unachievable goal.

As he saw it, he now had three options.

Firstly, he could simply commit suicide. Painless or agonising, swift or slow, whatever the method, the end result would mean he would no longer have to suffer in torment. There was an argument against it though - a major one. If he ended his life now, he would be denying his children their very existence.

It was true Stephen and Ann could not miss their lives if they were never born. However, Ian had held them both when they were only moments old. He had nurtured them through two decades of their lives. The memories of their achievements - the highlights of their being - lived on within Ian's mind. As far as he was concerned, they were already alive - like the sculptor who releases a statue from a block of cut stone. He would never kill himself.

The second option was equally simple. He could suffer in silence, making the best of every day, knowing his life would begin to improve in another nine years. Having passed his exams, he would begin on an educational path he had never encountered before. In seventeen years he would see his fledgling wife again. Three years after that, he would be reunited with the first of his two children.

Stacked against this option was the fact he could not bear to live like this for another day, never mind another nine years. He was physically weak; he would have to attend school to receive an education that would not stimulate one tenth of his brainpower; he had lost his independence; he would be denied adult conversation; he would be denied sex.

Even if he were able to cope, there had been two accidents so far; there might be others. He might finally be reunited with his family only to suffer another spasm in his sleep, returning him straight back here; to the age of seven. The risk was too great.

The third and final option was based only on theory. Ian had read somewhere that a person does not remember their lives between birth and the age of three. If he were to return to this period of his life, the mechanism that allowed him to retain his memory as a forty-eight year old man might reset itself. He would then live his life exactly as nature had intended, identical in every way to the first time - a disaster, save for the fact that, if the plan worked, he would be oblivious to everything that went before him.

The execution of this option would be easier, and probably more likely to succeed, if he were to return to the moment of his birth, rather than to any other point before his third birthday. It would be unnecessary to stop to check progress; he would simply shut his eyes, start the process, and keep going until it stopped.

On the face of it, this was the only viable choice, but for one overriding fear. What if he were to return to his body as a new-born baby, only to discover he still retained the memory of a middle age man? Lying naked on a blanket in the delivery room, he would be unable to see properly; he would be unable to turn himself over; he would be unable to speak; he would suffer the indignity of his mum stuffing a dripping nipple into his mouth. The more he cried, the more there would be comments made about him having a good pair of lungs. The frustration caused by not being able to make himself understood would surely be too much for him to bear.

Inside, he would be thinking of nothing else but suicide, but even that luxury would have to wait. By the time his body was mature enough to throw himself down the stairs, in all likelihood his mind would by then have broken.

Options one, two or three? The decision would have to be made, but Ian never having been one to act quickly, he decided to wait a day or two, in case something else popped into his head that he might not have considered.

At morning playtime the following day, Ian again sat alone, thinking to himself. Then it came. Suddenly, he knew what he wanted to do, more than anything else in the world.

'Debbie,' he whispered. 'I want to see Debbie.'

This was both a desire and a decision. With it, a new sense of purpose threw off the cloak of depression that had prevented his normal function. A weight had been lifted. From now on, he would act as he felt, not as his body would suggest he should. Then, when he was alone, he would plot; something he had become quite adept at doing of late.

At lunch, he accepted with relish, the vegetables that were spooned onto his plate, not seeing them as something merely to be moved around and separated in order to convince the teachers he had at least tried them. During the afternoon, he was asked to stand at his teacher's desk and read. He might have tried to ape the literacy of a seven-year old boy, but decided against it. Why should he not make waves? After all, he had no intention of staying around to ride them.

At home, Ian mischievously completed the crossword that his dad had abandoned on the kitchen table the previous evening. If his dad were to pick the paper up now, approaching the puzzle with a fresh eye, he would first wonder who had successfully unravelled the cryptic clues where he had failed. Then he would wonder whose handwriting it was, blocked out within the chequered grid in an adult's hand. It might even lead to accusations of his wife having an affair. If it did, it was of no consequence.

Following tea, Ian spent his time in self-imposed confinement, shut behind the door of his bedroom. Here, he was as far away from distraction as it was possible to be under the circumstances. Here, he paced and thought, sat and thought, lay and thought some more.

At seven-thirty, the instruction came that he was to prepare for bed. His mum was not to know she was ordering a middle-aged man to go to sleep three or four hours prematurely. It mattered not. The fact was he had pre-empted her, deciding it was time to retire, even before her call had risen up the stairs. Going to bed early would make it that much easier to rise early.

The first problem to confront him, when putting into practice his latest plan, was that he did not possess an alarm clock. He did have a wristwatch - a cheap, many-jewelled Russian one - but that was always silent, save for the soft ticking of the second hand. The only option was to rely on Mother Nature's own clock; a type of stopwatch to be reset only in the toilet.

Making his way down to the kitchen, wearing only drawstring pyjamas, Ian set about starting the bio-clock, drinking fresh tap water from a pint glass until every last drop had been ingested.

Before returning to his bedroom, he wished his parents 'goodnight' – both of them. There was no point punishing his dad now for what the man would do in the future. None of it mattered any more.

Relaxed by a sense of being in control, in circumstances where there should be none, Ian found no difficulty slipping into a state of sleep. There he remained until the dreams began.

A toilet had been placed in the corner of the lounge. Ian was trying to use it without the many occupants of the room seeing him. Then he was in the privacy of his bedroom, the facilities for relieving himself being entirely absent. Standing behind his door, he began to urinate a little at a time, allowing only enough to splash upon the rug as he judged it could soak up without being detected. Then he became disgusted by his own actions, questioning himself as to why he was not using the normal toilet, easily accessible to him along the landing. Then he woke up, his bladder telling him it was now time to get out of bed.

Despite the room being in total darkness, Ian threw back the bedclothes and sat up. There he stayed, patting the top of the bedside cabinet until his hand closed around his wristwatch. Then, having shuffled tentatively across the carpet, he drew back the bottom of one curtain, revealing a small portion of the window. A dim shaft of natural light penetrated the room, sufficient for Ian to be able to make out the position of the hands on the face of his watch. It was a little after four. The curtain fell shut once more and Ian made his way out of the room onto the landing. There he stopped at the entrance to his parents' bedroom, recalibrating his ears, sensitising them to the myriad lesser sounds of the night.

Through the closed door drifted a two-part slumbering melody: breathing - smooth and peaceful - accompanied by a harsh, rhythmic snore. Both his parents were sound asleep. Although impressed that his mum managed to sleep, despite the noise, Ian was aware that as a parent, she might have become immune to her husband's noise, while remaining attuned to anything else out of the ordinary. Ian had experience of this. Back in the future, he had always detected when either of his children had opened their door during the night, and had been there to guide them gently back towards their own bed.

Satisfied his nocturnal activities had not yet disturbed his parents, Ian made his way along the landing to the bathroom, grateful that the floorboards were free from squeaks.

Inside, with the door pushed to, he sat on the toilet, avoiding the need to aim in the dark.

The return journey to his own room was made with such a degree of care and sensitivity that, had the floor been carpeted with rice paper, not a single footprint would have shown.

Still protected by the cover of darkness, Ian dressed, choosing to ignore his school uniform in favour of casual wear. Jeans and a jumper would be far warmer than the shorts and thin cotton shirt his mum had hung from the handle of his wardrobe, ready for a new school day.

Downstairs, he donned his coat.

The plan now required he should take four additional items from the house: two cushions from the lounge; a pot of ground pepper from the kitchen; and his dad's bunch of keys from a hook in the hall.

Having come this far, Ian found himself confronted with a problem he had not considered when formulating his plan – how to exit the house in silence.

The front door itself presented two difficulties. Firstly, a chain had been applied as a secondary line of defence, clearly not designed with silent use in mind. Secondly, the sprung Yale lock had the potential to wake the dead when the door closed behind him. Neither problem was insurmountable: with time and patience the chain could be removed without making too much noise; the key could be used to operate the lock, ensuring silent operation. However, the door was not the primary concern.

Throughout the house, curtains excluded all external light. Not so the front door, the design of which incorporated three obscured-glass panels, their texture being that of small, clear pebbles, lain together in sheets. A faint light penetrated the panes, dimly illuminating the hall, and the nature of the problem that lay within it.

With a stroke of ill fate, one of Ian's parents had thought to leave two carrier bags, full of glass bottles and jars, on the doormat, fully within the arc of the door's swing. The bags had been left there with the best of intentions – as a reminder to take them to the recycling point in the morning. However, the consequences for Ian could not have been less helpful. Opening the door, even a fraction, would cause a cacophony of sound. Moving the bags clear of the mat would cause even more. There had to be another means of exit.

The natural second choice would have been the back door leading from the kitchen into the garden. However, Ian had witnessed for himself the force required to open it, usually applied with a swift kick from a booted foot. This was still the era pre double-glazing and the wooden door that was destined to be replaced with aluminium, was swollen and warped.

There remained one final option – the window in the lounge. Save for it being a metre off the floor, for all other intents and purposes, the butt-hinged sash of the casement window was very much like a normal door: wide-opening and large enough to permit the passage of a small boy; even a man. Secured only with a lever fastener at the side, a casement stay at the bottom, and no lock, it would allow for silent operation, and without the need for a key. The only drawback being Ian would have to leave the window partially open, allowing the breeze to funnel through the gap, causing the net curtains to billow unless he first pulled them to one side, gathered the material, and tied it about itself in a knot.

In no time at all, Ian was standing in the garden, under the stars, a bunch of keys and a pepper pot in his coat pocket, two cushions clamped between his arm and his side. Now he needed transport.

His bicycle was locked in the garden shed. Even if the tyres had pressure and even if he had the key to the padlock – which he did not – his destination was too far for a small child to cycle. Besides, there was a better way.

The family car sat on the drive at the front of the house. Having unlocked the vehicle by sense of touch alone, Ian opened the driver's door and climbed in behind the steering wheel. Mechanical adjustment, provided by the manufacturer, allowed the seat to move forward to the end of its runner, but the throw had been designed to accommodate adults of varying size; not children – hence the need for two cushions with which to provide the additional support he needed to be able to reach the pedals and to see over the dashboard. Even then, the young driver could only depress the clutch to the floor by stretching his foot to its extreme limit, and the road could be seen only by him pulling on the steering wheel to hold him upright.

Pulling the door gently to, avoiding slamming it, Ian turned the key in the ignition, and with difficulty, reversed the car out onto the road. Then, engaging first gear, he drove slowly away, stopping clear of the first few houses, beneath the yellow glow of a street light, in order to close the door properly, apply the seatbelt and find the switch for the headlights.

At this early hour, few other vehicles shared the roads. Of those that passed close by, only two drivers appeared to notice Ian's apparent youth. Both looked, looked away, and looked again, but the sightings were so brief both must have concluded their minds were playing tricks, and took no further action. Any subsequent call for witnesses might bring the two drivers forward, but by then it would all be too late.

It was inevitable a seven-year old boy – one who had crept from his parent's home in the middle of the night, stealing his dad's car in the process - would be caught. Ian knew that, and he did not care; as long as he managed to avoid capture for another five or six hours. Not wishing to make the job of the police unnecessarily easy, he parked the car in an anonymous street, two miles from his destination.

Unless his dad got up early to use the toilet, he would wake at six when the alarm clock sounded. At some point thereafter - possibly en route to the bathroom - he would discover Ian was missing from his bed. He would then, no doubt, begin conducting an ever more frantic search, during which he would notice the lounge window was open and the family car was no longer on the drive.

Ian could only imagine the sense of panic this would evoke and for this he was truly sorry.

There was no telling what theories might develop in his parents' minds during those first few minutes, but it was certain they would call the police without delay; in Ian's estimate, no later than six-fifteen.

Given the circumstances, the police could only treat the situation with the utmost seriousness: instigating an immediate search; informing all units to be on the lookout for a boy and a stolen vehicle. It might take hours to find the vehicle; it might not, but when it was, the police would no doubt use dogs to track him down - hence the need for pepper. Spread liberally inside and outside the car, there was a chance this simple, everyday condiment might put the animals off his scent. It might not be a complete success, but if it bought him time, Ian thought it worth the effort.

From here, the shortest route to his destination was a wide path running alongside the main road. Well lit and familiar to him, at least from a motorist's point of view, it would have been his preferred choice, but it was too exposed. By the time he reached his destination, dozens of pairs of headlights would have picked him out as a small boy, wandering alone, at a time of day when he should have been indoors, safely in the care of his parents. With his luck, some well-meaning busybody was bound to stop and question him. Worse, they might even insist he got in their car to transport him home.

Such confrontation could easily be undone, but it was better to avoid it in the first place by opting to take the back roads – a slower, but more discrete route.

Eventually, Ian's detour brought him back to the main road, emerging from a narrow, winding alleyway that cut through an otherwise impenetrable row of houses, to a point almost directly opposite the Wilhelm's Infant and Junior School.

A single panel of railings, set between road and path, prevented mothers with runaway prams accidentally careering out of control into the oncoming traffic. Turning to avoid collision with the crash barrier, they would be faced with a means of crossing the carriageway: a high, narrow, metal footbridge. The span was only as wide as the road itself. However, to reach the deck, pedestrians had first to ascend a shallow set of steps that formed ramps on either side, zigzagging back and forth, achieving ever-greater altitude.

Only the heaviest of traffic, coupled with a mind programmed to consider child safety, could persuade a parent to undergo such an ordeal four times a day. Ian, being neither technically a parent, nor remotely interested in self-preservation, and with the traffic being almost non-existent, swerved past the barrier and ran to the other side.

A short distance along the main road was the entrance to the school.

It was now nearly five-thirty. Ian knew his future wife would be in the playground of that very same school in as little as five hours. Until then, he knew he must hide. From half past eight, parents would be dropping their children off and the things Ian needed to say could not be done in front of adults.

Ian rolled his body over the barrier that prevented vehicles entering the premises out of hours. From there he crossed the playground, found a weakness in the boundary fence, and crossed into an overgrown meadow, choked with thistles, clumps of bramble, and beaten down grass.

Lying down on the far side of the small field, beneath the overhang of a hedge - a mixture of beech and hawthorn - nothing could be seen of the runaway boy. All that remained was for him to be patient and to wait for the hand bell that would sound the temporary release of children from their classrooms.

***

Ron Bradshaw did indeed wake up at six o'clock, just as his son had predicted. From that point on though, imagined scenario and reality set out on different paths.

Ron emerged from his bedroom dressed in a bathrobe, his hair a tousled mess, his face shadowed with stubble, his breath stale and unpleasant, even to his own nostrils. His priority was to make for the bathroom, not to check to see whether his son had been kidnapped during the night.

Twenty-five minutes later, Ron returned from the bathroom: washed; groomed; exhaling the aroma of spearmint. Ten minutes after that, he re-emerged from his bedroom, suited and ready for breakfast.

It was only when he got downstairs and experienced a draft that should not have been there that he began to suspect something was wrong.

On finding the net curtains tied back and the window ajar, Ron's first thought was that they had been burgled, but seeing the colour television still in the corner of the room, quickly downgraded the possibility to an attempted burglary.

His next reaction was to close the window, but with his fingers poised over the casement stay, his mind turned to the preservation of evidence, causing him to snatch his hand away.

Having looked through the window and determined there was no one immediately outside, or scrambling over the garden fence, he made a silent sweep of the ground floor, checking for intruders, while at the same time preserving his dignity in the event his wife subsequently provided an innocent explanation for the window having been left open. Other than the window, he found no signs of a break in.

Feeling more at ease, Ron climbed the stairs, intent on asking his wife if she could throw light on the subject. By now, he was confident her reaction would be one of mild shock, realising that by her leaving the window open, anyone might have got in. He would occupy the moral high ground, and she would never know just how much he had overreacted.

Agnes was by now sitting up in bed, consulting her to-do list, appending several new entries – a conscious step designed to blur the act of sleeping and the regime that accompanied every weekday morning; a means of easing herself gently into a new day.

Ron positioned himself strategically against a chest of drawers, his left elbow acting as a buttress, transferring some of his body weight through the furniture to the floor; his right hand supported by his left.

'Do you know any reason why the living room window might have been left wide open all night, with the net curtains tied back?' Ron asked, smoothly, a hint of sarcasm building in anticipation of his wife's answer.

If her husband's question had not extracted a confession, it had at least captured her full attention. There was nothing mild about her look of shock.

Ron was suddenly forced to reconsider his initial reaction, accepting either they had been burgled after all, or at least an attempt had been made to do so.

Adopting an infinitely more serious tone, Ron quickly related everything he had seen and done.

'What if they came upstairs,' Agnes whispered, pulling the coverlet up under her chin to ward off any would-be attacker. 'They might still be up here,' she continued, a solitary finger jabbing the air in the direction of the landing, the rest of her fingers maintaining a tight grip on the bedding.

'Look, there are no burglars in the house. I'm sure of it,' Ron responded, calmly, trying unsuccessfully to placate his wife.

'Have you checked Ian's room?'

The expression on her husband's face was sufficient enough that no words were needed.

Ron left the master bedroom having no expectation of there being anything wrong, feeling only the need to dispel the kind of doubt experienced by someone who could not remember whether they had turned off a tap, even though they were certain they had.

By the time Ron had reached the door to his son's bedroom, Agnes was at his side, in time for their discovery to be a shared experience.

'I'll call the police,' Ron said desperately, his chest heaving, his hands shaking uncontrollably. 'It's going to be all right. I promise.'

There was no opportunity for Agnes to argue who should do what. Having spoken his intention, Ron turned, grabbed the banister and opposing handrail, and slid downstairs, his feet barely touching the fitted carpet.

At the front door, he grabbed both carrier bags from the mat, shifting them clear with no regard to the nature of their contents. Then, instinctively, he grabbed for his keys – they were gone. Their disappearance was enough to fix him to the spot. He looked at the empty hook. Then he looked to his wife. Without saying a word, they expressed their fears; exchanged theories; decided upon action.

Ron tore at the chain, fumbling with the links until they came free. Then there was further frustration, lasting for a fraction of a second as he clicked the night latch off, having first tried to turn the catch, only to discover it would not operate. On the second attempt, the door flung inwards. Ron propelled himself through and ran to the spot where the car had been standing. He turned, his arms wide, his eyes looking towards the ground as if he might have overlooked its whereabouts. The nightmare had multiplied.

Coming to his senses, he ran in the direction of the telephone box, situated three hundred metres up the road. Inside, the air was rank with the odour of stale cigarettes and urine, but Ron did not notice. The index finger of his right hand dialled the 'nine' once, twice, three times. The minimal delay as the dial reset between each turn stretched the process to an unbearable lifetime.

'Which service please?' a woman asked calmly.

'Police,' Ron wheezed, his chest ready to explode, his entire world turned upside down.

***

Doors opened. Children came flooding out from many exits to fill the playground as efficiently as if there had been a fire drill. That was where the analogy ended. No neat lines sorted by class, or children waiting patiently to have their names called. Instead, games broke out spontaneously, boys running around wildly, girls skipping and performing handstands against classroom walls. No teacher could have organised such a level of activity in such a short space of time.

With the final act of his plan drawing near, Ian had leopard-crawled across the field, soaking and dirtying the front of his clothes from head to foot. No-one expected there to be a young, civilian-clad boy lurking behind tussocks of grass and bushes of thorn, but there was.

Systematically, Ian scanned the facial features of each and every girl in the playground, quickly discounting one before moving to another. Thankfully the girls seemed to stay within their chosen areas, while the boys weaved in and out between them. Twice, Ian moved position, remaining undetected. Then he saw her.

Debbie's features were unmistakable, even at this age, even at this distance. Her smile was the same - formed of a happy childhood; her dark hair complemented brown eyes - bright and defined; her skin tone reminded him of the ease with which Debbie developed a tan in the summer and retained it long into winter. Even though her maiden name – Sansom – did not bear witness, Ian fancied her lineage had its roots near the Mediterranean – Italy, possibly.

Positioned between two other girls of the same age, she stood with a length of elastic knotted about her ankles, loops of which ran round the ankles of her two companions. They chanted while Debbie jumped up and down, seemingly trying to increase the complexity of her bindings.

Without further delay, Ian revealed his position. Standing up suddenly, he walked to the fence. The number of people to notice him grew exponentially, but he paid no attention to any of them, other than the girl with a tangle of elastic about her feet.

Ian was a boy dressed in filthy clothing – coat, jeans and a jumper. He walked in a sea of uniform: boys wearing charcoal grey shorts, ash grey shirts, red ties and sandals; girls wearing grey skirt, white blouse, white socks and patent leather shoes. In short, he stood out from the crowd.

Heads turned towards the intruder. Curious pupils closed in behind him as he walked his unflinching course. The girl with the elastic about her ankles looked up and showed surprise. Her two companions looked too, their gaze quickly shifting from the grim determination on the face of a filthy boy, to the face of their friend. Unless they were mistaken, he was aiming directly for her.

He stopped several metres from her position.

'What's going on here?' the duty playtime teacher asked, dumbfounded by the sight of the intruder.

Ian ignored her.

'Debbie?' Ian asked, ridding himself of any lingering doubt she was indeed the person he believed her to be.

'Yes,' Debbie replied, curiously.

'I've got something I have to tell you.'

There was silence. Everyone wanted to hear what was so important, who this person was, and why he needed to speak to Debbie in particular.

248

'Seventeen years from now we will both attend a school reunion,' Ian began, choosing his words carefully, speaking them with precision. 'Not from your school, but from the secondary school I will land up going to. You will be introduced to me by my best friend, David Utteridge, and you will land up being my wife. We will have two lovely children who will go to university and make us very proud. I don't know what they will do after that because I was a fool and left them.'

'What?' Debbie responded, simply.

The teacher, so unnerved by what she had heard, placed herself between Ian and Debbie, ready to stave off an attack. Ian was not finished.

'I just wanted to see you one last time,' he said, tears beginning to run down his checks. 'I have to do something. I have to make a choice and I'm really scared. I'm so fucking scared, you just wouldn't imagine.'

Debbie stared at him, peering round the teacher, lost for what to do.

'Goodbye Debbie. I hope we shall be together again someday. I love you.'

With that, Ian closed his eyes. The buzzing sensation returned to the very centre of his mind. Low at first, the pitch quickly lifted – the final journey of Ian Bradshaw, a man with the ability to conquer time, had begun.

27

Despite his best efforts to remain calm, Ian was anything but, there being no telling how his bold plan might end. If his worst fears came to fruition, he would be left an intelligent adult, trapped inside the body of a helpless baby – as unimaginable as being buried alive, waiting for the release that only a slow death could bring. Alternatively, his life would reset, permitting him to live normally, from boy to man, free from the memories of his future that haunted his every waking moment.

The constant tone within his head continued, unfaltering. Then, for a brief moment, Ian experienced something new - a resistance, as though he was passing with difficulty through an invisible barrier. Caught off guard, he opened his eyes, halting the process.

Instantly, Ian felt old. He found himself lying in bed, his upper body angled gently upwards. Through milky eyes he could make out a man and a woman who appeared close to retirement, and two men in their mid-to-late-thirties. He studied the faces of each, his gaze moving slowly from one to the next. All four looked as though they had been crying, or were about to start.

The woman was holding his hand and was in the middle of speaking.

'I'm sorry,' she said, 'but they're stuck in America and can't catch a flight until the morning. We thought it best to leave Sam and Josh with the neighbours. Besides, they don't like children visiting and they only allow four in at any one time.'

Her words meant nothing; the names she spoke meant nothing.

'I don't know you. I have no memory of any of you,' Ian said weakly, surprised to discover he could hardly hear his own voice.

The woman pulled away, turned her head and began to shed fresh tears. The oldest of the three men broke away too, placing his arm around her shoulders for comfort. Brother and sister, or husband and wife, Ian knew not. Nor did he care.

Despite his physical condition being the worst he had ever experienced, Ian nevertheless retained the mind of someone half the age his appearance would suggest. His mind was still keen and he knew instantly that the woman's tears signified he was meant to know these people; meant to care about their feelings. They were clearly intimately connected to him; either directly, or indirectly related. With and despite that knowledge, Ian spoke again.

What he said, he said aloud. It would have been more sensitive to keep the words an internal dialogue, but to pass them between his lips went some way to overcome the aches and pains that sought to fog his thought processes. Besides, he owed these people nothing, and by now he had become used to upsetting people. It had become common practice to act on impulse and then delete his mistakes.

'That sensation I felt – it was the barrier between my future life and my past life. It can only mean one thing. I'm about to die aren't I?'

Now all but the older man were crying and he looked as though he wanted to.

The barrier of which Ian spoke he judged to be the domain between one life and the next. It seemed certain then that this was his deathbed and these people were his family, come to pay their last respects.

On the face of it, his plan had not worked. He had gone beyond his own birth, beyond the moment of his own conception, and still he retained the mind that persisted in torturing him. Perhaps though, this was the way his life would reset itself. He would die and be reborn, his memory wiped clean. If true, Ian's troubles would be over – at least until he rediscovered his ability in another forty-eight years' time. He could only hope that when the time came, he would not repeat the mistakes he had made.

Alternatively, there was still the possibility he would be reborn retaining the memory of his life-to-come. In that case, his greatest fear would become reality. He would be that screaming baby, his vision blurred, unable to communicate, unable to control anything, denied even the choice to live or die.

There had to be other options.

'Tell me honestly,' Ian asked, addressing the man he assumed to be either his son or his son-in-law, 'have I had a good life?'

The reply was muffled but nonetheless understandable.

'It's had its ups and downs like anyone's life, but on the whole, yes, you have had a good life.'

Reassured, the dying man wondered whether he could live it again, given he had no knowledge of it. By limiting how far back he went, he would avoid the problems associated with having a mature mind trapped in an immature body. He would still have problems integrating though. Friends' faces and names would be unknown to him. So too would his work. Of this he had recent experience, but then he had been able to jog a memory that had merely faded. In returning to an early period of his previous life, there was no question of restoring a memory that simply was not there. If he could not remember the basics, would he be able to duplicate the life his son or son-in-law had described? Then there was the matter of having to live through two world wars – interesting topics for the historian, but unpleasant to experience at first hand.

Although re-living a previous existence would not be ideal, it was comforting to know that if his plan to go forward did not succeed, he was operating with a safety net.

Feeling his life ebbing away, Ian accepted death willingly; hopeful, confident even, that it would be the answer to all his problems. He had experienced the effects of a general anaesthetic only once in his life. Dying seemed much the same – being conscious, then not, without any awareness of a transition from one state to the other.

Consciousness returned - a primitive consciousness that grew over a period of hours or days, time being immaterial. There was an awareness of a rhythmic sound: squishing, relaxing, ever present. In his dream, he could not feel fresh air filling his lungs, he could not see more than shades of light; he could hear only the ever-present beat.

Then, as though brought to his senses by a slap across the face, Ian suddenly realised what the beat was and where it meant he must be in order to experience it – inside his mother's belly. In his deliberations, he had overlooked one simple fact – obtaining consciousness does not accompany birth, it first appears while still a foetus.

Immediately he was aware that his movements were restricted, that his lungs were full of amniotic fluid, not air. A man waking to find he had been buried alive would be in a far better situation. Mistakenly being encased in a wooden box, planted two metres underground, would no doubt evoke terror, a frantic panic few would be able to comprehend. However, relief would always be at hand, nature providing an automatic escape route. In time, the air within the coffin would become poisoned, the unwilling captive being freed by a slow but inevitable death. Ian was similarly entombed, but the umbilical cord attached to his own belly would ensure his torture would be prolonged.

However, although the outcome of Ian's death was not all he had hoped it to be, the game was not over. Besides, he knew hysteria would solve nothing. The circumstances might have been unexpected, but they were not so far removed from the possibility he had already considered – being born an adult, at least in thought. He had accepted that risk, knowing he had a Plan B. It was not ideal, but at least it existed. Being reunited with his family now seemed a forlorn hope, but there still remained a chance everything would one day be returned to him. Without prior knowledge of his former life he would probably live it as the universe intended, and by the time it was done, his memories of Debbie, Stephen and Ann – of his current life – would have faded, in which case he might make his original choices, each at the right moment, eventually restoring all he had once enjoyed. Making a better life no longer mattered. He simply wanted to go back to what it had been, warts and all.

With nothing to be lost and everything to gain, Ian relaxed as much as was possible, and permitted the buzzing sensation to fill the core of his head. The sound was there as it should be, as it always had been, whenever he summoned it, but the response was far from normal. Time crept back painfully slowly until the immaturity of his brain brought an inability to concentrate, killing the process. Time then progressed forward again, restoring his ability and with it, the memories he had brought back with him from his life as a middle-age man. The barrier had somehow become impenetrable.

Throwing caution to the wind, Ian had travelled back from his life as a seven-year-old boy to the time of his birth at an unprecedented, unchecked rate. An impetus had grown, sufficient to punch though the membrane that separated his current and previous existences. Now he found himself flat against that membrane – that barrier - there was no run up; no distance in which to build up speed. The formula was a simple one. No momentum equated to no escape.

Understanding the prognosis only too well, Ian began to kick. His mouth was open. In his mind he was screaming.

28

Ian's panic attack had the potential to continue until he became exhausted, only to continue afresh once he had rested, and for the cycle to repeat itself until he was finally driven mad. What saved him was the sound of his mum's voice, penetrating her belly. She could not have imagined the torment her baby was suffering. Indeed, she was not aware of any torment at all; she simply spoke with her baby as was her habit, using the soothing tones of a mother who had begun caring for her child even before it had been born.

Ian stopped thrashing about, forcing himself to stay calm so he might consider his position and the best way forward – or back.

He first considered simply getting on with it, keeping his head down, and re-living his life in the hope that one day he would be reunited with his family. That was a big ask. There might still be months until he was born, and then it would be many years until he could hold an adult conversation. Even then, there were no guarantees. He might suffer to his adolescent years, make a mistake, and slip back to an earlier time in his life. Not to mention he was not sure if he had the willpower to live his life exactly as he had done before. There was always the option to abandon his original course and to make a new and possibly better life for himself. However, although the calendar told him he was decades into his past, his mind had not long been separated from those he loved and he was not ready to deprive them of the life he knew they could have.

Alternatively, he had the option to wait until he was strong enough, and then commit suicide, strangling himself with his own cord, but he could not present his mum with a stillbirth, deprive his wife two wonderful children, and rob those children of potentially fulfilling lives.

Ian's first solid conclusion was that whatever he chose to do, he promised himself he would never drink alcohol again; he would never get embarrassed, and he would never again look at old photos or memorabilia; three things that had brought him to this moment.

Plan B, quickly concocted on his death bed - to return to some point in his previous existence - undoubtedly offered the best solution. However, despite having restored his composure, nothing else about his circumstances had changed. He still lacked the momentum he had when travelling back at speed from the age of seven and therefore remained unable to break through the barrier. But in considering this his only option, Ian had overlooked the obvious.

Laying on his death bed, Ian had remembered nothing of the preceding years of his former life; no single detail on which he could fix and return to in an instant. Now, though, he had one very vivid memory of that life – the look upon the faces of those miscellaneous relatives that had gathered about his bed.

Without considering the possibility his next step might not work, Ian relaxed, thought hard about his former family, concentrating on recently formed memories of tears rolling down their cheeks, and then activated the process. The sensation at the very centre of his head lasted but a moment.

On opening his eyes Ian saw now familiar faces, and to their relief he formed a broad, if painful, smile across his face. For the wrong reason he had done the right thing, making everyone about him as happy as possible given the circumstances, all parties seemingly pleased to see each other and be together.

This feeling of togetherness lasted only another moment as Ian activated the next step of his hastily devised plan. Not having any other memories of this life, he would be forced to rewind for an arbitrary period of time before opening his eyes in order to ascertain how far back he had gone and how far back he should then go to reach the optimum point of his forgotten former existence.

Closing his eyes, Ian evoked the familiar buzzing sensation and began counting slowly. Having judged the first rewind to be sufficiently long, he halted the process.

What met his eyes struck him as being, at one and the same time, familiar and unfamiliar; familiar in that he recognised the room; unfamiliar that the decor was modern, and a paper-thin television had been affixed to the end wall, covering much of its surface. More surprising was the sight of a young woman he instantly recognised as his own daughter – an older version perhaps than the one he was most familiar with, but it was his daughter nonetheless.

'Ann?' Ian questioned, the muscles beneath his eyes tightening momentarily, his upper body rocking forward slightly as if this shortening of distance would help him comprehend the incomprehensible.

Ann looked back at her father, wondering what had caused him to suddenly mention her name half way through a sentence; a sentence that was designed to impart a fascinating fact related to whatever programme was currently showing on the television. Her look became a confused stare.

'Ann, is it really you?'

'Of course it's me,' Ann replied, a slight tremble detectable in her voice, her eyes scanning her father's body for symptoms.

Ian reached forward and took his daughter's hands in his. At the same time tears began to well in his eyes; eyes that remained fixed on hers. His lips began rolling in and out on themselves, shaking. In fact, his entire body had begun to shake. His breathing had become noisy; each shallow, rapid inhalation taken through a nose that was quickly filling with mucus. He sniffed.

'Oh God, I never thought I'd see you again,' he said, his voice fluttering.

'Christ Dad, what's wrong? Are you having a stroke?'

Ian fought hard to fight back the tears. As he did so his head shook quickly from side to side; the only answer he was able to provide. He stopped and gulped.

'This must seem so weird, but I assure you I'm okay; better than okay.'

Ann relaxed a little, but her face still showed great concern. Her father's words did nothing to help.

'Where's your mum?' he asked, his head craning round to see past his daughter.

'Are you sure you're okay, Dad? You told me when I got here she would be sorry to have missed me. You told me she's with her friend, Carol.'

'So, Debs is here too,' Ian commented, his head turning to one side as if this was necessary to store the information.

He looked back at his daughter.

'And Stephen?' he asked tentatively, as though it was too much to hope he might have been reunited with his entire family.

'At home with his family, I imagine.'

From his position, seated at one well-worn end of the sofa, Ian stared, incredulous.

'But...I don't...It's not possible,' he said, his eyes twitching, his head moving this way and that.

'Dad, you're scaring me. Are you certain you're all right?'

'To tell the truth, I'm not sure.'

He then cocked his head to one side, fixing his gaze on the middle distance while he tried to make sense of the situation.

Ann moved closer to him, placing a hand on his shoulder blade, bending her head down, tilting it up so that she could look into her dad's troubled face.

'Dad, you've got to tell me what's wrong?'

Ian snapped back into the room, turned to his daughter and put his hand on her knee.

'Tell me what you remember of your childhood. Tell me about uni.'

With a little more prompting, Ann was happy to reminisce about the childhood she had shared with her brother, Stephen, provided by her parents about whom she had only fond recollections. She then went on to talk about her years at university; her courses and friends. It was just as it should be. This was no parallel universe; this was the same life Ian had just left behind, although he had come back to it from the other end, the whole thing apparently a loop.

All of a sudden, everything made sense.

Ever since Mike Summerbee had revealed to him he not only rewound his own life, but the whole universe, he had wondered how one mind could be so powerful. It now seemed he simply possessed the ability to get his mind out of step with the rest of the universe that otherwise continued on a perpetual loop.

'Shall I make us a cup of tea?' Ann asked, still concerned that her dad, although smiling, seemed distant; troubled.

'Yes please darling, I need to think for a moment.'

Ann left the room just long enough to fill the kettle and set it to boil.

All the while, Ian remained seated; thinking. If his life was on one continuous loop, as he now suspected, then the people who surrounded his death bed had been known to him. Who had they been? How old had he been? Where was Debbie? They had spoken among themselves; they had given the names of people who could not be there, but he remembered none of the specifics. Someone had been stuck in America and two children had been prevented from visiting lest they became upset by seeing an ageing relative die, but that was all.

'Why did I not pay more attention?' he said aloud. 'I was so damned busy thinking of myself, I ignored everything around me. God, I'd give anything to go back and ask questions.'

His outburst served only to renew his daughter's concern. Her hands became locked together, her fingers contorting, writhing in anguish.

After a few minutes she left the room, but only once she had heard the switch flick off, keen to leave her dad alone for the briefest intervals possible.

She returned, carrying two mugs, a packet of biscuits and the sugar bowl.

'What's that for? Neither of us takes sugar.'

'I thought it might help. During the blitz they were always swigging hot sweet tea, weren't they.'

Ian produced a smile, directed at his daughter.

'This is not the blitz,' he said, mockingly, 'and I haven't been traumatised by the loss of my family, or my home.'

Ann was pleased to see the dad she knew was gradually returning to her. She smiled back at him.

'I need a piece of paper,' Ian said. 'I need to jot some things down. Something about all this just doesn't make sense.'

'You can say that again,' Ann responded, her eyebrows rising to their uppermost limit. 'As far as I'm concerned, none of it makes sense. There we were, talking about endangered pandas, when you suddenly call out my name as though it was the first time you've seen me in years. Then you start crying and you won't tell me why.'

'I'm sorry,' Ian replied, offering a sheepish smile. 'I don't know what came over me. I've been thinking about the plot of a book I want to write and it kept me up for much of the night. Maybe the lack of sleep made me a bit emotional; that and ideas for the plot flooding into my head – it's about a man who moves back through his own life and misses his family.'

'You silly old fool, Dad,' Ann responded, a note of anger in her voice, having been subjected to so much concern for such a petty reason. 'Firstly, I don't know why you would suddenly want to write a book. You've never shown any desire to do so before. Secondly, why would you want to do it if it's going to upset you so much?'

'Okay, please don't go on at me. I said I'm sorry.'

Ann could see by the fresh upset in her dad's face this was no time for admonishment.

'I'm sorry. It's just that you scared me. Now, what's this about you needing a piece of paper? You'd be better off dictating it.'

'Okay, but we'll still need a piece of paper.'

'I meant, dictate it to the TV. Honestly Dad, I don't know why you bought this thing. I've shown you a hundred times how to use it and you still have no idea what it's capable of. Why buy expensive gadgets if you don't use them?'

Ian looked more confused than ever.

Ann, realising she was going to have to go over the whole demonstration again, huffed, reached into a wicker basket down by her dad's side, and pulled from it a wireless head set. Seeing her dad staring at the device as though he had not the first clue what to do with it, she then jammed it onto his head, adjusting it so the pads covered his ears, the microphone was positioned in front of his mouth, and the movement detectors were placed directly in his line of sight. She then pressed a device into his hand, flicked an on switch and changed the TV source using the remote control. The television instantly became a computer screen; something Ian was more familiar with, although this was a much larger version than his desktop PC.

Following a few instructions, during which Ann was forced to grab her dad's head and physically guide it, a blank sheet of paper appeared on the wall, a cursor flashing to indicate it was ready to receive.

'Well, go on then,' Ann prompted. 'Say something.'

'Okay, dear; give me a moment to think.'

Those very same words immediately appeared on the screen in front of him. Ian looked surprised and frustrated.

'Wow.'

'Undo,' Ann said quietly, clearly indicating her dad should repeat the word.

He did and the sentence disappeared.

'This is brilliant,' Ian said, immediately seeing his spoken words translated onto the electronic page.

'Yes, but it can be annoying; especially when you sneeze.'

'Undo.'

Ann quickly demonstrated how her dad should coordinate his eye movements with the hand control, believing she was merely refreshing the knowledge she had given him many times previously. When she was finished, she indicated that her dad now had control and was free to compose. Ian settled back but said nothing. His daughter wafted her hands towards him, encouraging him to speak. Ian raised his right arm in response, his index finger pointing to the ceiling, indicating he needed a moment to collect his thoughts.

The optimistic, protective portion of his brain would have had Ian accepting his initial thoughts as truth, and be grateful; but another voice spoke to challenge his cosy proposition, raising an uncomfortable counter position.

'Is it a loop?'

Type appeared on the screen and the cursor then moved down a line in response to a click of the hand controller.

'Can't be.'

A green underscore indicated the program was not happy with Ian's grammar – the statement was a fragment. He ignored it and the cursor dropped another line.

Ian spoke slowly, with many pauses; the result of him formulating his argument as accurately and concisely as possible, before committing it to the screen. Such was the care he took with his thoughts that the written word rarely needed retraction.

'From the moment I discovered my ability, I found it impossible to go forward. Even once I had become so adept at slipping back into my own past I did so by accident, I still found it impossible to return to my family, despite being able to picture their faces and specific events in minute detail; despite my desire to return to them overriding any other. If the universe was truly on one continuous loop, by desiring to return to a specific point in the future, surely the process, if unable to go forward, would have me go backwards, through the barrier between the beginning and end of my life, and on until I reached the point at which I wanted to be.'

'Dad, why are you speaking as though this happened to you?' Ann interrupted.

Ian moved the microphone from his mouth.

'It's a complex plot,' he replied. 'It helps me sort it out if I imagine I'm the main character. There's nothing sinister about it.'

Satisfied his explanation had been accepted, Ian returned the microphone to its previous position and continued to download his thoughts onto the screen.

'Could it instead be a string of identical, or at least very similar, versions of the same life? Perhaps each one evolves from the last.'

This theory also had its flaws. At the cusp between his previous and current lives, the barrier would slice everyone else's lives in two, leaving only his undamaged. Ian added this additional thought to the screen.

'You sound as though you're well into constructing the plot,' Ann interrupted again, 'but you haven't been dictating it, have you. Please tell me you haven't written the whole thing out by hand.'

Ian looked to his daughter.

'There's no need to poke fun at me. I can't help it if I'm not good with all this new-fangled technology.'

Ian looked back at the screen, only to discover he had proved the point, his plea to his daughter having been faithfully recorded as text.

'Undo.'

Ann smiled and shook her head gently.

Ian posed another question.

'Is Mike Summerbee a threat?'

There followed a pause while Ian considered the answer.

'If this life is A to B and the original life is B to C, Summerbee did not discover his ability until part way between B and C. If this is a previous version of the same life, did Summerbee get his ability at the same point in it, or not until the next life? Or, in this life, is there someone else?'

After another pause, Ian removed the headset and then sat quietly for a short while, reviewing 'the plot'.

'All sorted?' Ann asked.

'In a way.'

In truth, there was only one conclusion of which Ian could be absolutely certain - no matter how much time he spent trying to determine an answer, it was an impossible goal. It was like wondering what lay beyond the confines of the known universe, then discovering that ours is only one of countless others, only to then consider what was beyond those. The ultimate truth was not mankind's to know.

Loop or linear; series or parallel; Ian had no choice other than to accept the life he now inhabited was close enough to the original so as not to matter.

As much as he would love to have sat with his daughter for the rest of time, Ian now knew what he had to do. In the short time he had been reunited with her, many questions had been posed, but none had asked the date. It mattered not, but for one thing. Up to this point, Ian had been the mind of a forty-eight year old man inhabiting the body of an ever younger self. Now he was perhaps physically fifty-eight and had no recollection of the period following the discovery of his ability. He had missed Stephen and Ann's graduation; his children had flown the nest and started lives of their own; they might even have produced offspring, but he had experienced and remembered none of it. Whatever the date, Ian had bypassed a sizeable chunk of their lives and an equally sizeable chunk of his life with Debbie. Even if he were told the past decade had been nothing but misery, he did not want to be denied a single minute of it. Besides, he was presumably still employed, but with no knowledge of his work, how could he hope to maintain a living? The problems he had encountered when he returned to the age of twenty-four were nothing when compared to those he now faced. Then he could rely on faded memories; now there was nothing.

Ian had no option but to go back further.

The decision was not taken lightly. If he were to ask a group of people what he should do, a large proportion would advise that he took what he had and be thankful. Yes he would relinquish a decade of precious memories, but he had his family; he had been gifted another chance to be with the ones closest to him. Why risk it for what could be described as merely the icing on the cake?

Ian was not a betting man, but he trusted logic and his ability to think logically. If he now fixed upon a moment in his past – his future past – he should return straight to the version of it in his current past. If this happened, all would be right in his world. However, if his current past was different, the process simply would not work and he would be locked in the present. It was the perfect failsafe; a mechanism that made it worth a try – nothing to lose; everything to gain.

Ian turned to his daughter and placed his arms around her, pulling her close. Instinctively, Ann reciprocated, bringing her arms up to embrace her dad, their faces becoming buried in each other's necks. After a while, Ian pulled back sufficiently to enable him to speak coherently.

'I've been such a fool,' he said. 'I thought I'd lost everything. As it is, I've still lost too much to bear and I must try everything in my power to get it back. If this works, I'm going to make you proud of me.'

Ann looked on, confused.

'But Dad, I am proud of you.'

Ian looked at his daughter's face and smiled.

'And I hope you will be again.'

With those words still hanging in the air, Ian pulled his daughter close once more and shut his eyes. He then thought hard about a vivid image that was close to the surface of his mind, and transported himself straight there.

29

Ian's eyes opened to the sight of a large fox, its eyes reflecting brightly the beam of Ian's torch; a torch which then beat against the side of the tent several times, encouraging the intruder to leave.

'Go on,' Ian said, twice flicking the device towards the animal as though throwing light at it, just as one would flick water from a hose.

The fox considered his options before turning and trotting away into the darkness.

Ian remained on all fours for a moment, the knuckles of both hands pressed into the grass, his right hand still clutching the torch which now sent its beam scudding across the surface of the field.

A moment was needed to take stock. After all the promises to himself that each rewind was going to be his very last, only then to breech every such promise in turn, Ian had finally reached a point he could truly believe to be the furthest back he would ever need to go. He still had the ability to go back further, but there would be no need. In fact, he would take active measures to ensure he did not. To prevent going back by accident, he would now be teetotal for the rest of time, and would shun memorabilia that tied him to his past. It would be a struggle, but reminding himself why he had adopted such drastic measures would surely keep him to his word.

This was to be a new beginning. He had not killed anyone, either by desire or by accident; he had not schemed; he had not been unfaithful – technically. A sigh of relief left his body, causing his chest to droop slightly between his outstretched arms. A gentle smile spread across his face.

Ian reversed back inside the tent, fastening the zip before returning to his original seated position.

'It was a fox,' he said, casually, as though the event had been nothing out of the ordinary.

'Cheeky little bugger,' David responded, cheerily.

Nothing more was said on the subject or on any other subject until after the first few spoonfuls of warming stew had been consumed and savoured.

'So,' David said, 'the butterfly effect has it that an insignificant little butterfly, beating its wings in some wood, somewhere, starts a chain reaction of seemingly insignificant events that land up providing some fella in Bangkok with a bowl of steaming hot owls' nest soup – no butterfly; cold soup.'

His four word summation was punctuated with two nods of the head; the first to the left, the other to the right.

Ian smiled.

'You and your owls,' he said, dipping his spoon into his tin mug, before delivering a steaming hot piece of minted potato to his mouth.

Ian waggled his spoon while the diced vegetable cooled sufficiently to be swallowed, the motion indicating he wished to have some say on the matter. Eventually, having breathed out many times through tunnelled lips, Ian's mouth was cleared.

'I entirely believe in the butterfly effect. Small things can cause a chain reaction that has a massive effect. Big things can cause even bigger effects. For the most part though, the final consequences will not happen until way into the future, so you'd never see them. Whatever the effect, it's unwise to try to manipulate the original cause.'

'Rubbish, we do it all the time,' David argued. 'Whenever I buy a lottery ticket, I do so hoping to cause an effect that will have enormous consequences, some of them within my own lifetime, and some I hope will help my children long after I'm gone.'

'Okay, I accept that,' Ian replied. 'If you buy a ticket and win - it's fate. What you must never do though, is try to outsmart fate.'

'And how could you do that? If you believe in fate, you would be fated to do whatever it was you did in trying to outsmart fate.'

Ian smiled, appreciating his friend's quick response, but he was not beaten yet.

'Even if you believe in fate, not everything has to be fated,' he countered. 'In life, there are two kinds of event: those that have an effect while you're alive; those that have an effect beyond your grave. My two kids are the next generation and by definition will affect life beyond mine. A few key events had to take place in order for them to be born. All of those have happened within my lifetime. You could consider each of those events to be acts of fate, but the rest is simply chaff.

'In order for me to have had Stephen and Ann, I first had to meet Debbie. To meet her, I had to attend the school reunion, and you had to have brought Debbie with you. For you to have introduced me to her, I already had to know you as a good friend. For us to have been friends, we first had to meet at junior school. Nothing else matters – choosing tea or coffee; holidaying in Burma or Bournemouth – nothing else matters. That's why my family means everything to me; it's the only thing that does really matter. I love my wife and kids more than anything else in the world and would do anything to protect them; make any sacrifice.'

'What about me?' David asked, feigning hurt.

'I love you too but given the difficult choice of losing you or my family, Debbie and the kids would win every time - sorry.'

'I know what you mean. I've always said that if anyone hurt my family, I'd do time for them. I'd kill for them.'

Ian fell silent for a moment. When he spoke, he delivered his response with unexpected gravity.

'All dads say that. Some would kill; some wouldn't. I know I could, but I also know that it's not the answer. Cause and effect, you see. A good man would be eaten with guilt; families would suffer as their husband and father was locked up in jail for the rest of his life; the ripples would spread far beyond anything you can imagine.

My advice is to cherish what you have and who you have. Family is far more important than material things. Never let greed blind you to that fact. Make the most of your life. It may not be the only one you have, but it's the only one that matters. Accept your mistakes and learn by them. Don't wish you'd done things differently; just be grateful for what you have. I could go on, but you get the picture.'

Ian said nothing more but sat wondering what his friend's reaction might be.

The roofer took the shipping clerk's words in his stride.

'All this proves one thing,' David observed.

'What's that?'

'Blokes don't need a pint of lager in their hand to talk utter bollocks; a mug of stew is just as good.'

Printed in Great Britain
by Amazon